LUXURY

F/2111874

By Jessica Ruston

Non-fiction

Heroines: The Bold, the Bad and the Beautiful

LUXURY

JESSICA RUSTON

headline
review

First published in 2009 by HEADLINE REVIEW
An imprint of HEADLINE PUBLISHING GROUP

1

Cataloguing in Publication Data is available from the British Library

Hardback ISBN 978 0 7553 4850 3
Trade paperback ISBN 978 0 7553 4851 0

Typeset in Sabon by Ellipsis Books Limited, Glasgow

Printed and bound in Great Britain by
Clays Ltd, St Ives plc

Headline's policy is to use papers that are natural, renewable
and recyclable products and made from wood grown in sustainable forests.
The logging and manufacturing processes are expected to conform to
the environmental regulations of the country of origin.

HEADLINE PUBLISHING GROUP
An Hachette UK Company
338 Euston Road
London NW1 3BH

www.headline.co.uk
www.hachette.co.uk

For my family

Acknowledgements

Thanks to my agent, Simon Trewin, who has been cheerleader, hand-holder, voice of reason and provider of much-needed encouragement throughout the writing and publication of this book. Also to his lovely and super-efficient assistant, Ariella Feiner. My editor, Cat Cobain, has played a huge role in the shaping of this book. I am extremely grateful for her clear-minded insights, her boundless enthusiasm and her unwavering belief in *Luxury*. And many thanks to everyone at Headline Review for all their hard work, in particular Emily Furniss, Jo Liddiard and Sara Porter. Also to Joan Deitch, who copyedited the manuscript and whose meticulous and thorough work means that any remaining errors are mine alone. Various people gave extremely generously of their time and expertise while I was researching the book, in particular Elizabeth Coulter, Sir Rocco Forte, Louise Mahon and Mike Wharton.

I am extremely lucky to have a very supportive family, both immediate and extended. Thanks to my parents, my sister and my in-laws for their love and support.

Finally, thanks to my husband, Jack, for his patience, his humour, his single-minded belief in my ability to do what I set out to do, and his much-needed reminders that 'it's all part of the process'. Thank you.

We are the music-makers,
  And we are the dreamers of dreams,
Wandering by lone sea-breakers,
  And sitting by desolate streams;
World-losers and world-forsakers,
  On whom the pale moon gleams:
Yet we are the movers and shakers
  Of the world for ever, it seems.

With wonderful deathless ditties
We build up the world's great cities,
  And out of a fabulous story
  We fashion an empire's glory:
One man with a dream, at pleasure,
  Shall go forth and conquer a crown;
And three with a new song's measure
  Can trample an empire down.

Ode, Arthur O'Shaughnessy (1844–1881)

Prologue

1981

From somewhere behind the hazy, green-blue blur of the horizon, a solidity began to form itself into the shape of a shore, a gently curving bay, a steeply peaked hill. As the boat drew closer, tacking round to approach from the west, it was as if an unseen hand was sketching in the details of the island – the deeper blue patches in the water indicating a reef off one side; then a spike of pale sand snaking its way into the sea; then a fuzz of flickering green – palm trees sprinkled down the slopes of the hill.

Logan exhaled. 'Oh, man. It's just like she said. Look – the jetty's still there. Take it round to that side.'

He pointed to the narrow structure of greying wood, its spindly legs rising up from the water, and motioned to his friends at the helm to head for it. The three young men were all tanned and relaxed from their summer in the sun – their 'last summer of freedom', as they had named it. They wore nothing but shorts and had let their hair grow long, in the knowledge that come the fall they would be in suits and short haircuts as they went off to begin their lives as adults, as Harvard graduates. This summer was a stolen slip of time between their student years and things 'getting serious', as they put it.

As Johnny leaned forward to bring the boat round, the muscles in his shoulders undulated under his skin. 'Looks pretty rickety,' he commented.

'How long is it since anyone was here?' Nicolo called from the far side of the deck.

'Not a clue,' Logan replied. 'Twenty years? More?'

They edged closer to the jetty.

'Let's stop alongside,' he told them. 'I want to see if it's sound.'

They slowly manoeuvred the boat so that it bobbed alongside the jetty. Logan hooked a leg over the handrail that ran round the boat's deck, and hanging on to it with one hand, he stretched forward and stamped on the jetty, testing its strength.

'Seems OK. I guess the worst that can happen is I get to go for a swim sooner rather than later.'

He swung his other leg over the side and hopped down on to the landing stage. There was a rustle of a breeze through the trees that lined the beach, and the faint swishing of the sea all around them. Otherwise, all was silent.

Johnny and Nicolo watched from the boat. The wood creaked as it absorbed Logan's weight, but it stood firm, and he spun round to face his friends, arms aloft and a wide grin on his face.

'Come ashore, my friends, my brothers. Welcome to L'île des Violettes!'

Putting his thumb and forefinger between his lips, Nicolo let out a long, high-pitched whistle. Johnny whooped with excitement and quickly secured the boat, then the two young men leaped off it to join him. The noise they made as they ran down the jetty and on to the hot sand startled the birds in the palm trees, who rose into the sky like a cloud of smoke, clacking and squawking.

They raced into the undergrowth, not caring that their legs were getting scratched. The air was cool and dry, and felt refreshing after hours spent on the boat.

'It's like a secret world,' shouted Nicolo.

'*Treasure Island*,' Johnny called back.

'*Lord of the Flies*?' responded Nicolo.

'Ha. Turning on each other?' Johnny chased after Logan. 'Not us, my friend, never us.'

Logan had stopped running and bent over to catch his breath. Johnny and Nicolo caught up with him.

'I feel like Robinson Crusoe – with two Man Fridays!' He was panting, his face a big grin, challenging his friends. Nicolo and Johnny looked at each other and shook their heads.

'Asking for it, don't you think?'

'Begging, I'd say, man.'

Logan chuckled, and before they could catch him he took off again, weaving through the trees. Whooping like savages, Johnny and Nicolo gave chase, until all three of them burst out of the glade of trees on to a rocky promontory. The view stopped them in their tracks.

'Wow.'

Without realising it, they had made their way to the highest point of the island, and from here they could see the shape of the whole mass. It was picture perfect. Blue skies, turquoise sea, leafy trees and sandy beaches. And as the three young men stood staring down at it, all of them felt a secret, powerful tug in their chests. All of them wanted it to be theirs.

'What's over there?' Johnny said suddenly, breaking the silence, pointing to a building. Even from a distance they could see that it was tumbledown, decrepit.

'Don't know,' said Logan. 'Why don't we find out?'

Later, the three of them lay on the sandy floor of the ruined building, a bonfire burning nearby, and the empty bottles of beer that they'd fetched from the boat discarded on the ground next to their sleeping bags. They gazed up at the sky. Tomorrow they would return to the mainland, give the boat back to its owner and catch their flight home. Back to real life, where Johnny would go to law school, Logan would begin his MBA as one of the youngest students ever to get a place on the prestigious Harvard course, and Nicolo would start work at a construction company in New York, learning the real nuts and bolts of the business. They'd got First, their fledgling hotel company, up and running, and it was doing well. They were raring to go. Their lives as men were beginning.

'So what do you think, Father Flores? Does she live up to your expectations?'

Nicolo leaned over and flicked the side of Logan's head with his thumb and forefinger. 'Don't call me that. And yes, she certainly does.'

'Why "she"?' asked Johnny.

'Fuck's sake, J. This place is a woman. A beautiful, uncharted, wild woman, just waiting to be tamed.'

'Ha. By you?'

'Yes, by me. No – by us.' Logan's voice was confident. He didn't doubt his words, and neither did his friends.

'We'll come back here, yes?' Johnny's words were stretched out, long with tiredness and alcohol.

'Yes. This is our future, guys. One day, we'll be back here – not as kids, but as men. As the men who own this place. And everyone will see that we made it.'

Logan raised his fist into the air. '*One man with a dream, at pleasure, Shall go forth and conquer a crown ...*'

Johnny followed suit. '*And three with a new song's measure ...*'

And finally Nicolo: '*Can trample an empire down.*'

Chapter One

2008

Logan Barnes stood on the edge of the building's asphalt roof, high above the Upper East Side of Manhattan. It was a clear, bright day, and the Hudson River was twinkling, sparks of white light glinting off its graphite surface. He moved closer to the edge and felt a flicker of fear as he looked down and saw the vehicles moving slowly through the streets beneath him. He pressed the feeling down, but not too far. A bit of fear was good – kept you focused on your goal. He looked up. Above him there was only sky. Below – everything. The city that he loved so much was spread at his feet.

He took another step, which brought him right up to the roof's edge – and then he jumped.

Seconds spent flying through the air seemed to last for ever. Time stretched and became luxuriously elastic. Logan felt absolute clarity. The world was in sharp focus as his body swooped down towards the uncompromising pavements of New York.

Four hundred and fifty feet below, a second man was scanning the roof for signs of movement. He had positioned himself so that he would have a clear view of what was about to happen. He checked the tiny video camera and then resumed watching the skyline. After a second he saw him, a tiny figure standing on the roof. He looked intensely vulnerable – exposed.

Johnny raised the camera and began filming as the figure tumbled from the roof, rolling like a hamster in a wheel through the air, falling into a somersault and then straightening and stretching his arms out like a bird. A few people noticed and pointed, or stopped dead in their tracks, but most people just carried on walking – too busy hurrying to lunch dates or back to the office to look up and see the falling man.

And then, just as Johnny was sure it was all over and was holding his breath in readiness for the inevitable, the parachute mushroomed upwards and caught the breeze, and Johnny exhaled with a relieved cry. A harried-looking businessman walked past, glancing at Logan briefly before hurrying on.

As he floated slowly down towards the ground, Logan used his body to steer himself towards a safe landing spot. The building he had jumped from faced Central Park, and as he glided over the grass, tourists in horse-driven coaches, and runners stopped and stared. He always enjoyed the look of surprise that spread over their faces as they registered the shape in the sky and realised it was a man, appearing as if from the heavens. It wasn't until he had drawn level with a tiny cluster of trees that he heard a terrible shrieking sound. He jerked his head over his shoulder, and a horse rearing up just behind him filled his vision, its rider fighting to rein him in and stay mounted as the animal's body bucked in fright. Pulling hard on the steering lines, Logan turned sharply, narrowly avoiding the horse's hooves as he landed. The rider eventually calmed the horse down enough to dismount, and stormed over to Logan, who had landed awkwardly due to the angle and was picking himself up. Shocked onlookers stared at the scene.

'You fucking lunatic! What in God's name do you think you're doing? You nearly killed me, and my horse! Where the fuck did you come from?' she yelled at Logan, her face puce.

'I'm so sorry.' Logan got to his feet and brushed the greyish dust of Central Park off his clothes. 'Are you hurt? Here, let me help you.'

'No – get your fucking hands off me, you prick.' The woman swiped angrily at Logan, but her hands were trembling, and he backed away, his face conciliatory.

A few yards away, Johnny was jogging easily towards them. The woman had turned pale now underneath her dark skin, and had begun to cry.

'I'm sorry,' she said, 'that was rude, I just . . .' She was looking at him strangely. 'Do I know you?'

He smiled. 'No, we haven't met. Look – you've had a bad fright. Here, sit down.'

Johnny neared them and took the bridle of the horse as Logan led the woman to a nearby bench. She was starting to feel calmer, and man, if anyone was going to almost crush her by falling out of the sky, Thandy was glad it was this one. He may not have been particularly tall, but the man had stature. His shoulders were broad and strong looking under the thin sky-diving outfit he was wearing, and his eyes were crinkled a little with concern. Dark eyes, kind, but with a steel in them, a strength. She shook herself. For good-ness' sake, she was getting carried away like someone out of one of those romance novels her mama read. She definitely recognised him, though.

'Do you work in the city?' she asked.

'Mm – yes.'

She narrowed her eyes. 'Do you work with – no.'

She started again. 'Oh, are you Jeannie's boss? At Bloomingdales? Homewares?'

'I'm afraid not.'

She looked at him suspiciously. 'You sure? You look a lot like ...'

Logan smiled and jerked his head at Johnny, who nodded in understanding and took out his mobile phone. Thandy listened as he spoke.

'Johnny Stokes here. We need a room, straight away.'

'What do you mean a room? I'm not going anywhere with you, you mighta killed me. I may recognise you from somewhere but that doesn't mean I'm gonna ...'

She trailed off. Oh. Johnny Stokes. She looked up at the other man, sitting next to her, her eyes wide. 'Oh my. You're ...'

Logan nodded. She had realised. It wasn't the first time it had happened – people often mistook him for someone they knew, waved at him in the street assuming they'd been introduced at a drinks party or that he was a neighbour or somesuch. He held out his hand. 'Logan Barnes. Pleased to meet you.'

The trio walked through the glass doors of the Royal Hotel, Johnny and Logan on either side of the bemused woman, whose horse had been led away by the owner of the stables after another phone call from Johnny. He knew someone almost everywhere in Manhattan, it seemed. There was little he couldn't arrange or get hold of within the city's parameters with a quick flick through his contacts list and a phone call, a handshake, or nod. They entered the building. A matching pair of uniformed porters wearing ivory gloves and deferential smiles greeted them. They swept open the glass doors in unison and their pale grey top hats nodded in synchronised greeting.

As soon as they entered the lobby, the concierge was moving towards them with a smile.

'Good morning, Mr Barnes,' the man murmured, awaiting further instructions.

'Morning, Matthew. Beautiful day, isn't it?'

'Indeed it is, sir. I have a suite ready for your guest as requested.' He looked over at the young woman on whom Logan had almost landed. 'If you'd like to accompany me, madam?'

Logan put a hand on her arm, and it was as warm as the smile in his dark eyes. She softened a little. He was an extremely charming man, and she had been annoyed to find her anger dissipating rather quickly in the park, when he had solicitously sat her down then whisked her to the hotel (one of the very best in the city, she knew by reputation) in the back of a chauffeur-driven car.

'I'm so sorry about earlier, really. Some fresh clothes will be delivered to your suite shortly. Your room has been reserved for you until the end of the week. Please don't hesitate to order whatever you'd like from room service. Matthew here is the concierge, and he will look after you – any reservations, or other help that you might need. Mr Stokes and I have somewhere we have to be.'

The concierge nodded at her and Thandy's smile widened. Well, look here. She, Thandy Stine, a secretary from Queens who saved up to ride in Central Park once a fortnight, in a suite in the Royal! Not only that, but as the guest of Mr Logan Barnes, from the TV. *And* Johnny Stokes, the one that all the girls in the office were in love with. She was going to phone her friends straight away.

As the concierge led her across the mink-coloured marble floors of reception, the cool stone inlaid with elegantly curving patterns of what looked like, but surely could not be, mother-of-pearl, she was already mentally planning the meal she would order on room service. A huge Porterhouse steak, bloodily rare, with mustard and fries. A plate of oysters to start, because she'd never tried them before. Some of those tiny pastel-coloured macaroons that looked so pretty and ladylike.

Turning round, she gave Logan a wink. If this was what came of people falling out of the sky and nearly killing you, then she didn't mind one bit.

Johnny and Logan left the overexcited Thandy in the capable hands of the Royal's well-trained staff, and headed over to the West Side, Logan Barnes International's hotel and club in the Meatpacking District of Manhattan. It was a totally different animal from his flagship property near Central Park, but no less successful in its own way. Where the Royal exemplified everything that was chi-chi and slick about Manhattan, with its pale marble floors and its opulent drapes, the West Side was its younger, trendier sibling. Black Perspex floors reflected neon spotlights that hung in clusters from the bare plaster ceiling, and the open-plan lobby was dotted with low seating covered in black suede. Black goldfish swam around square-cut glass bowls placed on black Perspex tables that rose up almost seamlessly from the floor, their frilled fins wafting through the water. A Damien Hirst sculpture of a sheep's heart pierced by a silver dagger was displayed in the centre of the room.

On the way, Logan checked his emails on his iPhone, while Johnny called to let the director know they were on their way.

'Yep, we'll meet you outside. No, that's fine, we'll do the tour as usual, and then the Check Out is at – four?' Johnny raised a hand to attract Logan's attention and raised his eyebrows questioningly. Logan nodded.

'Uh huh, four, then we head to London this evening. Yes, the three of us, plus Rachel and Kirsten. Come on, Chris, you know you can't. The plane's out of bounds. No way. Nice try though.' Johnny laughed. 'See ya.'

The plane was Logan's sanctuary, out of bounds to everyone apart from his board of directors, his personal assistant, Rachel and his family. It was where he recharged, regrouped, held confidential meetings and made the phone calls that he didn't want to be overheard. There was no way the camera crew were ever getting through those particular doors.

'Always pushing the boundaries, that guy,' Johnny said.

'Don't they all?'

'True. He wanted to come in the plane.'

9

'Ha.'

'I know.'

Johnny tutted, and picked up his phone again. He spent so much time on it, he tended to get through a new one every few months. Also, he got bored quickly. He was pretty bored with his girlfriend, Melissa, but he couldn't see an easy way to get rid of her, given her involvement in their TV series, *General Manager*. They had met at the 'Revolution'-themed party held to launch the Contemporary Museum of Art's retrospective of twentieth-century revolutionary art. He had gone as Che Guevara – who else? She had done a perfect Marie Antoinette – too perfect, he should have noted – and it was a sign of her social clout that she was the only one. No one would have dared tread on Melissa's brocade-clad toes.

The party was one of the major events of Manhattan's fall social calendar. The Metropolitan Museum balls were the grande dame, a long-established fixture that everyone made sure they were in town for, but the COMA had recently got in on the act. Realising how much publicity and cash clout the city's socialite clan had, they had started creating their own fabulous, themed balls timed to slot in with their big fall exhibitions. Tables went for $100,000 and upwards, costumes were minutely planned months in advance and the seating plan was of military detail and importance. Already this year Bunny Shawcross had left in a fury, her Romanov cloak dramatically gathered around her throat in a display of haughty disgust because her sight-line was obscured by a floral guillotine. The balls provided projects for scores of stylists, chauffeurs, doormen, florists, caterers, waitresses – the legions of men and women who staffed these events (and made a very nice living themselves out of them) were sought after and fought over for their skills. Aurelie Lezard, the organiser, was a willowy blonde whose fey looks belied her hard-nosed work ethic. She saw it as a matter of personal pride to make the ball the one that everyone was talking about. Johnny watched her work the room as he stood next to a vodka luge, an ice sculpture in the shape of a hammer and sickle which dispensed shots of the spirit from an opening in its base, spending her allotted thirty seconds with someone, giving them her full attention and the benefit of her large blue eyes and cloud of blond hair, then efficiently moving on.

Johnny and Melissa's eyes had hardly met across a crowded ball-room; he had trodden on the extensive train of her gown, which Melissa had purposely draped so that it was in his way. She'd had her eye on him for a while, having seen him at various parties and openings around Manhattan, and had asked about him. What Melissa wanted, Melissa usually got. They'd moved on to the Maotini bar, where he had asked if he could take her out for dinner, adding, 'I'd like to see what you look like without a birdcage attached to your head.'

He'd seen what every bit of her looked like after their date, as she lay diagonally across his emperor-sized bed after they'd made love (Melissa might have been New York royalty, but she was certainly no prudish princess) and then sat watching cartoons and eating mint-choc-chip ice cream.

Johnny was enchanted, although he might not have been quite so charmed had he heard her throwing it all up half an hour later.

It was Melissa who had come to Johnny and Logan with the idea for *General Manager*, a hotel reality show. She worked as an associate producer for her media mogul father, who had been looking for a new TV concept to rival *The Apprentice* and *Top Chef* and the various other prime-time shows that had proved so successful. Johnny had immediately loved the idea – he was always up for a challenge, for a new experience. Johnny believed that you only really regretted the things you didn't do in life. He'd taken it to Logan, unsure how his old friend would react; had talked up the potential benefits for the business as a whole, emphasised the wider customer base they would reach – but none of it had been necessary. Logan's eyes had lit up straight away. 'I love it,' he'd said, standing up and beginning to pace. That was when Johnny knew he was getting into the idea; Logan always paced when he was excited. 'Free advertising – who could say no? It could open up all sorts of avenues. Tell her yes.'

Johnny should have known he'd be up for it; Logan had always had a need for recognition, ever since they were kids. Doing things quietly was not in his nature. He'd always be the one badgering the teacher, pointing out his contribution to a class project, bouncing up and down on his toes while waiting to be picked for baseball teams, keen to make sure he wasn't forgotten about. His report cards all tended to say the same thing. *Logan's enthusiasm is clear. Logan is always eager to contribute his thoughts in class. Logan certainly has no problems sharing his opinions.*

It was Logan who had come up with the catchphrase. He'd approached his preparation for the project systematically, calling in DVDs of all the comparable recent shows and watching them, one by one, on his plane during flights, or at home late at night, or on his laptop in the back of the car. Figuring out what worked about them, what didn't, what could be improved upon. There was no way he'd just hand over the reins to the production company and show up for filming – in fact, Johnny wasn't sure that the producers had quite known what they were getting into when they got Logan involved.

'See here,' he'd suddenly announce, pressing Pause on the remote and pointing it at the plasma screen in front of him to illustrate his point. 'The contestants are called back in two groups – winners first, then the bottom three, who have to face the panel and explain where things went wrong. But in this one,' he pressed another button and switched to a different show, 'contestants go before the panel individually, and then are told the results as a group.' His brow would furrow as he considered the differing approaches, and scribbled notes on the pad at his elbow.

One morning, Johnny had been on a conference call with a lawyer in Tokyo and a real-estate developer in Beijing, when Logan had burst into his office and announced, 'Johnny Stokes, It's Time for You to Check Out!' And had stood in the doorway looking inordinately pleased with himself. There had been a conspicuous silence from Tokyo and Beijing, before one of them said, 'Um, Mr Stokes? Is everything all right?' Logan had clapped a hand over his mouth and gone away laughing.

The production company had loved it straight away and, when the show aired, so had the viewers. It was partly to do with Logan's delivery – masterful, without being melodramatic. Soon the phrase was popping up everywhere, in puns and jokes in media stories, spreading in the way that these things tend to do. People shouted it at Johnny when they saw him in the street, groups of students said it to each other in bars at the end of the night; it entered the everyday parlance of millions of people and helped make Logan,

Johnny and Mark – who made up the third member of the judging panel – household names.

Which was all great. Apart from the fact that, now she had managed to assign herself solely to *General Manager* (being the boss's little princess had all sorts of advantages), Johnny found himself seeing rather more of Melissa than he might have chosen to and, consequently, was becoming rather tired of her. There was always someone blonder, darker, curvier, slimmer, attracting his attention. But if he dumped her, it would be bad; he'd have to see her on set all the time, and she was definitely the type to bear a grudge. She was talking about moving in now, and he was definitely going to have to discourage *that*. The last thing he wanted was her in his apartment all the time. He was going to have to deal with it soon. But not yet.

When their car pulled up outside the hotel, the crew and director were waiting for them, cameras already rolling as Logan and Johnny got out and headed towards the glass doors. Passers-by paused, their attention attracted by the cameras and booms and the growing buzz of anticipation that surrounded Logan as he crossed the sidewalk and entered the hotel.

'Look, it's—'

'Logan Barnes.'

'It's the other one I like – Mark, the English one. Isn't he here? I just lurve that accent.'

'Oh Mom, hey, there he is – Johnny – you know, from . . .'

'Get your camera out, Marjorie – hurry up, they're going inside!'

'*General Manager*.'

'You *have* seen it. I watch it every week – yes, on Bravo. Yes, that one!'

'Alicia, please hand your room key into reception – It's Time for You to Check Out.'

The camera panned from the pretty yet stricken face of the blond-haired girl dressed in a white shirt and dark suit, to the panel of three men sitting behind a long wooden desk, one of whom had been the one to issue the verdict. Their faces were set firm, their minds made up. Silence.

The camera then moved to show the rest of the room. It was a large, square room, formal yet modern, situated high up in the building. The view from the large windows was one of neighbouring skyscrapers. The whole atmosphere was one of high-flying success. A group of four young women and three men sat in a line against the far wall of the room, their faces betraying varying degrees of relief, pleasure and smugness.

Alicia stood and smoothed down her skirt before heading towards the three men in front of her, her arm outstretched.

'Thank you for the opportunity, Mr Stokes.'

She shook the hand of the man on the left. He grinned at her – and was that a wink? She blushed. Johnny Stokes, always with a ready smile and a kind word, was known for being a ladies' man. As she had found out for herself one night not so long ago . . . She put that firmly to the back of her mind, and moved on.

'Mr Barnes. It's been an honour, sir.'

He nodded, his face unsmiling but not unkind. Finally, she took the hand of the third man, Mark Mallory – the Englishman with the pale blue eyes, the slender hands and long fingers. He was distant, cool, polite.

'Mr Mallory. Thank you.'

He smiled briefly, but there was no real warmth to it. The Brit contestants had all got on better with him than the Yanks, since he always seemed to be looking down on them, somehow. Mark Mallory, in his pale grey tailored suit and rose-pink shirt, his still thick hair with only a little grey combed back in a gentle wave, was LBI's Managing Director of Hotel Operations. It was his job to ensure that the group's properties were running smoothly, hiring and firing managing directors and individual hotel managers, resolving problems within the hotels' management structures with professionalism and a light touch. He had joined LBI years ago, when his aristocratic family had fallen on hard times. Their stately home in Dorset, Sternley, had been in a serious state of disrepair and about to be given to the National Trust in order to keep it going, when Logan had swept in, bought it up and transformed it into a luxury country-house hotel.

On *General Manager* it was Mark who set the hotel-management tasks, or who had the contestants racing to make hundreds of beds as they struggled to complete housekeeping challenges, or who got them to play bellboy and lug tons of heavy and fragile luggage up and down the stairs. Alicia had always felt that he enjoyed watching them suffer rather more than was seemly – there was something of the sadist in his eyes, she thought.

The girl's goodbyes completed, she turned to the line of other contestants now. 'Good luck,' she mouthed at Dominic, the big, camp man who was the only friend she had made during her three weeks in New York, and the one she would be rooting for to win. The rest of them could go fuck themselves. He blew her a kiss.

Picking up the handle of the suitcase on wheels that all the contestants were required to use, she walked to the back of the room and blinked away a tear. She didn't want to start crying now, since in a few months this episode would be shown on national television – well, international television actually, as it was very much a transatlantic production. *General Manager* was filmed in both New York and London, the contestants came from both countries, and the series was screened on the same day in both territories. It was an expensive way of doing things, and it meant a lot of to-ing and fro-ing, as well as headaches for the production company and editors, but it was all part of the show's ethos, which was to reflect the lifestyle of Logan Barnes and his right-hand men as accurately as possible. Part reality show, part fierce competition for a position working for LBI, the first series had been an instant hit, and this second series looked set to achieve an even greater success when it aired.

Taking a deep breath, Alicia prepared to leave through the big red doors that had become the symbol of the show in what she knew would be the final image of the episode. Every week someone was told to Check Out, and had to walk through those doors. Now it was her turn.

'OK, cut! Sorry, Alicia, dear, come back, come back – we're going to have to take that from the top. Can we have a bit more in the way of visible regret, please – you've just lost the opportunity of a lifetime! Really make us *feel* it. And Dominic, less of the kissy-kissy stuff in the background, please. You're not here to make friends, people. All right? Rolling . . .'

Alicia sighed, and put her case back on the floor next to her. She supposed this was what they meant by 'the magic of TV'.

* * *

15

Logan let the chatter of the crowd that was waiting excitedly outside the building by the time he, Johnny and Mark left fade into the background. He'd learned to turn the volume of it down in his head. At first it had bothered him that everywhere he went someone did a double take, or nudged their companion, or openly stared and pointed. He hardly noticed it these days. Even the camera crews, who were his almost constant companions for days on end, shadowing him in meetings and at dinners and in his office, he paid little attention to any more. It was surprising how quickly you adjusted, how fast you got used to even the most surreal of situations, and began to see them as perfectly normal. Being filmed while he viewed a potential new acquisition? Just another day. Turning on the TV at home to catch the news and seeing yourself negotiating with a contractor? His finger didn't falter on the remote control. Driving through Manhattan from JFK and seeing scores of billboards advertising the second series of *General Manager*, with his, Johnny's and Mark Mallory's faces blown up to the size of houses, their arms crossed, staring down at the camera with Logan's slogan, *It's Time for You to Check Out* emblazoned across the bottom? He didn't even blink any more.

As Logan stepped out into the heat that characterised August in Manhattan, the air hung heavily around him, thick and soupy, making his skin feel damp almost immediately. Office workers rushed between appointments, briefcases under one arm and a large skinny macchiato wedged under the other as they juggled phone and belongings in the scrum; a tiny, size-zero woman in her eighties, still in her floor-length fur despite the weather and a hairdo bigger than her bird-like skull, walked a miniature white Chihuahua; a black stretch Hummer limo drew up alongside a Foot Locker, music pumping, and let out a group of impossibly wide-shouldered black men, all in matching white suits, their hands shimmering with diamonds as they gestured, the jewels catching the sunlight. New York City. There was nowhere quite like it.

He reached the two limos that were idling in front of the hotel, one for him and his PA, one for Johnny, Mark and Kirsten Devizes-Brown. Kirsten was a tall, rangy brunette, and Logan's Head of Communications, Sales and Marketing. The eldest daughter of an old and notoriously eccentric English family, she was a PR genius, who could make anything and everything seem utterly, irresistibly desirable. Before

16

joining LBI she had worked on her own, masterminding the come-backs of pop stars who'd been busted doing drugs, or rappers caught carrying guns, running damage limitation for the reputation of young royals caught with their pants down somewhere they shouldn't have been, and babysitting a children's TV presenter through his drink-driving trial. She had a reputation for being tough, hardworking, knowing everyone, and also being great fun. Logan knew he was lucky to have her on his side. Apart from anything else, if she was working *for* him, he knew she couldn't be working *against* him.

Rachel was already inside the car, her ultra-thin laptop open on her knee, no doubt with a list of tasks and instructions and queries at the ready. She was an excellent assistant, he couldn't manage without her. She had been one of the contestants on the first series of *General Manager* – had been kicked off in one of the early rounds, mainly because she wasn't pushy enough for the show's producers. But he had spotted her efficiency, her calmness in the face of any kind of chaos, and had hired her straight away. It had proved to be a good decision, but then, his decisions usually did. He sat back. In a few hours he'd be home in London. Meet with Maryanne, give her a chance to go over the social arrangements for the next few weeks. See the kids if they were there – that was a good point. He turned to Rachel.

'Do I have a slot scheduled with Charlie and Lucia?'

She clicked the mouse to bring up Logan's digital calendar on her screen.

'Lucia, yes, tomorrow at eleven a.m., then lunch. I've booked you in at the Ivy Club. Charlie's not in London at the moment. In the evening you're hosting a dinner party at home.'

He nodded his approval. He could spend the morning with Maryanne, then check in with Lucia, see what she was occupying her time with (and hopefully be told that she had taken up the place at St Martin's College that she had been offered to study fashion design), maybe see if she had any news of what progress Charlie had made with his music recording (and hopefully discover that he was nearing completion and had got it out of his system), and then have a pleasant lunch with her before getting back on with things in his West End office. Good. The car sped them towards the airport.

* * *

17

The engines of his private jet whirred, and Logan shrugged off his jacket and rolled up his linen shirt-sleeves, as he and Rachel walked briskly up the steps of the plane that was waiting on the runway to fly them to London. His security detail gave the pilot the OK, having checked the plane over before Logan and his assistant arrived in his chauffeur-driven Mercedes, another shut the door behind Rachel, and the pilot prepared for take-off. Logan hardly noticed the team of bodyguards any more, he was so used to having them around, shadowing him, forming a tight band of experience and expertise around himself and his family. It was just part of the travelling circus of his life. He took security seriously, since the risks of kidnap and corporate sabotage were very real ones.

Logan dumped his briefcase down, pulled off his shoes and socks, and went to his fitted wardrobe to get a T-shirt for the flight. The long-range Boeing was just like another of his homes; with twenty-five properties scattered all over the world and a hands-on approach to hotel management like Logan's, it had to be. It carried him back and forth across the Atlantic, over the Caribbean, all around Europe – wherever he needed to meet clients, oversee building and renovation works, or meet with banks and business associates. As he changed, Logan continued to fire a steady stream of questions, comments and instructions at his assistant. She was well used to doing five things at once.

Logan selected a bottle of San Pellegrino from the assortment in the glass-fronted Sub Zero refrigerator built into a marble-topped bar on one side of the plane, and poured himself a glass.

'You have a three o'clock with the planning department regarding the Mall development, that's confirmed. Christian arrives at two tomorrow to discuss refinancing options and to put a proposal in front of you. Johnny's dealing with the legal issues remaining regarding Luxury.'

Rachel glanced over at Johnny who had wandered into the cabin, and who nodded in confirmation.

'We'll need to talk them through at some point. No major rush.'

Rachel continued as she, Logan, Johnny, Mark and Kirsten all gathered around the large oval table. The flight to London would be a working one – it was often one of the only opportunities they got to come together in the same place at the same time – otherwise meetings were held and decisions discussed and taken using the twenty-first century combination of conference calls and video screens, emails, iPhones and BlackBerries that they had all come to rely on.

'There's been a development with the lawsuit against the Vegas contractors: you have an update memo.' Rachel gestured at the papers Logan was going through. 'There's a request for you to chair a debate at Harvard Business, and a couple of charity requests. All the information is in your folder.'

Logan continued to look through the papers. 'Approve those.' He went on, 'The Pink brothers should have submitted the final selections for the guest cosmetics – chase that if they haven't come through. And I want to see where we are with the brochure copy. Also, the staff uniforms – when will I see the finished products?'

'Tuesday,' Rachel said. 'I'll confirm.'

'Is the film ready?'

'Yes.'

This was what they had all been waiting for.

Rachel pressed a single button and a plasma screen slid silently down from the ceiling as the lights around the room dimmed. The film began and Logan watched intently as a single word floated forwards out of the black background, the ornate lettering faintly shimmering as it came into focus, and then slipped away again.

LUXURY

Logan smiled. The word reappeared, gently pulsing on the screen. Rachel clicked another button on the remote, and out of the background emerged silhouettes of tropical birds of paradise sucking from flowers; limbs moving in a slow, sinuous dance; a ray of light catching a jewelled necklace; a thin curl of smoke winding up into the air from a pipe; liquid splashing gently against the side of a glass. All in the company's signature black and cream, all on the screen for just long enough for the viewer to decipher what the images were before disappearing just out of reach . . . back to black . . . and then the words:

Beyond your wildest dreams.
Every whim satisfied.
Every desire fulfilled.

In total privacy.

LUXURY . . .

The trailer they had spent months perfecting drew to a close. It was finally happening. The place that had fired his imagination and filled his daydreams for almost forty years, ever since Honoré, his beloved nanny, had first described it to him in a bedtime story, was his – and his alone.

'In the middle of the ocean, in a place where no one goes, there is an island . . .'

That was how the story had started, in Honoré's lilting Mauritian accent; the same every time, and Logan's neck would tingle in anticipation and he would hunker down into the duvet to listen. Honoré had worked for his parents for many years, and had taken on the role of nanny almost by default, the day Logan was brought home from the hospital. His mother had seen her role as being mostly completed at that point, and so Honoré had picked up the screeching little bundle in her arms and soothed him, rocking and singing softly to him. From that moment on, it had been she whom Logan went to for comfort, with a scraped knee or a shiny winged beetle he had discovered under a stone, she who taught him his numbers and ABC, she who dressed him in the morning and tucked him in at night – always with the story of the magical island of violets. But although the beginning was always the same, the rest of the story was always different. One day, L'île des Violettes would be at the centre of a battle raged by pirates who roamed the high seas searching for treasure; the next it would be the setting for a damsel in distress, complete with fairytale castle and dashing prince to rescue her; the next, a magical island where elves and warlocks inhabited the caves, and if you were quiet, a unicorn could be seen darting through the trees.

Every time a different tale, but every time the same backdrop of L'île des Violettes described so many times that Logan felt as if the geography of the place had seeped into his bones. He *knew* the place, knew its beaches and inlets as well as he knew the pattern of the cracks in his bedroom ceiling; knew where the hills and peaks were as well as he knew which of the wooden floorboards in the corridor outside his bedroom creaked and could give his midnight trips to the kitchen away.

20

So when he had finally gone to the island for the first-time, all those years ago, with Johnny and Nicolo, it had felt like coming home.

Rachel clicked through some of the brochure images. Rising up out of the deep blue of the Indian Ocean, the island had always gleamed with natural beauty, but now it shone with the gloss of many millions of dollars' worth of investment as well. Named for the surprising profusion of tiny purple flowers which grew all over the island, L'île des Violettes had once been the home of a reclusive film star, but after his death in the 1950s it had fallen into disrepair, and no one had lived on it since. Until now.

The first image showed the island from a distance, as the guests would see it when they arrived by boat. It sparkled with light, with life. Logan stared at the shoreline, the pale expanse of sand stretching out along the edge of the island, and he could almost hear the sound of the sea around him, feel the silky, caressing air on his face.

Rachel pressed another button and a new image appeared, again taken from the point of view of a guest arriving, drawing you into the place. This time, the photo was of the jetty, its glossy wood extending out into the sea towards the viewer. It was in the same location as it had always been, but rebuilt to make a solid platform for the distinguished guests who would be using it: smooth wood, with silver rails, and a uniformed attendant waiting to greet the ex-Senator, current Prime Minister or megastar who might be about to alight. Luxury was for the elite's elite. Sometimes it seemed as though anyone could be a celebrity these days; all you had to do was queue up for the latest reality TV show and you were almost guaranteed an interview in *Heat* magazine. Luxury was not for those people. No, she was for the top tier only – those who were rich enough and famous enough to pass the rigid security testing, to warrant the strict and tightly enforced privacy rules, to require a level of sumptuous indulgence that surpassed that of any hotel until now. People like billionaire hedge-fund managers, Russian oligarchs, Hollywood producers worth hundreds of millions. You didn't just book a room at Luxury, you applied for one, and waited to see if your request had been successful. You didn't deposit in order to be considered for a room. You didn't just get on a plane and fly there,

F/2111874

you waited until your reservation request had been processed and approved before you were told where you would be met from, by a limousine which would take you to a private airfield, where a company jet would be waiting for you. You didn't just go on holiday, you escaped to your own personal version of ultimate luxury.

Logan knew that the rich and famous enjoyed gimmicks and freebies. Indeed, in his long experience as an hotelier he had learned that the most shameless stealers of crystal ashtrays and bathrobes and items from the mini-bar were the wealthiest. He had once had to replace fifty thousand dollars' worth of items from a suite after it had been vacated by a famous pop star, as well as spending a considerable sum restoring the antique silk carpets her dog had destroyed. Dreaming up the little quirks and details was the fun part of the job, the bit where he got to play Willy Wonka with his hotels. But he also knew that what his guests valued above all was the ability to enjoy themselves and relax, secure in the knowledge that they were safe from the clicking shutters and scribbling pens of the media. To be confident that they would not be nagged for autographs by members of the public, or stared at like freaks while they were eating by people desperate to know what it was that Bill Gates, Madonna or Janet Jackson preferred to start the day with. Luxury's clientele didn't need just another luxury hotel – they needed *the* luxury hotel – and for them, that meant one that guaranteed them a refuge.

The beaches, with their smooth white sand that was raked every morning, looked perfectly natural, but were actually manmade structures. A crawlspace underneath allowed for internet access and iPod docking stations to be wired into the beach, situated at each cabana, as well as the sophisticated temperature-control system beneath the tons of sand which stopped it from getting too hot and burning delicately pedicured feet. Fire pits had been positioned every twenty yards or so along the top of the beach, which were lit at night, casting a bronze glow on the air. Guests could have their dinner barbecued on them by a private chef, castaway style.

Next came a close-up of the custom-made cream and black patterned silk that covered the walls of one of the small 'salons' inside the hotel. This was followed by a picture of a smiling, red-lipsticked, all-American girl, dressed in a retro striped cigarette girl outfit; the girls would serve cones of popcorn and miniature bottles of champagne with straws during the in-flight film on the private planes which would take guests to the closest airport to the island. Other features included the Nautilus mini-sub for underwater excursions, the custom-sprayed Harley Davidsons for more adventurous guests to borrow to ride around the island, and the matching buggies for those who preferred to drive more sedately. More images appeared on the screen. A violet velvet chaise longue on the balcony of one of the rooms, a fine sheet of transparent white linen falling in soft folds over its back. A walk-in wardrobe, with a rainbow of fine cashmere sweaters folded in a stack on one of the cedar shelves. A small caramel-coloured dog looking quizzically at the camera, its head tilted to one side: devoted pet-owners whose dogs had to remain at home because of quarantine laws could borrow one of the hotel's pets to keep them company during their stay, complete with accessories such as rhinestone-studded collars and their own pet sofas.

Upon approval of their application, guests would be required to sign a contract, drawn up by Johnny, which laid out the terms of membership. Absolute privacy, absolute confidentiality. No photos, no video cameras, no gossiping to the tabloids. A file was opened for each guest, and his or her personal details and preferences recorded. You would never have to explain how you liked your coffee at Luxury.

The slideshow ended and the screen faded to the company's curving black and white logo. Logan knew the project was an ambitious one. He knew what his detractors were saying – that it couldn't be done, that no one would jump through all of the rumoured hoops that the arrogant Logan Barnes was putting in place. He didn't care. He'd been surrounded by whispers all his life. He wasn't going to start listening to them now.

This was it. This was his magnum opus.

The trailer ended. Logan was standing in front of the plasma screen and facing his most trusted executives, the group of men and women who formed the foundation of his company. His best friends. They might be the board, but this – Luxury – was very much Logan's baby. And Johnny's, of course. But still, Logan was the driving force, the instigator of everything. He waited for their reactions.

They all stood up, cheering, Johnny and Mark rushing forward to clap him on the shoulder, squeeze him in manly hugs; Kirsten and Rachel kissing him on the cheek, Kirsten leaving smudges of plummy lipstick in her wake.

'It's wonderful, Logan, just awesome.'

'Many congratulations, old boy. You've done a hell of a fine job.'

'You did it, man. You did it.'

Logan breathed a sigh of relief and pleasure. He minded what they thought; he respected everyone in the cabin, and would have given any reservations they might have had serious consideration. But they loved it. They really loved it. There was just something nagging at him . . . He pushed it down. Suddenly he felt very tired, and glanced at his watch. He would try and take a nap before they landed in London.

'OK. The press release is going out tomorrow. It contains the hotel's particulars and outlines our unique reservation processes; it also gives the basic website and contact details. The launch party is mentioned, but no details are given. I want it to hit everyone at the same time, when it happens. So please remember that we're still keeping all information regarding this completely confidential. I know I don't have to remind you, but humour me.'

He smiled at his team. God, he was excited. This was what it was all about; this was why he did it. The adrenaline of forthcoming success.

'As a brief aside, we're opening advance applications the day after tomorrow, and our reservations teams are primed and ready to take calls. I have every faith they'll do so with great efficiency. On to the party. As you know, we have a very high-profile event planned. We're anticipating a huge degree of interest from the press wanting to get in. As well as all the usual socialites, reality TV 'stars' and hangers-on.'

There was a murmur of laughter from around the table. Logan Barnes's parties were glamorous, fun and just a bit wild, and were always one of the hottest tickets in town.

'We're keeping the guest list tight. There are going to be plenty of people – including some big names – who can't get in. I know this is a bit of a gamble, turning away people who can normally get in anywhere they want to. But the theory is that this is going

24

to make them want it even more. And of course, anyone really important whom we've turned away will be the first to be let through when it comes to reservations for the hotel itself. We don't want to completely alienate them – just make them work for it a little. I'm confident this party's going to be our best yet. I'm really excited about it, and I hope you are as well.'

He looked at Rachel, who now took over.

'The system to ensure that the exclusivity of the event is maintained is as follows. Invitations are being sent out tomorrow. They're being hand-couriered to the invitees, who will then have twenty-four hours to reply. Anyone who hasn't replied within that time will not have their invitation validated, and as such, will not be given the final part of it, which contains details of the location. There will be no plus ones, no last-minute changes to the guest list. No one will be allowed in who hasn't been personally invited and replied within the allotted time-frame.'

Mark Mallory inclined his slightly weak chin a little.

'Mark?'

'Is that wise? Journalists and celebrities are both used to getting what they want. They can become very . . .' he smiled thinly '. . . vocal, shall we say, if they feel they're being sidelined. It's inevitable that some of them simply won't be able to respond in time.'

'You're right. And that's just the point. Like I said earlier, I want people to realise that not everyone will get into the party – just like not everyone will get into Luxury itself. And the way to do that is to put our money where our mouth is, which inevitably means some people will be disappointed. But by doing this, we'll prove our brand identity right from the off. Luxury is exclusive. It's private. It's not for everyone. But once you're in, you're in. And we protect *your* privacy. Anyhow, the ones who don't make it will be even more intrigued by the hotel itself. While we're on the subject, Steve, I want to go over the security arrangements with you. Can you send a report to Rachel for me to look at?'

'Not a problem.' Steve Bigby was sitting in the corner of the cabin, absolutely still and silent until he was spoken to. He was Logan's head of security; a slight man, with one of those faces that you could never quite recall once he had left the room. Shadowy. An ex-casino conman, he had grown up in a trailer park on the outskirts of Las Vegas and knew all the tricks. He had the ability to slip into any situation and adapt himself to it. Flitting around the sidelines, sliding in between the cracks. Nothing could get past Steve. Logan trusted him absolutely.

'Mrs Barnes has approved the menus, both for the party and the following events, but I have the florist's presentations here.' Rachel passed the laptop to Logan as he sat at the table, and he scrolled through images of shallow pools of water dotted with floating candles and the palest pink orchids, lit so that the water glowed, jewel-like; of olive trees strung with tiny fairy lights.

'Perfect. Send the menus to my laptop as well, please.' He noted the look of surprise that appeared briefly on his assistant's face before she assented.

That was strange, she thought. Maryanne usually took sole charge of the food and design details at Logan's parties, both business and private; she always had done. It had been said more than once that she had played a role at least as influential in Logan's success as Johnny Stokes. Rachel had never quite believed that, but she tried to give the woman the benefit of the doubt – she hadn't known her in the early days, after all. Maybe it was true. If it was, how Maryanne must have changed since then . . .

'This is something new. Something no one has ever done before. It's going to be great.' The excitement of his long-held dream finally nearing realisation showed in Logan's face. He held his weight on the balls of his feet, full of energy. 'And if a few hacks get their noses put out of joint because they've missed the free canapés and champagne . . .'

A confident, rich drawl interrupted, 'Well then, they should have replied in time, shouldn't they?' Johnny Stokes looked around the room, his smile easy and charming, but behind it lay an iron strength, just as his casual dress concealed a body tightly muscled from years of training. Johnny loved to run, jump, kayak, windsurf – anything physical, and the more dangerous the better. He held Mark's gaze, his eyes bright and challenging him to disagree.

Eventually Mark nodded his head briefly in acquiescence, and looked away.

* * *

26

The meeting over, Logan announced that he was going to have a rest.

'And Kirsten, can I have a word, please?'

'Of course. I have some documents for you to look over, also.'

He headed to his bedroom at the back of the plane, Kirsten following. As usual, her clothes were both smart and quirky; today's suit was deep charcoal and had a tight, nipped-in waist and flared, asymmetrical skirt. Logan pulled his tie off as he went.

'I've put some ideas together for people you might want to consider giving interviews to when we launch,' Kirsten said. 'Not too many, just a balanced selection of some big names, along with some more unusual choices – smaller publications, but ones that reach specific demographics.'

Logan opened the folder and glanced over the list of names. She was right, there were some magazines and websites on there that no one would expect him to give interviews to. But he trusted her judgement; Kirsten had an unerring instinct for PR and trends.

'There are also some thoughts on how best to handle your personal PR profile.'

Logan glanced at her, noting her expression. 'No need for you to feel embarrassed, Kirsten. I'm well aware of the potential issues that my family life might pose. Thanks.'

She nodded.

'So here's the thing,' he went on. 'Am I making a mistake with how we're running the party? It's not too late to say. You know I want your input.'

She shook her head. 'I don't believe so. Your thinking is right. People will talk about this more because we're going against the grain – even the ones who don't get in. It's ballsy, but I think we can pull it off.'

'That's how I like it.' He smiled.

Logan's voice was as confident as ever, but Kirsten noticed there was something else behind his words – some slight wariness, maybe? Perhaps he was just tired.

Logan felt unsettled. The beautiful island, his paradise – he was opening it up to the world. Was it the right thing to do? Would the world appreciate it as he did? Well, no one could do that . . . but would they see the splendour of it?

'Have I got it right this time, Kirsten?' he asked slowly.

'The party? Yes, I told you—'

'Not just the party. The whole thing. The hotel, the island – have I made all the right decisions?'

The young woman stood in front of him and looked into his eyes. For the first time in seven years, she could see uncertainty in them. *He was scared.* The realisation startled her. The island must mean a very great deal to him.

'This isn't just another hotel, is it?'

'No, not this time.' He seemed relieved that someone had recognised it. 'It's – I can't explain it. L'île des Violettes is the most beautiful place in the world, and I'm opening it up to the world. And what if the world doesn't like it? Tell me honestly, Kirsten: is what I'm doing to the island going to ruin it? Is the island going to ruin *me*?'

She took a deep breath.

'Honestly? I have no idea. No one has any idea. This project – well, when you first told me about it – the whole board – we all thought you'd gone crazy. An island you have to apply to go to, that journalists can't publicise, that provides its guests with anything they want, whenever they want it? No one thought you could get this far. But you have.'

'At what cost though?' Logan murmured. 'At what cost. Ignore me.' He shook himself. 'Something's spooked me today, I'm sorry.'

'Don't apologise. Everyone's allowed to be unsure of themselves, now and again.'

Logan smiled. 'Not me.'

'Yes, even you. Even perfect you.'

She paused. Damn. He was silent for a moment, he let it slide past, and for that she was grateful. She continued, 'Anyhow, nothing's going to go wrong. You're Logan Barnes, remember? You can't *get* anything wrong.'

'I got it wrong once before.'

'That was then. This is now. The finance is structured differently now, you're older – wiser . . .' She shrugged.

'True.' But he still looked unsure.

'Hey – and you didn't have me back then,' she teased him, lightening the mood. 'I think that's what it was all down to, you know.'

'Good point, well made.' He laughed. 'Thank you, Kirsten.'

'No problem. I believe in Luxury, Logan. It's happening – you're making it happen, it's going to be perfect.'

'It's a big gamble.'

'You think? I think it's what they call *a sure thing*.'

Chapter Two

'After making London their base just a few months ago, the American hotelier and star of hit show *General Manager*, Logan Barnes, along with his glamorous wife Maryanne, have taken the city by storm. Top of everyone's dinner-party wish lists, their fabulous Summer Garden Party was the most hankered-after invitation of the year.'   *Tatler*

'Social butterfly and power wife Maryanne Barnes was on sparkling form last night at the opening of new Mayfair eatery Carousel. Accompanied by her muso son, Charlie, who is tipped to be in demand by some of the big labels, Maryanne joked that she was checking out the competition on behalf of her husband, Logan, before leaving for a private dinner engagement.'
                                                    OK! Magazine

'Is a certain over-privileged "socialite" recently landed back in London, and making sure everyone knows it, going just a bit too heavy on the happy pills? Our sources tell us her doctor can hardly keep up with her demands, she's cracking through her supplies with such enthusiasm …' *www.tittle-tattler.com*

'Maryanne Barnes, wife of hotel tycoon Logan and mother of rock musician Charlie and hot young model and It-girl Lucia, presided over a lavish ball to raise money for the new wing of the Royal Ballet School. Injecting some Manhattan-style gloss into the London arts scene, she hosted a small drinks reception at the family's Eaton Square mansion before the evening continued with dinner and dancing for 300 guests at the nearby

LBI-owned Chesham Hotel. Maryanne, whose personal style has secured her place near the top of the best-dressed lists for over 15 years, wore a full-length, strapless black silk gown with a lace overlay and small train. Hot-pink Louboutin heels and a rare pink diamond necklace completed the outfit. Expect to see more from inside the ball later this year, as the event was being filmed as part of series two of *General Manager*.'

Hello! Magazine

Maryanne Barnes lay flat on the silk chaise longue in her dressing room, her head hanging off one end in a move intended to help blood flow to her skin and therefore increase radiance; her legs were raised to help blood flow away from her ankles and therefore reduce puffiness. Her eyes were covered with a mask infused with an aromatherapy oil that contained an extract of a flower found only in the mountains of Nepal, and which claimed to 'Naturally Relax, Revive and Restore serenity and bliss'. She concentrated on practising the breathing exercises her yoga teacher had given her; trying to make her body soft like the snow, flowing like water. Inhaling slowly through her perfectly sculpted nose, subtly reshaped by Mr Langhorn of Harley Street, she focused her mind on attempting to make her breath become part of the energy of the wind. It just made her want to pee.

Sighing, Maryanne pulled the mask from her eyes, took a bottle of pills from underneath the pillow and swallowed two with a swig of Sancerre, before padding over to her Venetian glass dressing table. Leaning down, she opened the small glass-fronted fridge that had been custom-built into the side of the table, and refilled her glass. Then she twisted her hair on top of her head, stuck a pin in it, and sat up straight to examine her face in the mirror. She was still beautiful, and the soft mocha of her silk tunic flattered her skin tone. Her eyes had always been her best feature, but she had to concentrate not to let the skin at the corners of her eyes contract and display the fine lines there. She lifted her chin. Was there a faint sagging under her jawline? Damn. She stared into the mirror. Maybe it was just a bit blurred. Everything was a bit blurred these days, come to think of it. Ah, well. Blurring was a good thing, kept everything soft focus. No sharp edges.

But even the wine- and pill-saturated soft-focus lens couldn't hide the ever-deepening lines that ran from her nostrils to the corners of her mouth, or the slackening and loosening of the skin on her neck. She was getting old. Should she move her Restylane appointment forward by a couple of weeks? Putting her hands on her cheeks, she gently stretched the skin back, smoothing out the lines which were made worse by the way she slept, all hunched in on herself, squashing her face up. She'd slept like that since she was a child and, although she'd tried hard to train herself out of it, nothing worked. There was a new sort of face lift that she'd read about – subtler, apparently. She should look into it. Face lifts were one thing, but no one had invented a hand lift yet, had they? When did she get old lady hands?

The double photo-frame that sat on her dressing table displayed a picture of her in her late twenties in one side, and her daughter, Lucia, in the other. In the photo Maryanne was wearing a clingy Alaïa minidress, spinning round in Logan's arms, her hair choppy, her head thrown back and her red-lipped mouth wide open, laughing. In the other picture Lucia wore the same dress, having unearthed it from the nether regions of one of Maryanne's wardrobes and worn it to a film premiere, with high boots and a leopard-skin coat. She was standing on the red carpet, about to enter the cinema, pouting and posing for the cameras. They both looked so young.

Maryanne poured another glass of wine. She would definitely move her appointment forward.

It had all happened without her noticing. Half her life had happened without her noticing. She took a deep breath. *No no no. No self-pity for you today, Maryanne, that's not on the menu. You made your bed ... isn't that what they say? And what a silken-sheeted, goose-down-pillowed bed it is ... Come on. Time to shake a leg and take part in the day.*

Jewellery! Yes, that would cheer her up. Sparkly things, glittering rings. She slid open a drawer and looked down at the selection of baubles lined up inside. Pearls? Hmm, no. Cassie, with whom she was lunching, always bloody well managed to outdo Maryanne on the jewellery front. It was tacky, really. She just seemed to chuck everything she owned on, like a Christmas tree, and then make snide remarks about how 'subtle' Maryanne's choice was. Well, today *she* was going to show *her*. Maryanne started picking pieces out of the drawer and holding them up to her face. Sparkle sparkle.

Two hours later and Maryanne Barnes had finished her assessment of her face, and was rifling through her temperature-controlled shoe room, pulling Perspex boxes from their shelves. Her maid, Clara, flinched as each pair clattered from its carefully catalogued places to the polished parquet wood floor. Oyster-coloured satin, crystal-encrusted Jimmy Choos, scarlet leather ankle boots, hand-made and hand-tooled cowboy boots – they all hit the floor as she stood on a stool in her search for the one pair of shoes she had decided she could wear. Where *were* they? She had to find them or her outfit would be spoiled and the whole thing would be pointless; she might as well cancel her lunch plans and go back to bed. As well as the whole jewellery thing, Cassie Malone always wore the most fabulous shoes. Yards of column inches seemed to be dedicated to her and her bloody shoes. She and Maryanne were good friends in the uneasy way that women are when their relationship is at least partly founded on attempts to outdo one another, and Maryanne was damned if she was going to turn up wearing anything that was less than perfect.

She wobbled slightly on the stool.

'Careful, Mrs Barnes, please . . .'

'Oh, for goodness' sake, I'm fine, Carla! I just need the candy-striped Blahniks.'

Crash. A pair of patent pumps hit the floor. Carla bit her tongue and bent down to move them out of the way as Maryanne scooted the stool further along the rack.

'Oh, damnation!' She stamped her foot in frustration.

'Mrs Barnes, I really think you left them in New York. You remember you wore them at the tea party for Miss Elizabeth?'

Maryanne turned slowly and gave Carla a steely look.

'Don't be absurd. I didn't do any such thing, I wore the . . .'

Oh, fuck it. She *had* worn the striped shoes to that party, of course she had. She remembered now because Elizabeth de Mouton had particularly commented on them, as she was bemoaning the toll pregnancy had taken on her previously slim feet. However, there was no way she was going to let the maid know she was right.

'I wore the polka-dot slingbacks; Elizabeth made a point of

admiring them.' Her eyes dared Clara to disagree. The young woman, however, well aware of who paid her salary and kept her in second-hand designer jeans, simply began to tidy the shoes up.

'Of course, I remember now,' she said neutrally. 'How silly of me to be so forgetful. Shall I pick you out another outfit?'

'No. It's all spoiled now. I'll pick something new up on the way to lunch.'

Three-quarters of an hour later, Maryanne's impatiently waving fingers indicated her rejection of outfit after outfit as they were proffered to her in the private dressing rooms of Harvey Nichols. Her oversized Chanel sunglasses did little to conceal the look of disapproval on her face as she talked on her mobile phone.

Click, click, click went her fingers. She broke off her conversation with a guttural noise intended to express her irritation.

'I said I needed something for lunch with a friend. What in heaven's name makes you think that would be an appropriate choice?' She waved her hand dismissively at the black, layered ensemble the girl was holding up in front of her.

'Must go, darling, the girl here seems to be quite unable to follow simple instructions. *Ciao ciao.*'

She turned her face back towards the increasingly fraught-looking girl in front of her, and raised her eyebrows.

'Well?'

'McQueen, Mrs Barnes? Some new pieces have come in today.'

Maryanne shrugged one shoulder and turned her attention to a magazine. The personal shopper serving Maryanne knew that this was as positive a reaction as she could hope to expect, and rushed out of the room to find something that would satisfy her client's whims. Maryanne poured herself another glass of Veuve Cliquot, and carried on flicking through *Vogue*. She reached the social pages at the back of the magazine, and as she did so, a photograph from a recent book launch caught her eye. It gave her an idea. Flowers, for the party – hadn't Logan said he needed to decide on them? Yes, he had, when she had had dinner with him in New York last week. Well, here was the perfect thing. She'd better let him know straight away. She picked up her mobile again.

'Rachel, put me through to Logan. Well, wake him up. No – *don't* put me through to— Oh, for God's sake. Johnny! That girl is impossible, you know? Anyhow . . .'

The dresser reappeared, displaying a dress made from a very pale grey silk, teamed with a darker grey jacket. Maryanne raised an eyebrow and inclined her head slightly in approval.

'Listen, I've changed my mind about the flowers. I think they should be all one colour.' She could hear the sounds of New York travelling thousands of miles down the phone line as she waited for his reply. Cab horns blaring, music as he walked past a busker playing the violin.

'I'm pretty sure we've already approved them, Maryanne. But you know this isn't really my area.'

Isn't my job, is what he meant.

'No, but I can't get hold of Logan. You'll speak to him before I do, so tell him they should be all pink. Or red. No, pink. Hot pink. Elton did it for David's last birthday – it'll be striking.'

'I'll try and remember.'

But Maryanne had already hung up and was taking the outfit from the dresser.

'Fabulous. Now, find me some shoes to go with it. Louboutins, don't you think? Well – go along then. Chop chop!'

Forty-five minutes later, the black Mercedes pulled up outside Scott's in Mayfair's Mount Street, and the doorman stepped forward and opened the door. Maryanne took another of her pills from her bag and put on her large black-framed sunglasses. Everything felt very spiky suddenly. She wasn't really in the mood for lunch any more. Rebalance – that's what she needed to do. It was all going to be fine. She opened a bottle of mineral water and took a sip, then swallowed a Co-codamol. That should get rid of her headache and smooth out the edges a bit.

'Ma'am.'

She got out of the car, sliding her legs elegantly to one side to avoid the grimy puddle on the road and glaring at the back of Henry's head as she did so. Her outfit would be ruined if it got splashed. Honestly, one puddle in the whole street and he managed to park right next to it. Was everyone conspiring against her?

*　*　*

'Maryanne, how lovely.'

'Cassie! I can't – mwah – tell you – mwah – how much I've been looking forward to this.'

Maryanne sounded so sincerely pleased to see her friend that she almost convinced herself. She quickly scanned the room over Cassie's shoulder. A few actors with their agents, the notoriously wayward son of a minor royal chatting up a starlet at the oyster bar, and a very serious-looking meeting taking place in the corner between three of the most powerful men in the media. She was the best-looking woman there, though, and heads turned very slightly to gaze at her as she sat down at their table. A gossip columnist spotted her and nipped to the downstairs loo to send a quick email to his editor from his BlackBerry.

A waiter appeared at Maryanne's elbow and poured her a glass of champagne from the bottle of Krug chilling in an ice-bucket.

'I couldn't resist – naughty of me, I know,' Cassie said, picking up her glass and raising it. 'To fun.'

'I'll drink to that,' said Maryanne, tilting her glass to return the toast. 'I've had the most terrible day.'

Two hours later, Cassie and Maryanne had finished their meal of octopus carpaccio and lobster mayonnaise – both starter-sized portions, neither of which they finished. They'd finished the champagne, however, and Maryanne was now on her third glass of Meursault. Cassie had raised an eyebrow at the second glass – Maryanne had seen her over the top of the menu – but she knew better than to say anything. Screw her, anyway.

'So I was thinking, her fourteenth birthday party should be something really special, magical. You're so clever, will you do it?'

'I'm not doing any private projects at the moment, Cassie. I just don't have the time. What with all the preparations for Logan's launch, I'm completely overwhelmed. I can't commit to a thing apart from that.'

Maryanne occasionally 'did' parties for her friends and acquaintances on an ad hoc basis. Cassie pouted and clasped her hands together.

'Please? Pretty, pretty please? Oh go on – say yes. It won't be the same if anyone else does it, I know it won't. Say you will or I shall weep, right here.'

Maryanne laughed and held her hands up in surrender. She did like it when people owed her a favour, after all.

'All right! I'll do it. I'll put some ideas together and we can go from there. I'm thinking *A Midsummer Night's Dream* meets *Cabaret*. Now, I need you to do something for *me*, darling. Can you ask Mikael to write me another prescription? I'm running low.'

Cassie had a tame private GP with whom she was having an affair, and who sometimes helped Maryanne when she ran out of the pills she had come to rely on more and more. In repayment, Maryanne made sure Cassie was invited to some of the glitzier events that she would otherwise have struggled to get into – Elton and David's recent bash, for example. Quid pro quo. Cassie and Maryanne had become very good friends.

Logan's plane arrived from New York at 6 a.m. He'd got to the Barnes family's London home – a double-fronted townhouse in South Kensington – at seven, showered, changed his clothes and then gone straight to his West End office. Maryanne was still asleep when he got in, so he hadn't disturbed her. Hadn't needed to – they had their own suites of rooms, each with their own bedroom, bathroom, dressing room and drawing room, so they could quite often go for days without bumping into one another. And quite frequently did. 'We need the space,' they had told each other when they first started sleeping in different rooms. When was it? Logan couldn't remember now, a few years ago.

'I come in so late sometimes,' he had said. And, 'Yes, and I need my beauty sleep!' she had replied. And then they'd both smiled brightly at each other and turned away, and wondered how and when they had ended up so far apart from each other, and from the boy and girl who had happily slept curled up together in a tiny single bed, limbs entwined so that when they woke up they were never sure where one ended and the other began.

Maryanne had spent the morning sleeping and the afternoon preparing for the dinner party. A manicure at three o' clock, a blow dry at four, and then the florist arrived at five, after which she went upstairs to choose her outfit and do her make-up. She was tired – so tired, today. She took a nap and woke at six, feeling groggy and confused, and lay for a moment, wishing that she could just stay there for ever. Never getting up, never having to go downstairs and be Mrs Barnes, Logan's wife, never having to talk and be charming and laugh and smile . . . Then she pulled herself together. Poured herself a stiff gin and tonic, then made it a bit stiffer. Reached into her medicine cabinet for a Prozac and a couple of painkillers – Pethidine, Vicodin, Codeine? Ip, dip, dog . . . Pethidine today. Her favourite. Not that she had favourites, not really. Clever little pills, all of them. She got in the shower and let the warm water run over the outside of her body as the warmth from the pills spread up inside her. She would be fine. It would all be fine.

Maryanne put her head around the door of the dining room of their London home. Mink-coloured silk covered the walls and provided a neutral backdrop for the deep purple glassware. Candles in the matching crystal candelabras shone a soft light that reflected off the highly polished silverware. The butler was just finishing placing little silk-covered boxes at each place which contained the gifts that Maryanne had become known for giving to her guests. Tonight, the men were going home with silver Asprey letter-openers in alligator-skin cases and the ladies with silver lipstick holders, also from the Bond Street store. Maryanne had the current catalogues of all the fine goods stores carefully filed in her office – Asprey, Tiffany, Cartier and Smythson – and before each important dinner they gave, she selected luxurious little favours for their guests and had Henry go and collect them.

Closing the door, she headed next for the kitchen, to make sure everything was on track for the dinner. As she went, she put her hand to the discreet pocket that was sewn into the hem of her softly draped jersey dress and felt for the little bottle of pills tucked inside. One more, before she went in. One more for luck.

' . . . off to Necker on the thirteenth for two weeks with the family, bit of a break, *sooo* relaxing there . . .'

' . . . couldn't believe the cheek of it, but Caroline said that Beatrice had insisted . . .'

' . . . Jebb's current girl's on the way out, and I hear he's trying to buy Archie Rathcomb's old place in Ireland. Rathcomb's having none of it . . .'

' ... opened a new restaurant in Covent Garden, absolutely bombed, poor thing, so he's gone off to Cambodia to lick his wounds ...'

The babble of conversation ran in and out of Maryanne's ears; she couldn't catch hold of the sentences long enough to work out how to respond. She turned to the man on her left, who was looking at her expectantly, but his face was all shifting and fluid and made her dizzy, so she had to look down at her plate again. She tried to concentrate on her breathing, calm and slow, calm and slow, but it just made her feel seasick. The words weren't even making sense now, they were all muffled and stretched out and she could only make out floating fragments.

' ... Paris ...'

' ... can't bear it ...'

' ... incredibly beautiful girl ...'

She tried to drag herself out of her daze and smiled in the direction of the voice. 'Thank you, so kind.' The plate of langoustine ravioli shimmered in front of her, and the smell rising up from it made her feel nauseous.

She took a sip of wine and searched through her head for something to say. The man on her right was a banker, wasn't he? Must be, they all seemed to be bankers.

'The markets.'

'I'm sorry?'

'Markets. Emerging. How are they?'

The whole room seemed to go quiet all at once, and everything came back into focus in a rush. She could see faces staring at her from further down the table. Why had they all stopped talking? The man looked uncomfortable.

'As far as I'm aware they're still, well, still emerging.'

She nodded. He looked terrified.

'You're not in banking, are you?' she said.

He looked at her kindly. 'History. Well, historical novels really. The Elizabethans, Spanish Armada – that kind of thing. Complete dunce with numbers, I'm afraid.'

There was a horrible pause. Neither knew what to say next and Maryanne could feel Logan's eyes heavy on her from the end of the table. She couldn't bear to look at him. Oh, God. She was good at this; this was her talent, her strength, her *job*. Dinners, parties, lunches; she knew things about people, always knew the right thing to say, the right question to ask. And now she had got it so mortifyingly wrong. If she couldn't get this right any more, then what could she do? Her cheeks felt hot and she was all shaky. A hand reached down to one side of her arm and she jumped in fright and pushed her chair back suddenly.

There was a terrible clatter as Maryanne's chair shot back into Linny, the Thai maid who was trying to clear the plates from the table, and the beautiful crockery smashed to the floor.

'Oh!' Linny went pink and looked devastated. 'Sorry, Mrs Barnes, my fault, so clumsy, so sorry . . .' She was trying to hold her tears back as she gathered up the shards of china.

Maryanne stood and watched her for a second, appalled at the mess she had made, and ran from the room, muttering something about finding the butler to help Linny.

'She's been on some antibiotics for a chest infection and it's knocked her for six. Thank you so much for coming . . . thank you, Jim – yes, I'll be in touch about that meeting . . . Joanie, thank you, I'll pass that on to Maryanne, she'll be touched . . .'

Halfway up the staircase, hidden from view by the curving wall, Maryanne listened to Logan making excuses for her as the guests left. The cup of herbal tea that Linny had made her sat beside her, undrunk. What was happening to her? She dragged herself upright, and wandered across the landing into her study. The Rolodex sat on the Oriental desk in the corner of the room, taunting her. It was where she kept all the details of the people with whom she and Logan socialized. She knew almost everything in there off by heart. What they did for a living, how many children they had, whether the flowers she sent should be a romantic hand-tied bouquet of roses and peonies, or whether an architectural display of spiky exotic blooms was more 'them', who was having problems with their elderly mother and whose business had run into troubles – she prided herself on knowing all these little details of her guests' lives, and people always commented on it. It was her. It was what she *did*.

Going to the desk now, she rifled through some papers. Half-written thank-you cards sat waiting to be finished and put into their tissue-lined envelopes. It wasn't so long ago that she would write such cards on her return from an evening, before she even took off her make-up. Now there were dinners from a fortnight ago that she hadn't acknowledged. Invitations that had been ignored, left unanswered.

'Such an amazing memory, Maryanne has. I don't know how she remembers everything, and she always gets it just right.' People were flattered by her attention to detail; it was one of the things that made an invitation to dine with her and Logan at any of their homes so highly sought-after. 'The Original Power Hostess', she'd been called by an article in W Magazine last year. A journalist had written that she was *the ultimate tycoon's wife – at least as successful as her über-hotelier and property developer husband in her area of expertise. Her social manoeuvrings are executed as efficiently as a military campaign, the difference being that her operations really do win hearts and minds.*

And now look at her. Sent to bed early like a small child because she was unable to negotiate a simple dinner party in her own house. She flopped back on to the chaise longue, and reached under the pillow for one of the vials of pills she kept there. What was the point in pretending any more? She was a washed-up failure. Logan would be better off without her. He could remarry, would be sure to do so, someone more befitting his status.

Logan would be so angry with her, she thought, as she counted the little white tablets into her hand. Ten, eleven, twelve ... He hated people who couldn't control themselves and keep their head when it mattered, she knew that. But she also knew that he couldn't possibly hate her any more than she hated herself. Maryanne wept as she sat looking at her rings, watching how they sparkled in the light: her engagement ring was a rare chunk of pale pink diamond, flanked by two white diamond shoulders. She remembered the night he had given it to her. That night in Marmande. Replacing the cheap scrap of silver she'd worn for more than five years with the chunk of rock she was looking at now.

Maryanne gulped a sob and a pill back into her throat at the same time. Next to the engagement ring was her simple platinum wedding band and an eternity ring, while on her right hand she wore more gems – a diamond Cartier trilogy ring and an aquamarine and

41

diamond piece. She took another swallow and another pill. Her fingers were weighed down with jewels while her heart was weighed down with shame and sadness.

Logan stood in the corridor outside Maryanne's room, as he had done so many times since she had first got ill and this whole sorry mess had started. He could hear her crying through the door and couldn't decide whether to go inside or not. For once in his life he felt totally and utterly helpless.

The depression diagnosis had been meant to signal a new start, an acknowledgement that there was a problem – a solvable, treatable problem. Logan did what he thought he did best – he tried to solve the problem. He had made appointments for his wife with the top psychiatrists, had booked her in for spa weekends, had sent her to every kind of alternative and conventional therapist. Things he had read about, things he didn't believe in, things he had never even heard of. Anything was worth trying if it would make her better, stop the dreadful wracking sobs that came from her at night. Stop her hand trembling as she poured his coffee, stop him having to see the look of confusion in her eyes when she woke up after a drinking binge and struggled to work out where she was. But it was just the beginning of a cycle of more drugs, more prescriptions, a never-ending search for the one that would finally work, that would make it all better. They all had a side-effect and Maryanne wasn't good at being patient and waiting for them to subside, so she'd take another pill to try and get rid of the tiredness, or the insomnia, or the jitters, often without telling Logan what she was doing, and he was away so much that he lost track of what she was taking at any given time. Oh, that was no excuse, he knew that, but it had always been easier to pretend she was in good hands. She had worked her way along Harley Street in her increasingly desperate search for a magic panacea for her pain, but nothing was effective. She just lurched, weeping desperately, from one drug to another, one doctor to the next, until no one seemed to know what she was taking or when. She had changed. The light had gone out behind her eyes and he couldn't reach her any more. When he tried to talk to her she just said she was fine, not to worry about her. And so eventually, at the end of his tether, he had stopped trying.

Logan could run a hundred hotels, manage employees, negotiate deals with equally tough businessmen, handle politicians with finesse and bullishly take over flailing companies and turn them around into thriving interests. But he felt utterly lost and helpless in the face of this black struggle his wife was facing, and that he was leaving her to face alone.

How much of the responsibility for the state Maryanne was in now lay at his door? Some of it? All of it? His hand rested on the door handle but he couldn't bring himself to open it.

Instead, he turned away and walked slowly down the corridor. There were things he had to do, he told himself. Important things. As he walked on the sound of Maryanne crying faded away.

Chapter Three

'Your new iPod, Mr Flores. If I can just take a moment of your time to show you the playlists we've loaded on to this one?'

Nicolo nodded, and listened with a portion of his attention while his household manager – who was fully trained by the Starkey International Institute of Household Management in topics as many and varied as the identification of his employer's 'flavour profiles', cigar service, food and wine pairing, care of Oriental rugs, intelligent home technology and closet organisation – listed the specially designed selections of music that would sonically enhance every conceivable aspect of his life. William, as his household manager called himself – his real name was Dwayne, but he had taken the decision that his given name would not help him rise to the top of the Personal Service ladder, and had changed it to the more suitable William – continued to speak in smoothly modulated tones as Nicolo let his eye run down his appointment schedule for the day.

Nicolo's mind was as compartmentalised as his playlists. Currently, part of it was listening to William, storing the information away in the back of his mind for when he needed it. Part of it scanned the business news that appeared on the ticker of his computer screen. Part of it looked ahead to the day in front of him. And another part of it, as always, looked down on himself, coolly observing everything that was going on. Nicolo was constantly aware of his movements, of his composure, of how he appeared to others. It helped him project his preferred impression to other people – that of a calm, confident and controlled businessman.

It was 7 a.m. Nicolo was always at his desk by then. He woke every day at 5.30 a.m. with no need for an alarm, stepped out of his eight foot bed and straight into the wet room that was positioned at the far end of his bedroom, behind a single pane of glass that could be lit to either conceal or display the bather behind it. He liked to be able to lie in bed and watch a woman washing herself, readying herself for him, but never allowed them the same privilege. He would spend five minutes under cold water before stepping out, drying himself and putting on a pair of shorts, then taking his private elevator downstairs to his personal gym. Nicolo's apartment occupied the entire top three floors of his hotel in West Hollywood, the Residence Flores. It was one of the finest hotels he owned, a sparkling white building that seemed to have been created as a testament to Californian cool. From the climate-controlled underground car park, with individually assigned spaces for guests, and electric ports for the more eco-conscious drivers to recharge their Priuses, to the rooftop infinity pool and public gym with 360-degree views of the city, the hotel was high energy and always in great demand. Nicolo kept permanent homes in three other hotels – in London, Tokyo and a villa in his complex in Bali. When he needed to visit other countries, other properties, he took over the penthouse suite. He hadn't spent a night anywhere than in one of his own hotels for almost fifteen years.

Five days a week, Nicolo's trainer would arrive at 5.45 a.m. for an hour of training, the specifics of which changed each day. The man was a Brit, a former Royal Marine and a big wall of solid flesh who pushed Nicolo through his paces with no sympathy for aching muscles or fatigue. Nicolo didn't like him – he was a thug – but that was an advantage: he pushed himself harder out of irritation and a desire to prove that he wasn't some preening wimp, that he could work as hard as anyone. There had been a woman trainer for a few months but it hadn't worked out; fucking her over the weights bench had been an interesting addition to his workout but had ultimately proved too distracting. And Nicolo didn't like distractions.

After his session finished at 6.45 a.m., Nicolo would take his second shower of the day before dressing in one of the two sets of clothes that had been laid out for him. Once a week, Nicolo and William met to go through the appointments that he had scheduled into his diary in the next seven days, and William would plan a series of outfits that fitted the 'Style Profile' Nicolo wished to portray, that of a sleek, urban businessman, from the photo library on the computer system in which every item of clothing that Nicolo owned was catalogued, with details of designer, size, date purchased, and events it had been worn to.

This morning the outfits laid out for Nicolo in the mirrored changing room were both casual; they consisted of an all-black outfit – soft trousers, a brand-new black T-shirt and thong sandals – or a grey silk knit V-neck with loose jeans that had been artfully distressed by the designer so that no two pairs were the same, and hi-tec running shoes. All of today's meetings and appointments were to take place in his apartment; later, he would change outfits for the party he was attending at the home of one of Los Angeles' hottest young pop stars. Today was one of the days in the month that he had allotted *not* to the running of his hotel chains or any of his other businesses, projects and offshoots, but to dealing with his personal life – his household staff, family affairs, social and charitable concerns and business matters of a more delicate nature.

Nicolo glanced at his watch. 7.30 a.m. And, right on schedule, there was a quiet but firm rap on his office door.

'Come in.'

The door opened and William's stout, uniformed body appeared in the doorframe, holding in both hands, The File. The File contained all the invitations, requests and enquiries that made their way to Nicolo via his letterbox, email inbox, answering service or personal delivery. Like most rich, successful and good-looking men, Nicolo Flores was a prime target for charities wanting injections of cash, fundraisers wanting patrons, ball committees and press launches wanting guaranteed appearances, designers wanting endorsements. Unlike most people he insisted on seeing all of the letters himself. So everything went into a large black file that was brought to him once a day, wherever he was in the world; if he was abroad, all requests were copied, and then filed using exactly the same method, and The File was presented to him as usual. Once he had been through it, his assistant would update his diaries accordingly, and ensure there were no clashes.

Now William handed the large black folder to Nicolo, poured him a glass of sparkling water, and left the room.

Nicolo spent the next hour at his desk, going through The File, scribbling his instructions on each page as he went.

Invitation to the premiere of the new Bond film and VIP after-party. *Yes, plus one.* He rather fancied that.

Invitation to a special performance of *Cosi fan Tutte* and Neapolitan banquet in aid of the Italian-American Women's Association. *No.* A load of Mafia wives and girlfriends flashing their baubles at each other – he saw enough of that in his casinos.

Request for a donation to the Republican Party. *Yes, $50K.*

The usual request for donations to the big charities – the Red Cross, Unicef, AIDS research. *Yes – $50K each.*

On and on it went – requests, invitations, suggestions, ideas, thank-yous. The minutiae of the life of an international entrepreneur carefully filed and annotated and double-checked.

Nicolo closed the book just as William rapped gently on the door once more.

'Ms Morton, sir.'

'Thank you, William. Helen – thanks for coming.'

Nicolo stood to greet the personal art consultant, passing The File to William as he did so.

'Mr Flores, good morning. I have some recommendations that I think you'll find exciting.'

During the course of the next fifty-seven minutes Nicolo selected three pieces of art for his personal collection, plus a set of Tracey Emin drawings and half a dozen paintings for his various business ventures. He had also agreed with Helen Morton that she would arrange viewings of some pieces that were not, and would never be, available for sale on the open market – pieces the origins of which the owners were keen to keep concealed.

The meeting finished on time – everything in Nicolo's life started and finished on time – and was followed by one with his personal bank manager, then his style consultant, armed with sheaves of images of the new season's collections. After that, he went downstairs to the hotel's oyster bar and ordered lunch; he didn't like to eat alone in his room.

When he'd tipped the last sip of salty liquor down his throat and drained his glass of white wine, Nicolo checked his watch before taking his private lift back up to his apartment and ordering coffee before his next appointment began. He stirred two cubes of brown sugar into the double espresso, before knocking it back in one swift gulp, wincing at the heat and strength of the drink. As he was putting the cup back on its saucer, the door opened and his girlfriend Vienna entered the room. She was classic LA – so thin that her head looked too big for her body. She sat on the edge of his desk.

'Can we go for dinner tonight?'

'Why? You never eat anything.'

She tutted. 'Dinner's not about eating. It's about the vibe.'

The vibe. What did that even mean? he thought impatiently, then said, 'Fine, book somewhere, whatever. Was there something else you wanted?'

'What's up with you?'

'Nothing. I'm just busy.'

'You're always busy.'

'Yes. That's how come you have so many pairs of shoes. It's how it works.'

'OK, OK, I'm going.' Vienna got up to leave. They had been together for a year or so. Nicolo found her attractive, and she played by his rules, knew what he wanted out of a relationship, which wasn't a lot. It worked for Nicolo well enough, she was pretty and unambitious and didn't place too many demands on him. He didn't love her, but then Nicolo didn't love anyone. Not any more.

'Oh, before I go – you know what I overheard today?' the girl said. 'A businessman, sitting downstairs, having a brandy with his colleague. Just chatting, you know? And I was walking past, and something caught my ear. Logan Barnes.'

Nicolo's head jerked up but he remained silent. Vienna smirked.

'Thought that might get your attention. Your old friend, isn't he? They were talking about this new place Logan's opening. The hottest hotel in the world – ever, they were saying. No one knows where it is, but apparently he's announcing it soon.'

And having delivered the news that she had been saving and savouring for the last few hours, Vienna sauntered out of the door.

Nicolo was unusually distracted during the rest of his afternoon meetings. His mind kept returning to Vienna's words. *The hottest hotel in the world . . .'*

He knew she had said it to get under his skin, but it didn't matter. It had worked. The old resentment had started up again. It was nothing to do with the publicity – Nicolo knew that was fickle, easily enough achieved. It was the old feeling that Nicolo just didn't,

48

and never would, quite measure up against his old friend and rival, Logan Barnes, golden boy, with his golden wife and family. Hell and damnation. He tried repeatedly to drag his attention back to what the faces that kept on appearing in front of him were saying.

'Your personal wealth, Mr Flores, is considerable, but might I suggest that with additional investment in the futures market ...'

' ... and your cousin sends her love and wanted me to tell you how grateful they all are. Teddy's doing so well at college now, and they'd never have afforded it on a caretaker's salary ...'

'These are some samples of the work produced by students whose art college fees have been paid by the Trust. Of course, Mr Flores, we always ensure that your privacy is protected, so the students never know who is behind the Trust ...'

But eventually he couldn't do so any longer.

'I'm sorry – you're going to have to leave,' he interrupted the man from Nissan, just as he was getting warmed up with his pitch, trying to persuade Nicolo that a fleet of their four-wheel drives would be the perfect choice for his staff cars.

'Excuse me?'

'Something's come up and I need you to leave now. Please reschedule with my assistant on your way out.'

And Nicolo left the confused man standing in the middle of his office, his laptop open, presentation still running on its screen, and walked down the corridor to his den. Closing the door firmly behind him, he then locked it for good measure. The den was the place where Nicolo allowed himself some rare symbols of his success, a little self-congratulation. Ordinarily he hated such outward displays: he thought they made people lazy, complacent, slow. Bragging was for those who needed to remind others of their importance because they weren't impressive enough on their own.

But here, in this room that hadn't been colour-coordinated and created through careful construction of a mood board by an over-paid interior designer, but that Nicolo had decorated by just choosing things that he liked, he kept a few souvenirs of his career. A framed photo of himself with the Governor of California at a private dinner. His Harvard graduation certificates. One of the architect's drawings of his first hotel, framed. Tucked into the corner of a book-shelf, the paperwork confirming his purchase of number 13 Geary

Lane, the house he had grown up in and that he had bought back from the bank after they repossessed it when he was just seventeen. Next to it, the toy that had enabled him to do so – a little pastel-coloured creature that squawked and talked when you pressed a button inside its ear. He reached down and did so now.

'Hi, I'm a Squeaky Squeezy. Can I be your friend?'

He pressed again, in a different place, on the foot this time, and it juddered gently.

'I'm cold. Can we snuggle?'

The high-pitched, slightly Mexican-accented mechanical voice took him back. Nicolo had discovered the cheap fluffy toys in a back street. A wholesaler was going bust and selling off its stock, and Nicolo was a bright, ambitious teenager whose father had died and whose mother couldn't pay the bills by taking in paying guests any longer. Nicolo had gone out looking for a way to keep them afloat, and with the crates of talking toys he had found it. He had given them a cute name and created a craze for them in his home town which had spread to the entire county, and then, to the surprise of everyone, including the self-assured teenager who had lit the touch-paper, the state. Soon Squeaky Squeezies were everywhere – every kid wanted one. Nicolo quickly sold out of the first batch, and had to source another manufacturer, putting in orders for different colours of toy, different voices and lines.

Within six weeks, there was no longer any question about whether Nicolo would be able to afford to go to college; in six months, he'd made enough money to buy his mother her home back, and in a year the pair of them would never have to worry about money again. Nicolo was a successful entrepreneur before he was out of his teens, and he had caught the moneymaking bug.

He put down the toy that had paid his way through his years as an undergraduate at Harvard, studying engineering. That had got him started on the road to where he was now, standing in the best apartment in one of the best hotels in Los Angeles. Owner of scores of properties, of restaurants, clubs, casinos, of a goddamn private plane, for crying out loud. No one could say that Nicolo Flores hadn't made it. And so why was he standing here feeling like a failure, because of the mention of one man's name?

Chapter Four

1973

Johnny Stokes and Logan Barnes met on the second day of Mason High School, Michigan, ninth grade, in the queue for lunch. 'Met' might be overstating their initial encounter – they were shoved together in the middle of a scrum of older kids, all hustling to get their food, loud and confident and full of hormones and bravado, and Johnny and Logan looked at each other, each recognising a fellow amateur at the art of not-waiting-in-line. They had both recently turned thirteen, but neither was large for his age. A big, acne-faced lump of a youth pushed in front of Logan, stepping on his foot as he did so.

'Hey!'

The boy turned. He was wider than he was tall, and he wore a snarl that made it clear nothing got between this kid and his food.

'What?'

Logan shrugged. 'Nothin'.'

The boy glared, and continued trampling on the obstacles between himself and his end goal. Johnny and Logan looked around at the sea of smelly T-shirts, and boys and girls who looked as though they'd been here for ever, and who somehow knew all the rules that were still a mystery to the new kids, and realised they needed to take action. By some unspoken agreement they stood tight together and hunkered down, using their lack of height to slip through the crowd and work their way forwards in line, dodging jabbing elbows and ducking under damp armpits.

When they reached the serving station, they both stood for a second, a little dazed by their journey, and the bright fluorescent lights and clattering of pans. The lunch lady looked down at them, her polyester uniform covered with specks of what they assumed was gravy. Gravy seemed to be everywhere, on every dish of food. The room was permeated with the smell of it.

'Whaddayawant – meatloafchillisloppyJoefiestasalad?'

They stared.

'Meatloaf,' said Logan, taking the lead. Johnny was impressed with his choice, and nodded, holding out his tray for the same. In reality, it was the only word Logan had been able to distinguish from the stream of syllables uttered by the lunch lady. But he kept quiet about that as they paid their ninety-five cents and carried their plates of meatloaf with mashed potato and gravy, buttered corn, dinner rolls and glasses of milk over to a table in the corner of the room, dodging flying food and sprawling legs as they went.

They sat opposite one another over the Formica table, and ate. Both wondering what to say.

'Didn't see you at lunch yesterday,' ventured Logan.

'I didn't eat lunch yesterday,' admitted Johnny.

There was a pause while they both shovelled forkfuls of potato and gravy into their mouths.

'Me neither.'

And that was how a friendship began that would become, in many ways, the most important relationship in both their lives, spanning decades to come. That discovery, on their second day of high school, that they were more effective together than separately, was proved to be true time and time again. They just made a good fit – similar enough to have common goals, the same sense of humour, values in line with one another's, yet different enough to spark off each other, with different tastes in girls, different strengths in enough crucial ways that where one faltered, the other could take up the slack, where one held back, the other bounded forward to take his place.

They both loved sports of all kinds, as adventurous and extreme as they could get, pushing each other further as they pursued the adrenaline rush of closely escaped danger, spurring each other on to jump off, out of and over ever higher and more perilous objects. Discovering new ways to feel that elusive scooping sensation in their chests as they dived, paraglided, snowboarded, sky-dived their way through the elements.

They were both ambitious, determined to be not just successful in a small-town way; owning a business that turned over a few hundred K with a nice house and a bit of land in their home town wasn't going to satisfy either of them. No, they were going to be the sort of successful that meant people knew their names – people outside Mason, outside the state, outside their country even. They were going to travel the world, see their names on the Forbes 500, form a powerhouse that would become known as the benchmark for the highest of standards of achievement in the world of – well, that was the bit they weren't quite sure of yet. At thirteen they both knew there were some gaps that would need to be filled in their plan. But they also knew, after just a few months of friendship, that whatever it turned out to be, they would be doing it together.

The two friends were closer than siblings. Logan was the only child from his parents' marriage; there was a much older half-sister called Annabel from his father Peter's first marriage, but as brother and sister were separated by three marriages and over thirty years (his father had been through two more unsuccessful unions by the time he met his fourth wife, Logan's mother Elizabeth), the pair did not seem destined to have a close relationship. Annabel sent him cards at Christmas and on his birthday, but the photos of her children that she included showed that they were closer to his age than she was, and only served as a reminder of the differences between them rather than forming a bond. She would have had more in common with Logan's mother, since they were a similar age, but the two had never met.

Logan had always been popular and found it easy to make friends; growing up with a much older father and no readymade playmates in the form of brothers and sisters had meant that he had looked outside his family for company, but he had never found a best friend until he met Johnny.

Johnny did have a brother, Bobby, who was three years younger than him, whom he loved fiercely and of whom he was deeply protective, but Bobby would never be the one with whom Johnny shot hoops in the backyard, or rang the neighbours' doorbells and then raced away down the street. Bobby had been born prematurely and had spent weeks in an incubator in the hospital, cocooned in a tangle of tubes, watched over by a team of nurses and his distraught parents as he struggled to stay alive. Johnny didn't remember this, he was too young, but as he grew up he was always aware that Bobby was different, needing more care and help than his friends' younger brothers and sisters. When Bobby got a little older and his contemporaries began to take their first steps, and it became clear that Bobby wasn't going to do the same, Johnny would sit with his younger brother and play with him, glaring at anyone who looked like they were going to ask questions about why he wasn't walking yet. When Bobby was four his parents were told by the doctors that it looked unlikely that he would ever walk, and they got him a wheelchair, which Johnny took great pleasure in whizzing around, pushing it as fast as he could until Bobby squealed with excitement and their mother called to him to be careful, not to tip Bobby out on the sidewalk or she'd ground them both for a week! When he heard that, Bobby would grin up at Johnny, thrilled to be grouped with his big brother like that.

The first time Logan went round to Johnny's house one blustery October weekend, two things struck him – how new everything was, and how busy life there seemed to be. In contrast, the Barneses' home was a big old detached building, which had been in his father's family for years. It had a wraparound porch and a huge oak tree in the backyard that was perfect for climbing. The rooms were big, and full of old paintings and furniture, and the corridors were lined with family portraits. His mother didn't usually emerge from her bedroom until late morning. She spent her days playing tennis or lunching at the country club, and her evenings at cocktail parties or playing bridge. His father was usually around the house somewhere, but was rarely present. Peter Barnes would have his first 'official' drink at eleven – a 'pre-prandial snifter' as he called it – but he would often have sunk a couple in secret before then, and he tended to pass his days snoozing in a wing chair in the library, or occasionally making it to the country club for a round of golf. The only time Logan really saw his parents was in the early evening. From when he was a small boy he had been taken downstairs to say goodnight to his parents while they had their first drink of the evening, before being put to bed by Hororé. Now he was too old for a nanny and Hororé had retired, but the custom had continued. His father would ask him about school, about what sports he had played and what he had learned that day, and his mother would roll her eyes at her husband and tell Logan to make sure he had fun, and asked who the prettiest girl in class was, and if he was going to bring her home. Logan would tell his mother that he couldn't, because they'd be too cross to be outshone by her, and she would laugh and kiss his cheek, and he would inhale the familiar scent of Diorissimo and hairspray and cigarettes, and then he was free for the evening.

The Stokeses' house, on the other hand, was a new ranch-style house, just three years old, with a wide driveway and an attached garage. Inside, there were no fusty portraits of dead relatives; it was all modern and shiny. Johnny's mother used a Cuisinart to chop up vegetables, which she was demonstrating to some friends in the kitchen when Johnny took Logan through to the den.

' . . . and you just feed the vegetables in at the top, and it chops them all up for you. You can use it for almost anything. I swear, I'm never chopping another onion as long as I live, so help me . . .'

Johnny's parents, Mike and Ginny, were different. His dad always seemed to be around, chatting to the boys, showing them his latest gadget, buying them tickets for a ball game or sneaking them a chocolate bar before they went out in the yard. He was a young father and liked sports, liked to know what his kids were into; he went running before work and wore fashionable clothes. The house was always full of music and people, it seemed to Logan. He was always welcome there as the Stokes had an open-house policy, and it didn't take Logan long to slot in. He would turn up on Saturday mornings while his parents were still sleeping, wolf down a bowl of the cocoa pebbles that he loved but that his mother said were vulgar so refused to keep in the house. Sometimes Johnny would still be in bed, and Logan would just hang out, waiting for him to get up. Johnny's parents treated him like part of the furniture, but not in a way that made him feel ignored, like he did at home. Somehow, the way they did it, he felt accepted. Comfortable. There was only one time that Johnny's dad made him go home – when Logan turned up after his mother had phoned the Stokeses and told them Logan was to be sent straight home again, as her family were visiting. Logan had been hoping to escape the terminal dullness of the family weekend by pretending he'd forgotten, and hoping he wasn't missed. Mike, Johnny's dad, had been raking leaves in his sweatpants and T-shirt, and had shaken his head when he saw Logan heading into the backyard.

'Sorry, buddy. Your mom's already been on the phone.'

Logan sighed. 'Oh, man.'

'Yeah, I know. It's not fair. Life isn't.'

Logan stalled. 'Can I just use the bathroom? I'm busting.'

Mike stopped raking and looked him in the eye. Logan sighed again. When adults did that, it didn't usually mean anything good was coming.

'I know it's not always that easy for you at home, pal.'

Logan shrugged and looked at the ground, saying, 'Whatever. I just don't wanna spend my entire weekend with my stupid mother's stupid family. None of them care about me, so why the fuck should I? They just ignore me, and my dad'll be so drunk he won't even know I'm there. What's the point?'

He stopped, shocked. He hadn't meant to say all that – any of it.

Mike put a hand out and squeezed his shoulder. Logan's lip was trembling. He and Johnny both played the big man – hey, they were teenagers, it's what they were meant to do – but underneath they were just kids.

'The thing about being a man', Mike went on quietly, 'is that sometimes, you just have to do the right thing. You know?'

Logan breathed in deeply, then nodded. Yeah. He knew.

'It's important. Do the right thing, and life'll turn out good in the end. You'll see. Now, go use the bathroom and get outta here.'

Logan had gone upstairs and wiped his eyes, and then he'd gone home and suffered through the weekend of his doddering, useless father and his shallow, self-obsessed mother and her family who only cared about how things looked and what other people thought, and it was somehow kind of OK, because he really did feel like he was doing the right thing. '*Do the right thing, and life'll turn out good in the end.*' He had held on to that, because he believed in Mike and Ginny more than he believed in anything else in the world. They were proof that not all families were fucked up.

But that was just one weekend. Most times when he turned up on Saturdays, Mike would wave and throw them a few bucks, and then he and Johnny would hang out with Bobby for a bit before

heading out on their bicycles to the Dairy Queen for their favourite
peanut butter parfaits, the tall ice-cream sundaes made from layers
of smooth whipped ice cream, chocolate sauce and crunchy nuts
that were just forty-nine cents if you went up the counter and said,
'Scrumdillyishus!' to the server. They would only do this if the
server was old Mrs Briggs, with her old-fashioned fifties glasses
and her ever-present scowl. If it was Mindy Marshall, they would
pay full price and sit at the counter, leaning forward to try and
catch a glimpse of her legs when she bent over the grill. Mindy
was sixteen, with bouncy curls and a bouncier bosom; the town
pin-up and the object of almost every young boy's first stirrings
of lust between 1972 and 1975, when she left town amidst a storm
of scandal, with the married head of the high school in tow and
a bump that she could no longer conceal beneath her Dairy Queen
tunic.

When Johnny and Logan had been going there and mooning at
her over their sundaes for six months, Mindy took pity on them –
or took advantage of them, as Johnny's mother would have seen it
– and led them to the car lot behind the building where she charged
them a dollar each to look down her top. She had been wearing a
lacy pink bra, which she had pulled to the side, so they could see
her nipples. They were fourteen years old, and it was the first time
they had seen a girl's breasts in the flesh. Afterwards, they had
retreated, pink-cheeked, to the bandstand to discuss the experience,
sitting with their backs up against the ornate sides.

'Very . . .' began Logan.

'Very nice, I thought,' provided Johnny.

'Oh, yes.'

'Quite . . .'

'Quite . . . friendly looking.'

'Uh huh.'

They shifted their weight from side to side a little.

'So, I'm gonna . . .'

'I'd better be . . .'

They both spoke at the same time, then stopped.

'Yup.'

'See you later.'

And they picked up their bikes by the handlebars and cycled off to their respective homes and bedrooms to deal with the after-effects of viewing Mindy Marshall's breasts.

That was the first of many firsts that they experienced together. A few months later they smoked their first cigarettes, again with Mindy, behind the Dairy Queen, bought from the machine inside while no one was looking. She showed them how to inhale, and then pretended not to notice when they turned pale and had to struggle not to vomit. They had become sort-of-friends with her by now, but not so much as to not mind what she thought of them. After all, she was seventeen.

When they were fifteen they got drunk for the first time. This, they didn't do with Mindy, aware that it was unlikely to show them at their coolest, and by now, this was a primary concern, especially for Johnny, whose mild crush had transformed into a full-blown obsession. He was planning on asking her out on a date, where he would ply her with alcohol and persuade her to make out with him, and so he had decided that he needed to ensure he would be able to remain sober enough himself to take advantage of the making out part of the evening. They bought a bottle of vodka from a kid at school, who had an older brother and a nice little sideline supplying booze to underage drinkers, picked up some Coke and lemonade from the Seven Eleven, some plastic cups and a few bags of potato chips, and took their stash down to the old birdwatchers' hut by the lake. They'd had alcohol before, wine with dinner and the occasional glass of beer at a barbecue at home, but never spirits. They were ready to become real men.

After their first drink they weren't sure they could see what all the fuss was about, so they made the second round stronger. After the third drink they had decided that vodka was the best thing that had ever been invented, and that the secret to their future success should be drinks factories. After the fifth drink, they were both bemoaning the lost years when they hadn't been friends, and pledging eternal loyalty to one another. And then they were both violently sick, and woke up an hour later having passed out on the dirt floor of the hut, heads pounding and hands trembling and vowing that they would never drink again. It was only a few weeks after this that Mindy left home in the incident which would keep chins wagging and the town gossiping and speculating for the next year, so Johnny never got a chance to find out whether she would have gone on a date with him, or whether his seduction plans would have worked. Later in his life, he realised that this was probably a good thing.

At sixteen, they went on their first double date. Carly and Karen were sisters, and Carly was in Johnny's history class. The girls had long straight hair that fell down their backs to their waists and shone like mirrors, and they wore a different headband every day, matched to their outfits, which were always perfectly pressed, and they smelled of fresh cotton. There was no chance that Carly and Karen would let Johnny and Logan get them drunk and make out with them. But somehow, that made them all the more enticing. They were clean and smart and good. They were the sort of girls that Johnny's father would call 'the marrying kind', as opposed to the 'dilly-dallying kind'.

Logan and Johnny spent the whole week before the Friday that they were due to take Carly and Karen out getting nervous. They were picking the girls up at 6 p.m. and taking them to see *Jaws*, partly in the hope that the girls would be scared by the sharks and the atmospheric music, and that they would be required to comfort them with a protective manly arm round the shoulders. After the movie, they would take them to Arby's for roast beef sandwiches and shakes. It was the first official date either of them had been on, though Logan had kissed a girl from his parents' country club, and Johnny had got to second base with Suzanne at school, but that didn't really count, because everyone had got to second base with Suzanne.

They had agreed that Logan would go to Johnny's house in the afternoon so they could leave together. For convenience's sake, they had nodded, both privately relieved that they would have the reassuring presence of the other beside them, and would not have to walk up to the sisters' front door alone. When Logan arrived at Johnny's, the latter was in the bathroom shaving, his mom said, 'Though how he can take nearly an hour to get rid of that bit of bumfluff sprouting out of his chin, I do not know.'

'I heard that,' hollered Johnny from upstairs.

'So hurry it up then! We all have to go out tonight as well, and I need to wash first.'

Ginny was helping Bobby to eat a snack of peanut butter and jelly sandwich cut up into little triangles. The boy's muscle control was often poor and his movements jerky, meaning that mealtimes could be a messy business.

'Hey, Bobby,' said Logan as he hopped up on to a stool at the breakfast bar.

Bobby stopped eating to raise a hand for Logan to high five.

'So, the big date, huh?' teased Ginny. 'You wearin' your lucky pants?'

She passed Bobby, who was giggling, another section of sandwich. 'Lucky pants,' he guffawed. Logan could feel the heat in his skin as he blushed down to his collar.

Ginny smiled. 'Sorry. Just teasing.'

Logan decided to change the subject quickly. Man, he hoped he grew out of this blushing thing soon. It was *so* not cool.

'Where are you off out to?' he asked.

'To the hospital, to talk to some people who've had premature babies. Let them meet Bobby, see that things can turn out all right even if you have a bad start.'

That Bobby's situation could be seen as anything other than all right was not something that his mother acknowledged. To Ginny Stokes, it would always be miraculous that he was alive, however hard day-to-day life was, and she knew that on her visits to the hospital she did manage to give hope to parents who were still shell-shocked after delivering a baby weeks, sometimes months before they were expecting to. She glanced up at Logan.

'Don't worry, we're going straight there and coming straight back again, so we won't be wandering around town, cramping your style.'

'I wasn't . . .'

She laughed. 'Yes, you were. Come on then, where are you taking those lucky young ladies?'

'Cinema, then Arby's.'

'Good choice.'

'You think?' said Johnny, as he came into the kitchen, skin pink from showering and shaving. 'Oh man, then we should do something else. Something the mothership likes is so not cool.'

Ginny dropped her jaw in mock outrage. 'Johnny Stokes. I'll have you know I was voted Hippest Girl in Class the year I left high school.'

'Yeah, like, a *million* years ago, maybe.'

The front door opened and banged shut, and Mike stood in the kitchen doorway, loosening his tie and unbuttoning his shirt collar.

'What was a million years ago? When we were young and in love and didn't have any of these pesky kids tying us down?' He leaned over and kissed Ginny on the top of her head, and then Bobby. He put an arm round Johnny's shoulders.

'Exactly. I've sacrificed my looks, my figure, my life as a movie star for you lot, and this is the gratitude you show me?' Ginny winked at Logan as she took Bobby's plate over to the sink.

'Yep.' Johnny was leaning into the fridge, foraging around.

'You can't possibly be hungry, J-J, you had lunch two hours ago.'

'I know. Two hours! I'm a growing boy.'

'Growing outwards,' squeaked Bobby, who then dissolved into hoots of laughter at his own joke. Speaking was hard work for Bobby, so he tended to choose his words carefully. He might be physically disadvantaged, but there was nothing wrong with Bobby's mind. Logan watched the four of them. Relaxed, easy together, with none of the stiffness and formality that characterised his own family. And for a single, tiny moment, he felt a shameful emotion that he wanted to wash away as soon as he recognised it for what it was. It was a black feeling, a sticky pool of tar in his heart that wanted Johnny's family to be destroyed, broken up; it was too perfect, too close. Of course it wasn't perfect, Logan knew that. He knew how hard it was for Johnny's parents, caring for Bobby and making sure Johnny didn't feel sidelined; he knew they would have loved to have more children but were too afraid of having a second child who was disabled. But to him, right here, right now, it felt perfect, and he was briefly but totally consumed by jealousy.

He felt sick.

They left the cinema both holding the hands of their dates, the girls' hair as glossy and swingy as ever, and only a little mussed up from the boys' arms snaking round their shoulders in the darkness of the auditorium. Arby's, the fast-food restaurant specialising in roast beef sandwiches where they were going afterwards, was just a few blocks down from the movie theatre, and they decided to walk, Logan and Johnny giving Carly and Karen their jackets to wear on the way. The evenings had grown chilly in the last week or so, and it wouldn't be long before winter was setting in.

As they neared the corner of the sidewalk and waited to cross the road, Johnny felt for the first time like he was becoming a man. He was walking his date to dinner – holding her hand and making sure she didn't step into the road before it was safe. He had his learner's driving permit and was starting Driver's Ed. in a few weeks, along with Logan. The part-time job he had found in the hardware store meant he could save for his first car, and his dad had promised to match every dollar he earned. He was doing good at school, he had his best friend and the two of them had big plans. Yes, he was really and truly growing up. Making ready to step into the road, he held tightly on to Carly's hand. And as he looked to his left to check for traffic, his childhood ended for ever.

The Stokeses' long brown station wagon, with its distinctive back end that had been modified to carry Bobby's wheelchair, was lying on one side across the road, its bonnet crumpled and partly open, and acrid black smoke coming out of it. There was an ambulance to one side, and two police cruisers, one directing the traffic around the accident, and one parked up to one side. The driver's side of the vehicle was mostly concealed by the front of the truck that had ploughed into it. There was a crowd of people standing on the sidewalk, watching. No one was talking. A tall man had taken his hat off and was turning it round and round in his hands. His face was pale.

The noise Johnny made when he saw the scene sounded like the noise a paper bag made when you blew it up and then clapped it between your hands. *Crumph.* And then he ran, faster than he had ever run on the football pitch, faster than he had known he could run, his heart bursting inside his chest.

Logan stood for a long moment, quite unable to move. Watching Johnny take off down towards the pile of mangled metal and flashing lights. Watching him slam into the solid body of a police officer, who headed him off before he reached the car. Watched as he fought, battled against the stronger man, scrabbling at the man's chest as if he could work his way through his body and somehow reach his family. Watched as he finally gave up, his legs buckled beneath him and he crumpled to the ground, a small figure at the centre of the chaos who suddenly looked far younger than his sixteen years.

'Oh my. Is that his . . . Oh wow.'

Carly's voice brought Logan back to reality, and now he was the one running, towards the crash and towards his friend, towards the horror that he knew would await him. But nothing could have prepared him for what he saw when he neared the vehicle – the sight of Bobby's purple wheelchair dangling from the back of the station wagon, and the boy's twisted and atrophied body still slumped inside it.

They found out later that Johnny's father, Mike, had died immediately, from the force of the truck slamming into the side of the vehicle. Johnny never saw his body. Ginny was still alive when the paramedics arrived at the scene, but died on the way to the hospital. And little Bobby died still strapped into his wheelchair, crushed by the very chair that had been designed to keep him safe.

Afterwards, people said that it was a blessing that they'd gone quickly, together. Johnny never did understand that. How could anything about his family's death be a blessing? All that it meant was that they had all died at once, his whole family wiped out for ever in one terrible moment – and they had left him behind. A truck driver had caused the accident – he'd been at the wheel for too many hours and had been taking sips of whisky to make the time pass. A single moment where his eyes slipped shut was just long enough for him to obliterate Johnny's entire family.

At the funeral, a steady stream of people had approached him. Well-meaning friends of his parents, colleagues of his dad's, ladies from his mom's tennis club, all wanting to shake his hand and clap him on the shoulder, to tell him what a great guy Mike had been, how much they'd miss Ginny, how tragic, how they just couldn't believe . . . Johnny just let it all flow past him. He didn't know why they were bothering. He knew all of that. Did they think he didn't? Yes, his dad had been great, his mom had been beautiful. Bobby had been – no. He couldn't think about Bobby. Too much, it was too much. So he nodded and thanked them and said yes, he would be sure to call if he needed anything.

Of course he didn't call, because why would he need to? He had Logan. Anyway, it wasn't like he was a kid. He was sixteen. Logan's parents had agreed to sign the papers that would make them his official guardians. Logan had gone to a lawyer and paid for the consultation himself, to find out what would happen next, just a few days after the accident. Johnny had said he didn't care, he would just stay in the house by himself, but Logan knew that something would have to be arranged, and that the alternative might mean Johnny being shipped out to some distant great-aunt or something. There wasn't anyone close. Mike and Ginny had both been only children; Ginny's parents had died when she was young, Mike had never known his father, and his mother had recently died of cancer. The last thing Logan wanted was for Johnny's agony to be compounded by complex legal issues. So he went to the lawyer, got the necessary papers (having lied to the attorney, telling him his parents had already agreed to take over Johnny's care), and then taken them home.

He knocked on his father's study door. There was a noise from inside which Logan knew would be the man trying to rouse himself from gin-sodden sleep. He waited for a moment, and then opened the door.

By the time he came out of the room, he had promised himself that he would never ask his father for another thing.

Mr Barnes had been surprised to see Logan, and had looked at his watch – checking, Logan knew, that he hadn't slept through the afternoon and that it wasn't now early evening, Logan's traditional time to appear before him. When he realised it only 2 p.m., he had looked confused. Logan waited.

'Something wrong, boy? I'm rather busy, as you can see.' He swept an arm around his study.

Logan looked at the room. So many times he had been told this, ushered out of his parents' way by nannies and minders, told they were busy, that he mustn't bother them. Busy with what? Logan asked himself now. It was just a library. There was a large mahogany partners' desk, a few wing chairs, a globe. It was full of the sort of old books that you could buy by the yard from dealers. No one had ever read them. Logan had looked at the atlases, tracing his finger along the contour lines of mountains when he was a young boy, but that was it. Peter Barnes hadn't done a day's work since he had been retired from the US Navy because of ill health – an event which had always been shrouded in mystery – and that had been decades ago. Since then, he had taken on a few directorships, which seemed to mean going out for long lunches every few months, and sat in this room, doing nothing, as far as Logan could figure out. But his father was always 'rather busy'.

Logan took a deep breath. 'I need your help with something, Dad.'

His father had looked surprised at first, then baffled. 'Well, I'm not sure ... Are you having trouble at school? Don't you have someone you can talk to there – a teacher?'

'School's fine. It's about Johnny.'

'Johnny?'

Logan stared. 'Johnny Stokes. My best friend. His parents were killed a few weeks ago, in the car accident.'

His father's eyes were steady, but Logan could tell that behind them his mind was working to remember.

'Of course, of course,' he said finally, nodding. He didn't have a clue what Logan was talking about. He was bluffing. 'Johnny. Fine kid. Terrible business. Is your mother out?'

Logan bit back the frustration. He couldn't allow his feelings to show. 'I need her to help as well. I've asked her to join us.'

'Right.'

They faced each other for a long moment. Logan's father standing, legs apart, hands behind his back, the posture of a military man – a military man who hadn't been anywhere near the military for a lifetime, his son's lifetime – and his son, who was asking him for something for maybe the first time in his life. Both broad-shouldered, with thick hair and strong features. Logan wearing a button-down shirt and slacks rather than his preferred T-shirt and jeans, his father in his usual blazer and flannel trousers, a Hermès silk triangle folded in his breast pocket. Neither of them with the faintest idea of what to do next. Eventually, Logan took control.

'Shall we sit? Mother should be here at any moment.'

'Yes, yes, excellent.' His father looked relieved. 'Very good.'

Logan busied himself with taking the documents that he had had drawn up by the lawyer out of the folder he had been carefully carrying them around in. His hand was shaking a bit as he did so.

Why so nervous? he asked himself. *This is your father – you should be able to go to him with anything.* But the man sitting in front of him in uncomfortable silence didn't feel like the person he should be able to turn to first, the person who had brought him into the world. He felt like a stranger.

Logan, darling, what is it that can't wait? I've got a hair appointment in half an hour and the Black and White Ball tomorrow.'

Logan sat up, papers in hand, and watched his mother sweep in, all brightly patterned chiffon, filling the musty library with perfume and colour and fluttering hands. She declined to sit with her husband and son, but stood leaning against the desk, fidgeting, obviously keen to get away. Her life was not in this house, at home; it happened elsewhere, and she wanted to get back to it.

Logan cleared his throat and launched into his planned speech. 'OK. As you both know, Johnny's family was killed a few weeks ago. He doesn't have any other close relatives. There are some distant cousins, but they're in Idaho and he's never met them. And his parents never appointed guardians. They didn't make a will. All that side of things is going to take a while to get straightened out, but what would make it simpler is if Johnny had an official guardian – or guardians.'

He looked up. His father was gazing into his lap, about to doze off. His mother was looking at her reflection in the shiny brass of the desk lamp, smoothing down her hair. He carried on.

'I've been to see a lawyer. If you were to sign these papers and become Johnny's legal guardians he wouldn't have any problems staying in the house while everything goes through. It would only be for two years – not even that – just until he's eighteen. But if they made him move house, or move towns to go and live with some relatives he's never even met, then I don't know whether he could take it. Please. Will you sign?'

Logan waited. His mother tore her gaze away from her reflection and came over to where Logan was sitting, a distracted look on her face.

'Darling. You know I don't understand any of this legal talk. I'm sure your father will know what to do. Won't you, Peter?' And she patted him lightly on the shoulder, obviously desperate to get away.

He looked over to his father, whose expression was approaching terror. 'I must run, sweetheart, I'm going to be so late.'

'But Mum, will you sign—'

'Oh, here.' She reached one hand over and took the pen that Logan was holding, and scrawled her name, hurriedly, next to the pencilled cross he was pointing to. He watched. She could have been signing a birthday card for all the importance she attached to the decision – in fact, a birthday card would probably have received far more attention, thought Logan; his mother had always been a dedicated sender of celebratory missives. She leaned down and kissed his head.

'It'll be lovely having your friend here to stay, won't it, Peter? The least we can do.'

'No, he's not coming to stay. He's—'

But she had gone; he could already hear her picking up her car keys and shutting the front door behind her. His father stared after her.

'Right. Well, if your mother thinks it's all right.'

And his father signed too.

Logan was just sixteen, yet at that moment he was all too aware that he had been the only one thinking like an adult during the conversation he had just had with his parents, if you could call it that. And everything that had happened recently told Logan that it was time for him to become a man. Johnny's parents were dead, and for all the good they were to him, Logan's might as well be dead too. He and Johnny were on their own – and he was ready.

Chapter Five

1977

Maryanne Curtis was sitting on her hands, in the hope that the rough material of her dress would rub against the red, swollen skin and stop the itching, if only for a few seconds. It felt like her skin was lined with Velcro, its tiny spears rasping against her flesh, pushing red lumps and weals up into angry, ugly bumps. The rash was agonising for Maryanne and infuriating for her mother. It wasn't enough that the girl was wilfully shy and ungainly, of course she had to be the sort to get prickly heat as well.

Maryanne knew full well that her rash was at least as irksome for her mother as it was for her, and that gave her some small satisfaction as she writhed in discomfort. Sativa, as her mother had recently renamed herself, was ignoring her as usual, holding her large-brimmed straw hat on to her baby-blond hair with one hand and gesticulating with a Sobranie cigarette with the other, as she leaned in to the man next to her to whisper something in his ear. He took the opportunity to slide a deeply tanned arm round her waist, his white shirt rolled up to show off the heavy gold Rolex on his wrist, and stroke the curve of her hip. She was practically purring with pleasure. God, he was disgusting, she was disgusting – it was all revolting.

Maryanne glowered and sank deeper into her seat, the orange plastic squeaking sweatily against the back of her legs as she did so. The plumpness of her legs was something else that irked Sativa – oh, honestly, she couldn't think of her as that, it was absurd. But what else could she call her? Mom? The thought was laughable. Her 'real' name? It had been Candy in the sixties, while Maryanne's father had still been around; before that, it had been something else. What child didn't know her own mother's name? Maryanne, that was who. Oh no, now she was coming over.

'Will you stop *squirming*, for goodness' sake!' Maryanne's mother hissed in her ear, the cloying scent of Opium mixed with cigarette smoke clinging to her body like a cloak.

'I can't help it – it HURTS.'

'Darling, these things are sent to try us. And it's certainly bloody well trying me.'

Maryanne sighed and took a sip of her Fanta, which had gone warm in the hot sun, and grimaced.

'Want me to perk your drink up? A little bit of vodka might make the afternoon more fun for you.'

Maryanne said sulkily, 'No. *I* don't need alcohol to have fun.' Actually, vodka made her feel sick, but she couldn't tell her mom that; she would despise her even more than she did already. Sometimes she managed to force it down, but she knew that in the heat it would make her ill.

'Well, aren't we Little Miss Goody Two-Shoes. As usual. You don't look like you're having much fun now.'

'That's. Because. I'm. Not.'

Sativa glared at her. 'Impossible girl. If you can't at least pretend to be having a nice time, you might as well go back to the hotel. You're going to ruin my chances with Carlos.'

'FINE.'

Maryanne turned her head away and let her fringe fall in front of her eyes so that her mother wouldn't see the tears forming as she pretended to struggle to untangle her cardigan from the chair legs where it had fallen.

'For God's sake, Maryanne, why can't you find a friend – someone of your own age to hang around with?'

Maryanne still didn't look at her. She wouldn't let her see, couldn't let her see. She freed her cardigan and put it on, then stood. Her mother sighed.

'Oh, go on then, off you go. Leave the door on the latch if you go to sleep.'

Then Sativa walked back over to the bar, laughing as Carlos clasped his hands to his heart, saying, '*Che bella, bellissima . . . mi amore ...*' He stretched out his hand and she twirled into him.

Ugh. The guy was a sleazeball. Man, her mother could pick them. No one noticed as Maryanne made her way through the throng of people drinking champagne and celebrating their wealthy, carefree existence in the seafront bar. She emerged into the unnaturally clean streets of Monte Carlo and headed in the direction of their hotel. The city was like a theme park for the rich. Everything was shiny, well-kept, there was no unemployment, no strikes, no punks here like there were in Britain. Just champagne and roulette and Mercedes Benz taxis. It made Maryanne feel nervous all the time. She was terrified that they were going to be found out.

'*Why can't you find a friend ...*' She'd stopped bothering to hide her face now that she was away from the bar, and the tears were falling down her cheeks. Why *couldn't* she find a friend? It wasn't just here, it was everywhere they went. Ever since her father had left and she and her mother had begun their unsettled existence, moving from one place to another as one relationship after the other didn't work out, and Sativa zoomed in on the next perfect place to snag a rich man, Maryanne had been the outsider.

Always on the outside, even within her own family. Her parents had always been a unit of two, looking towards each other. Her father only had eyes for her mother, and on the rare occasions that he did notice Maryanne, he saw her through Candy's eyes. And the image was not a flattering one.

Maryanne was five when she first realised that her mother did not want her.

She was playing with her doll's house by herself, as usual. She was in the middle of sitting her doll family down to eat. The mother was serving the father with an extra large helping of potato salad and the big sister was helping her little sister hide her broccoli. Candy's voice floated up with her cigarette smoke from the garden where she was drinking Martinis on the patio with her friend Lorna, as the men stood poking slabs of meat on the grill and smoking.

'You're so lucky, Lorrie,' Candy was saying. 'No one clinging on to your ankles. No one crying in the middle of the night and breaking up the party. No ruined stomach muscles ...' She paused, and Maryanne knew she would be blowing her smoke out in a steady stream, creating a veil of fug around her face.

'Oh, but she's lovely, Candy. And not too noisy or annoying at all.'

'You don't have to live with her.'

Oh. It was her. The 'she' they were talking about was her. Maryanne concentrated hard on her family dinner.

'Come along, Daddy, pass the potato salad to everyone,' the doll's-house mother was saying in a jokey voice.

'Sorry, darling, but your cooking is just so *yummy*,' said the father. Maryanne sighed.

'Children are just so – so everywhere,' her mother was saying now. 'All over the house, her toys and clothes, and we can't go anywhere without making some arrangement. In fact, I can't even go to the damned bathroom without her whining for me, and it's just . . . God, it's just relentless.'

'Here. Have another cocktail. Lovely vodka! Makes everything better.'

The women laughed. Maryanne tried to concentrate on getting her little models to eat their dinner, but they had lost their appetite.

Maryanne walked quickly through the streets, trying to reach the relative sanctity of the hotel so she could run a tub of cold water and immerse her enflamed legs in it. As she crossed the road and stepped up on to the opposite pavement, her shoe caught the edge and she stumbled, her arms flailing in a vain attempt to stop herself falling.

'Oh! Damn you!'

Dumb platforms that her dumb mother made her wear to make her dumb legs look longer. She threw her bag on the ground next to her in temper, and wept, her pudgy legs stretched out in front of her with the stupid shoes stuck on the end of them. She could see that the one that had tripped her up had a broken buckle. Good – she wouldn't have to wear them again. Her arm was grazed from the wrist up to the elbow where she had tried to break her fall, and her crocheted bag had spilled its contents all over the pavement. Perfect.

Maryanne stared glumly at her belongings. Some cheap lipstick that she never wore because it made her lips feel all tacky, her small beaded purse holding a bit of money, her Donnie Osmond Fan Club membership card, a photograph of her father, some plastic beads, her hotel room key – and finally, her tattered copy of Harold Robbins's *The Pirate*, which Sativa had passed on to her and which Maryanne had turned her nose up at first and then devoured. She picked it up woefully. Things like this never happened to the heroines in those books.

'*Puis-je vous aider, mademoiselle?*'

Maryanne looked up. A slim hand with long tanned fingers was reaching down towards her. She took it and stood up, conscious that her own hand was sticky and grimy.

'*Cela vous fait mal?*'

Maryanne tried to remember something from her French lessons as she stared into the kind, dark eyes of her saviour – anything at all that would help her communicate with this extraordinarily good-looking boy in a pale yellow sweater that looked soft as a newborn chick, and his shiny tan leather shoes.

'*Je suis ... Il y a ...*' It was no good. All the French she had learned in the long hours spent in the classroom dissolved into thin air.

'Oh, good, you're not French at all. I thought you were because you looked so chic. I'd just about exhausted my repertoire and was going to have to resort to asking you where the post office was.'

The boy spoke quickly, the words tumbling out of his mouth in a rush to be heard. He grinned at her, and stuck out his hand again. She quickly wiped hers on the back of her skirt, and he took it and shook it with a confidence far beyond his years.

'I'm Maryanne,' she said shyly.

'Hey, she speaks! I was beginning to wonder. I'm Nicolo. Nicolo Flores. American, like you. And you look like you need a drink.'

Nicolo was her first proper, real friend. The first person that she had met by herself, rather than being pushed into it by Sativa. Nicolo was the first person who wanted to spend time with her, who was interested in what she had to say. Someone listening to her and asking her opinions was an entirely new experience for Maryanne, who felt her confidence grow stronger every time she saw the dark, good-looking boy. She could never quite believe he wasn't embarrassed to be seen walking down the street with her, but on the contrary, he seemed proud to do so. That first day that they met, he had taken her off to a bar where he ordered them Campari and soda, which was bitter and made Maryanne's mouth pucker inside, but it looked so beautifully jewel-like that she didn't care.

The two of them spent the afternoon drinking cocktails and walking through the streets of Monaco, talking. Nicolo insisted on carrying her bag, and she laughed at how the small, hippyish pouch looked dangling from his slim shoulders. He'd played up to her laughter, mincing along the street, pretending to be wearing high heels and miming applying lipstick.

They ended up, three Camparis later, at a table outside a tiny backstreet café, away from the glitz and the wide streets that were so clean they looked like they'd been Hoovered rather than swept. Maryanne felt much more comfortable here, out of sight of the rich yachtsmen and their trophy blondes, of whom her mother might be one, but Maryanne felt she had about as much in common with them as with aliens.

At this point Nicolo asked her about her life, and it all came pouring out. How her father had left after discovering his wife in bed with one too many of his friends and colleagues – it was his boss that had proved the final straw in the collapse of their marriage – and had packed his bags and never looked back, not even to say goodbye to Maryanne. How she missed him, but not as much as she felt she should, because when he had been there he had always been looking at her mother, never at Maryanne, whom he rarely noticed. So she thought maybe it was the idea of him that she missed really. How she was ashamed of her mother, because she knew she was a gold-digger, and it embarrassed her when she saw other women looking at her sideways, and standing closer to their husbands when she was around, or when she saw the glint in Sativa's eyes as she spotted a potential sugar daddy. How she was scared that children always turned out like their parents, and that one day she would become that woman, whether she liked it or not. How she felt happiest when she was drawing or painting, how it seemed to take her to her own little world, as she coloured in the detailed line drawings of parties and flam-boyantly dressed women in hats with ostrich feather plumes and beribboned shoes.

And Nicolo listened – not looking bored, or waiting for her to finish, or staring over her shoulder nodding politely – but really *listened* to what she was saying. Eventually she ran out of steam and sat, feeling like she had just run a race, slightly out of breath and amazed that she had just told an almost stranger every detail of her life, but exhilarated as well. She felt lighter. And anyway, he didn't feel like a stranger or even almost a stranger, he felt like her friend.

'I'm sorry. I haven't asked anything about you and I've just dominated the conversation,' Maryanne said.

Nicolo laughed. 'Dominated the conversation? How formal.'

She blushed. 'My mother sent me to etiquette classes. She said no one would want to spend time with me unless I could learn to conduct myself properly.'

'How dull. I think conducting oneself *im*properly is much more fun.'

He winked, and Maryanne's blush deepened. Was he flirting with her? She didn't know. No, of course he wouldn't be, he was at least three years older than she was; he was sure to have some glamorous girlfriend back home, wherever that was.

'Don't panic, I'm not flirting with you.'

Oh God, was she that transparent? Suddenly she felt very gauche and uncomfortable. He was laughing at her, he must be. He was sophisticated, even though he was young, good looking, obviously the child of wealthy parents who travelled the world … he was clearly just killing time, amusing himself for a few hours with the podgy little girl who'd fallen over on the street. She stood up quickly, and reached her hand out for her bag.

'I should go. Thank you for a nice afternoon. My mother will be wondering where I am.'

'What? You said – oh hell, I've upset you.'

'No, no, not at all, I just should go to my hotel now.'

'It was the flirting thing, wasn't it?'

She looked up at him. He was smiling, and a sudden surge of anger swelled up inside her throat. Screw him! She might be unsophisticated and childish, but she didn't deserve to be laughed at.

'Look, I know you've got better things to be doing than sitting here with me, so why don't you go back to your rich friends or family or whoever you're here with and we can forget we ever met each other. It's unkind to mock people, you know.'

And, with as much dignity as she could muster, she took her ragged bag from his hand and stomped off down the street.

'Hey, Maryanne. Maryanne! Wait up!'

Stomp, stomp, stomp. Who did he think he was? She walked more quickly, her feet fumbling to keep up with her legs. But he was quick, and now he was alongside her, keeping pace easily.

'What do you mean, my rich friends? Why are you running off? Will you stop?' He grabbed her elbow and she stopped, and whipped it away.

'Get off!'

'Fine! Jesus, why are you being such a bitch?'

'Me? You're the one who's been sitting there laughing at me all afternoon, getting me to tell you all about my pathetic little life so you can go back and tell everyone about this sad girl you met...'

She trailed off. Listening to herself, she sounded ridiculous. Nicolo was looking at her in astonishment.

'What *are* you talking about? You think I've been hanging out with you so I can laugh at you?'

She didn't reply.

'Well?'

Maryanne nodded. She felt rather silly, all of a sudden.

'Fine. Go back to your hotel. Wait for your mother to roll in at God knows what time. I don't care. But if you'd bothered to ask, you'd know why I wanted to talk to you, to hang out with you.'

Oh, God. Now she really did feel ashamed. He was right, she hadn't asked anything; she didn't even know where he lived. She *was* a bitch.

'I'm sor—'

But he didn't let her finish.

'You want to know why? Because I'm lonely. I'm here by myself, and I just got sick of pretending to be worldly and walking around by myself. I wanted someone to talk to. Someone normal. Never mind. Just forget it.'

Now it was Nicolo's turn to take off down the street, walking with his slim shoulders hunched over and his hands shoved into his pockets. Shit. Maryanne ran after him. She had really messed this up.

'I'm sorry, Nicolo, I'm so sorry. I just thought – oh, I'm such an idiot. I thought you were flirting with me, then I realised you couldn't be, I mean, why would you, and I'm sure your girlfriend's lovely, and I just got into a big muddle . . .' Her words were coming out in big gulps.

Nicolo stopped, and sighed. 'What girlfriend?'

Maryanne shrugged again.

'You know something, Maryanne?'

'What?' She braced herself for the 'fuck off' she felt sure was coming. And which she deserved.

'If we are going to become friends, you're really going to have to learn to ask me questions rather than just filling in the gaps yourself inside your funny little head.'

They did become friends. They spent the rest of that evening eating burgers and frites after they had gone back to Maryanne's cheap hotel so she could write a note for her mother ('Not that she'll be back before me, but still . . .'), and now it was Nicolo's turn to talk, to tell her about his life back home. He told her about his business, about how his father had died, and his mother had struggled, about his sudden success and his newfound notoriety in his home town as a result, and how he'd decided to take himself off on a grand tour of Europe for the summer, before he had to go back to high school to complete his final year and deal with the effects that he knew his sudden wealth would have.

'My friends – well, there aren't that many, but the ones I had before don't really know how to act now, you know? It's like I'm a different person. I make them uncomfortable. And the rich kids don't want to know me – I'm new money, you see? All very embarrassing, actually earning your cash rather than just being a member of the Lucky Sperm Club.' He blushed. 'Sorry.'

Maryanne shook her head and laughed. 'It's fine. I've heard the word "sperm" before. Live with my mother and you hear it a lot.' She bit into her burger and tried to stop the slick of grease from dribbling down her chin.

'My mother would freak if she heard me say that. She's kind of old fashioned. Anyway, I'm sure they think it's some kind of scam,' he said, wiping the salt from around his mouth with a paper napkin, and handing one to Maryanne so she could do the same.

'Your business?'

'Yeah. A con, or whatever. You know, I'm too young, it all happened too quick, it must be something dodgy. It's not. It's just, I feel like I've kind of found what I'm good at. Having ideas. Selling them to people. Convincing them they want what I've got.'

He paused, looked down at the pavement. 'I don't know. Maybe that *is* a con.'

'I think it's a talent. A pretty cool one, too.'

'Thanks.'

They were silent for a few moments, listening to the sounds spilling out of the nearby bars.

'Hey, you know before?' he went on. 'With the whole, um, flirting thing?'

'Mm.' Maryanne put a handful of frites in her mouth so she didn't have to say anything else.

'I wasn't *not* flirting with you because I have a girlfriend. I don't. And it's not because I don't think you're cute. I do.'

He paused. Maryanne didn't say anything. Was she meant to talk now? What was she supposed to say? 'Thank you'? But to her relief he carried on.

'It's just you're kind of young. And I don't know what's going to happen when I go back home.'

Now he was looking at her like he was expecting her to say something. She could only manage a slightly strangled 'OK.' God, this was *so* embarrassing.

'OK.' He looked relieved. 'I just didn't want you to think I was laughing at you. Because . . .'

She couldn't bear it any longer. 'No, really, I don't. It's fine. So, what's the next stop on your big trip?'

A few days later, Nicolo went on to Italy, where he planned to spend a fortnight backpacking around and seeing all of the works of the Great Masters that he had only ever seen in pictures. Before he left, he and Maryanne had discovered their shared passion for art, and he had promised to send her postcards of the highlights. She and Sativa returned home a few days later, back to the family home in Ohio which Maryanne knew they would not be able to afford to stay in for much longer. It was rented, and the money her father had left Sativa with had almost run out, spent on a year of futile attempts to find a rich man. Maryanne knew this because she sneaked looks at all of her mother's correspondence – partly because she knew it was the only way she would find out what was going on, and partly because she was secretly hoping that there would be something from her father. There never was.

But this time, when she sat on the bottom stair, with her cardigan wrapped round her in the chilly house (there wasn't much furniture left any more, since Sativa had sold much of it to pay for their flights to Nice, and the gas had obviously been shut off while they were away), going through the mail looking for the bill to see if they could afford to pay it, although there was still nothing from her father, there was something from Nicolo. A postcard from the Uffizi in Florence, of a painting she recognised: Botticelli's *Birth of Venus*. She gazed at the beautiful woman rising out of the sea on a huge shell, her hair twisting around her shoulders in great thick ringlets, covering her between her legs, but not concealing the fact that she was naked.

She turned it over.

Saw this and thought of you . . . read the confidently inscribed letters in black ink. She turned the postcard back over and stared at the image again. The woman was definitely, indisputably naked. A nipple peeked out from between the fingers that she was holding, loosely, at her breast. Maryanne flushed dark red. She didn't look anything like this gorgeous woman – did she? She got up from her place at the foot of the stairs and went to the mirror that ran along the hall wall. Taking the clip from her ponytail, she shook her hair free. It was the same sort of golden-blond colour as the Botticelli nude, and it was thick and wavy like hers as well. Maryanne twisted it back and over one shoulder, tilting her head to one side, holding the postcard up next to her face for comparison. A shiver ran down the back of her neck. Was that how he saw her? Could it possibly be?

'What's that you've got there? What are you doing?'

Maryanne jumped. 'Nothing. Just had something in my eye.'

She shoved the postcard down her top. Luckily Sativa was too groggy to pay much attention, and as she pushed past Maryanne on her way to the kitchen the girl could smell the sweetness of hash mingled with the sour undertone of vodka. Her mother's very own signature scent.

'Hello, this is Mrs Curtis. I'd like to speak to my account manager please.'

Maryanne breathed deeply as she attempted to keep her voice steady and sound older than her fourteen years as she stood in the phone booth, one eye on her mother who was standing on the sidewalk, smoking.

Making the calls to the utilities providers and the bank herself, pretending to be her mother, was the only way Maryanne could think of to keep things from falling apart completely. Sativa seemed to have descended into a pit of drunken despair, and was refusing to deal with anything, or get a job. Maryanne didn't know how much longer she could go on like this. In a couple of weeks summer would be over and she would have to go back to high school – and what would happen then?

As she waited for the bank manager to come on the line, she put a hand to her bag and pressed it, feeling for the thick envelope of postcards that she had amassed over the last few weeks. It seemed that every day brought another card, as Nicolo picked out paintings and sculptures, mostly of women with long golden hair, and sent them to her. She raced down in the morning when she heard the mail drop through the letterbox – not that there was any need as far as hiding the cards from Sativa was concerned, since her mother never rose before lunchtime any more. But they brought a flash of excitement to her day, seeing where he had been this time, what card he had picked out. She would take them upstairs to her bedroom and crawl under the covers with them, imagining him in the gallery gift shop, selecting that day's card for her, his hand hovering over different ones before eventually landing on this one. Then, she thought, maybe he would go and sit in a café in a piazza, and drink a cup of coffee while he wrote the message on the back. They were always short, usually just one line. *Ate tripe. Advise you don't bother. Venice beautiful. But stinky.* And then the most recent. *Homesick. Booking flight back today.*

Her heart had leaped when she read that. Now it leaped again, but this time with nerves rather than excitement, as the bank manager came on the line.

'Mrs Curtis?'

She cleared her throat. 'Yes, this is she. I need to talk to you about my account.'

'Indeed you do, Mrs Curtis. I've been trying to reach you on the phone but it seems it has been disconnected.'

'Yes, there was some confusion with—'

'There was no confusion. The phone was disconnected because your bill hasn't been paid. For six months. And the cheque you tried to pay it with most recently was refused. By us.'

'Yes, I wanted to talk to you about that. I'd like to transfer—'

'Mrs Curtis, there's nothing to transfer. Your savings account is empty. All your accounts are empty. Unless you can pay in . . .'

The manager continued talking but Maryanne was no longer listening. Everything was swimming around. She'd known it was only a matter of time before they ran out of money, but she'd thought they had a bit longer, had hoped she could hold on for long enough to get her mother back on track and persuade her to look for a job. She'd imagined her working at a beauty salon, maybe, giving people manicures and doing girls' up-dos on prom night. She looked out now at her mother, her face bloated, no make-up, her clothes unpressed and a bit grimy. And Maryanne hung up the handset and began to sob like the little girl she used to be.

Maryanne and Sativa arrived in London one damp, dank morning in September. The grey runway and wet, grey air matched Maryanne's mood as she stared out of the plane's window, her mother snoring lightly beside her. Maryanne had made the call to the only person she could think of who might help them – if not out of affection then at least out of some sense of obligation. That day in the phone booth, once she had stopped crying, she had flicked through her mother's address book until she found the number, and had managed to work out the international dialling code and get through.

The voice on the other end of the phone had been unfamiliar; even her accent was unlike any British accent Maryanne had heard on the television. They were either plummy and posh, or jovial, cheery Cockneys – this was rasping and harsh.

'Yeah?' it had said, when the line connected, sounding bored.

'Is this Mrs Westbrook?' Maryanne asked.

There was a snort. Maryanne could hear the derision in the voice from thousands of miles away.

'Is this Missus Westbrook? Well, I suppose it is, though Mister Westbrook ain't been seen round 'ere for a fuck of a long time. Who's this?'

Maryanne swallowed. This woman didn't sound like she was going to be willing to help them. Still, she had to try. What choice did she have?

'This is Maryanne Curtis calling from America.'

There was a pause.

'Your granddaughter.'

Chapter Six

1978

Nicolo's bags were neatly lined up in the hallway of his mother's house, the plain brown leather of the matching set standing out against the cream and gold patterned wallpaper behind it, and the pastel shades of the silk rug beneath it. Mama Flores didn't understand her son's preference for simple design, be it in clothes, furniture or architecture; for her, quality was in workmanship, and workmanship was best displayed in the ornate, the slightly ostentatious. When she was choosing new things, Nicolo always said to her, 'Mama, what about this one? It's subtle, you can see the quality.' Ach, but those things just looked bland, dull. It wasn't that she wanted to brag about her son's youthful success, but – well, what was the point in being able to afford nice things if no one could tell? She still couldn't believe how well he had done. It wasn't as if he'd shown particular promise as a small child. He'd just been average, really. But after his father had died and things had gone downhill for them, it was as if he had been transformed. He wasn't a boy any more, hadn't been for some time. And now he was off to Harvard, the best university in the whole of the United States of America. Back in Malta, she had never dreamed that she would have a son who had not only made enough money by the age of seventeen to buy his mother a brand-new house, fully furnished, but who was also going to Harvard. She sighed happily, and took one last look at his luggage, lined up in height order, before going off to make his favourite meal for dinner. She was very proud. It was just a shame he had been so depressed these last few months. She didn't know why. Girl trouble, most likely, she nodded to herself, as she went in to the kitchen to start the pastizzi.

Mama Flores was right – the reason her son Nicolo had been miserable was girl trouble, of a sort. Maryanne had got under his skin, somehow. While he was travelling around Europe he'd got used to sending her postcards, had taken pleasure in finding the perfect one each day, and sitting down at a café with a coffee to write it. It had become a ritual almost, a way of punctuating his day. And more than that, the slightly pudgy fourteen year old, whose puppy fat had not yet dissolved into womanly curves but whose skin was luminous and whose hair fell in thick soft handfuls over her shoulders, had somehow entranced him. She was a child still, and yet she wasn't childish – probably down to having to take care of her mother. They had that in common – absent fathers – though hers had left and his was dead, but there was a mutual understanding even so. And she was so full of life, so enchantingly excited by his attention, so open . . . That was it, he thought now as he sat on the edge of his bed in his almost empty bedroom. That was what was most attractive about her – her openness. Her thoughts spilled out of her mouth as soon as they entered her head; you could see her emotions in her body, in the way she stood and the way her hands moved. She was transparent – a lie would be impossible for her to tell, even if she wanted to. She was honest, and she was real, and he realised during his travels that, quite against his better judgement, he had fallen in love with her.

He'd been so looking forward to seeing her again when he returned home. He hadn't bothered to give her his address when they were in Monaco because he hadn't known when he was coming back, and would be on the move until then, so he had just taken hers. He'd also, if he was honest, quite liked the mystery he had imagined this gave him, and the power of being able to be the one who was in control, who would send her missives from around the world and then sweep back into her life when he was ready to do so.

It had somewhat backfired. He'd tried phoning at first, but the number had been disconnected. He'd tried again, thinking maybe he'd dialled it wrongly, but had just got the same unobtainable tone. The phone company had refused to give him any more details, wouldn't even confirm the name the number had been registered to, saying that it was 'protected information, sir'. Then he'd sent a letter, giving his number and address, telling her he was back in the country and asking her to get in touch. After a week, he'd written again, telling himself that the first letter had probably gone astray. Two weeks after that, having lost his appetite and as a result, half a stone in weight, despite the best efforts of his worried mother to feed him up, he had sent a telegram, ticking the box that meant delivery required a signature. Two days later, the telegram was returned to him, unopened, with *Not known at this address* scrawled on the back.

If Nicolo had been a different sort of person, less defensive, slower to jump to negative conclusions, he might have made the journey from his home in New Jersey to Maryanne's old house, and, if he had done so, he might have bumped into a neighbour who could have told him that the girl and her mother had left, suddenly, and that the bailiffs had come knocking. And he would have realised that they had been forced to leave in a hurry. If he had done this as soon as he returned, or within a fortnight, he would have got there before the new family had moved in, with their boxes of belongings and toy trucks and trampoline, and who had paid a professional cleaning company to come and give the place a thorough going-over and get rid of the smell of cigarettes and incense and the pile of unanswered post that had been building up behind the front door. And he would have realised that Maryanne had never received his most recent letters, instead of thinking that she had given him a false address, and that he had been sending all those postcards into the void, or even for other people to laugh at. He might even have found a small piece of pink notepaper tucked under the doormat by Maryanne just before they left, half-poking out so it could be seen, with a hastily scribbled London phone number and address inside its folds, and his name on the outside.

But he didn't do any of those things, so the note flew away when the doormat was shaken out to get rid of the dust, and then was picked up and thrown in the trash by the cleaners, and Nicolo never read it, and so went on thinking that Maryanne had lied to him.

Nicolo hated liars. The only thing he hated more than liars was being laughed at. So what he perceived as Maryanne's cruel taunting of him, in a way that seemed utterly at odds with the girl he had met on the street in Monaco, plunged him into a bitter funk. He had dragged himself through the fall and winter, burying himself in his studies. He was miserable in school, he still had no friends, and his current mood didn't help matters; during his summer travels he'd promised himself that when he returned home he would make a renewed effort to meet people his age, in school, out of school, it didn't matter. He would take up a sport, join a club, it didn't matter what as long as it brought him into contact with new people, who didn't just think of him as the sallow-skinned, slender boy who had made all that money out of a cheap toy, and who looked at him slightly askance because of it. He'd never imagined that success would be so complicated. He had thought that he could just buy his mother's house back from the bank and that life would continue as before, except in greater comfort. He'd been very wrong.

After the initial excitement had worn off, his mother had decided that she didn't want to live in the old house any longer, that it was too full of memories, too rickety, too many stairs. She wanted a good address and a boy to come and mow the lawn, not creaking floorboards and a rundown park at the end of the road. So Nicolo had gone to the realtor and ascertained which were the best streets in town, found a new-build house on one of them, and bought it. But the same problem had followed them here, as it did at Nicolo's school. The new neighbours were stuck-up, were suspicious of them, didn't respond well to his mother's little gifts of Maltese pastries when they moved in. Didn't want to make friends. And her old friends thought themselves not good enough for her any more, thought that she was the one who had become stuck-up, who had moved higher up the ladder than they could reach, and so they didn't trust her any more, and smiled politely when she visited but treated her as they would treat the priest or their husband's boss. Not letting her back in. So she and Nicolo were stuck, in limbo, alone together. And it was suffocating him.

That was partly why he'd gone away, and when he returned it was no better; nothing had changed – if anything, it was worse. He had seen so many wonderful things in Europe, so many incredible buildings, had filled thick leatherbound notebooks with diary entries and scribbled sketches and thoughts. And he had met Maryanne.

His disappointment was written in his body; in the hunched way he held his shoulders as he walked to his car every morning to drive himself to school. For the next few months he had just got up, gone to school, come home, studied and gone to bed. In a daily cycle.

Grindingly tedious it might have been, but it had stood him in good stead, because in December he had applied to Harvard, to study engineering, and a few months later he received notice that he had been accepted. His mother had kissed him five times, and had sent him off to 'go and tell his friends'. Nicolo had driven to the drive-in and watched *Superman* while drinking a chocolate milkshake to celebrate, then he'd driven home and started to draw up his reading list. He had been determined to ensure that he went to Harvard well prepared.

And now, as he stood in the hallway of his mother's house (and it was her house, since he had put it entirely in her name) ready to leave he was confident that, academically speaking at least, he was up to the mark. He had read every book recommended by the school, as well as a long list of volumes whose titles he had found in the bibliographies of those books. He had read all of the books published by the men who would teach him, and had researched their careers. He had read biographies of successful men and had analysed why others had failed. His brain was at the peak of its fitness, like an athlete's body shortly before a race. He was ready.

When he arrived at Harvard the next day he realised he was not ready. He wasn't ready for the swarming mass of unfamiliar faces and cacophony of voices, all shouting, laughing, calling, chattering. He wasn't ready for the piles of paperwork and forms he was required to fill in, the avalanche of timetables and study group choices and optional lectures and additional classes. He wasn't ready for the buildings, the miles of corridors and staircases and lecture rooms, carved stone and looming statues and hundreds and hundreds of years of academic brilliance in the air around him, in the very bricks of the place, it seemed. He wasn't ready for the staggering, swaggering confidence of his fellow students, who all, it seemed, knew where they were going and with whom and why already, swirling around him as he stood under a tree in Harvard Yard, struggling to hold on to his armful of papers and carry his luggage and decipher the photocopied map with a pencilled cross marking the dorm he had been allocated to, and that would be his home for the next year.

'You've got it upside down,' a voice pointed out from behind his shoulder, and Nicolo turned around. Standing next to him and gesturing at the map was a young man of his own age, or so it appeared, but of very different appearance. Whereas Nicolo was of medium height, slim, elegantly built, he was tall, with broad shoulders. A muscular forearm protruded from the rolled-up sleeve of a worn shirt and the big, tanned hand that was waving a cigarette at the map Nicolo was grasping was in sharp contrast to Nicolo's slender limbs and carefully pressed sleeve under a layer of dark green cashmere V-neck. The stranger had messy light brown hair that stuck up at odd angles, making Nicolo's wave of dark hair that always fell back into place look almost feminine by comparison. But the biggest difference was in the self-assurance that this fellow student exuded; he looked completely comfortable in his surroundings, in his own skin, with everything that was going on, whereas Nicolo was all too aware that his awkwardness and uncertainty were plain for all to see.

'Oh look, you're with us – weird, huh? Lucky I found you. Come on, it's this way.' And the other guy loped off ahead, a trail of smoke flowing behind him and his long legs covering half the courtyard by the time Nicolo had gathered his luggage together to follow.

'It's four of us – me, Logan, and now you, and some other guy who hasn't shown up yet,' he went on. 'We've been wondering who we were gonna get. Some of the dorms've got six people, but I think it's better to get in a smaller one as it's not so long to wait for the shower.'

'Who's Logan? Actually, who are you?'

'Oh, sorry! Johnny, I'm Johnny. Logan's my best friend, from back home. They don't usually room you together but his old man is alum and so he pulled some strings. Well, he doesn't know that – we faked his signature.'

Nicolo nodded, trying to take it all in, then introducing himself. 'My name's Nicolo.'

'I know, it said on your map.'

Nicolo looked at the piece of paper that he was still grasping. So it did. He pushed it into the pocket of his dark navy wool jacket. They arrived at the end of a corridor and a wooden door, which Johnny shoved open as Nicolo tried to take in all the information that had just been added to the already overflowing pool of stuff he had been told since he arrived, barely an hour ago. Behind the door was another narrow corridor, with more doors leading off it. Nicolo dropped his bags on the floor and followed Johnny, past a door with his own name on the cardboard tag, towards an open area at the end with brown and yellow tweedy couches that looked as though they would be scratchy, arranged around a dark wood coffee table covered in ringmarks. Sitting on one of the couches was the boy who Nicolo figured must be Logan. He stood and faced Nicolo, his expression unsmiling but not unfriendly. He was dark-haired, stocky, with a good looking and somehow far more adult face than any of the other students Nicolo had seen so far. His friend Johnny had an easy, slightly crooked grin, and a boyish look, but this guy looked like a man, not a boy. Nicolo squared his shoulders and stuck out his hand.

'Nicolo Flores.'

'Logan Barnes.'

They shook hands, Nicolo noting that Logan's grip was firm, his handshake practised.

'Man, look at you two. Like a couple of statesmen. Chill out.' Johnny threw himself on to the couch and flipped his legs up to rest on its back.

Logan broke into a smile. 'Yeah. Good to meet you, Nicolo. Woman from Admissions came by. The other guy's not coming, after all. Some mess-up. She said they were going to allocate someone else to the room, but it's the strangest thing – when she looked at her files, this dorm was listed as just a three-roomer. She must have been mistaken.'

Nicolo looked confused, and Logan winked. It was the first time, but would be by no means the last, that Nicolo was to witness Logan's extraordinary talent for getting his own way.

'So,' Logan said, sitting back down and picking up a pack of cards that was lying on the coffee table, 'looks like it's just going to be the three of us. Fancy a game of poker?'

Just the three of them. That's how it had been, from then on. The two friends had swept Nicolo up into their tight little world, expanding their duo into a trio. Or so he had thought.

It didn't matter now what he had thought back then, Nicolo reminded himself as he sat in his den, the words of the poem that had once been the trio's war-cry, their emblem, floated into his head. *'We are the music-makers, And we are the dreamers of dreams.'*

Fucking Logan Barnes, insinuating his way into his life, his thoughts even now. He needed to clear his head, straighten himself out. Picking up the phone, Nicolo pressed the button that connected him directly to his personal and private assistant.

'Phone the agency, will you,' he said, 'and tell them not to send the one I had last time. She was too fat.'

Without bothering to wait for a reply, he hung up. He was agitated, and it wasn't just down to his confrontation with Vienna earlier. He couldn't put his finger on what was wrong. Going over to the polished wooden sideboard that served as a bar in the corner of the room, he poured a glass of Pétrus from the decanter. He swirled it gently, warming it slightly in his hand. It was almost exactly the same colour as that nail varnish all women seemed to wear now – Rouge Noir. Ruby red, with a hint of black underneath. He sat, and drank while he waited.

He'd never played poker before that day, had never gambled. His mother didn't approve of playing games for money. But he'd loved it, and been quite good at it, had found it challenging and interesting. He wasn't as good as Johnny, who had the mathematical sort of brain that could calculate probabilities and percentages more quickly than most people could add a simple sum, and Logan had the advantage of having been taught bridge and other card games at a young age by his mother, who had wanted a partner to practise with at home in order to reign supreme at the country club tournaments, but he could hold his own. They had fallen into the habit of playing most nights, after class had finished and they had completed the work their tutors had set, sitting around the battered coffee table in their dorm. Chatting, eating, drinking, smoking while they played. It relaxed them, it became their nightly ritual, a pocket of calm in the hectic lives they were leading as freshmen finding their feet in the hothouse heat of Harvard.

89

Nicolo was happy at the university, properly happy for the first time in his life, apart from the period he had spent travelling, but the memory of that had been tainted now, so he refused to let himself dwell on it. Here, he could be himself, a better version of himself. Freed from the expectations and constraints of his loving but suffocating mother, of the watchful eyes of everyone who lived in his hometown, he could be just another student, not the boy who had made good. He was loving being stretched academically, taught by the best, absorbing everything around him like a sponge. Everything about Harvard thrilled him – the sense of achievement, of competition, of hard work; the late-night debates, the student magazine, the history and beauty of the place.

But most of all, he loved the fact that he had friends, real, true friends, with whom he could laugh and joke and drink beer, play cards, make plans, talk about the future and the past. Over the first few months the trio had formed a strong bond, forged in the intensity of the life into which they had been plunged. Sitting up late, playing cards, Nicolo had heard about their families, listened to Johnny talk about his brother Bobby, watched as he fought not to cry as he told Nicolo how his family had died. He told Nicolo the whole story, standing at the window, blowing cigarette smoke out of it into the cold air outside, and then he never mentioned his family again. There was an unspoken understanding that they didn't talk about it. Johnny's way of dealing with what had happened was to keep it inside, keep living his life to the max and not look back. Logan and Nicolo both knew it couldn't last for ever, that he was burning the candle too fast, too hard, but they also knew that there was nothing either of them could do to change things for Johnny. He would have to face his demons in his own way, in his own time. Meanwhile, he studied, rowed, partied, womanised, gambled. And an anger burned somewhere behind his eyes, driving him forwards.

He had heard about Logan's parents, watched and laughed as Logan had mimicked his mother's bored drawl and his father's gruff confusion. They had talked about what they wanted to do with their lives, and Logan and Johnny had shared their plans for high-flying success with Nicolo, had included him from then on when they talked about how big they were going to make it. It was a given, now, that he would be part of it all. They would pool their resources, make it happen together, the addition of his strength to their cluster of complementary talents making them stronger still. And in return, he had told them what he knew about his own father, how he had died when Nicolo was too young to remember him, and what it had been like growing up with just him and his mother, about how he had always felt like an outsider. He'd told them about the things he had seen when he had been travelling, had even told them about the girl he had met, and the disappointment he had felt when he'd realised she had lied to him, and they had sympathised and clapped him on the back and poured him another drink. And he had known that they would never let him down as she had.

He hadn't told them about the money he had made, though. He didn't know why not. He had kept it to himself, hugging the secret tight inside.

Sighing deeply, Nicolo opened his laptop and clicked on an icon on his desktop that brought up a media viewer programme. Clicked on the Play button.

The credits rolled. They opened with dramatic backdrops of the streets of London and New York, and gradually moved closer in, cutting between the fronts of LBI-owned properties in the two cities. The glitzy glass front of the West Side, the majestic architecture of the Chesham in London, the grande dame that was the Royal back in Manhattan. The scenes were filled with action, energy. Then, walking down the sidewalk, facing the camera and looking more like male models than hardworking businessmen, came Logan, Johnny and Mark. They came to a stop, looking down into the lens, their eyes hard in a deliberately fierce-looking pose. And the titles slashed across the bottom of the screen in bright red. *General Manager*.

Nicolo snipped the end off a cigar with a silver cutter and lit it, savouring the taste.

The image of the three men was replaced with a glamorous female presenter, standing in the function room-cum-studio that they used as the show's base.

'Hello, and welcome to this week's *General Manager*. Coming up, Denis can't stand the heat in the kitchen.' An image of a man sweating in his chef's whites as he struggled to balance two huge trays of food across his big arms.

'And Paula gets into hot water with housekeeping.' The screen showed a harassed-looking woman stuffing piles of bed linen into an industrial washing machine.

'But, first, let's welcome the judging panel. Johnny Stokes, Logan Barnes – and Mark Mallory. What a powerhouse of business expertise these three men are!'

Nicolo puffed on his cigar before shutting the laptop. Since he'd first seen the trailers for the series, he hadn't been able to stop watching the show. Seeing Logan and Johnny everywhere, so powerful and famous and fucking smug, had reignited that fire in his soul that he thought he had managed to quench years ago. He wondered if they ever thought of him as they sat there, arrogantly pronouncing the fates of the poor bastards who were auditioning for a job in front of the whole nation. Did they ever look at the third seat at the table, and think it should have had another person sitting in it, and remember why it didn't?

It should have been him. It just – should have been him.

One Friday night, in their second year of college, they had been playing cards as usual, surrounded by the debris of takeaway pizza. They had moved into one of the houses for second- and third-year students, but had managed to retain their group of three. The dorm was another suite of rooms with a kitchen and bathroom, and Johnny had been lying on the sofa with his legs over the back, as was his habit, flicking through a book of poetry, a set text from the elective he was taking in literature, in addition to his core math classes. Every so often he read a line or two out loud, fragments of poems by Oscar Wilde, Poe and Tennyson: '"O beautiful star with the crimson mouth! O moon with the brows of gold" ... "By a route obscure and lonely, Haunted angels only" ... "Out flew the web and floated wide; the mirror cracked from side to side."'

'Shut up, Jay,' muttered Logan, 'I'm trying to win here.'

'You're not going to win,' Johnny replied good-naturedly, 'as you don't have the cards.'

Logan glared at him, while Nicolo smiled secretly to himself. Johnny's memory for numbers was amazing.

'Hey, listen up,' said Johnny, flipping himself upright and leaning

92

forwards. Logan pulled his cards closer to his body, and Johnny saw and shook his head.

'I'm not trying to look at your cards, you fucking dumbass.'

Logan threw a cushion at him, but the other boy caught it before it hit his head.

'No, really, listen to this.' He started to read. Johnny had an actor's voice, rich and clear.

> 'We are the music-makers,
> And we are the dreamers of dreams,'

Logan and Nicolo fell quiet. There was something compelling about the way he was reading.

> 'Wandering by lone sea-breakers,
> And sitting by desolate streams;
> World-losers and world-forsakers,
> On whom the pale moon gleams:'

Now Johnny held up a finger, signalling for the others to pay attention.

> 'Yet we are the movers and shakers
> Of the world for ever, it seems.'

Logan smiled, leaned back in his seat, lighting a cigarette. He glanced over at Nicolo.

'Yeah, baby. Movers and shakers.'

They high-fived.

'Wait, wait – there's more.' Johnny waved at them to be quiet again.

> 'And out of a fabulous story
> We fashion an empire's glory . . .'

Logan was sitting forward now, a glint of excitement in his eyes. Talk of their future success was always sure to get him fired up. Johnny stood now, his voice rising in volume as he read the next lines.

> *'One man with a dream, at pleasure,*
> *Shall go forth and conquer a crown;'*

He leaped up on to the coffee table, with Logan and Nicolo looking up at him.

> *'And three with a new song's measure*
> *Can trample an empire down.'*

And then Johnny raised his arms and threw the book above his head, whooping as he caught it. The other two were on their feet, clapping and cheering.

'What do you say? Are we going to fashion an empire's glory?' Johnny cried.

'Damn fuckin' right we are,' Logan replied, his face flushed. They were high on life, on youthful confidence, on the promise of great things to come.

Johnny hopped down from the table and Logan rested one hand on his shoulder and one on Nicolo's. The three stood – a triumvirate of bright young things.

'The three of us,' he said. 'No bullshit, no messing around. We trust each other, yes?'

The other two nodded solemnly. 'We're going to build something great. I can feel it, you know? We do it, and we don't wait until we leave here with our MBAs and our law degrees, like everyone else. We start now. Today.'

Johnny and Nicolo's eyes were on Logan. He was almost hypnotically inspiring; energy seemed to flow from him into them.

Logan looked at Johnny, saying, 'We've always said we were going to start a business – build an empire. And now we've got the engineer to help us build the foundations.'

'We never decided what the empire was gonna be, though,' said Johnny.

'I've been thinking about that. How about hotels? Top-class, high-end, luxury hotels. People always need a place to rest their heads. And now we've got the perfect package – or we will have. There's you, Johnny – a lawyer who can make anyone feel at home and like they've got a friend.' Logan had warmed to his pitch now and he was orating, sounding far older than his years. He gestured at Nicolo. 'An engineer of buildings but also of far more than that, I have no doubt. And then there's me – a businessman, an organiser, a man behind the scenes,' and he tipped his hand to his forehead in mock salute.

'What do you say, my friends? Shall we build the greatest group of hotels the world has ever seen, together?'

'Yes!' Their voices rang out, and they laughed. 'Hell yeah!'

Logan grabbed a beer and shook it up, then opened it, showering them all with foam.

'Today, it's Bud. Tomorrow – champagne!'

Later, they went to the Irish bar near campus to toast their big plans with more cheap lager and whisky chasers. Johnny picked up a girl. Johnny usually picked up a girl. She hung around for a bit, then got bored of all the talk about corporations and IPOs, of listening to three nineteen year olds act as if they were kings of the world.

They slumped back in the wooden booth, suddenly tired and glassy-eyed. The intensity and pace of their schedules left little energy over for much else, and the rush they had become caught up in earlier had left them wrung out. Johnny was tearing a beer mat up into little pieces and arranging them in a pile.

'We need a plan,' Logan said, his voice slightly thick.

'Mm.' Johnny nodded.

'We're going to have to work out the best way to get started. We could get some experience, maybe look for a summer job in one of the big hotels? Then try and persuade a bank to back us.'

'I've got some money,' Johnny proposed.

'Yeah, me too. But it's not enough. We wanna start with a splash. A small splash, but it needs to be something decent. And we'll need to employ good people. Right now, *we* know we can do this, but who's going to back three students with no experience?'

'No one.' Johnny picked up the pile of shredded pieces and let them fall through his fingers.

Nicolo had been quiet up until this point, but now he raised his head and looked Logan straight in the eye. Usually he was the quietest of the three, deferring to Logan, letting Johnny make the jokes. But now he felt confidence surge through him. It was time.

'Not quite no one . . .' he told them.

Nicolo drained his glass. The smooth Claret was a far cry from the sandpapery whisky chasers they'd drunk back then. That had been the moment, really, with hindsight. He remembered how proud he had felt, how he had puffed out his chest as he told Logan and Johnny that there *was* someone who would invest in their project, in them. That they were looking at him. And he had confided in them about the money he had made and the marketing skills he had learned while doing so, had gleefully watched their eyes widen as they realised just how successful he had already been, and what this could mean for the three of them.

Well, he had certainly learned from *that* mistake. Pride really did come before a fall.

A soft knock came at the door and Nicolo shook himself out of the past. Good. He would spend an hour with whoever they had sent, purging himself of this black cloud, and then he would get back to his life – the comfortable, high-achieving life that he had created all by himself.

But when he opened the door, it wasn't to a statuesque blonde, or a beautiful Latino girl with a smile on her face, but a tall, tanned boy directing the full wattage of a bright, white smile at Nicolo. He was dressed in a black and white bellboy outfit, complete with piping and pill hat. Between his outstretched hands was a silver plate, covered with a traditional silver dome of the sort removed with a flourish by waiters in smart French restaurants.

'Good afternoon, Mr Flores.'

'Who the fuck are you? Is this some kind of a joke?'

The boy's smile faltered. 'No, no joke. My apologies, sir, I hope this isn't a bad time. I have a special delivery for you.'

He gave a little bow and then, holding the platter with his left hand, deftly used his right to remove the cover, sweeping it behind his back in one graceful movement. In the centre of the silver plate was a glossy black Perspex box, with *Nicolo Flores and Vienna Chatters* engraved on the top in silver cursive lettering. He stared at it. Without investigating any further Nicolo knew who would be behind this. It was something to do with Logan Barnes. For a second he considered just closing the door, walking away from the interminable dance he and Logan had locked themselves into. But only for a second. Reaching out his hand, he lifted the box from the tray.

Inside his den again, he sat down at the desk in the corner and stared at the box. Its shiny surface and its sharp lines invited you to touch it, to run a finger along the edges, to open it. He resisted. It was as if something in him knew that by opening it, he would in some indefinable way, be submitting.

There was a knock on the door. He ignored it. Finally, sighing, he opened the lid. A rectangle of thick black card lay inside, with a single word inscribed in the centre of it, in the same elegant lettering, this time in cream:

LUXURY

He flipped the card over. The writing on the back was laid out in the more usual style, black on cream.

A unique new hotel experience. Absolute luxury.
Absolute privacy.
Absolute confidence in confidentiality.

And then:

Your presence is requested at the grand opening of LUXURY.
To attend, you must reply to the number below by 8 a.m.
on 13 September.
You must be available to travel on 15 October.
This invitation is for the addressee only.
Further information regarding arrangements will be made
available upon confirmation of attendance.

The inside of the box was divided into four sections, each with individual lids made out of soft cream leather and numbered one to four. Nicolo lifted the lid of the first. A small silver-coloured locket was inside. On opening it, in place of the usual photographs or curls of hair, he found a tiny silver key, a diamond set at one end

97

of it. The second boxed-off section contained a hundred-dollar bill, neatly folded to fit into the square. He took it out of the section and examined it. It appeared to be real. The third, a casino chip, in the same black and white as the bellboy's uniform, with the words LUXURY – *A Logan Barnes Hotel*, around the outside. And finally, a small dark chocolate. He popped it into his mouth, which was immediately filled with a rich, slightly alcoholic-tasting caramel, flavoured with a hint of something floral . . .

And then he knew. Violet. *L'île des Violettes*. Of course. He should have known that would be the big project Logan was announcing. The beautiful, seductive island the three of them had visited all those years ago, had planned to turn into a luxury resort of a kind the world had never seen. Logan – and Johnny – had done it. Nicolo picked up the casino chip and turned it over in his hand, running his finger over the embossed lettering.

Despite himself, Nicolo admired the stylish design of the invitation, the way it made you curious, the way it lured you in. Very apt, he thought. Logan had always been a master of the art of seduction.

Chapter Seven

Maryanne waited impatiently for the queue of people to progress through customs. She wouldn't allow herself to believe she had finally escaped until she was 100 per cent officially back in the States. She shuffled forward a little, pushing her bag ahead of her as she did so. How had she managed to choose the slowest-moving queue? People who had joined adjacent queues at the same time as her were going through, while she was stuck here. *Hurry up*, she willed the uniformed customs officer in the booth. *Get on with it!*

Eventually she made it to the front of the line and stood before the officer with an inexplicable feeling of guilt, as if she was about to be found out – but for what? She hadn't done anything wrong; she was hardly an illegal immigrant – she was coming home. But even so, she didn't breathe easily until she had stepped over that magic yellow line, looking down at her feet as she did so. She watched them as, clad in hightop Converse with hot-pink legwarmers, they returned to their native soil, and she laughed out loud and wiggled her toes in joy. Home. With only a single backpack and five hundred dollars to her name – but free.

Things had taken a sharp turn for the worse when she and Sativa had arrived in England.

Her grandmother had not been happy to have her daughter, who she thought she had got rid of years previously, turn up on her East London doorstep, along with her teenage offspring. Ada Westbrook had never been a maternal woman, and five pregnancies to a handful of fathers hadn't changed this fact. Candy – or Linda, as she was named on her birth certificate – was her fourth child, and by the time she was born Ada had given up any responsibility for the child's health and education, preferring to leave it instead to her older kids. So little Linda, as she had still been then, had scrambled her way through her early life, learning to eat whenever she got the chance and stay out of the way of her mother's loutish boyfriends and not a lot else. No one made her go to school and so she usually didn't bother. She had run away when she was fifteen and had never looked back.

Running all the way to India, where she had grown tanned and thin, running out of money to pay for her next move, running into trouble in a dimly lit back street, and finally running into the arms of Maryanne's father, a travelling salesman who picked her up and took her back to Ohio with him.

Her mother had never bothered to look for her, glad to have seen the back of her. So it came as something of a surprise to both of them to find themselves thrown back together again.

Maryanne realised she might have made a terrible mistake when they arrived at the squalid little house in the depths of a council estate in Bethnal Green. The windows were smeared and the net curtains were stiff with dirt. Swallowing the lump in her throat, she hoisted their luggage out of the taxi and on to the pavement in the rain, watched by the driver, then coaxed her mother out of the car. They stood and stared at the depressing-looking building for a moment as the taxi drove away. It was cold, and there was a smell of old frying oil in the air. Maryanne took a deep breath, grasped her mother's arm and led her towards the gate, which was hanging off its hinges. They were here now, and they were just going to have to make the best of it.

And that's what she had done, for almost four years. Made the best of it, kept her head down, gone to the local comprehensive school and then, when she was old enough, left, got a job and started saving. She had made a chart, counting down the months until she would turn eighteen and could leave, and as the months turned into weeks, and then days, she had booked her ticket. She hadn't allowed herself to dwell on how miserable she was; on how her mother had allowed everything to fall apart and their lives to meander to a full stop, or on how her father had just abandoned them. If she had let herself think about any of that she would have crumpled – and she knew that she couldn't allow that to happen. If she did, she would never escape this awful house, its blaring TV and the permanent stink of cheap cigarettes. She got up, she drank her cup of tea and she went to school, then after school and on Saturdays she got on the train and went to her job in a shoe shop on High Street Ken. She did that every day for years, apart from Sundays, when she would make a packed lunch and take herself off somewhere. She would find a corner, in a park or on a bench or at a gallery sometimes, and she would draw, for hours and hours, losing herself in the motion of her pencil, letting herself slide into a meditative state as she concentrated on committing people, buildings, birds to paper; making the time pass in a flash as she filled pages and pages of sketchbooks.

It was only now, as she looked out of the window of the bus that was trundling her into New York, that she thought back over the last few years and acknowledged the sheer, lonely wretchedness of them. And she also admitted to herself that she was scared. She might be home in one sense, in that she was back in the States, but New York was new to her; she had only been once before on a trip with her father when she was eleven. Yet it was about to become her home. Six months ago, she had sent a selection of her drawings to six art schools in America, and then she had crossed her fingers and waited. She hadn't had to wait long; after just a few weeks she had been offered a place at all of them and a full scholarship at four, including the New York School of Design, which was where she was headed now. Everything was paid for, even her flight. The terms of her scholarship allowed for one flight home per year for international students, but she had told them she wouldn't be needing that, and so they had agreed to put the money towards a cost of living allowance instead. She would be studying interior architecture. She wanted to make beautiful places for people to live in.

Maryanne rested her head against the seatback and watched as the outer boroughs disappeared and the bus rolled into Manhattan – and the brief moment of fear turned into excitement. There was something about the city that raised her heart-rate and got her blood pumping. It was packed full of life, of people, of opportunities. Finally, her life was her own; at last it was truly beginning.

She reached a hand into the side pocket of her pack. She had brought as few things as possible with her – not that she had had much to start with, as all her money had been tucked away into her savings account, not spent on clothes and records like the other girls at school did. But one thing she would never have left behind was the thick envelope of postcards that she wrapped her fingers round now. A wodge of postcards from galleries and cities all over Italy, places that she dreamed of visiting one day. All with a single line on the back, all of which she knew by heart. The envelope had become her talisman, her cornerstone; she always carried it with her. Despite the note she had left behind when they fled, she had never really expected that Nicolo would find it, because surely he wouldn't bother traipsing all the way to her house when he got back to America. She had no way of knowing whether he had continued to write after they'd left even – maybe he had simply got bored and forgotten all about her. But even though she had lost him, there had once been someone who had thought she was worth talking to, listening to, spending time with. Had thought she was beautiful, even. And that thought had kept her going through all of the nights when she went to bed in her clothes to keep warm, through all of the times when she had locked herself in her room because she was afraid of the men who were in and out of the house at all hours, visiting her mother and her grandmother, through all the times she sat up late at night to finish her homework after she had worked a long shift in the shop. Through those long and lonely years Nicolo Flores had been her saviour; his words had kept her company and somehow, someday soon, she was going to find him again, and she was going to thank him.

'Thank you. Thank you . . . oh, oh God, thank you!'

Nicolo lifted his head from between Maryanne's legs and looked up at her pink cheeks, damp with sweat.

'You don't have to thank me, you know. Making love to a woman as beautiful as you is hardly an arduous way to spend an afternoon. And you certainly don't have to thank God. What did He have to do with it? I don't want Him stealing my thunder.'

He pulled himself up on one arm and pushed Maryanne's hair off from her face. She was damp and warm in his arms, and her breathing was still fast. She took his hand and laced her fingers through his. They were lying on the pull-out bed in her tiny studio flat, which was so small that you had to clamber over the bed to get to the kitchenette – or indeed, to anything, as it took up most of the room. Her clothes were suspended from a system of wires and coat hangers that she had rigged up, as there was no room for a wardrobe, and she had to wash her dishes in the bathroom sink, but to Maryanne, the room was a palace. She had painted the walls white and used them to display (and store) her drawings for college. She'd picked up a few yards of heavy unbleached cotton at a warehouse sale and had dyed it herself in her bath, a deep ruby red. Candles in coloured glass jars lined the small windowsill in the bathroom, casting their jewel colours on to the tiles.

'I still can't believe I found you.'

Nicolo smiled. 'And I still can't believe I lost you. Tell me how you found me again?'

'I've told you so many times!' Maryanne laughed. 'I told you the first night.'

'I like hearing it.'

'Once I got to New York and registered at college, I went to the library and looked up the high schools in Hackensack, New Jersey.'

'Because . . .'

'Because I remembered that's where you lived.'

Nicolo smiled at the thought. She had remembered him, remembered the details of him.

'And then?'

'Then I got on the phone and pretended to be someone from your college needing copies of examination certificates. Of course it was difficult because I didn't know which college you'd gone to, or if you'd gone to college at all. But eventually I got through to your old school, who confirmed you'd been there, and I asked them what course they had on record that you were enrolled in, because there had been some administrative confusion.'

She giggled.

'I lucked out. The woman was real busy and just wanted to get me off the phone, so she told me you'd gone to study engineering at Harvard.'

'Clever girl.'

'Clever boy! My Harvard boy.'

Maryanne reached behind her and stroked his shoulder. He kissed the top of her head.

'Once I knew you were there, or had been there, it was easy. I called them up, and this time I asked for the Alumni Association, and they put me on to the Registrar's office for your course. They confirmed that you had attended, and had graduated, but wouldn't tell me where you were now.'

'A dead end.'

'That's what I thought.'

'But you didn't give up.'

'I *couldn't* give up. So I did what I should have just done in the first place, and called your mother, who gave me your address and number straight away and said she was sure you'd be pleased to hear from an old friend and to drop by any time I was in the area. So really, it's not like I performed some miraculous feat.'

They both laughed, and then Nicolo fell quiet. 'But you did. It doesn't matter how you found me, you found me, after I'd stupidly let you go.' He rolled over on top of her, and looked into her eyes. 'I won't be letting that happen again.'

Nicolo was flying. As he walked down the street in Boston towards the construction site that he was to visit, he felt like dancing. When he sat talking to friends they were constantly teasing him for staring into space, his mind filled with thoughts of Maryanne and the next time he could see her. Life couldn't be better. He was twenty-one, he had plenty of money, he had just started work with a large property developer and construction firm in Boston, he had the beginnings of a flourishing business with his two best friends. The three of them had spent the remainder of their undergraduate years setting it up. They'd all invested what money they could, Nicolo putting in a considerably larger share than the others, because that's what he could afford, and splitting the shares equally between them. They had bought a small hotel in nearby Boston, and had done it up. Within three months of opening for business, they were doing well enough to take on a second property and, not long afterwards, a third.

They had good managers running the hotels day to day, and things had been going so well that they had taken a month off in the summer after graduating. A magical month, spent sailing around the groups of islands in the south-west Indian Ocean that Logan had talked about, had promised them was the most wonderful place on earth. He hadn't been wrong. Together, the three of them had discovered the island that Honoré had described to Logan in bedtime stories, the tiny capsule of wild natural beauty that was L'île des Violettes, and they'd all fallen in love with it. One day, it would be theirs, they'd decided. One day.

But most of all, best of all, he had Maryanne. Oh, Maryanne. His heart melted into his chest whenever he thought of her. She was the sweetest, most beautiful girl in the world, and she had come back into his life two months after they had returned from their travels, and Nicolo had started at the construction firm. She had walked back into his life and, if he was happy with his lot before, now he felt like the luckiest guy in the world.

Every weekend he rushed to New York as soon as he could decently get away from work, not wanting to waste a single second that he could be spending with her. His day job wasn't suffering – he could do it easily, and was really only working for the large construction firm for the experience, to prove that he had done it, and while he decided whether to continue as an entrepreneur, or to go and study for an MBA next year, like Logan was already doing. Nicolo wasn't sure. It all sounded a bit tedious. Sure, Harvard was great and he'd enjoyed his three years there, but he was ready to get out there and *do* business, not spend another two years learning about it from books and in lecture halls. Anyhow, he had already proved he knew how to make money, had done so before the others had even left high school. On the odd occasion when Nicolo felt just a little bit inadequate next to Logan and Johnny, his delicate good looks outshone by their all-American style, his gentlemanly good manners brushed aside by Johnny's readiness with a joke and Logan's forceful charisma, that was what made him stand tall next to his friends – the knowledge that he had already proved himself worthy, that, indeed, they relied on him.

He walked past the pale grey frontage of the public library, an American flag flying over the wide steps. He liked Boston. He liked the wide streets and feeling of space, liked the history and class of the city, the fact that it was one of the oldest cities in America. The buildings brought him joy daily; all he had to do was look up, and there was a constant source of inspiration. One day, he would be walking to his own building here, he felt sure. Maybe after Maryanne had finished her studies in New York she would move here; he knew she would like it. It would be a good place for them to build a life together.

Don't get ahead of yourself. There's plenty of time for that. But he couldn't help smiling to himself at the thought of walking down these streets holding her hand, maybe going to work together – with her interior design skills and flair she would be a brilliant addition to First – the name he, Logan and Johnny had given their little hotel chain. Because it was a chain already; in less than two years they had managed to open three hotels. That was something that was suffering a little, he acknowledged now. Logan and Johnny were starting to grumble about the time he spent visiting New York rather than working with them, as they had done every weekend since Maryanne had come back into Nicolo's life.

The hotels were relatively small, aimed at business travellers who wanted an efficient service without the uniform feeling of the large chains where once you were inside the foyer you could be in any city in the world and not know the difference. First properties were definitely American in flavour, and aimed to provide their clientèle with 'first-class perks as standard'. The boys had decided that part of the reason people really wanted to fly first class, or would pay to upgrade their rooms in a hotel, wasn't just for the extra space or comfort, it was for the first-class freebies – the meals cooked to order and the in-flight bags full of socks and embossed with a gold logo: to be able to take a souvenir home to their kids and tell them that it came from a smart hotel suite. So they had created a concept for their hotels whereby everyone felt like they were getting these perks. Even in the cheapest single rooms there was a choice of pillow fillings, and a different complimentary chocolate on their pillows every night, rather than the single mint many of the customers would be used to getting. They were trying to provide a higher level of service for everyone. And, so far, it was doing well. The travelling salesmen and conference-goers who were checking in seemed to like the amenities and the fact that they were treated as individuals, rather than being handed a name badge and herded along in a mass of beige suits. They liked that the food was American, familiar, no Continental breakfasts, but pancakes and grits and eggs.

So far, so good. But it was hard work, harder than any of them had really bargained for, and they were all trying to fit the business in around their other commitments. Now that Nicolo had added Maryanne to his life and put her as his top priority, his attention to First had wavered. Still, he wasn't worried. After all, other than a small amount of investment from each of them, it was his money that was behind it. But more importantly, Johnny and Logan were his friends. They understood. They were happy that he had found someone so special.

She *was* something special. Logan was struck by it as soon as he saw her. It was as if there was a light around her – oh man, as soon as the thought came into his head he realised how cheesy it was. But it was true. Johnny had always been the ladies' man, out of the two of them, drawn to women like a magnet. He went for the obviously sexy types, couldn't resist a pretty face, a flash of cleavage or a great pair of legs. In a bar, he would make a beeline for the girls all the men were eyeing up, whereas Logan would seek out someone quieter, someone who didn't put it all on display. He liked the process of discovery, of delving below the surface. And one of the things he had discovered, and which kept him seeking out the girl who had slightly mousy hair next to her bright blonde friend, or the one who looked a bit uncomfortable and shy, was that once you got them going, these women tended to be absolutely filthy in bed.

There was nothing quiet about this girl's looks, however. Her natural beauty couldn't help but announce itself. Logan was waiting for Nicolo outside the small office they ran First from, on a crisp Saturday morning in April, 1982. The three of them were due to meet the general managers of their three hotels, evaluate progress so far and begin the decision-making process as to what they would do next. Their original business plan had only taken them up to three properties; now they needed to figure out whether they were going to continue to expand, and if so, how.

Logan had arrived early and, as he didn't have the keys to the

107

office, was sitting behind the wheel of his car, using the time to catch up on reading for his marketing class. The pressure of studying for an MBA alone was considerable, without the added workload that he had taken on by setting up First, and he had to use every second of the day to get things done. But Logan was thriving on it. He was up at 4.30 a.m. and never in bed before midnight, yet he woke up every day raring to go. He had chosen to go straight into Business School rather than taking time to work and save as many students did, mainly because he could. He'd been advised by his tutors that he would be accepted, and his parents would happily pay for it, as long as it kept him at arm's length and somewhere prestigious that they could boast about at the country club dinners and on the golf course. And he planned to use the time to learn more, make contacts, make plans, and build up First with Johnny and Nicolo. He hadn't anticipated how much he would enjoy the course, and how much he would also enjoy doing what most people would consider to be far too much work. It was addictive – the more he worked, the more he wanted to take on. There were never enough hours in the day.

Which was one of the reasons why it drove him insane when other people couldn't be punctual. He didn't have time to waste, and if he could get to places on time, so could they. Even though he had been early for the meeting, he was becoming more and more annoyed each time he glanced up from his textbook to see if the others had arrived. And it was with one such glance that he saw her. She was walking along the street towards him, thick curls of golden-blond hair swinging around her shoulders, wearing a loose patterned blouse that displayed her slender collarbones and blue jeans, and she was laughing and holding Nicolo's hand. They stopped a few yards away, oblivious to anything but one another. Kissed. Looked into each other's eyes. Kissed again. Then, with obvious reluctance, they let go, and she began to walk off down the street, past Logan's car, waving to Nicolo as she went.

On impulse, Logan got out of the car quickly and strode over to his friend, who stood staring after her. 'So that's the girl who's been taking up all your weekends, is it? Aren't you going to introduce me?'

Nicolo turned to him. 'Oh, I didn't know you were here. Yes, hang on.'

He held a finger up in the air for Logan to wait, and ran after the girl. Logan knew he should have stayed in his car, pretended he hadn't seen her. He shouldn't be standing here watching her walk towards him, a broad, open smile on her gorgeous face, with his knees trembling and with treachery in his heart. Because as soon as he had seen her he had known that he was at a crossroads, but one where there was no real decision to be made. There was only one road he could follow.

When she reached him, she held out her hand, saying pleasantly, 'Hi, I'm Maryanne. Nicolo's told me so much about you.'

And as he took her small, soft hand in his own, he felt his heart expand in his chest, and knew that he had met his future wife.

From that day on Logan made it his business to find out everything he could about Maryanne, subtly probing Nicolo, discovering where in New York her apartment was, where she went after college, what she spent her free time doing when she wasn't with Nicolo. It wasn't difficult; Nicolo was full of his new relationship with the pretty blonde art student, desperate to talk about her at every opportunity. Within a few weeks Logan knew and had filed away in his memory Maryanne's address, her favourite place to get art supplies, her preferred brand of coffee and what she thought about everything from hem lengths to the situation in the Falklands. Almost every sentence out of Nicolo's mouth began with the words 'Maryanne thinks . . .' But now, instead of being irritated by this as he was previously, and feeling annoyed that this girl was the focus of Nicolo's attention rather than the business, Logan encouraged it, winkling information out of him. And Nicolo, not suspecting for a moment that Logan wasn't asking out of anything other than friendly interest, sang like a nightingale about his beloved Maryanne.

Logan was ashamed of himself – but not enough to stop. He knew that what he was doing was wrong, morally speaking. Knew as he was sitting across the road from Maryanne's college and watched her coming down the stone steps carrying her books, chatting with her friends, that his friendship with Nicolo would end if he continued with this course of action. But nothing could stop him. From the moment his eyes had caught hers and he had felt that connection between them, nothing else mattered apart from owning her.

Logan approached the seduction and acquisition of Maryanne's heart like he did everything in life, with careful research and planning, applying the rules that he would later apply to his business empire during hostile takeovers and when making new property deals. Do your homework, plan your attack, and then go in hard and fast, giving your target no time to stop and think. However much he enjoyed observing Maryanne during his research phase, as he thought of it, he still felt uncomfortable about it, like one of those lonely men who hang around in the shadows spying on someone, like a Peeping Tom. But he reminded himself of the necessity of it, and took pleasure in the grace of her movements, the easy flick of her hips as she walked, the creamy blondeness of the curl of hair that fell from her widow's peak. Years later she would spend hundreds of dollars a month having it blow-dried into submission, but for now it sprang free and she just pushed it back and tucked it behind her ear.

That was exactly what she was doing the next time that Logan saw her, tucking it back as she barrelled along the street on her way home from class. He waited for her to near the juice bar where he had positioned himself, and then, when she was a few metres away, he stood up, gathering his newspaper and belongings as if to leave.

'Oh, hi!'

He turned, his expression friendly yet slightly confused. 'Hello . . .' His face said he recognised her, but was trying to place her, so she helped him out.

'Maryanne Curtis – Nicolo's girlfriend?'

Now the look on his face changed to embarrassed recognition. 'Of course, Maryanne – great to see you!'

He held out his hand and she shifted her armful of papers to the other side so she could take it. As their skin touched she shivered slightly, and wouldn't meet his eye. So it wasn't just him, she felt it as well. 'I'm so sorry, you must think me incredibly rude.'

'Not at all, we only met briefly. I've just got a good memory for faces.'

'No, it's unforgivable, I was just miles away. Can I buy you a drink, make up for it?'

She hesitated.

'Go on. The coffee's great here.'

She nodded. 'It's my favourite. I live just round the corner.'

'Oh, really?'

'Yeah. OK, coffee would be good, thanks.'

They had sat in the café for an hour, drinking smoothies and talking, until Maryanne had suddenly felt uncomfortable and had made her excuses and left. As she walked home, she wondered why. Logan was a friend of Nicolo's – it wasn't like she'd picked up some stranger. But she couldn't shake this feeling. She'd worked out why it was by the time she turned into her street. It was because she felt so comfortable with him. Silly, for comfort to cause discomfort.

But somehow in that hour with Logan – she couldn't have explained it, but she felt as if he knew her, really knew her. Understood her in a way she didn't really even understand herself. The questions he was asking, about what she wanted from life, where she was heading ... she'd felt a connection, as if – oh, it was stupid. She mentally shook herself as she unlocked the front door of her apartment. Nicolo was her boyfriend. She loved him. The only reason she had felt so comfortable with Logan was because he was Nicolo's friend. She could feel safe with him. But she couldn't shake off the feeling that, from the moment she had agreed to sit down at the café table with him, she had been agreeing to a whole lot more.

It had all happened very fast, too fast to stop and think about what she was doing. She had fallen head over heels in love with Logan. She'd never believed in soulmates, or love at first sight, not really. She'd read about it in the cheap romance novels she stole from her mother, but had always written it off as lust, or delusion. But when she met Logan on the sidewalk with Nicolo, something had shifted inside her. And when she had sat down to drink coffee with him, the whole world had disappeared into the background.

For three weeks she and Logan had met in secret, and only during the day, so that if they were spotted it could be explained away more easily. He would drive through the night to visit her in New York, and they would lie awake, not wanting to waste a second together. One weekend she made the train journey to Harvard, and he took her out into the countryside to walk through the woods, twigs crunching underneath them as they made love in a clearing, giving her scratches on her back that lasted for days and which she had to conceal from Nicolo by making up a story about having her period. Their meetings were difficult to arrange, given their busy schedules and need for secrecy, and they spent hours on the phone, making plans, telling each other everything they had done and seen and thought that day, trying to absorb each other's lives down the lines. She would lean her head against the wall, the handset tucked into her shoulder, and close her eyes and listen to Logan breathe, drawing the essence of him in close to her.

It was an intensely physical sensation, falling in love, she realised now. It didn't just happen in your head or heart, but in the space between you that shrank away so you could join together, in your arms and legs, through the pores of your skin and deep in your belly. She ached for him when they were apart; it was as if the cells in her body were crying out to be taken to him, to be fed and nourished by closeness to him.

They spent one excruciating evening with Nicolo, on a double date with a friend that he had insisted on setting Logan up with. The four of them had gone to a movie, one Sunday in Boston, which Maryanne had pushed for so as to cut down on conversation, and she'd spent the whole time watching Logan out of the corner of her eye, trying to see if he was looking at her as well without Nicolo seeing. Then they'd gone for dinner in a restaurant that was too quiet and which only emphasised the awkward atmosphere at their table. She and Nicolo had rowed in the car afterwards, him accusing her of being frosty to Logan and not making an effort with his friend. She had had to keep her mouth shut, not tell him that the real reason why she had avoided Logan's eyes all night was that she couldn't look at him without longing. Tell him the reason she hadn't talked to Logan was because she was scared that if she started, she would not be able to stop, be unable to keep from saying, 'I love you.'

They returned to Nicolo's apartment in silence and went to bed without making love. He was obviously confused, hurt. She couldn't help it. She lay next to him in his narrow single bed, and cried herself silently to sleep. The next morning, he was keen to make up, bringing her coffee and juice in bed, and kissing her tenderly.

'Nicolo?' she had said, intending to end it, end it now. Maybe she could just finish it, walk away. Not tell him the reason why, not hurt him like that. But something stopped her.

'Yes, angel? What is it?'

'I'm sorry,' and she had burst into tears. She couldn't get the words out. He had hushed her, apologised as well, assuming she was sorry for their cross words. And so they had made love, Nicolo trying to comfort his treacherous girlfriend, she with her eyes shut, unable to look at him, wracked with guilt. She knew this must be the last time it happened; she couldn't do this again. Every time he touched her she wanted to recoil, because he wasn't Logan. Every kiss, that only a few weeks ago she had relished, was wrong, because his lips weren't Logan's. It wasn't fair, what she was doing, she must stop it. Nicolo deserved more than to be making love to a girl who wanted to be somewhere else – in the arms of his best friend. Oh, God. That was it. She leaped from his arms and ran to the bathroom, where she was sick.

A couple of hours later she escaped, telling Nicolo she was going to go and buy some supplies she needed for her course. Instead, she had run to the nearest phone booth. As soon as he answered, she couldn't help it, she cried and cried.

Logan sat on the bed in his room and listened to the woman he loved sob her heart out down the phone, and felt as if his own heart would break. He couldn't let her go on like this. It had only been a month since they had sat down for that coffee, and two months since he had first met her, but it didn't matter; he knew with more certainty than he had ever felt before that this was the right thing to do.

'Maryanne, Annie, sweetheart, calm down. Deep breath. Tell me where you are. Exactly.'

Eventually she managed to stop crying enough to tell him, through deep ragged gulps. Then: 'But Logan, what do I do? I don't know what to do.' She began sobbing again.

He couldn't bear it. 'Just wait there.'

'I have to get back, he's going to wonder where I—'

'*No*. Listen, Maryanne, do you trust me?'

'Yes.' No hesitation.

'All right. I'm going to take care of this, and I'm going to take care of you. All you have to do is wait there for me.'

He'd never driven so fast in his life as he did that morning, racing desperately to get to her. When he arrived she was sitting on the wall next to the phone booth, a forlorn-looking figure with puffy eyes and a furrowed brow. He didn't think he'd ever seen anyone more beautiful.

'Maryanne, hey, it's OK,' he said, leaving his car parked at an awkward angle with the door open, not caring, only caring about her, about looking after her.

'Oh, Logan, I can't. I don't—'

He gathered her into him, holding her tight. 'I told you, you don't have to do anything.'

He could feel her heart slow back down to a normal pace. She took a deep breath, and smiled weakly up at him.

'Sorry. For being such a mess.'

He shook his head. 'You're not. You're lovely.'

Logan reached into his pocket. 'I love you. I love you too much to carry on like this. I want us to be together properly – no sneaking around, no lies, no hiding.'

She nodded. 'That's what I want as well.'

'Good.'

'Yo, buddy! This your car? Move it!' An irate driver was leaning out of his car window, waving at Logan, honking his horn. Logan glanced over quickly, and then turned back to Maryanne. Held out his hand to her. In between two fingers he held a thin silver band.

'Maryanne, will you marry me?'

She couldn't speak. She tried to, but the words got stuck somewhere. So she just nodded, and held out her left hand so he could slide the ring on to her finger, and then wrapped her arms round his neck and kissed him, letting him lift her up off the ground. The driver's angry shouts turned to whoops and applause.

'Yeah! Hey, it's just like in the movies! Now move yo' fucking car, dude!'

Logan laughed, and ran to his car, waving an apology. Maryanne stood on the sidewalk and watched, holding on to her new engagement ring, looking at it. He returned to her, took her hands. She smiled. No tears any more.

'I can't believe it. I can't believe we're doing this.' She held her hand up for Logan to admire in its newly adorned state.

'I can't believe it. I don't believe you've done this.'

They both turned at the same time, two guilty faces looking at the man they had betrayed. Nicolo was standing a few feet away, a newspaper tucked under his arm and a lit cigarette halfway to his mouth, staring at them. More specifically, at her hand. She had never seen total shock before, complete disbelief. It was as if his brain simply would not allow what his eyes were seeing to be processed. All the usual synapses and responses had slowed to a fraction of their usual response rate, to protect him from the terrible blow that was about to hit him.

'Oh, God.' Maryanne felt a cavernous thud in her sternum. Nicolo was still staring at her hand. There was a long silence. She didn't dare move, hardly dared breathe. What would he do?

'Nicolo? Say something,' she whispered. Nicolo closed his eyes for a moment, then slowly raised his head and looked straight at Logan. His gaze was steady and his eyes were black.

'I will never forget this. And, I promise you, neither will you.'

And then, without looking at her, he turned round, and slowly walked away.

When he got back inside his apartment, Nicolo shut the door behind him and locked it. He lit a cigarette and sat on the floor, his back against the door. There was nowhere else in the small suite of rooms that he could bear to put himself; nowhere that she hadn't sat, or touched, or lain on. Tears ran down his face. He would let himself cry this one time, then that would be it. Now it was Nicolo's turn to reach into his pocket and take out a small black ring box. He opened it and looked at the tiny sapphire ring inside. He snapped the box shut again, and with it, closed up his heart, for ever.

Logan took Maryanne back to his shared house where they celebrated their sudden engagement with a bottle of wine in bed, listening to Pink Floyd. Shut out the world.

'What will we do?' she asked him.

'What do you mean?'

She sat up, pulling the covers around her against the slight chill. 'I mean, where will we live, and what will I do? A year ago, I had a plan. I was going to do my design course, that was the next four years sorted. Then I found Nicolo again, and I had a boyfriend, and my apartment, and it was all normal. Now I'm engaged to someone I only met a few months ago, Nicolo will never talk to me again, and I don't know if I like who I am. I don't even know if I *know* who I am.'

It all came out in a flurry. Logan drew her close to him. Kissed her hair.

'OK. I'll tell you. You're a talented, clever, beautiful woman. You're going to do whatever you want to do. We're going to do it together, whatever it is. We're a team. And you're going to be my wife. Good enough?'

Maryanne turned to him. Suddenly she felt at peace, and very, very tired. She rested her head on his chest and closed her eyes. 'More than good enough.'

Logan lay awake for hours that night, as she slept on unaware of the burden he was burying within himself. Because just before Maryanne had phoned him from the callbox outside Nicolo's apartment, Logan had received another phone call, this time from Nicolo himself.

He had sounded happier than Logan had ever heard him.

'I wanted you to be the first to know,' he'd said.

'Know what?'

'OK, it's not official, but it will be soon. I want you to be my best man – well, one of them.'

'You . . .'

'Yes. I'm going to ask Maryanne to marry me.'

He had done a terrible thing. He knew that. And he regretted the way in which it had happened. Seeing Nicolo's face when he came upon them had been awful. But as soon as Nicolo had uttered the words, Logan knew he had to get in there first. Nothing in the world was more important than making Maryanne his. So he had driven, stopping off briefly at a drugstore to buy the ring, not caring that it was cheap and tinny, caring only that he got to her first, and he put it on her finger before Nicolo had a chance to do the same. And yes, as he lay awake holding her, he regretted causing his friend so much pain, but he wouldn't have changed anything, because now she was his, for ever, and he would never, ever regret that.

A few weeks later, Johnny and Logan went to the bank to raise the money to buy out Nicolo's share in the partnership. Then Johnny drafted a letter to Nicolo informing him that this was what would be happening, and enclosing a cheque equal to the value of his investment. He outlined the terms on which they were doing this – saying that, as per their original agreement, his own and Logan's combined interests outweighed Nicolo's, and so they could force him to give up his stake. It was all fair, it was all above board. But it still left a nasty taste in their mouths.

Still, it had to be done. Nicolo couldn't remain part of First any longer, and that was the end of it. A new agreement was drafted, to reflect that the company was now owned solely by Logan and Johnny, in equal shares, and they went to toast it in their old student bar.

'Feels strange to be drinking to the end of things, in this place,' remarked Johnny.

They both looked towards the table in the corner where they had drunk to the beginning of their business with Nicolo, only a few years ago; where they had made so many plans, held their first 'board meeting' even.

'Onwards and upwards, eh?'

They clinked their glasses together, and Logan drained his.

'I'd better run. Maryanne's down for the weekend soon.'

Johnny nodded. He missed the weekends that he and Logan had used to spend together, sitting up late drinking whisky and playing cards. But he was OK. He was glad Logan had found someone. And he had no shortage of female company. In fact, he had a date himself, with a very hot freshman.

Logan waited for Maryanne on the station concourse. He couldn't wait to see her. He had plans for the weekend involving a long fuck, a quick dinner and then more sex with a bottle of champagne. Logan and Johnny were both enjoying the fruits of their labours at First which, despite taking up a huge amount of time and energy, was enabling them to have a far nicer lifestyle than many postgraduate students.

But when Maryanne walked through the barriers she looked pale and tired, with dark circles under her eyes. It was clear the only thing she was going to be doing in bed that night was sleeping.

'Hey. What's the matter? You look exhausted. Working too hard?'

She looked up at him with worried eyes from under the brim of her little red beret.

'No, not exactly. I'm . . . well, I'm pregnant.'

Logan cried out with joy, and swept her around in his arms. 'That's amazing! Oh, Maryanne. A baby!'

He put her down suddenly, looking concerned. 'Sorry, is that OK, I didn't hurt you, did I?'

She smiled. 'No, It's fine. I'm just tired, that's all. Are you pleased, then?'

He took her overnight bag from her hand.

'Pleased? My darling girl, I've never been happier in my life. Aren't you?'

'Oh yes, of course. I just wasn't sure – with your studies and everything.'

'It's perfect. I'll finish next year, just in time – when's the baby due?' He took her hand and led her through the busy train station.

She paused, and swallowed before answering. 'Sorry, I just feel a little sick. June, I think. The doctor couldn't be completely sure. My cycle . . .'

But he wasn't listening, he was too busy making plans for the future.

'Perfect timing. May – I'll finish at school, you'll have the baby, and then we can do whatever we want, go wherever we want. All we have to do now is squeeze in a wedding. I don't want my son born out of wedlock.'

'Your son?' She rolled her eyes. 'How do you know it's going to be a boy?'

'I just do.'

Logan had been right. Maryanne gave birth to a healthy seven pound, three ounce baby boy three months after their wedding. They named him Charlie. By then, Maryanne had left art college and had moved in with Logan for the last months of his Masters degree and her pregnancy. They'd planned their tiny wedding over hot chocolate late at night when he had finished revising for his exams and doing whatever business he needed to deal with for First. He'd come into bed with mugs for them and wake up Maryanne, and they would sit and talk until she couldn't stay awake any longer. It was a hard, busy time, but they were happy.

They married on a cold, bright day in February, 1983. Maryanne wore a pink suit with a swing jacket to accommodate her bump and a miniskirt, to show off her still slim legs. She carried a little posy of white roses and wore a pink bow in her hair. She looked even younger than her twenty years. Logan wore a dark suit with a sombre tie. In years to come they would look back at their wedding photos and joke that he looked like he was on his way to a business meeting – in fact, although he didn't tell Maryanne, he had just come from one. Johnny was the groomsman and witness, and his current girlfriend the second witness. Neither of their parents came. Maryanne had sent a telegram to her mother and grandmother, telling them she was getting married, but hadn't really expected to hear anything back, and didn't. Logan had written to his parents to invite them, and was not surprised when they politely declined, sending a cheque. So it was just the four of them, and afterwards they went to Fired Up, the grill restaurant that Johnny and Logan had bought next door to their first hotel, for a wedding breakfast of steaks and Martinis.

Three weeks before Logan and Johnny graduated from business and law school, repectively, Maryanne gave birth to a son, a little earlier than expected, but with no other complications. He was healthy and blue-eyed. The next day, Logan, full of pride and whisky from wetting the baby's head, travelled to New York and put a deposit down on a place for them. Manhattan was to be the little Barnes family's new home – and Johnny's. He'd rented an apartment and was preparing to move there too. Logan, Maryanne and Charlie would follow as soon as Maryanne had recovered from the birth. It was time to put the next stage of their plan into action.

The first time Maryanne saw the apartment that Logan had bought was the day she moved in. She was standing on the sidewalk holding her baby in her arms and looking up at the filthy grey facade of the block on the Upper West Side. The street was down-at-heel,

119

dangerous, even. She would never have ventured to this address when she was a student in New York, so why on earth was she here now – with her infant son? She couldn't believe it. For the first time in her short marriage, she thought that maybe she had made a terrible mistake.

'Spare a dime?'

There was a tramp tugging at her skirt and she leaped backwards, looking in horror at the pile of trash at her feet that had come to life and was staring, wild-eyed up at her. She burst into tears and fled.

'I am *not* living there. I will not bring up our son in that godforsaken hellhole!'

When Logan had arrived at the building to find that Maryanne was not there, and the removals van was waiting outside to be told what to do with their small collection of furniture, he guessed what had happened and went off to find her. It didn't take long. She had made it as far as the diner two blocks away, and was sitting at a Formica table giving Charlie his bottle and drinking coffee, her cheeks still flushed. He approached carefully. He could see how angry she was, and he wasn't wrong. As soon as she saw him, she let rip.

'What are you thinking? Have you gone completely insane? It's dirty, it's dangerous, it's dangerous, it's—'

'It's going to make us a very great deal of money,' he interrupted.

'Is that all you think about? Everything's all right as long as you're making money? Well, it's not. It's not all right. *I'm* not all right.'

Logan nodded.

'I'm sorry you feel that way,' he said, 'but this is where we're going to be living. I suggest you get used to it. I also happen to know that you'll like it very much. I'll be helping the guys unload the furniture when you're ready to come and have a look around.'

What was she, an accessory, a pet, to go where she was told? Like it very much? She didn't think so! How could he know so little about her, to think she would be happy living in such a dive? The thought brought a tear to her eye again. She'd really believed he knew her better than that. She looked down at Charlie, who had gone to sleep. Logan was stubborn. He would be expecting her to give in. Well, she just wasn't going to. She could be stubborn as well.

She lasted for another two hours in the diner, and then it started to rain and get dark and Charlie started to grizzle, and she realised she was going to have to swallow her pride. So she ran all the way to the apartment, the baby tucked inside her coat to keep dry, and banged on the buzzer to be let in. Logan opened the door with a smug expression on his face. She pushed past him furiously.

'I've got a key for you, you know. You don't have to use the buzzer every time.'

'Oh, go fuck yourself!'

And then she stopped short. She was standing in the centre of an enormous room. It had huge, high ceilings and ornate, if crumbling, mouldings on the plasterwork. The floorboards were bare and needed sanding and varnishing, but they were original. Their voices echoed around the room – the pieces of furniture they had brought with them were completely swamped by its massive proportions.

'Oh, Logan.'

'Ha. Am I allowed an "I told you so", or is it too soon for that still?'

She shot him a dark look. 'Don't push your luck.'

'Hmm. Thought so.'

But she wasn't angry – how could she be? The room was one thing, but she was completely captivated by the view. She carried Charlie over to the windows. There were eight immense rectangles of glass, standing proud in a line, like sentries. They started around her waist height and soared up to near the ceiling. How could simple panels of mucky glass be something so wondrous? She had no idea, she just knew they were. And she knew Logan had been right. She was going to love living here. The things she could do to this place . . .

He appeared behind her and snaked his arms round her, lifting Charlie up into the crook of her arm.

'OK, I admit it. You were right. It's amazing.'

'I know it's a mess. But you can make it come alive, can't you?'

'Oh, yes.' Her head was already bubbling over with ideas.

'And I promise you, this is a good buy. The area is on the up –

121

all right, I know it couldn't really be going down – but I swear, this is where it's at. I'm seeing another property tomorrow. I've got a good feeling about this, Annie.'

'I trust you. Really. I'm sorry I didn't. But don't go too fast. One step at a time, yes?'

Logan didn't answer, just kissed the top of her head and held her close.

One step at a time didn't get you anywhere. Logan went forward in leaps and bounds. He and Johnny bought the building after their visit the next day, using their company as collateral, because this time they weren't just buying an apartment, they were buying a whole building in midtown Manhattan. It was an old warehouse, and they planned to turn it into a hotel, slick and efficient and with every mod-con. People said they were mad. The area was rundown and insalubrious, but they were fitting out the property with a huge gym and an expensive sushi restaurant like the ones that had started to spring up on the Upper East Side.

People said it was too much, it wouldn't work, no one would pay those prices to stay there. But it wasn't, it did, and they would. Logan and Johnny managed to turn around the renovation very quickly by paying their workers time and a half, and they opened their first New York hotel in the spring of 1984. They celebrated the opening with a huge party in the club underneath the hotel. It was the first big event Maryanne taken complete charge of since she and Logan had decided she should have more input into the business, and she worked sixteen-hour days in the run-up to make sure everything went smoothly. It paid off – she managed to get Grace Jones to sing, Janice Dickinson and Mick Jagger appeared in public together for the first time, attracting a mass of paparazzi, and the next day, a photograph of Logan, Johnny and Maryanne appeared in the *New York Times* with the caption *The Three New Musketeers of Manhattan's Hotel Industry?* Maryanne had it framed, and a few weeks later, as they toasted Charlie's first birthday in their apartment with champagne and friends, she hung it on the exposed brick feature wall, next to the Keith Haring drawing she had bought with the fee Logan had given her for masterminding the party. Charlie was crawling around on the dhurrie rug she'd had shipped from India. She had worked hard to turn the apartment into a stylish home, and she had succeeded – photographers from *Manhattan Style* magazine were arriving the next day to shoot images for a feature they were running on the Barnes couple. Logan appeared next to her.

'You look miles away.'

'No. No, I'm right here. And I wouldn't want to be anywhere else.'

The business went better than they could ever have predicted. The three of them worked well together. Logan found new properties, drove the deals; Maryanne dreamed up brilliant concepts for the hotels, beautiful designs, sourced unique furnishings; Johnny took care of the small print, made sure everything was above board and the taxes were paid, and met with the zoning officials.

New York was booming. Wall Street was expanding at a rate no one had predicted, and with that expansion came a market for more and better hotel accommodation. The bankers wanted smart bars, restaurants, gyms and impressive hotel rooms for their clients. First opened a hotel in the Financial District specifically aimed at traders who didn't have time or inclination to go home and who just needed a room to crash in for a few hours before heading back to the floor. They opened an art hotel on the Upper East Side, where every room contained a unique piece, many of them by hot up-and-coming artists. They opened a block of luxury condos; they bought the old and rundown Grand Hotel and renovated it to its former glory, celebrating its reopening with a nineteenth-century-themed ball; they opened a nightclub with rooms above it for weary partygoers in a disused shoe factory in the Meatpacking District.

Every time Maryanne had a new idea for a themed hotel or design concept she would take it to Logan, who would find the site, and Johnny would take care of the rest. They were rolling out fast. In the space of three years First had a portfolio of twenty-three hotels, more than a dozen restaurants, a sports club, night clubs, bars, and even a parking lot which they had snapped up from its elderly owner and turned into the vehicle-storage facility of choice for the city's new breed of Yuppies.

They spread out beyond New York. Logan became keen on golf, so they opened a golf resort. Maryanne went through a phase of going roller skating, so they opened a roller-disco bar. Johnny got into smoking cigars, so a chain of cigar bars joined First's portfolio. Their lives became the business and the business was their lives. Money poured in and poured out again into new projects, but that was fine; it was turning over at such a rate that the banks were happy, payments were made on time and it seemed as though there wasn't a project that the three of them could dream up that they wouldn't be able to raise finance for and make a glorious success of.

Once First had fanned out all over the East Coast, they branched out further, making trips to sites in San Francisco, Los Angeles and San Diego, as part of their plan to dominate the West Coast as well. It was Johnny who found the building in LA, an apartment block that he thought had potential to be converted into a hotel. Logan looked over the floorplans and decided he was right, and the three of them, with Charlie and his nanny in tow, as well as the construction consultant and the PA that Logan and Johnny shared, all flew out there to look the place over. The entourage required when the First team travelled was growing.

'*The Three New Musketeers of Manhattan's Hotel Industry?*' The caption beneath the photograph taunted Nicolo every time he saw it, which was every day, because he kept the cutting attached to the front of his fridge with magnets. Every morning when he went to get milk for his coffee he would bend down and see the wide white smiles of Logan, Johnny and Maryanne grinning back at him. Why did he keep it there? It wasn't like he needed a reminder, might forget what had happened without it. It was more like picking at a scab. Seeing them every day gave him a few minutes of self-abuse. *A nice bit of masochism with your morning coffee, sir? Oh, yes please, young man, I do like a good serving of self-hatred. Starts the day with a bang, don't you find?* He slammed the fridge door shut. Fuck. Maybe he was finally losing it? He looked at the picture one more time. It was all wrong, that was the thing. It should have been him with Logan and Johnny, not Maryanne; it should have been him with Maryanne, not Logan. But somehow, his place in both partnerships had been taken, leaving him out in the cold.

After Nicolo had received the cheque from Logan and Johnny

for his share of First, he had left his job in Boston and headed to San Diego, where he lived now. There was no point working for the construction firm any more, he was keen to leave the city as soon as possible, and there was no way he was heading home to Mom, so he picked the beach town almost at random, went down there and took the first serviceable apartment that he found. After a couple of months of moping and drinking, he got bored, so started to think about what he was going to do next and, by chance, did so in a bar which was for sale. It didn't take him long to decide – nothing did, these days. It wasn't like there was a lot at stake any more. He bought the bar with some of the First money and put the rest into property in Los Angeles, a handful of condos that he rented out. And that was him done. He had a place to live, a car to drive, a bar of his own to drink in, and money coming in every month. And plenty of time to think about just how deeply he had been wronged.

Once, Nicolo had been ambitious. Now, he found that any immediate ambition had been sucked out of him. He had no one to build an empire for, his previously solid confidence had been damaged, and he was drifting. He could feel himself sinking into a rudderless life, living above a bar, maybe opening another one a bit further down the coast. Ending up as one of those sixty-year-old men with nothing to show for their lives but a pocketful of bar tales and a lot of broken capillaries. He didn't want that, thought men like that were pitiful, but at the moment he couldn't quite summon together the presence of mind to do anything else. So he opened up every morning, mixed mojitos and cracked open beers, and watched the world go by from his safe little corner of California. And fuelled his hatred daily, with the help of a newspaper cutting stuck to his fridge.

The next day, he drove into LA to take a girl out for dinner. No one special, just one of a phonebook full of women he killed time with when he felt so inclined. Women who didn't ask anything more of him than a good night out, and who needed no bullshit romancing to persuade them to do the quite specific and unusual things he liked to do at the end of the night. Ones who would leave the motel room before the sun rose.

He was early, and decided to pay a visit to the Hustler store opposite the Rainbow, and pick up a few things for later. Things he wanted her in. Strippers held tiny bits of metallic string up to themselves, selecting their workwear, as he browsed the aisles. He picked up a couple of movies and a restraint that would constrict the wearer's movements by attaching their wrists to their neck behind their back with thick bands of leather, and went to pay.

The cash desk was in the front of the store, and he stared blankly out of the glass windows as he waited. He was looking forward to his first beer of the night, and maybe a bowl of the Rainbow's famous chicken soup, thick with tender meat and waxy potatoes. His anticipation was interrupted with a jolt by the appearance of Maryanne into his field of vision. He inhaled sharply and audibly, and the checkout girl's nail extensions stopped tapping against the cash register.

'Um, that's fifty-nine dollars and—'

She didn't get a chance to finish; Nicolo was already out of the door. Maryanne. For half a second, maybe not even that, the possibility that she was here to see him filled his head. That was the impulse that propelled him out of the shop only to stand, frozen, in the street as the realisation that she was not alone took over. Even if she had been, why did he think she might be coming here to find him? Stupid. She had made her choice – she was with Logan now. And here he was, the man himself.

Nicolo watched as the couple moved down the sidewalk, then stood back in order to get a better view of a building a little way down the street. Logan was pointing up at its facade, and Maryanne was nodding, sketching something in the air with delicate, fluttering movements of her slim fingers that were painfully familiar to Nicolo. The building was a rundown one with a shabby entrance and dingy windows. Nicolo knew immediately what they were doing here: they were discussing how they would renovate it. He could almost see their mutual vision of what they would turn the place into, rising up like a Technicolor mirage in the air between them. *No.* No, this was *his* territory. They had New York – that was their place. He knew how ridiculous the thought was. California 'his'? *Nicolo, you fucking idiot.*

But still. He didn't want them here, didn't want to have to worry about whether he was going to bump into them every time he came into LA. Watch them open more and more hotels while he ran his little bar along the coast. So Logan was going to take over the place that he thought of as his town, as well as what he had already taken over – his love. Why was he standing here torturing himself by staring at them? He had thought that he would react violently when he next saw Logan, but now all he felt was an overwhelming desire to get away. They looked so happy. It was fine. He could pretend he hadn't seen them, get back to his car and drive home to the safety of his bar.

Too late. Whether Logan had felt Nicolo's eyes on him or whether it was chance that made him turn, Nicolo didn't know. But suddenly Logan was looking at him, and then Maryanne was turning as well, following his gaze across the street to where Nicolo stood uselessly. Her hand went to her mouth in dismay. He could tell that she instantly recognised the pain Nicolo would be feeling, and she looked from left to right as she went to cross the road. She was stopped by Logan's hand reaching out and taking her elbow, holding her back. Nicolo saw his lips move. He couldn't hear what he was saying, of course he couldn't, but it was as if he could.

'No, Maryanne, don't. I don't want you going over there.'

Her forehead wrinkled. 'Why not?' he could see her saying. 'Logan, don't be silly, he's not going to do anything. I can't just ignore him. *We* can't just—'

'I'll go.' His hand still holding her arm.

That was it, the catch that opened the floodgates. Watching himself being talked of as a danger, a liability, someone to be avoided, was too much, and all his anger and rage returned in a rush. *He* was not the person they should feel wary of, it was the other way round. *He* was the wronged one. Not just his future wife, but his business, his life – he should have been riding the wave of success, but instead he was running a crappy beach bar while they enjoyed the profits of the business that he had made happen. First would never have got off the ground without him; it would still be a pipe dream that they talked about after a few drinks.

He was across the road and slamming into Logan in seconds, his full body weight knocking Logan on the sidewalk underneath him. Maryanne yelped as the two men fell to the ground.

Nicolo had the advantage of enraged adrenaline and the first blow, but Logan was stockier and stronger, and it didn't take him long to push Nicolo off and get to his feet.

127

'Nicolo, I don't want to fight—'

His words were interrupted by Nicolo flying at him again, this time shoving him back against the wall of the hotel Logan and Maryanne had just been studying.

'I don't give a shit what you want,' Nicolo spat. 'I don't care what you think, or need, or do.'

His arm was pinned against Logan's neck. Logan had decided to let Nicolo release some of his anger, and didn't fight back against his taut body, pumped with fury.

'I don't care where you go, or what fucking hotel you buy, or whom you have dinner with. I don't care. About any of you.'

He didn't look at Maryanne when he said this, couldn't look at her, but his meaning was clear, and she flinched.

'Just stay the fuck away from me.'

Logan looked him straight in the eye. Nicolo was breathing hard, his clothes crumpled, his hands trembling. In contrast, Logan was completely still. Calm and silent. He leaned forward, slowly, until his temple was next to Nicolo's and his mouth was at his ear.

'You will never be good enough for her.'

The day they found out they had won the contract to develop the site in Vegas, building a brand-new mega-resort in prime position on the Strip, was Logan and Maryanne's fourth wedding anniversary. It was 1987. Maryanne had never been happier. She was working hard with her husband and Johnny; she had taken charge not only of much of the overall design of the hotels, but of events within the company. She organised meetings with important clients and ensured that they ran without hitch, as well as board meetings and Logan's personal dinners that he gave. She had introduced and planned facilities for weddings and other celebrations, offering different types of packages according to the different hotels, tailoring them efficiently so that the larger, cheaper hotels offered affordable, basic packages that were still stylish and included all the essentials, while the more upmarket hotels could cater for the grandest society wedding or the most exclusive celebrity do.

They were well off, money was pouring in, and they spent their evenings in some of New York's best restaurants, where they would talk for hours about work, new projects and their future. Maryanne would pore over the menus, noting down ideas for the hotel chefs to experiment with, new canapé ideas to offer at her parties, and drawing quick, elegant sketches of innovative ways people were presenting food in the black leather notebook she carried with her everywhere she went. They filled each other with enthusiasm; their life centred around their work and their love, and Charlie, their much adored son.

When the call came into the office confirming the contract, Logan had put the phone down and given a great roar, then picked Maryanne up and twirled her around.

'Logan, put me down! Stop it, everyone can see my panties!'

They could as well; she was wearing a full, gathered skirt that flew out as he spun her, and Johnny led the office in a cheer and cacophony of wolf-whistles. Logan dropped her, laughing, and she gave a little bow to the crowd. Someone was sent out to buy champagne and they drank to the success of First – 'Past, present and future,' as Logan said, 'because this is just the beginning of a journey we're all taking together.' Everyone had cheered again, and Maryanne had felt so proud of him. He inspired the whole team to do better, reach higher.

Later, they stopped home to kiss Charlie goodnight and tuck him in, and then went to Marmande, a chic Manhattan eatery, where on Logan's request the chef had created a special tasting menu for them, and the waiters had appeared from the kitchen bearing course after course of exquisitely crafted dishes: a single scallop resting atop a light potato rosti and garnished with shiny black caviar butter, a forkful of truffle risotto with a curl of Parmesan melting on top of it, a leg of tea-smoked squab stuffed with a smooth foie gras mousse.

The final course was served on a white porcelain Limoges plate edged in old rose; a selection of five delicate rose-inspired desserts. A soufflé of rose and strawberry, the palest pink with a single crystallised petal balanced on top, a square of rose and pistachio baklava, sticky with honey and rose syrup, and in the centre, a box made out of white chocolate that had been coloured pink, and inside, a pile of pink sugar on which rested a large, rectangular pink diamond ring, surrounded by smaller white diamonds.

'Maryanne. Marry me? OK, stay married to me?'

She'd laughed. 'You idiot. Oh, Logan.'

'Four years. Doesn't seem it, does it? I bet you thought you'd never get a decent engagement ring.' He'd slipped it on to her ring finger above her delicate wedding band.

'It's beautiful. It must have cost you an absolute . . .'

' . . . fortune. Yes, it did. We're going to have to do the washing up to pay for dinner.'

'I love it. I love you. What with the Vegas news, and this . . . Well, I've got some new of my own. I'm pregnant again.'

Logan had been overjoyed, again. The year had passed quickly for him, less so for Maryanne. This pregnancy was more difficult than her first; she ached and felt sick and heavy all the time. She began to suffer from migraines as well, and spent days lying in a darkened room, unable to bear anyone coming near her. Logan was away in Vegas a lot of the time, as was Johnny, and when she wasn't lying low, she realised how little social life she had of her own. Unable to work, she was bored and restless and lonely.

One day, she was lying propped up in bed reading a magazine that she had rested on her growing bump, when she stopped short. Nicolo's face was staring out at her, a thin smile on his lips. The picture showed him standing in front of a perfectly made bed in a hotel room, arms crossed in front of him, wearing a dark blue suit and gold tie. As ever, he looked more like a member of some European Royal Family, his hair in its smooth wave, his nails perfectly imperfectly manicured. The headline read *Boy wonder Nicolo Flores is back in the hotel game, and he wants you in his bed* . . . It made her shudder. For a moment as she looked at the picture, it was as if the headline was talking to her, as if *he* was talking to her, taunting her. *He wants you in his bed.* It was like a challenge. She had a sudden, horrible feeling of foreboding,

She threw the magazine to the floor. Pregnancy hormones. They made you crazy.

Chapter Eight

1991

Heat and noise. The two near-constant elements of Las Vegas hit Logan and Maryanne full in the face as the door of their limousine was opened. Before he got out, Logan turned to Maryanne and pushed a blond curl gently back behind her ear.

'Who'd have thought it?' he said. 'You and me. Owners of one of the biggest new hotels in Vegas.'

He kissed her forehead. She flapped him away.

'Careful of . . .'

'The face, I know, I know. Ready to show them how it's done?'

'You betcha.'

Logan grinned and got out of the car, before walking around to the other side to open Maryanne's door. They stepped on to the red carpet, and the flashbulbs began to pop. Behind them was the reason for all the furore – Piccadilly Circus – the latest casino to hit the Strip, and Logan's biggest project yet. Vegas was booming. Since the opening of the Mirage two years previously, the Strip had become a frenzy of construction sites, with ever larger and more elaborate hotels and entertainment complexes laying their foundations almost daily. The cash tills in the eyes of property developers and hoteliers were ringing up the zeros as quickly as the dials on the slot machines that the punters were flooding into town to play, and Logan was ensuring that he was at the epicentre of the explosion.

'Logan? Mr and Mrs Barnes . . . Over here, Maryanne . . .'

Flash, flash, flash. The hottest couple in Vegas, for the night at least, smiled and posed. Logan slid his arm round his wife's slender waist and kissed her flamboyantly for the cameras.

'They love you as usual, Mrs Barnes.'

'Me? Oh, I'm just a passenger, Mr Barnes. You're the main attraction here tonight.'

They made their way towards the resort's entrance – a scaled-down version of Tower Bridge that stood proudly over a River Thames shining with the reflected glow of streetlights just like London's old father Thames did at night. Beyond, they could see hundreds of guests already inside, waiting for their arrival.

Maryanne squeezed Logan's hand.

'Nervous?' he asked her.

'No. Excited.'

'It's only the beginning, my love. It's only the beginning.'

As they walked over the bridge towards the party, the guests began to applaud, their clapping getting louder and louder until it was joined by the sound of a string quartet playing the opening bars of 'A Nightingale Sang in Berkeley Square'. The perma-tanned comedian who was compèring the event stepped forward to greet Logan and Maryanne, holding a microphone, and led them towards the Tower of London that was in the centre of the resort. All around were London landmarks, recreated for the Vegas audience. Scaled down Houses of Parliament, perfect in every detail (although Big Ben's hands never moved – time stands still in Las Vegas), gardens modelled on Hyde Park, an abridged version of Shakespeare's complete works that ran in the replica of the Globe Theatre four times a day, a spectacular 'Gunpowder plot'-themed fireworks display every night at ten ...

Logan appeared in the turret of the Tower of London, and the compère raised his microphone to speak. 'Ladies and gentlemen, it is my very great pleasure to introduce you to the man behind the magic – the incomparable, the charming ...'

Logan motioned to the presenter to hurry up.

'The extremely impatient ...'

A ripple of laughter from the audience.

'Mr Logan Barnes.'

A roar of applause. And he took the stage.

He had made his speech. It had gone down brilliantly. Everyone had loved it. Loved him. And then he had declared Piccadilly Circus officially open, and the party had begun. What a night it promised to be.

He and Maryanne made their way through the crowd, greeting friends, acquaintances, business associates. They were both buzzing with the high of success, of knowing that they were catching the wave of something huge. They could feel it all around them. Piccadilly Circus was going to be a hit.

'Awesome use of space,' a revered architect was saying to his boyfriend.

'Oh look, cute, the slots are in the Golden Mile!' exclaimed a teen actress with a champagne cocktail in each hand.

'Chin, chin, old chap,' said an Oscar-winning director in a terrible English accent and they passed him, raising a red, white and blue layered shot to the couple, who tried to stifle their giggles.

'I'm just going upstairs to check on the kids,' Maryanne said, once they had squeezed through the throng.

'Don't be long. The show's going to start soon,' Logan replied.

'I know. I won't be.'

Logan watched her walk towards the lifts, her gold beaded dress clinging to her curves. She turned her head back to him, and made a shooing motion.

'Go see your public!'

He blew her a kiss, and turned his attention back to the party.

Five minutes later, in the backstage corridor that ran between 10 Downing Street and Pall Mall, Logan was getting the best blowjob of his life from between the expert lips of Georgia Hardy, one of the dancers who was about to take part in the grand show that was to be centrepiece of the night. The place was stuffed full of celebrities and the press. Everyone who counted in Vegas was there, and was going to be talking about this party for weeks. He was a legend, he was on top of the world. Fuck everyone who had said he couldn't do it – he had proved them all wrong. It was no good being a pussy, or surrounding yourself with them if you wanted to succeed; you had to take risks, you had to push the boundaries. He knew how far he could push things, how much he could risk, always had done. He hadn't been called Golden Boy at college for nothing. He had the Midas touch, all right. Christ, but so did this girl … Logan groaned, and wrapped her hair around his fingers, pulling her head in towards him and forcing himself deeper into her throat. He felt her gag a little, but ignored it. She could take it.

The music soared to a climax, gearing up for the final moments of the display.

Dressed in the tight Lycra costumes of red, white or blue, the dancers wove their way into the finale. From a scattered, disparate spread of colour, they gradually came together and arranged themselves into the shape of a rose, red with blue petals, surrounded by white, and then they began to move on to a tiered structure at the back of the stage. Gradually, bit by bit, they transformed themselves from a collection of individual bodies into a single image of the Union Jack, rising up from the stage and fluttering, undulating as if being blown by a breeze. The band had accompanied the dancers through their complex routine with a medley of London-themed songs, and now, as they segued into 'London Calling', the whole audience were on their feet and cheering with excitement.

The flag remained on display as the fireworks began, a thunderstorm of coloured light and sparkle in the sky. F-I-R-S-T spelled out against the darkness, followed by Catherine wheels, screaming rockets and showering fountains of gold.

'Happy Birthday,' Maryanne whispered in his ear, and Logan felt like he was King of the World.

And then, as everyone was savouring the moment of Logan's triumph, there was a terrible creaking and splitting sound, and the flag was rent apart. Screams from the dancers mixed with those coming from the audience, who watched, appalled, as the display came tumbling down in a jumble of limbs and heads and bodies all muddled together. And at the bottom of it all lay a thin, pretty woman, whose hair was still messed up from her encounter with Logan only a few minutes earlier, and whose neck was bent at an angle it wasn't designed to; her spinal cord, as they would discover later, when they had finally unearthed her from the rubble, was irreparably damaged. Logan stared at the stage in horror, and knew he was watching not just the wooden structure, but his very empire, crumble.

And Nicolo Flores, who stood in the shadows at the back of the auditorium, leaning against the doorframe, drank in the chaos on stage and let it fill his heart with malicious satisfaction. *It had begun.*

Piccadilly Circus was intended to be the jewel in Logan and Maryanne's crown, but instead it became the albatross around their necks – a symbol of doom and despair. The small crushed woman at the bottom of the pile survived, but was permanently paralysed. Many others were injured – suffered from broken arms and legs, a punctured lung, head injuries. The incident made headlines all over America, the dazzling spectacle of opening night in Vegas brought down, quite literally, to earth.

Logan was crushed. The glittering gold of his business, his life, had been permanently tarnished. People were talking about Piccadilly Circus, but no one was visiting. The structure had obviously been unsafe, and hand-in-hand with that came the suspicion – only slight, but enough to do damage – that the whole hotel might not be as well-built as it should be. Bookings were cancelled. The high-rollers stayed away, eager not to be seen gambling in a sinking ship. It was surprising, even to Logan, how devastating an effect the accident had. And then the lawsuits began to roll in from the dancers.

Still, Logan felt sure he could salvage if not this hotel, then his business and reputation. When the damage cases went to court Logan hired the best lawyers, but insisted that he would not see the dancers' medical bills go unpaid, did not want a reputation as someone who wouldn't clean up his own mess. He ignored the advice from his legal team that he must fight the cases if it was not to look like he was taking full responsibility for the accident. He was, at heart, an honourable man, and he paid the dancer whose case was due to come to court first a generous settlement.

The recession hit. They were mortgaged up to the hilt. The whole company was built on borrowed money, and as the numbers of people across America willing and able to spend money on fancy hotels diminished, their payments increased. They were just hanging on, by their fingernails, to the company. Johnny worked through the night, most nights, trying to keep them afloat. They put properties up for sale, ones that hadn't been doing great business, but they didn't sell. No one was buying.

A group of dancers had formed a team and were suing him together, an action which meant they were able to afford an excellent lawyer to represent them. Logan, having paid the first settlement, had opened himself up to liability for all of the injuries suffered by the performers on that night. And suddenly, he found that he owed a very great deal of money indeed. And then the news came that there would be no insurance payout, because the investigators suspected sabotage. Nothing could be proved, the structure was too damaged following its collapse to determine what had occurred during the collapse and prior to it. But the result was the same – no money to cover medical or legal bills, and no clearing of Logan's name. Logan might suspect the involvement of Nicolo Flores, the police said, but there was no evidence that he had anything to do with the incident. Surely he would not have anything to gain, they said, looking at Logan with raised eyebrows and an unspoken implication that he, as the owner, would.

He tried to mortgage further, but struggled. The banks had become wary, and suddenly he didn't look like such a sure thing any more. Everyone was tightening their belts. But still they hung on. He mortgaged their apartment in New York, which was by now worth much more than he had paid for it, which injected some cash into the business, and some of the hotels were still doing well. He'd made good decisions, he was sure that would see him through this dark patch. He had the knowledge that he was doing the right thing on his side, the support of his wife, and the conviction that they would get through this crisis together. Surely there was enough confidence in the brand that he had worked so hard, so bloody hard to build, for them to weather this particular storm?

Then something strange began to happen. Complaints of food poisoning and skin problems resulting from bedbug bites began to be raised by guests staying in his other hotels. Logan couldn't understand it. His hotels had always been immaculate; he had always paid his housekeeping staff well, much more than his competitors, because he knew that they had the worst, but one of the most important jobs in the industry. A grimy bathroom or a dusty lampshade made all the fancy trimmings and well-run reservations departments irrelevant. People remembered dirt. So when more court cases were lodged, one by the parents of a child who had been hospitalised following a bout of sickness caused by poor food hygiene at a First-owned hotel, another from a woman who claimed she had been bitten by bedbugs so severely that the bites had become infected and she had needed hospital treatment, Logan's worst nightmares were coming true. How had it gone so wrong? And the complaints just kept on coming.

An accident was one thing, it could be recovered from, in time. Accidents happened, after all. But with these new problems came the whispers that First hotels were anything but first class, that they were dirty, badly maintained, and just not safe. And as a result, First slid slowly but surely down into the swampy mire of bankruptcy.

Two years after Piccadilly Circus had opened and closed in quick succession, they were all in a bad way. The string of lawsuits and bad publicity had brought the company to its knees, and Logan had been forced to declare bankruptcy. Maryanne knew she would never forget the look on his face the day he had come back from signing the forms that dissolved First and officially declared him bankrupt. He looked smaller, somehow. She touched his hand when he came in through the door of their rented apartment – the loft apartment had long since disappeared in a mass of debt – but he had just walked past her, absently stroking six-year-old Lucia's hair as he went towards the bedroom, where he shut the door behind him. Maryanne had tried to tell him that it was OK, that this happened in business – but he just shook his head. And went back to work.

He worked all the time, coming home to the small apartment they had moved into to sleep for a few hours, occasionally. More frequently he would crash out at the office and just come back to shower and eat before going back out to work. The week that Maryanne reached breaking point, he had spent a total of twelve hours at home. She had counted them up as the week went on. It wasn't as if she had anything else to occupy her mind – she was at home looking after Charlie and Lucia while Logan struggled to keep the company from going bust and then to rebuild it. Her strength was in the aesthetics and the creative side of hotel management, not in the financial. The apartment was cramped and the children were picking up on the tension between their parents and reacting to it. She never got a break. The scant few hours that Logan was at home weren't enough to hand the children over to him. When he was there, his head was elsewhere, he was on the phone or buried in a pile of paperwork . . .

She tried to help – well, once.

'Can't you ask your father, your parents, for help?' She had suggested. 'Surely they wouldn't want to see you – us – struggle like this?'

'No.'

They were in the kitchen and she was trying to persuade Lucia, who was a picky child, to eat more than a few spoonfuls of supper.

'I know you're not close – obviously, I've never even met them, but still . . .'

'I said no.'

'Logan, you can't just make unilateral decisions like that. Things are bad. It's not just about you. You've got children now, responsibilities . . .'

'Don't you think I know that? Jesus Christ.'

He had slammed his fist into the cupboard door so hard that it went straight through the cheap fibreboard and splinters of laminate scratched his skin. He cried out in pain. Lucia screamed, and dropped her spoon on the table. Maryanne went over to her, kissed the top of her head and then took her hand and ushered her out of the door. She and Lucia and Charlie went to spend the night with a friend.

The next day, when they returned home, Logan took her in his arms, tucking her head in underneath his chin.

'I'm sorry. I'm sorry I lost my temper. But I won't go cap in hand to my parents. We sink or swim on our own.'

He kissed the top of her head. God, he was stubborn. So stubborn. He was always elsewhere. He hardly slept. When he did come to bed he tossed and turned all night, his skin hot to the touch, radiating nervous energy even as his body tried to sleep. His brain whirred, all the time, never resting. He had to do it alone, or not at all – even if it cost them everything, he would risk it all for the sake of being able to say *he* had done it, no one else.

Maryanne stood leaning against him for a moment, with her eyes closed, trying to pretend everything was normal, that it was going to be OK. But she couldn't quite make herself believe it.

She'd never realised how lonely it was possible to be with children as your only source of company and conversation. There was no spare money for her to go out and shop, or take them to the zoo, and they got tired of walking around the park. So most of the time they stayed in, scratching on each other's nerves. This wasn't what she had thought it would be like – motherhood, her life as Logan's wife. She had imagined it would be hard work at times, testing of her patience. But she had envisaged them doing it together, working as a team to nurture the company and their family at the same time. Instead she was by herself with a son who hardly said a word and a daughter who had violent, rage-filled tantrums. They were violent enough to get the three of them thrown off a bus, on one of the few occasions that Maryanne attempted a day out. She had ended up sitting on the sidewalk sobbing, with her two children weeping along with her. When she had gathered the strength to get up again, they had walked to Logan's temporary offices, a bedraggled trio making their way through Manhattan.

When they arrived, Logan was in a meeting with a group of bankers whom he was trying to persuade to finance a new project. She sat in his office with the children, waiting for him to finish. The room was small and bland, and she could hear the meeting going on through the thin walls. It wasn't long before Lucia got bored of waiting, and started whining to get Charlie to play with her. He was listening to his Walkman and turned his back on her. Maryanne had no energy left to entertain her daughter and, eventually, the child reached up and began playing with her mother's earrings. But Lucia was fidgety and when she tripped over one of Maryanne's shoes, her hand was still holding tightly on to the silver hoop in her mother's ear.

Maryanne screamed in pain and couldn't stop herself from flinching, which upset the girl and frightened her. Her wail was high-pitched and plaintive, and soon turned into a full-blown tantrum.

'What the hell is going on? What are *you* doing here?' Logan was in the doorway, trying to keep his voice low but unable to disguise his anger.

Maryanne looked up at him and then burst into tears again.

'Jesus, Maryanne, what's the matter?'

'We got thrown off the bus, and so we came here, and ...'

He exhaled. 'I thought something awful had happened.'

'It *was* awful.'

'Look, I don't have time for this. This is your part of the deal, OK? I can't do everything. Go home, feed the kids, I'll be back later.'

And he walked out of the room, shutting the door behind him. As she gathered the children up she could hear him, his work voice, explaining her away to the men in suits in the meeting room.

'My wife, yes ... so sorry – she gets these crazy ideas about coming to visit ...'

He was trying to make light of it. But she could tell by their silence that they were unimpressed.

That night he came in late, and she was already in bed. He smelled of whisky and tobacco.

'They said no.'

'Because of us?'

There was a long pause.

'They just said no.'

She didn't ask again.

In the morning, she had settled the kids in front of the TV with a video, and picked up the phone.

'Nicolo? It's Maryanne.'

It was the biggest mistake she had ever made. They had spoken for almost an hour. She didn't even really know why she had phoned. Just to talk to someone who knew her – not as a mother, or Logan's wife, but *her*. And someone who knew Logan as well, who wouldn't tell her how wonderful he was, how inspiring, how charismatic. Someone who she knew still loved her.

After that, they had spoken every day. Nicolo understood. He had time to listen to her talk about how she felt, how her day was. What the children were doing. He wasn't bored by her, like Logan seemed to be now. Then he started sending her money. Not much, a hundred dollars or so at a time maybe. Telling her to spend it on herself, not the children, buy herself a new pair of shoes. She didn't. She rolled it up and kept it in an empty shampoo bottle. Running away money, like her mother had always said she had in the back of the wardrobe. And she had planned to run away. Back West, back to the sea and the sunshine and away from the stress and loneliness and unhappiness. They had it all worked out, she and Nicolo. She would fly to Los Angeles, by herself at first, and he would meet her at the airport. They would send for the children afterwards. He told her they couldn't come straight away, he didn't have the room. She didn't want to leave them, not really, but then she looked at the apartment and their faces, so needy, so dependent, and told herself that a break would do them all good. Make her a better mother when they came to join her.

Later, she realised that she hadn't been thinking clearly. Looking back on that time, it was as if she had been in some kind of alternate reality, another version of herself walking through her life. But by then it was too late. She had left the children with a neighbour, a woman with kids the same kind of age. They helped each other out sometimes. She got the train to the airport and, with a last look back at the city, had boarded the plane.

He hadn't come. She had waited for three hours before calling. Sure that the traffic was bad, that he had got lost, that he had stopped to fill up with gas. When she phoned his apartment, though, Nicolo picked up on the first ring.

'I'm here, I'm at the airport,' she said. 'Where are you?'

'Clearly, as you've just phoned me here, I'm at home.'

'But I . . . I thought you were going to meet me.'

'Yes, I was. And I thought you were in love with me once. Things change.'

And he had put the phone down.

Chapter Nine

2008

Colette Hardy flopped back on to the slightly grimy beige sheets that covered her foldout and watched Anders, the guy she had picked up last night in her favourite rock bar on the Strip, the Rainbow, stand and pull his black jeans up, buckling the snakeskin belt around his waist in one quick movement. He clearly couldn't wait to get out of here. Whatever. It was hardly like she was desperate to make pillowtalk with him. She ran a hand through her peroxide-blond hair and lit a cigarette. Lay back, one leg crossed over the other. She wiggled her toes, which made the tattoo of a swallow that covered her left foot look like it was flying.

'I'm off, babe. Thanks for the ride.' He leaned down to kiss her, all tongue and bare chest, his long black hair falling over his face, bringing the smell of sweat and whisky down to her face with him.

'Just get the fuck out of here.'

He shrugged, laughed, and left. Story of her fucking life. She stretched her arms out above her head, and then flipped herself up. Picking up the metal bar underneath the mattress, she folded it back up into its daytime role of a settee. Turned her iPod up loud while she finished her cigarette, and pulled on a pair of jeans and an old Guns 'n' Roses tour T-shirt that she'd found on Melrose. Then she stepped over the piles of dirty underwear and magazines and empty cigarette packs, and went through into the tiny galley kitchen of the apartment.

'Colette? Who was that?' Her mother's light voice came from her bedroom – the only bedroom in the apartment.

'No one. I'm making you coffee. You want toast?'

There was no response, just a faint sigh from her mom's room. Great. It was going to be one of those days. One where her mother sighed and gave Colette baleful looks, as if the fact that she was in a fucking chair was somehow her fault, and made remarks about how it was nice for Colette to be able to go out in the sunshine whenever she wanted. The whole emotional-blackmail, guilt-trip bit, designed to get Colette to stay by her side every minute of the day, never to leave, never to go out and God for-fucking-bid, never to meet a guy and have fun. Then Colette heard her mother coughing, and felt bad. It wasn't her fault, after all. It was only one person's fault . . .

Colette poured a cup of coffee and took it through to her mother's room. She opened the curtains, let sunlight in, cranked down the bars on the side of the bed ready to get her mom washed and dressed. Georgia Hardy just lay in bed, staring; now the room was light Colette noticed that her hair was lank and greasy. She would have to wash it later. Colette tried to put it off for as long as she could, it was such hard work getting her to the bathroom, supporting her over the tub while she arranged the shower head just right, kept the suds from going in her mother's eyes. But she couldn't put it off for ever. Her mom used to have such pretty hair, she remembered being so jealous of it when she was a kid, light nutty brown and so shiny, while her own was a dark blond. Mousy.

Colette had grown up in a series of rented houses in the suburbs of Los Angeles, moving on to the next one whenever her mother got bored, or defaulted on the rent for too long, or was hospitalised again and Colette had to be taken into care. Georgia was a single mother, an actress, model and waitress – and also a manic-depressive. The combination did not make for a stable lifestyle for either of them. Different houses, different faces, different streets – Colette had got used to moving on, sometimes in the middle of the night, as her mother bundled her up like a sausage roll in her quilt and laid her on the passenger seat of the pick-up with its brown peeling paint and tan leatherette seats that had turned orange and cracked with age.

Later, Colette had become an actress as well, but that was after everything else that happened. She did better than her mother, despite the fact that she was also having to be a full-time carer to

Georgia by then. Maybe it was because she was willing to go 'that extra mile' as some of the directors put it, in her determination to get a part. And eventually, after playing various girls in horror movies who ventured into the basement/attic/woods armed only with a flashlight, or nurses delivering such well-crafted lines as 'Doctor will see you now, Mrs Molloy', and teenage drinkers at frat parties that went wrong, she landed a part in one of the smaller lunchtime soaps, playing a bored housewife with slightly psychotic tendencies. It had paid for a nicer apartment and a part-time nurse for Georgia, and had kept Colette in designer jeans and the television magazines for a few years. But then the director had been sacked when the finance department had finally caught up to what everyone on set had known for the past three years – that his 'expense' account was out of control, since every hooker and dealer in Hollywood had been overcharging their services to it, and the new director had wanted to 'take the show in a new direction' and 'really push the boundaries of what *Gardenia Grove* can be'.

Life in LA as an ex-soap star was far, far harder even than life there as an aspiring one. No one wanted to know you if you were just the girl who *used* to be in that show. 'You know, the one Jodi James is in now?' Ugh. It was too depressing for words. She wanted to get out. She was a has-been now, pouring drinks in a music bar where the rockers and porn stars didn't care what show she used to be in. But she needed to get away. She didn't want to be the girl who used to be someone any more.

An hour later, when she had given her mom a bath, washed her hair, dressed her and installed her in front of *Oprah*, she lit another cigarette and sat at her laptop with a coffee. She checked her messages first, then flicked to Google and typed a name into the news search box. Nothing new today. No matter. She would check again tomorrow – and the next day, and the next. One day soon, she was sure she would get another email, another communcation that let her know it was time. She was waiting. Patiently waiting for she wasn't sure what – the email, the phone call, the sign that the time had come. She didn't know what it would be yet, but she would know it when she saw it. The chink in the armour of the man who had ruined her life.

Chapter Ten

Logan had been at the office for a couple of hours when he got the call. The voice at the other end was high, frantic.

'Mr Barnes, you come home quickly. Is Mrs Barnes, she . . .' Linny was sobbing. Logan could hear a commotion in the background, voices.

'Linny, what is it? What's the matter with Maryanne?' He waited for her to calm herself enough to speak.

'She sleeping, Mr Barnes, deep sleeping. We think she take some pills, but she can't wake up.'

As he drove through the busy London traffic, the Fulham Road gridlocked, willing it to move more quickly, Logan remembered the night fifteen years ago that he had come home and found Maryanne curled up on the couch in their New York apartment, sobbing.

'What is it? Annie, what's happened?'

She had sat up and stared at him. And through jagged, wretched breaths had told him everything – how she had planned to leave, to go back to Nicolo, how she had betrayed him, then been tricked and punished herself. Her face was contorted with guilt and misery. Logan had gathered her up, held her, gently rocked her.

'You hate me, don't you?' she wept. 'You hate me for betraying you, and you always will.'

He had denied it, of course he had. How could he hate the woman he loved so much for trying to escape when she was backed into a corner? He knew all too well how miserable he was making her, how hard it was for her. And yet – oh, he didn't know, maybe part of him *did* hate her for it. He'd been hurt, that was definitely true – deeply hurt. But he'd told himself that she was confused, exhausted, he hadn't been paying her enough attention. God knows, that had been true. He couldn't blame her for wanting to escape, and he could hardly be angry that the person she tried to escape to was Nicolo. It wasn't as though Logan had any right to take the moral high ground. And yet . . .

When she had calmed down, he told her the news that he had come home to give her – that his father was dead. There had been more tears, but he had hushed her, comforted her again. It was a relief, in a way, he had admitted. Part of him had always felt guilty for never visiting his parents, for turning his back on them and getting the hell away. Even though he knew it was the right thing to do, knew that if he had stayed, he would have been suffocated.

At the time, that night had seemed like a turning-point. He and Maryanne had come back together, pulled together to rebuild their lives. Logan's father's death had brought an unexpected windfall – a small hotel situated on the Upper East Side that Peter Barnes had bought years ago, when he retired from the US Navy with a lump sum, and put in trust for his youngest child, Logan. The trust was the only reason the hotel passed to Logan – to his mother's shock and disgust, the rest of the estate was rendered almost worthless by the debts his father left. Elizabeth Barnes had always turned a blind eye to the mounting bills and, following her husband's death, had turned her back on them for good, remarrying quickly and leaving with her new husband for Australia.

The building was in a mess, run into the ground, but the structure was solid, and Logan's instinctive flair led them forward. With a new project to focus on, he regained his energy, stayed up late into the night working on business plans and spreadsheets, got up at dawn to run, pounding the streets before heading to the site. Maryanne took strength from his energy; she pushed all the unhappiness away and focused her energies on supporting Logan and helping him and Johnny rebuild the business. Slowly, slowly, they had pulled themselves back up and out of the abyss. They had been more cautious this time, taking on less debt, treading more carefully. They had rebranded the company, putting Logan himself at the centre of it, naming the new company after him alone. They were older now, wiser – and they waited until the hotel was breaking even before taking on another property. This time, Logan was determined that all of his hotels, and the company's future, would be built upon unshakable foundations.

And now, in 2008, as Logan gave up and called a limobike to whisk him to the Chelsea and Westminster hospital, leaving his Lexus parked in a side road, he wondered where it was during those years that Maryanne had started to falter again. He had married a kind, smiling girl who dreamed up crazy ideas for parties and somehow managed to make them happen, who was a bit wild, and free with her heart and her time. She used to be so vital, always alert, catching hold of an idea and blowing life into it. When they were living in New York, when the children were young, she had infused their childhood with magic, sneaking them downstairs to catch a glimpse of the grown-up parties going on in the apartment, their eyes wide, their little bodies hot and soft in their sleep-rumpled pyjamas, before whisking them back to bed before they had woken up properly. In the morning they'd wonder if it had been a dream, if all those ladies in wonderful dresses, so glamorous and full of perfume, had really been here, in their home that was now full of morning light and the smell of coffee and newspaper print. Maryanne would have been up since 6 a.m. cleaning up the debris before everyone else woke, full of energy. When had she stopped doing that? he asked himself. When had she stopped being the girl who would come to his office to surprise him at lunchtime and take him to Chinatown for noodles, or to the stationery cupboard, for sustenance of a different kind?

Maryanne's body was flat on the hospital bed, an IV drip in the crook of her arm. Her head was resting on a thin pillow and her hair tied loosely back from her pale face; indigo smudges like thumbprints hovered below her closed eyes. Logan stood by the curtain that surrounded her cubicle and watched her chest rise and fall softly underneath the sheets. It was noisy in the busy casualty department – the NHS didn't make any concessions to wealth in an emergency, and famous socialites and tycoons' wives went to A&E like everyone else.

In the next cubicle he could hear a man swearing at a policeman, and the clatter as he struggled and slammed his handcuffs against the metal bedrails. 'Cunt! Fucking cunt! I'm going to fucking top myself, I am, and when I do, it'll be your fault, you pig. I'm gonna pin a fucking sign to my chest saying *PC Cunt Face did this*.'

The small area of floorspace around Maryanne's bed was still scattered with the wrappings from syringes, and a pair of latex gloves had been dropped and abandoned.

She wouldn't be here for long. The private ambulance was on its way now to transfer her to one of the intensive care beds at St John and St Elizabeth, where she'd receive the very best care, in comfortable surroundings. Logan didn't want her to wake up here, he thought, looking with distaste at the smeared mirror above the small, stained sink, as he threw the gloves in the bin.

Maryanne's eyelids flickered as the man in the next cubicle continued his tirade against the silent police constable guarding him. 'Cock-sucking arsehole! I'm a sick man, I am, and the system just wants to get rid of me, because there's no time for Trevor. Trevor's no good to you, is he? Well, you can stick your fucking system up your Jap's eye, you—'

Trevor was interrupted by the force of a fist slamming his face against the bars of his bed, squashing his fat mouth shut.

The PC jerked to his feet instinctively, then looked at the situation in front of him – Logan's face full of rage as he held the man down, the fine cut of his suit, and the look in his eye. Then he shrugged and sat back down again, crossing his ankles and grinning as Trevor's legs twitched. It was the only part of him that he could move, as the weight of Logan's body pinned his torso to the bed.

'Shut the fuck up. Shut up now.' Logan wasn't shouting; his voice was deep and slow and certain. 'My wife's asleep in the next bed. She's ill. She'll be leaving soon, but if you wake her up before she does, you'll wish you hadn't. Are we clear?'

Trevor gurgled, and Logan removed his arm and brushed off his sleeve, before leaning over and shaking the hand of the policeman. 'Fine job you're doing here, Officer.'

'Thank you, sir. We do our best,' he replied, as he slipped the folded fifty-pound notes that Logan had slipped him into his back pocket.

In the corridor, Dr Hayley Metcalfe looked nervously at her notes as she talked to Logan. She was a petite woman, just over five foot tall and very slim, an attribute which she had greatly enjoyed while she was a medical student, as it had meant she had been able to buy children's clothes and save on the VAT, but now, as a qualified doctor in A&E, she felt it put her at something of a disadvantage when dealing with arrogant consultants or difficult patients. Or their families. Taking a deep breath, she tried to stand up straighter, and spoke with as firm a voice as she could muster.

'The thing is, Mr Barnes, when Mrs Barnes was brought in here, she was very poorly. And the lady who came in with her, Ms ...' she checked her clipboard, '... Ms Santhisawan, was very distressed and, well, to be honest, her English isn't very strong. The triage nurses had some considerable difficulties ...'

Logan interjected. 'Linny's been with us for fifteen years. Her English is fine. And your staffing issues really are none of my concern, Doctor.'

Hayley wasn't going to let this man talk down to her, however rich he was and however important he thought he was. Even if he was Logan Barnes, from *General Manager*, and more famous and popular than Alan Sugar and Gordon Ramsay combined. God, her flatmate would not believe it when she told her ... *Oh honestly, Hayley, pull yourself together. You are a doctor, and he is the husband of your patient. That's all.* Pushing her shoulders back, she looked him square in the eye.

'Well, Mr Barnes, I'm afraid that at the time we were unable to ascertain the exact degree of Mrs Barnes's problems from your employee.'

Logan's face was thunderous, and she decided to continue quickly. Her confidence only went so far in the face of such force of personality. She cleared her throat.

'Although she *had* brought with her a pill bottle which she had found near Mrs Barnes. Which was very helpful. The bottle had contained an opioid painkiller ...'

'My wife has some sleeping problems. We live a high-pressure lifestyle and she sometimes has trouble switching off.'

Why was he justifying himself – justifying Maryanne – to this girl? Logan thought irritably. She didn't even look old enough to be in medical school, let alone let loose on patients. She barely looked older than Lucia – and God knows, he wouldn't trust *her* to treat anyone for a sprained ankle.

149

'Well, painkillers aren't really the best way of tackling sleep problems,' Hayley told him. 'I'd be happy to recommend some things that Mrs Barnes could try, to help her sleep better. Some simple—'

'There's no need. We have perfectly ample medical care already, thank you.'

She gritted her teeth. Bloody hell, the terrifying demeanour you saw on TV wasn't an act, then. He didn't shout and swear like some of them, there were no displays of histrionics on *General Manager*. But he brooked absolutely no argument, either. What he said went, no question about it, and now she understood why.

Logan had made it a rule, throughout his adult life, never to show weakness. It was the way he had built his company – and rebuilt it; it was the way he had run his family. 'Pure, unadulterated arrogance,' as one TV critic had said recently. Logan knew that was how many people saw it, but they were wrong. It was up to him to make sure things stayed under control. He had a family who looked up to him and relied on him, he had hundreds of employees who needed him at the helm. And he wasn't the sort of person to shirk his responsibilities. Right now, his responsibility was to Maryanne. His own anger with her would have to wait, as would the feelings of shame and confusion that he was so carefully concealing from the doctors and nurses. For now, the priority was getting his wife somewhere private, to make sure that the family presented a united front.

The doctor was talking again, glancing at her notes every so often. ' . . . and because of the medication she was brought in with, and the symptoms that your wife was displaying at the time of her admittance, we treated Mrs Barnes with a drug called Naloxone. It's proven to be very effective in reversing respiratory depression caused by an opioid overdose. We administered Naloxone to Mrs Barnes intravenously, and her breathing improved rapidly. The drip that Mrs Barnes is on now is just fluids – she was quite dehydrated when she came in. And she's still sedated. She should start to come round in a few hours.'

'I'll make sure the staff at John's know.'

Dr Metcalfe looked up at him sharply. 'You're having her transferred?'

'Of course.'

'Mr Barnes, there really is no need. I can assure you we have all the facilities necessary here—'

'That's as may be, but a private ambulance is on its way already.'

She was getting annoyed now. 'I don't recommend that you do that, Mr Barnes.'

He looked at her, his gaze intent. He really was very attractive. She swallowed. And he was obnoxious, and quite possibly putting his wife in danger. She was going to tell him that he was being short-sighted and selfish, and – and then he smiled at her, and put his hand on her arm.

'Look, I do appreciate the care you've given us, really. You're clearly a very conscientious doctor. Please don't see my decision to move her as having anything to do with you, or this hospital.'

She faltered. 'Right, well, it's very nice of you to say that, Mr Barnes, but the fact remains that—'

'Dr Metcalfe, can I be honest with you? I'm really worried about my wife – about Maryanne. Like I said, she's been under a lot of pressure, and she's obviously not coped with it as well as I thought. Now I know that she just got confused, took too many painkillers – but the press . . . well, I'm a big fan of the UK, but your tabloids aren't exactly known for their sensitivity in situations like this.'

She could hardly argue with that.

'I just want to protect Maryanne from any unwarranted intrusion that could put her under more stress, and endanger her health further. You're a doctor – a good one. I'm sure you understand.'

Hayley sighed, and Logan knew he had won her over.

'You should be aware that as the dosage wears off, respiratory distress could recur,' she warned him. 'Also, because this drug essentially reverses the effects of opiates, it can precipitate withdrawal if the patient is addicted to—'

'Is there anything I need to sign? The ambulance will be here shortly, and I'd like to be able to leave straight away.'

She held out a form. It was still against her better judgement. She'd be far happier keeping an eye on Maryanne Barnes herself – the woman was clearly addicted to painkillers, and quite possibly a lot more, but there wasn't much she could do about it. It was his call, at the end of the day, and he wasn't wrong about the press, at least. They'd be all over it in seconds.

Logan's pen whipped across the clipboard, before handing it back to her. 'Doctor – thank you. For your professionalism and your kindness. I only wish there were more like you. I'd like to make a donation to the hospital. Help keep things ticking along. I know you struggle in the face of real adversity. My assistant will be in touch.'

With a final, brilliant smile full of those all-American teeth, he turned and walked down the corridor to his wife's cubicle. Hayley watched him go. She had just been well and truly steamrollered. And, if she was honest with herself, she had rather enjoyed it.

Logan paused in the corridor outside A&E. The girl had just been doing her job; he knew that. Just as he knew how to switch seamlessly from hardball business mode to full-on charm assault in order to get things to happen in the way he wanted them to. All in a day's work. So why, when he was so adept at resolving conflicts, leading by example and inspiring great achievement in his workforce, did his family seem to be in such a state of absolute fucking chaos? For once, Logan didn't have any of the answers.

When she began to float up from her sedated sleep, the first thing that Maryanne became aware of was pain in every part of her body. Dragging her eyes open, she saw that she was in a large room, decorated in bland pastels designed not to alarm or distress. Its pale wood furniture and prints of flowers and countryside scenes were chosen to have a generically pleasant visual appeal to most patients – but they were infinitely more offensive to Maryanne's discerning eye than the most lurid graffiti or experimental modern art. What idiot had put her in such a place?

She tried to sit up but a sudden weight was pressing down on her chest, expelling the air from her lungs and rendering her immobile. She breathed in, but somehow the breath didn't want to come. That was strange. She tried again. She felt oddly distant from the process. Unpanicked. She couldn't breathe, she thought, and it struck her as almost funny. Maybe she was going to suffocate in this room staring at some God-awful fucking Monet print. She would have laughed at that, if she had been able to get the air.

The monitor next to her bed detected her respiratory distress, and automatically released a dose of Naloxone into the IV drip in the back of her hand, and as the oxygen swooshed back into her blood cells she dropped back into the thick haze of unconsciousness.

Chapter Eleven

Charlie Barnes lay sprawled over an old armchair in the corner of the studio in West Hollywood, his laptop on his knees, updating his band's Twitter feed and replying to add requests on MySpace. As he did so he kept one ear on what the producer and engineer TJ Burke was doing in the background as he tweaked and trimmed, adjusted levels and reshaped the song from a nice idea and a sweet melody into a commercially viable piece. Charlie had been writing songs in his bedroom since he could strum chords on a guitar, but he knew he was still learning, still had a way to go. His trust fund could buy him the best bits of kit, and the time of one of the hottest producers working in Hollywood right now, but it couldn't buy him what he really needed to make it in the music industry. Only experience, talent and time could do that. That was fine by Charlie. He had no intention of being known as 'Logan Barnes's son, wannabe rocker Charlie' for ever.

> *'In your clothes from sixty-eight,*
> *While you play dress-up and make me wait,*
> *Vintage Violet,*
> *Vintage Violet . . .'*

Charlie listened. His voice sounded better on the track than he knew it did in reality. Live he sounded fine, he could carry a tune and he had a slight drawl that added to the California-cool vibe of his songs, but he was well aware it was nothing a thousand other guys didn't have. It was when he played guitar that he stood out from the crowd. Charlie was good – really good. And he knew he could make it, he felt sure of it. It was the reason he'd stuck to his guns so far, hadn't given in and gone to work for his dad; he knew Logan thought the whole thing was just a waste of time and was waiting for Charlie to get it out of his system and get a proper job. He wasn't going to wait much longer, either; he was getting impatient at the lack of progress as he saw it. Charlie himself knew that the band was getting better all the time, and soon they'd have something they could start to showcase. In the meantime, he tried to stay out of his old man's way as much as possible.

The other guys in the band were getting bored. Two weeks in the studio with not much to do was getting to them. At the moment they were messing around with a video camera. Matt, the bassist, was holding the camera and filming his brother, Brandon, who was the band's drummer, and who had drawn a huge moustache on to his face with the burned end of a cork, and was inserting the inside tube from a biro up into his nasal cavity. The studio smelled of burgers and beer and boys. 'Man, you guys are sick,' complained Charlie. 'Can't you make a movie of something that doesn't make us look so fuckin' mental?'

Matt and Brandon sniggered, and the biro tube shot out from the latter's nose. Matt zoomed the video camera in on it on the floor.

'You've got some grim shit up your nose, Brandon my friend. See, viewers, the lesser-spotted slugs that reside inside the nasal cavities of . . . *The Brandon.*'

Charlie rolled his eyes, leaned over and flicked the video camera off, then smacked Matt on the side of his head. 'Shut the fuck up. Go and get us some food, or something.'

'Could use a burrito.'

'Whatever.'

As the two sloped out of the door, TJ looked over his shoulder at Charlie. He wasn't a bad kid, for a rich kid; he'd certainly worked with worse.

'You're going to have to keep them in line if this goes anywhere, you know.'

Charlie shrugged. 'They're OK.'

'Maybe. The days of pissing about in the studio for a bit and then sitting back and watching the dollars roll in are long gone though. No record company's going to push you if your guys spend all their time videoing their snot.'

'Mm.' Charlie knew he was right. Behind his laid-back beach boy image he had his dad's work ethic, even if their interests lay poles apart. And Matt and Brandon? Well, they just didn't.

'You could do well, you know. Think about it.'

Charlie thought about it.

He carried on thinking about it as he walked from the studio on La Brea to his black Porsche SUV that was parked outside. Charlie checked his hair in the rearview mirror – he never could get rid of that cowlick at the front, so he just ruffled the whole thing up – and pulled a new T-shirt out from a Fred Segal shopping bag on the back seat. As he changed, he dialled a number and clicked his mobile phone into the hands-free speaker. It was part of the security system of the car – wired to a call service, the system was able to detect any impact to the car, and immediately connect to the emergency services. Charlie was used to living with such high-tech safety measures. Apart from the bit where things went wrong and his family were poor for a while, which he didn't really remember much about, he'd grown up in a shiny bubble full of gadgets designed to protect or entertain. The first time he had played with a remote-controlled car had been with a Formula One racing driver who was a mate of Johnny's and who had taken Charlie to the track for the day, where they had rigged a car up for him to drive with a joystick from the pits. Most kids remember the first time they go abroad as an exciting and much anticipated event, but Charlie and Lucia travelled so much with their parents as kids that they had no concept of the distinction between abroad and home.

He pressed one of the speed-dial keys and waited for the call to connect.

'Hello?'

'Hey. I'm finished.'

'Are you coming over?'

'There in twenty.'

Charlie's and Belle's bodies were entwined as soon as she opened the door of her sugar-pink pool house, and they were tugging at each other's clothes as they backed into the hall. Belle was fifteen years older than Charlie, but her tight, dancer's body was still a perfect size four, and her breasts were expensively natural looking and dotted with freckles like chocolate sprinkles on cupcakes. Charlie pulled her kimono over her shoulders to free them and cupped one in his large hand, his fingers finding her small, hard nipple and pulling on it gently. He reached behind her with his other hand and lifted her on to the granite worktop of the kitchen island. She sucked her breath in as her bottom touched the cold marble surface. She pulled back for a second to look at Charlie. His face was flushed with excitement and he leaned forward to kiss her again, but she put her hand on his chest, and held his gaze while she unbuttoned his jeans. Their breathing quickened as she pulled him close, and guided him inside her, slowly, holding back, making it last.

'Belle . . . Oh shit, Belle . . .'

She smiled, put a hand on either side of his face, and held it. 'Hi,' she whispered.

He looked at her face. She wasn't young any more, but she was still so, so beautiful. There was so much more in her eyes than in those of the vacuous starlets who followed him around Hollywood hoping for a quick fuck, a fuck that might make them a member of his entourage, get them closer to the privileged lifestyle that they could see he was used to. Charlie never really knew whether they wanted *him* as well. Being the son of Logan Barnes meant that there was always something to live up to, and Charlie had never really felt as if he quite made the grade. But with older women, ones who were already successful, he didn't have to wonder whether they were with him in order to get into the VIP areas at clubs, or for the kudos of saying they were sleeping with Charlie Barnes, or whatever. And with older, married women, he had even fewer concerns, because they were more worried about keeping their extra-marital liaisons quiet than anything else. Lucia told him they were just after his body. She was probably right. That was fine with him – at least his body was his own, and not his father's. And when they looked and fucked like Belle, they could use him for his body as much as they liked. He stroked the delicate pink skin of her cheek. She liked to feel that he was completely absorbed by her. Wrapping her legs tightly round his back, gently squeezing him inside her, she stroked his tanned chest as he moved between her legs.

A recorded clip of Charlie's band playing the opening chords to one of their songs began to play. He twisted his head towards a chair a couple of feet away, where his cellphone lay along with his wallet and keys.

'Leave it.'

He turned back to Belle, distracted. She unhooked one of her legs from behind him, and lay back far enough to lift it up so her slim ankle was resting on his shoulder. He kissed the instep of her foot and she giggled, lying back on the counter so her body was stretched out in front of him. The song started again. He grunted with frustration.

'Charlie, leave it.' Her voice was playful.

'Argh, I can't. Oh, screw it.' He went to pick up the phone but it was out of his reach, so scooping up Belle, who squealed and clung on to him to avoid tipping backwards, he waddled to the chair, picked up the phone, and then sat down in the seat to answer it.

Belle wriggled, repositioning herself on top of him. She circled her hips, grinding into him.

'Dad – hi. It's not a good time, man. No, I'm in LA – kind of in the middle of something.'

Belle giggled. 'Or of some*one*.'

Charlie held a finger up to her lips to try and quieten her. She began to suck on it as she continued to move on top of him. He sighed, opened his eyes and looked at Belle, his face telling her that no amount of grinding was going to get things underway again now. The moment was gone.

'OK, fine. Yes, I'll be there, Dad.' He clicked the phone shut, ran his hand through his thick blond curls in frustration. 'Fuck it.'

'Daddy calls again, huh? What is it this time? You know, Charlie, one of these days you're going to have to grow up and cut the apron strings. It's not even as if you work for him.'

He didn't reply. There was no way he was going to tell her that the reason his father had called him back to London was that his mother had taken an overdose.

Belle stood and walked out through the glass doors of the pool house angrily, and Charlie heard her dive into the water as he pulled his T-shirt back on. He didn't think they'd be seeing each other again.

* * *

As the door of the dark saloon car opened in front of a hotel in a back street of London's Soho, the clacking of flash bulbs began, and the photographers started to call Lucia's name, even before they could actually see her.

When she emerged, it was with a harried expression on her face. She was clinging on to the arm of a tall man, wearing jeans and a dark brown overcoat with the collar turned up and a knitted hat pulled down as far as it would go. Neither of these things did much to conceal the fact that he was Gerry Davies. Not much would, since he had one of those faces that was instantly recognisable. Maybe that's what true star quality was. Either way, the paparazzi were going mad for it. Gerry Davies was in the same league as the likes of Tom Cruise and Will Smith, but he was a good twenty years older than Lucia – his children were closer to her age. His marriage of fifteen years was thought to be one of the few success stories in Hollywood. What a coup!

Lucia looked shocked by the flashes, and dropped Gerry's arm quickly, holding a hand up to keep her face partially concealed.

'This your new boyfriend, Lucia? Going to introduce us, are you?'

Flash, flash, flash.

'No, no comment. Excuse me.'

They were up in her face, she could smell their damp wool coats and smoky breath.

'Like the older man, do we, darlin'? Good girl.'

'Stopping off for a quick afternoon tea, eh?'

'Didn't know they hired the rooms out by the hour in this place, did you, lads?'

Filthy chuckles all round.

Lucia and Gerry ducked into the lobby of the hotel. A few of the paparazzi attempted to follow them, but were firmly held back by the doorman. Lucia clicked her compact open as they walked towards the lift. The hotel manager sidled over to greet them.

'Ms Barnes, Mr Parr asked me to bring you to the meeting room.' He gave Gerry Davies an obsequious little bow. 'Mr Davies, always a pleasure. Your usual suite is ready.'

Gerry turned to Lucia. 'Nice doing business with you, Ms Barnes.'

They shook hands. Their entrance had been arranged by their publicists and the hotel. Gerry Davies got the best suite in the house for as long as he wanted it, Lucia got a nice fee, and she and Gerry both got plenty of publicity. If things went well and they received enough coverage as a result they might take it to the next stage. Gerry was thinking of getting a divorce anyway, and a tantalising romance with a young, nubile blonde might be just the thing he needed in the run-up to the UK premiere of his latest movie. But that would all be something for other people to negotiate. Lucia Barnes had spent the majority of her life being treated like a perfect blond-haired doll. The end result was that now, nothing much was expected of her other than to look pretty, dress well and be charming. She was very good at fulfilling all three expectations.

She'd always been Daddy's little princess; Logan had been completely smitten with his daughter from the moment she was born. He hadn't expected to fall so utterly in love so quickly. He had always felt that he would be a better father to boys, since they were a known quantity: he would know where he stood with a son. And when Charlie was born, that had been confirmed. He loved him straight away, wanted to give him every opportunity in life, wanted to teach him everything *his* father had never taught him. But it was, despite the universal shock of new parenthood, broadly as he had expected. He felt pride, love, fear, exhaustion in equal measures.

When Lucia was born, however, it was immeasurably different. As soon as he saw her he was filled with an emotion that he had never experienced before and could not name. The closest he could get would be to say that he was awestruck. There was something miraculous about the fact that he, Logan Barnes, had produced this perfect little girl – a girl! He'd never imagined himself as the father of a girl, had just assumed that their second baby would be a boy as well, so when the midwife turned to him and said, 'Here you are, Mr Barnes. Meet your daughter,' he had asked her to repeat herself.

The woman had laughed. 'It's all right,' she'd said, 'it's a little girl, not an alien,' and had turned back to Maryanne who was lying, flushed and damp and proud, on the hospital bed.

'Oh,' Logan had said eventually, and through her Pethidine-befuddled exhaustion, Maryanne had looked worried.

'Darling?'

He hadn't been able to reply straight away, was unable to form the words. How do you respond when someone has placed perfection in your arms? But eventually he had managed it. 'She's perfect,' he had whispered, and had brought her over to Maryanne. 'Look.' And they had both gazed into her crumpled, bloodstained, purple face, seeing only indescribable beauty.

Which was pretty much how things had stayed – from Logan's side, at least. He was blind to Lucia's faults. Furious if anyone suggested she was anything less than perfect. Shortly after she was born he had come home raging one night, after having been at an industry black-tie dinner, brandishing the small photo that he carried around in his wallet.

'I'm never talking to that prick Saul Masters again,' he had raged.

'What on earth happened?' Maryanne asked, looking up from the TV show she was watching.

He had waved the photo at her. 'Khrushchev! Can you believe it? He said she looked like Khrushchev!'

Maryanne had stifled a giggle. 'Oh Logan . . .'

Much as she loved her daughter, and thought she was the most beautiful girl in the world, Maryanne was a little more realistic than Logan, and didn't expect everyone else to share her opinion.

'Poor little thing.' Logan had flopped down next to her, still holding the photo of Lucia. 'Compared to a fat, bald Commie.'

'Well, she is bald,' Maryanne said calmly. 'And quite round. Which is a good thing in a baby.'

Logan had smiled. 'True.'

And he had carefully tucked the photo safely back inside his wallet.

As Lucia grew up, she realised that her father was quite unable to say no to her, so it was always Maryanne who had to be the bad guy, insisting that Lucia did her homework, or giving her a curfew, or disciplining her when she was caught misbehaving. Like the time when Lucia was nine years old and Maryanne had found out she was paying the housekeeper to tidy her room for her out of her extremely generous allowance, rather than doing it herself as she was supposed to. Logan had just laughed, and said that at least she was enterprising. Maryanne had wondered, if she was like this when she was nine, what on earth was she going to be like when she was nineteen?

Appearing in her first lingerie campaign and taking full advantage of the many red-carpet invitations and boys bearing gifts that came her way, had been the answer to that. Lucia had basically spent the last three years, since she had left high school, partying. She had gone to college to study fashion design but had left after six months, telling Logan and Maryanne that she just couldn't devote enough attention to both studying and her career to do both justice. The truth was that she sucked at fashion design. It was much harder work than she had anticipated, and she had far more fun wearing the clothes than pinning the patterns for them together. So Lucia had carried on appearing in commercials and print campaigns, even doing the odd runway show, and generally having a good time.

The only thing was that recently she had started to feel just a little bit bored.

Lucia floated through her life in a fragrant bubble of perfume that smelled of candy floss and a haze of menthol Marlboro Lights. From within this portable cloud came a stream of almost constant chatter and fidgety activity. She was always talking – on her mobile phone, or to one of the clique of girlfriends who followed in her wake, or to her dog. Right now she was doing all three at once. Perched on the edge of her publicist's desk, she was flitting between petting Ratbag, her Chihuahua puppy, debating her evening plans with Tamara, who sat cross-legged on the floor at Lucia's feet like a pilgrim at the feet of an unusually blond and skinny Buddha, and discussing her personal branding and PR strategy with Jonty Parr, her publicist.

Jonty's office was a small room above a café in Soho, where they had headed once the paps had dispersed. The walls were covered with shelves crammed with box files full of magazine cuttings of his clients, and the tiny window had a view of Old Compton Street, if you leaned right out of it and angled your head far enough to the right. Lucia had signed up with him when she moved to London with her parents, keen to make sure that she made her mark on the UK. So far, she'd got plenty of modelling work, mostly underwear and jeans campaigns, appeared in a few music videos and plenty of gossip columns, and could command a healthy fee for public appearances at parties and openings. But she'd got most of them off her own bat, through friends and acquaintances. Jonty hadn't proved his worth yet, and she would have got rid of him already, if it weren't for the fact that he had an in with the director who was shooting the campaign for a new fragrance that Crescat were about to launch; it was called Heiress. There were a number of other girls up for the job, but Lucia *knew* she was the best choice. She just had to convince the director and the cosmetics company. And if Jonty could help her do that, then she was going to make sure she kept him around till the ink was dry on the contract and the money was in the bank.

'Jonty, here's the thing.'

Jonty glanced up at her. 'Yes, babes? Tell Uncle Jonty what's on your mind.' He grinned, and leaned back in his swivel chair, his legs spread unnaturally wide, as if to accommodate some enormous appendage.

Lucia smiled sweetly at him. 'I need the Heiress campaign. I'm the best girl for the job, and I need the money.'

Jonty raised an eyebrow. 'Come off it,' he drawled, 'don't tell me you're scrabbling down the back of the sofa for pennies.'

Lucia looked coolly at him over the top of her sunglasses. God, he really was an insufferable twat, with his 'babes' and his slang that he thought made him sound young and 'street'.

'No, clearly I'm not. But I have plans, big plans.'

'Do you now?'

'Don't mock me, Jonty. Yes, I do.'

'Can't you just go to Daddy?'

She glared at him. 'No, I can't. Not for this.'

He shrugged. 'OK, chica, keep your knickers on. Or don't.'

Jonty's eyes roamed suggestively down to the hem of her flippy little summer skirt. Lucia shifted her weight so it hitched up a little, parted her legs very slightly, and gave him a good look. Then she stood, picked up her bag and her dog, and waved a hand in Tamara's direction. 'Come on, let's go.'

Tamara scampered to her feet.

'Don't panic, babes, Jonty'll get you the gig, I promise. Just tell me one thing.'

Lucia turned back to him.

'What do you need the money for?'

'Oh, you know,' Lucia said lightly. 'A girl can never have too many shoes.'

As Lucia walked out of the door, her phone rang. 'Charlie, I'm busy. What do you want?'

'Listen, something's happened.'

'That's kind of how life works, Charlie – stuff happens. People do things, they go places, the world turns. Hold on.'

Lucia's other mobile phone was ringing. She snapped it open and pressed a button, all business now.

'Yeah, Ranj? OK, thanks, I'll look over it asap and come back to you. I know, and I appreciate it.'

From the first handset, Charlie's voice was urgently calling her. She sighed.

'Luce – fucking listen!'

'Ranj, I'll call you later. Charlie, what *is* it?'

'Mom's in hospital. She OD'd. Dramatic enough for you?'

Lucia paused. 'Yes, Charlie. OK. Where is she?'

As he spoke, Lucia wrote down the address of the hospital in her looping handwriting, dotting the 'i's with small hearts as usual, although they were a bit wobbly this time, because she couldn't quite stop her hand shaking as she wrote.

'Mum? Mum, wake up.'

Maryanne's hand with its skin chemically smoothed by regular scrubs and peels looked tiny as Charlie held it in between his larger, tanned ones, their skin roughened and blasted by sun and sand. She lay still, savouring the sensation for a few seconds before opening her eyes. 'Hi.'

Charlie's dark blue eyes were wrinkled at the edges with concern as he said huskily, 'You had me worried.'

'I'm sorry, darling. What are you doing here?' Maryanne pushed herself up on her pillows. Still in the same room, she noticed. But something was different, she was sure of it. The Monet prints had vanished, and the room was full of flowers. Charlie saw her look of bemusement and smiled.

'I took the prints down. Didn't think you'd be best pleased if they were the first thing you saw when you woke up.'

Maryanne laughed, then coughed. 'You know your mother too

well. Hey, you're meant to be in LA.'

'I came back. You've been asleep for a while. Lucia's been here. She had to go.'

Maryanne took a deep breath, inhaling the scent of the flowers. The sweet, floral freshness quickly turned to a cloying fug in the back of her mouth and she was overcome with nausea.

'Are you all right?'

She shivered. 'Open the window. I need some fresh air. Oh, God.'

Charlie opened the window and a breeze carried a wave of traffic noise and distant police sirens into the room. A sheen of sweat had broken out on Maryanne's smooth forehead. She was flushed, but still shivering.

'I'm getting a nurse.'

'No, I'm fine.'

She concentrated on taking the fresh air into her lungs in deep, slow breaths. Gradually, the waves of nausea subsided.

'Honestly. I'm all right.'

Charlie sat down again and a little furrow appeared by his left eyebrow, as it always did when he was worried or grumpy. Maryanne reached up a hand and tried to smooth it out.

'You'll get wrinkles.'

He shrugged her off. 'I don't care. Mom . . .'

Here we go, she thought. Emotional blackmail, overreaction. Her family were always trying to control her. If it wasn't Logan, which it was most of the time, then it was Charlie. Even Lucia had got in on the act recently. Nagging her, getting at her. Making her headaches worse, so much worse, was it any surprise she had to dull the pain with something? She shouldn't be angry with them – how could they be expected to understand what it was like? No one could. But the incessant eyes, watching her . . . They forced her to be secretive. Don't do this, don't take that. We'll help you, they said, we'll support you, darling, Mummy, Mom, Maryanne, Mrs Barnes. When had she acquired so many names? So many versions of herself. Once she was just Maryanne, Maryanne Curtis, plain and simple. Her life was plain and simple. But that was a long time ago. Before everything . . . before Logan.

'You know I love you. And that I'll always be here for you – right?'

Maryanne smiled up at him. Her beautiful boy. His face was so stricken. For a moment, she felt terrible guilt. It was her fault that he looked like that. So much sadness in his dark blue eyes.

'But . . .'

Here it came. She stamped down on the feelings of guilt and remorse. She must be strong now. He was going to try and stop her doing what she needed to do. And she had to make sure he didn't. These days, it was that simple.

'But I can't watch you do this to yourself any longer.'

She looked down so he couldn't see the irritation flare in her eyes. He's just a boy, she told herself. Don't be angry with him. He's trying to do what he thinks is right. He's just too young to understand.

'I'm not going to try and talk you out of – of this – any more.'

Maryanne looked up, surprised. This was new. Was he tricking her? No, it didn't look like it. There were tears in his eyes. *Oh my poor baby, don't stop. Just stop. Breathe.* She breathed.

'I know this isn't your fault. You have an illness.'

She nodded. 'Oh Charlie.' Now her eyes were filled with tears, but ones of gratitude. 'It's such a relief, that someone understands. The doctors seem to have given up on me. Everyone has, really.'

Suddenly Maryanne felt terribly sorry for herself.

'No one's given up on you, Mom.'

'If they could just find out what's causing them, I'm sure I'd feel better. I worry so much, you know, and that makes it all worse, I know it does.'

Charlie sat back. He looked confused. 'Causing what?' he asked.

'The headaches, of course. My awful headaches.'

Charlie stood up, and shoved his hands deep into his pockets. He shook his head. 'No, Mom. No!'

Maryanne gave a tiny gasp. 'What do you mean, no?'

He was fighting to keep his temper now, she could tell, he had that hunch in his shoulders. She wanted to tell him to stand up straight, that it was so important to look after your back . . .

'Not the headaches, Mom. They're not the problem. It's you – no, I mean, the illness I'm talking about *isn't* the headaches.'

He looked straight at her. 'It's the addiction that I'm talking about.'

There was a silence. He had shocked both of them. It was the

166

first time anyone in the family had said the word. Eventually, Maryanne took a deep breath and spoke.

'I'll forget that you said that, Charlie. It's all right, I know you're upset. I know I messed up, but I'm not—'

'*Mom!* Stop. I spend half my time in LA, you know? I'm not a kid any more. You don't have to be embarrassed. Hey, some of my best friends are in NA.'

He tried to smile at his own weak joke, but it faded.

'I want to help you, I really do. But I can't do that until you help yourself. None of us can. And I can't watch you kill yourself. I love you too much, and it's . . .' He broke off and rubbed his hand over his eyes, wiping away tears with his fist. He looked so young. 'It's just too hard, Mom. When you do something about it, I'll be here. I promise.'

He turned quickly and walked out of the room, shutting the door gently behind him. She could hear his sobs coming from the corridor and it tugged at her heart. Somewhere, beneath the denial and the anger and the need, the increasingly desperate need, to swallow something, anything, to divert her from the growing pressure in her head, she knew that he was only trying to help. They all were. But they just didn't seem to be able to understand that no one *could* help her.

Maryanne left the hospital of St John and St Elizabeth two days later in the time-honoured way of the drug-ravaged or newly cosmetically enhanced celebrity – behind a large pair of dark glasses in the back of a discreet limousine that was waiting for her by the ambulance bay at the back of the building. The staff were well used to such arrangements; they helped her into the car, while Henry held the door open and kept an eye out for any lurking photographers. Today, though, she was in luck; the coast was clear.

Logan was sitting in the back seat waiting for her. She leaned against the leather headrest and closed her eyes – she already felt exhausted – before reaching to stroke the back of Logan's hand with her index finger. He resisted the urge to move his hand away.

'Thank you, darling,' she sighed.

'What for?'

'Looking after me. Transferring me. Making sure I didn't wake up in some unspeakable hole of a hospital.'

'It's what anyone would do.'

'Mm.' She turned away. Ouch. That hurt. So he'd just done what 'anyone would do'? Just what you might do for a stranger, a random acquaintance. She swallowed and rummaged in her handbag, looking for something to distract herself with; found a pot of lipbalm and started to apply it.

'So silly, I still don't know how I managed it. What a fool I am.' She tried to laugh but it was too high, too tinkling. They both knew it was false.

Logan glanced at Henry in the rearview mirror. The driver understood his meaning, and pressed a button. A partition silently went up between driver and passengers. Logan turned to his wife. 'You're no fool, Maryanne.' His voice was hard.

'Well, thank you. I think.'

'You're an addict.'

There was that word again. Why did they keep saying that? She fumbled with the lip balm and it fell to the floor. 'Oh, damn.' She leaned down to pick it up.

'Leave the fucking thing on the floor. Just – leave it.'

'OK.' Her voice was small now, with a little tremor in it. She sounded a bit scared. That was good. She hoped it would shock him, get him off her back. It didn't.

'How long has it been?'

'What do you mean?'

'How long? Since the first lot of anti-depressants? That's when it started, isn't it? Or was it before then, even?'

'Oh Logan, I just take some painkillers occasionally. You know I get migraines. I'll have you know I suffer a great deal, every day. Not that anyone notices.'

He ignored that. She continued, 'I got the dosage wrong, that's all.'

She was convincing. He looked into her eyes. They held his gaze. With anyone else, she would almost certainly have got away with it. But he knew her too well.

'Again. This isn't the first time something like this has happened, is it? Last year, you passed out in the bath. Linny found you – how that woman hasn't left us yet I have no idea, with what you put

168

her through – and what was it you said that time? Oh yes, it was the heat. You fainted because you'd made the bath too hot.'

'We have an extremely powerful hot-water tank.'

'And now you do it again, and again poor Linny has to get you to hospital, call me and tell me what's happened. Did you do it on purpose?'

'No! Of course not.' She looked away.

'So it was accidental – because you were drunk? Well, I guess we both know you were drunk, don't we? After the little scene at dinner. Or was it that you were drunk *and* high? Too high to remember how many you'd already taken?'

Maryanne blinked, tears filling her eyes. 'No, I . . .'

'Because the doctor seemed very sure that you've been taking these pills for quite some time.'

'Oh, don't be absurd, he can't possibly know that.' Maryanne surprised even herself with the confidence in her voice. She was sure, quite sure, they couldn't know.

'Can't? Why? because it's not true?'

She faltered. 'Yes, exactly. It's not true.' But she sounded like she was trying to convince herself as much as Logan.

He exhaled in frustration and disappointment. 'You're lying to me, Maryanne,' he said.

'I'm not! I'm not lying. I got confused, I took the wrong pills – too many pills. I won't do it again.'

She was sobbing now, a thick lump in her throat and she tried to swallow it and regain her composure. She opened the window, hoping that the fresh air would help calm her. *Breathe in. Slow. He doesn't know. He can't know. It will be fine soon, you're almost home, and he'll go back to work. Then . . . But first, concentrate on calming down.* She took another long breath. *Better.* And turned back to him, forcing herself to give him a weak smile.

'I'm sorry, I really am.'

Logan stared at her dispassionately. It was like looking at a mask. He knew she was lying – knew it beyond all doubt, for God's sake. The doctors had told him at the hospital that the drug they had given her to bring her round from the overdose only precipitated withdrawal if you were dependent on drugs. Heroin, Methadone, or Pethidine. They even used it to diagnose dependence. And

Maryanne had all too quickly displayed the classic signs of it, her body beginning to tremble and convulse as the opiates were leached out of her system and her body noticed their sudden disappearance and began to start crying out for the drug it had come to rely on. She had sweated and vomited her way through a fast withdrawal that he hadn't been able to watch. It hadn't been his wife lying in that hospital bed, couldn't have been. And now she was telling lies, over and over again, shamelessly.

'Oh, come *on*, Maryanne. Do you think *I'm* the fool – is that it? You think I'm a stupid man?'

He was raging now, all the frustration of the last year, and before, coming out. And now she was scared. His face was hard, furious.

'Of course not.'

'Really? Because it certainly looks that way to me.'

'No, I just . . .' She started to cry again. He rolled his eyes.

'Oh, please. That's not going to work this time,' he snapped. 'Save it.'

She bit her lip. He could be very, very unkind, her husband. But so could she. 'I wish I'd never married you.'

Logan laughed.

'What's so funny?'

'Is that meant to hurt me? Cut me to the core, shock me into saying, "Oh darling, poor *you*, let me make it all better"? Well?'

It rather had been, actually.

'You wish you'd never married me, hmm? In that case, can you even *begin* to imagine how *I* feel?'

'I . . .'

'I've given you everything. Everything you wanted, everything you asked for, and didn't ask for. And still, all you can think about is yourself, how *you* feel.'

Suddenly he didn't think he could bear to be in the car with her any longer. He pressed the intercom button to speak to Henry.

'Henry, drop me here. I'll call you if I want you. I need to walk.'

The car slowed and pulled up next to the entrance to St James's Park. Logan got out. He spoke to Maryanne without looking at her.

'Henry will take you home. There's a nurse there. You'll be well looked after. As usual.'

Maryanne watched him walk down the busy street, and become

170

part of its human traffic. A few heads turned as people thought they recognised the dark-haired man from somewhere, then put it out of their minds. Probably just one of those people who looked familiar.

She would be well looked after. As usual. As Henry slowly and smoothly pulled away from the kerb she watched as the only person whom she wanted to look after her walked away.

Logan stormed down the street, not seeing anything or anyone beyond his own anger. It was the lying that was the worst of it. How could she look him in the eye, and tell such blatant lies? How long had she been hiding this from him? Years. On and off, for years. He'd brought up the time she passed out in the bath, almost drowning herself, but that wasn't the only incident. There had been others, dozens of smaller things, that he had explained away, told himself were nothing, let her brush off. It wasn't just Maryanne he was angry with, it was himself. Why had he buried his head in the sand for so long? When Linny had phoned him, telling him that Maryanne wouldn't wake up, he had honestly thought she was going to die. And part of him hadn't been surprised – he'd realised that he had been half-expecting this for a long, long time. And yet he hadn't admitted it to himself, hadn't allowed himself to acknowledge that his wife was an addict, and an alcoholic.

It hardly reflected well on him, did it? All-powerful, all-conquering Logan Barnes. To see past Maryanne's perfectly made-up face, with its features that he knew and loved so well, past the memories of their years together, the history they shared, the lives they had built, and to look beyond that to see the truth of her addiction and the depth of her unhappiness, would be to acknowledge that he had failed. Failed in the most fundamental and important of ways, as her husband. He would have to stand up and admit that he had not been able to make her happy, to fulfil her, to give her what she needed, despite the fact that he had tried so hard to do so. That not once, but time and time again, he had let her down, disappointed her, and so she had sought refuge and solace in the bottom of a pill bottle.

As he walked, Logan's anger started to subside. He still had time to put things right. He would make her better, he would fix her. He

171

owed her that. And, apart from anything else, Logan did not want his marriage to be a failure. Logan Barnes did not do failure.

Then an unwelcome thought bubbled to the top of his mind. That wasn't quite true, was it? There was someone he had failed, very badly. Someone whom he still saw in his dreams. Not every night, but just occasionally, without warning, she would appear. The top of her head as she knelt in front of him, bending her neck to take him in her mouth ... the cry that came from that same mouth as the podium collapsed ... her body crumpled beneath it as the paramedics fought to save her life. The way she had looked at him the one time he had visited her in hospital, all wired up to machines. Worse, the look on her daughter's face as she gently wiped her mother's brow with a damp towel. Just nine years old and having to care for her mother like that. He hadn't been able to face going again. So he had turned and walked away, and left it to the lawyers to agree on a settlement. There wasn't anything else he could do. He tried to tell himself that when she appeared in his nightmares, over the years. He couldn't be responsible for them both for the rest of their lives.

Somehow, though, it didn't make the nightmares go away.

Chapter Twelve

The warm air blew through the car's air vents and rushed past Mark's cheeks as he drove his vintage red Porsche out of the Eurostar train and up the ramp. He accelerated past a group of blokes in a white mini-bus who he assumed were on a stag weekend, judging by the neon-green mankini one of them was wearing, and overtook them, enjoying the sensation of the car's engine opening up as he hit the pedal to the floor. They made wanker gestures at him as he sped up on to the autoroute, immediately slipping back into the habit of driving on the 'wrong' side of the road. He'd grown up driving between the two countries; trips down to Nice and Monaco, weekends in Paris and through France to Brussels. He liked to drive, hated to fly, and would always travel to the Continent in his much-loved old 911 if he possibly could. Especially as it meant he could hit the sorts of speeds that would get him banned for years in England.

He pressed down harder on the accelerator. He was keen to get to Le Touquet as soon as possible.

'*Rien ne va plus.*'

The gamblers whose hands still hovered over the felt, too late to place a bet, withdrew their chips and watched the silver-coloured metal ball as it ratcheted around the wheel, gradually slowing. The croupier stood at the far end of the table, his face blank and his body held stiffly inside his neatly pressed white shirt and bow tie, waiting patiently for it to choose its landing place. Mark picked up the stack of chips in front of him and, one by one, dropped them back down on to the baize.

He had a stack of chips on red, representing 20,000 Euros, a 10,000 stack on the central 'douzaine' – the column of numbers running down the middle of the board – and chips worth 5,000 each on three individual black numbers, eight, eleven and thirty-one. Two chips on the eight, as he'd won on that on the last spin of the wheel. Always leave a winning bet on the table, his father had taught him.

Toc-toc-toc-toc-toc-toc-toc.

Mark craned his neck forward. The ball slowed to a stop.

'*Huit.*' The croupier placed the marker on the winning number and cleared the other piles of chips off the table. He nodded to Mark, who smiled. A double win – one on the eight and it was in the middle twelve of the board, so he picked up the win for that as well. It was turning out to be a pretty good night. And he had plans that he anticipated would make it even better.

Two and a half hours later, Mark was down to his last stack of chips. He was in his shirt-sleeves now, his blazer over the back of his stool. No one else who had been at the table when he came in was still there – in fact, no one who had been there even half an hour ago was still going. The croupier looked over at him. His expression was deliberately blank, but Mark knew that underneath it concealed contempt. Mark could see it, like the skull beneath the skin. He didn't blame him. The guy spent his whole life standing at the end of that table, sweeping chips towards him from out of the pockets of poor fuckers on their uppers, still trying to claw back some of their losses, as desperate and whining as a dumped teenager. Mark wasn't on his uppers. He just didn't care.

He signalled to the croupier that he would be returning to the table, and went to the cash-point machine in the casino foyer. Another 5,000 Euros later and every single one of Mark's chips was back in the hands of the casino. Ah, fuck it. It was time to call it quits.

He tapped the end of a packet of cigarettes on the beaten-metal surface of the bar and lit one while he drained his drink. Around him, off-season tourists finished off their after-dinner liqueurs; week-enders here for the golf, mainly. A few couples obviously on illicit trips away from spouses. Mark looked at his watch. It was late. His wife would have been asleep for hours by now, tucked up under her Cath Kidston duvet, her face carefully coated in night cream, her hair neatly brushed. He should have divorced her, should have done it years ago. Then she could have found someone else, would have had time to build another life with a nice man called Phil or Tim, a solid, reliable type. A chartered surveyor maybe, or a solicitor. They could have lived in an old rectory in a little English village, and June would have been perfectly happy. June wasn't perfectly happy now, Mark knew that. But then, neither was he. At least he gave her the satisfaction of knowing that they were both as miserable as each other. The difference was, it was his fault. His weakness.

She had married him in good faith, had walked down the aisle in her modest Catherine Walker wedding dress – nothing too low-cut or, heaven forbid, strapless, for June – ready to stand by her man; for richer, for poorer – well, that part had been fine; in sickness and in health ... to be fair, she couldn't really have been expected to predict the sort of sickness she would be dealing with. There were the children, who had been born in the Lindo Wing and announced in *The Times* – two boys, an heir and a spare – Sternley House, the Mallory family home, had been sold to Logan, and she had stood by him, and then a bit later she had got into local politics, and he had stood by her, as he had promised to do, and they had all posed for photographs on the steps of their townhouse and he had known that he was trapped.

The barman passed another Martini to him with a pot of salted almonds that he waved away. Time to go, he was getting morose.

He walked slowly down the narrow alley. The girls hissed at him from the shadows, cat calls, whispered come-ons. '*Bonsoir, m'sieur ...*' His eyes slid sideways, assessing the qualities of their flesh as they parted coats and hitched up skirts. No. Not here. There was nothing for him here.

It was the sound of one of them tripping that first alerted Mark to the men behind him. A scrape and the sound of a shoe scuffing and a muffled '*Merde!*' and he'd known what was coming straight away, had turned and raised his right arm to cover his face as the three youths had suddenly been upon him, their hands rifling through his pockets, their feet kicking at his shins so he stumbled forward on to his knees. One of them, the one who seemed to be the ringleader and who was stockier and better-built than the other two, grabbed his wrist as he did so and roughly pushed his jacket sleeve up. Mark felt the static of the boy's cheap sports jacket crackle against his skin, before he spotted the expensive Rolex and deftly jerked it off Mark's arm. The boys leered at him.

'Get off – get . . . *ooof.*'

Mark bent over, winded, as one of them planted a foot in his stomach. They laughed, showing their badly looked-after teeth. The girls had melted away; they didn't want to risk being there if the police turned up. Not that they were likely to. It was off-season in a seaside town. No one was coming. The leader walked up to him, pocketing Mark's cufflinks and watch, and spat in his face.

'*Putain.*'

And Mark was left kneeling on the cobbled ground, in the muddy puddle that he had landed in, his shirt-sleeves flapping as he laughed and laughed and laughed, until he leaned forward suddenly and vomited on to the street. He was the husband of an MP, a successful businessman, one third of the power trio that was making waves in the hotel industry – and here he was, kneeling in the gutter, surrounded by his own blood and vomit. And he knew that, somehow, that was where he truly belonged.

Chapter Thirteen

Elise McAllister sat at the green baize table in one of the *salles privées* of 33 Duke Street, a small but perfectly formed casino – one of those that had sprung up in London in the last couple of years. She kept her body still and relaxed. From her manicured but unvarnished fingernails to the ends of her straight, shiny hair, she was motionless. Her silk shift dress drew no attention to itself and yet flattered every line of her body to its best advantage. Tucked away in a quiet corner of Mayfair, with no sign outside to advertise its presence, and situated in an eighteenth-century building, the club was entirely of the twenty-first century. The bar was presided over by a young, hot mixologist – an Old Harrovian who had rebelled against the family tradition of law and appalled his parents by mixing and stirring his way around the world.

The design of the club rooms was avant-garde, zany, a bit Willy Wonka. When Elise had first come here she'd been entranced by it, by the energy and sense of fun in everything, from the tiny pin-lights strewn across the classical ceiling mouldings, to the crystal-encrusted basins in the loos and the deep purple, suede-covered bar. She'd paid the sky-high member's fee immediately. Her love of the place had only deepened when she had had her first big win at the poker table here. Ten thousand pounds. She recalled the thrill as she looked around the table at the four players whom she faced now. Hedge Fund Boy opposite had already folded, as had The Heiress, to his left. The nicknames Elise gave her opponents were inspired either by their play or by titbits of information she picked up about them, or just by the way they looked. It helped her to see them less as real people and more as moving caricatures, a collection of behavioural patterns and quirks, like a children's mix and match book.

The Actor, the flashy, good-looking man to Elise's right, whom she had underestimated the first time she had come across him, because his acting skills were far better at the poker table than they were on television, grumbled before throwing his cards into the middle of the table. 'Fold.'

He flopped back in his chair and rifled through his pockets for a handkerchief before blowing his nose loudly. The Heiress wrinkled her smaller and more delicate nose in disgust. And Hedge Fund Boy smirked, and shifted slightly in his chair so he could get a better view of The Heiress's cleavage. But Elise didn't take any of this in, because as soon as The Actor had folded she had trained all her focus on to her sole remaining opponent.

The Sparrow (so-called because he handled his chips and cards with jerky, staccato movements, and his head bobbed forwards every so often) peeled the corner of his cards up and stole a look at them, before staring at the cards that lay face up in the centre of the table. Elise laughed silently to herself. Stop pretending you're trying to calculate the odds, she thought. You know perfectly well what you've got, or haven't got, by now. There was still one card remaining to be dealt. She knew that she had seven possible outs, or chances, to make her hand. She could make a straight, or a flush. Or her luck could fail her and she could make nothing. Thirty-eight cards remained with the dealer. The odds of her getting one of the seven she wanted weren't the best, but they weren't the worst either. But it all depended on what The Sparrow had.

As they stared across the table at each other, she brought to mind what Anoushka had often repeated to her as the two women had played together during the evenings that had become an escape for Elise, a space where she could direct all her concentration on the cards and could forget about everything else. In her thick, Eastern-European accent, her mentor Anoushka repeated the mantra, 'In any bet, there is a fool and a thief. Don't be the fool, Elise; and don't be afraid to be the thief.' *Don't be afraid to be the thief.* Elise knew that reducing poker down to two basic elements like this was oversimplifying things – some players were brash in their bets and overconfident in their calls; some played tighter, quieter games, and some played in an entirely unemotional way, refusing to use their senses or instincts at all, simply doing the maths, playing the percentages. But in the end, poker came down to a single bet, with a winner and a loser. A fool and a thief. Elise took a long, cool look at her remaining opponent. Who are you? She thought. A fool? No, almost certainly not, not having reached this stage of the game. But was he a thief? He held her gaze at first through his glasses, and then his eyes flicked down to the table and his shoulders seemed to tense very slightly. There! That was it, the tiny sign she'd been looking for.

'Raise ten thousand,' she said, and pushed a pile of chips towards the centre of the table.

'Call.' The response came quickly, his voice emotionless. He added his pile to the pot of brightly coloured chips that tumbled over the table.

The dealer turned the final card over, smoothly.

'Queen of Diamonds.'

And Elise leaned forward to draw the pile of chips towards her.

In a small room lined with video screens, situated in the basement of the building where Elise was now leaving the room to cash in her winnings, the security manager on duty leaned back in his chair, impressed.

'She's good,' he said. 'Really good.'

High praise indeed, from a man who had spent decades of his life sitting in rooms such as this one around the world, watching for cheats and illegal play at private games with the highest of stakes at the World Series, in clubs and casinos and hotels. He'd seen Chris Moneymaker come out of nowhere to win the WSOP, he'd watched as Amarillo Slim lightened Larry Flynt's pockets by almost two million dollars, and had witnessed the greatest poker players in the world beat each other, money flowing back and forth between them like a long and constantly moving tennis match.

But the woman he'd just watched could hold her own against most of them, he believed; could better many. She had that coolness about her that the real pros possessed – a splinter of ice in their soul, that enabled them to stay calm despite monumental losses, to face their opponents with a visage that betrayed none of their inner turmoil, to return to the table time and again without it being a compulsion and descending into the frenzied play that marked a player who was ruled by their impulses rather than the incalculable blend of head and heart that marked the real talents. He'd observed her take control of the table smoothly, subtly, with a grace that touched even the cynical old soul of a man who'd spent his life around men and a few women who had seen it all and then some.

Elise's key was stiff in the lock, and she fumbled slightly as she pushed the heavy front door of the penthouse apartment open. The wall facing her was made up entirely of floor-to-ceiling windows, looking out over the river from the building's Battersea location. It was a slick, modern flat in a prestigious, architect-designed building, chosen by her husband. All mod-cons – a wet room, fully-equipped kitchen with stainless-steel-fronted cabinets that the housekeeper polished with baby oil daily, a temperature-controlled wine cooler, enormous, almost industrial-sized sinks, surround sound every-where, plasma screens above the baths and remote-controlled everything. Everything you could need or want. But Elise hated it, hated its minimal rooms with their concrete floors and metal doors and acres and acres of glass windows. Large pieces of modern art of a style she particularly disliked covered many of the walls – cold, detached pieces with no personality, no flair. Just technical skill. She didn't see the point – why not just take a photograph? Frequently when she entered the apartment every tendon and joint of Elise's body instinctively wanted to turn away and run. But she didn't. Danny. Danny kept her there.

Now she looked around the hall with its sweeping staircase leading up to the mezzanine level, and just felt cold and sad. She dropped her baby-blue Marc Jacobs tote bag, and its metal buckles and studs clattered against the pale limestone floor. Then she kicked off her heels and padded barefoot through the living area, wishing she could replace the statement pieces of art bought as investments with holiday snapshots propped up behind books or stuck into the frames any-old-how next to clumsy coil pots made by her son to keep pencils in. She didn't bother to turn the lighting system on as she made her way to the kitchen; it was too complicated. She usually ended up flooding the whole apartment with light by accident. She was starving. She took the perfectly presented plate of sushi left for her by Ines, Danny's nanny, from the fridge, and stood by the open door, picking at it.

Suddenly she froze. What was . . . ?

She turned slowly towards the other side of the room. Bill McAllister sat silently at the end of the glass table, deep in shadow, his striped and tailored cotton shirt still buttoned, his white cuffs as crisp as ever. Bill didn't do relaxed, laid-back. The end of what she knew would be a Montecristo cigar flared crimson as he drew heavily on it. She could hear his lips suck disgustingly around its end. He pushed the smoke out of his mouth slowly and steadily, not looking at Elise as she reached for the light switch and flicked it on. Relief flooded through her.

'Jesus, Bill, are you trying to kill me off?'

He didn't look up, but rolled the ashy tip of his cigar gently against the lacquered walnut ashtray. Elise poured a glass of red wine and took it over to the table. The relief solidified into something else as she felt the anger emanating from him, forming an almost visible aura around his body. He clearly wasn't waiting up for her in order to chat about her day. His mouth was a sulky frown and the look in his eyes was scathing, marring his preppy, American college boy looks. She reached out and rubbed his forearm.

'Hey,' she said gently.

His voice was harsh. 'You know what sort of family I come from, don't you, Elise?'

She laughed, with surprise rather than amusement.

'I'm vaguely aware, yes.'

'And you remember your son? Danny, six years old, upstairs, asleep? *My* son, as well, as a matter of fact, and my parents' only grandson.'

'That is how it tends to work, Bill.' What was this about?

'Who has been uprooted from what's familiar to him, who's still settling into a new school, and who every day asks for a little brother or sister?'

'We've talked about that before, and—'

Bill held up a hand, stopping her.

'That's right. We started talking about it four years ago. You didn't want a second baby, you weren't ready. You'd had a difficult time when you were pregnant with Danny. I knew that – I accepted it.

And I waited. Then we were offered the move from New York, and once again, it wasn't the right time. Right, I accepted that. I didn't want to put you under unnecessary pressure. Jesus, how much pressure can there be for someone who doesn't work, has a nanny, has all of this?'

His voice was bitter.

'Now we're settled, it's the right time, for everyone. And still, you're stalling. You won't sleep with me. God knows when we last had sex. Once again, I try to accept that all marriages go through phases, different stages. I'm an understanding man. Things will work themselves out. But then . . .'

Elise held her breath and waited. 'Then what, Bill?' she said, after a while.

'Then I find out where you've been going at night.'

She looked over at him. 'I go out for dinner with friends when you're at work events. I go to my book club. You know all this.'

'Bitch!' he shouted, his voice ringing out, bouncing off the hard edges of the room. 'Lying bitch!'

'Bill . . .'

'Tonight, Elise, tonight you haven't been having dinner, nor have you been at a book club, or whatever bullshit excuse you make for getting out of this house as much as possible, have you?'

She took a breath. Calmed herself.

'I haven't been to those things tonight, no. I've been at my club.'

'I know where you've been. I followed you.'

'You followed me? How dare you, Bill! Am I not entitled to—'

He pushed his chair back from the table and slammed a fist on to its glass top in one swift, violent movement. Elise flinched, and then watched as his cigar dropped to the floor. She wondered if it would mark the tiles.

'No, you're not entitled. You are not entitled to fucking anything, you stupid whore. How dare I? I want you here, at home. Being my wife, being a decent mother to our son, and yes, I want another child. You waltz in at two a.m. like some kind of slut, sneaking around in the kitchen, because you've been out in a sleazy fucking club playing cards all night. Shit, Elise, you're all class, you know that?'

She didn't say anything. It was always a toss-up when Bill was in a rage like this, whether to stay still and quiet and hope that it burned itself out quickly, or to argue with him, or to try and mollify him. Not the second option this time, she decided. He'd been sitting here for hours probably, working his anger up slowly, nursing it along with his glass of peaty single malt.

'Say something. Tell me why I shouldn't just throw you out. Your life isn't exactly arduous, Elise, now is it? You don't have to work for those pretty dresses and shoes you like so much. Don't exactly have to struggle to put food on the table, do you? Answer me, goddamn you!' His face was contorted and ugly with rage.

'No. No, I don't.'

He smiled. Crossed the room to where she stood. Touched the soft curl of chiffon at the neck of her dress. She stood still. She was good at staying still. This was where she had learned the technique that served her so well at the poker table.

'Are you losing all my money at those tables? What is it, Elise? You think maybe I don't work hard enough, think I need help to get rid of all that cash?'

She shook her head, no.

'Lots of people would say you had it easy, wouldn't they? You have a beautiful apartment . . .' His voice was low now, as his hand swept over the silk dress, brushing her stomach lightly, pushing the fabric up over her thigh in a swift, smooth movement. His other hand went to her throat, and he stroked her neck slowly. 'A wardrobe full of designer clothes. Diamonds on your pretty ears. A lovely son asleep upstairs. Innocent. Happy. Secure.' He was standing close now, his heat palpable, his mouth next to her ear as he spoke.

She turned her face away slightly.

'No, no, look at me, Elise. Look at me.'

She dragged her eyes back to his face. It was gloating now, and somehow this was worse, uglier than the anger. He was enjoying every second of his power over her. She felt only utter despair. She could never leave. She would be trapped by this man, by her love for her son, for ever.

And as Bill shoved her roughly against the metal cabinet, making her cry out as her shoulder was jammed against the sharp corner, tearing the delicate fabric of her underwear as he ripped it aside, Elise thought of the times she'd rushed back from somewhere to be with him, how she'd longed for him to return from work so that she could bury her face in his shoulder and breathe him in. As he wrapped a handful of her hair around his fist and tugged, forcing her head back and exposing her neck as he drove himself into her, pounding against her body, she remembered how, when she told him she was pregnant with the baby that became Danny, his face had taken on a strange look she'd never seen before, and he'd clasped her hand and promised to be the best father, the best husband she could have wished for, and that she would never, ever regret marrying him.

And as he climaxed with a shudder, and finally released her, she thought of everything that had happened since then, and she turned away and walked quickly out of the room, so he wouldn't see her start to cry.

Bill stood alone in the huge kitchen, hands in his pockets. He ground the smouldering cigar into the tiles and poured a whisky. Someone would clear it up tomorrow. Shit. He didn't like losing his temper with his wife. It wasn't as if he enjoyed these scenes. But she drove him to it. He flicked through the pile of mail at the end of the kitchen table, and his eye was caught by a glossy black Perspex box, engraved with the words *Mr and Mrs W. McAllister*. Intrigued, he picked it up and ran his finger over the lettering, wondering who might have sent them such a strange and beautiful thing.

Upstairs, Elise stood in the doorway of Danny's bedroom, looking at his small body splayed out underneath the duvet. The nightlight cast a soft blue glow over everything in his room. Watching him sleep calmed her, centred her once more. Everything else receded into the background. She blew him a kiss, and then turned to go. As she did, he stirred.

'Mommy?'

'Shh, sweetpea. Go back to sleep.'

'Tell me a story.'

She smiled, and went to kneel by his bedside. She smoothed out the wrinkles over the embroidered circus animals on his bedcovers – a red and white striped big top, a dancing horse, dotted over the white cotton. He was circus crazy, cuddling his toy clown; where so many children found them frightening, seeing something sinister beneath their white face-paint and grinning red mouths, Danny liked them. They made him feel happy, he said, which was good enough for Elise. The child's bedroom was the one place in the house where Elise felt comfortable. Even Bill hadn't been able to insist that his son's bedroom was a testament to minimalism.

'Which one?'

'Balloon story. Balloon story going to the circus.'

His eyes were flickering shut with tiredness, but he was battling to keep them open.

'Shut your eyes then, otherwise the magic won't work.'

He closed them, his face serious, concentrating.

'OK. One day, you come back from school and go upstairs to take your uniform off, and when you've folded it up neatly and put it away like a good boy . . .'

Danny giggled.

'Yes, like a good boy, to make your mummy happy, you go outside to play in the garden and there, just floating in the warm air, is a big, beautiful red balloon. Where did it come from? You reach out your hand, and take hold of the string. And you feel a little tug in your hand, and then the balloon starts to pull a little harder. And you hold on to the string – hold on very tightly – and it starts to rise up, up in the air, taking you with it . . . Sleep now Danny boy . . . my Daniel . . .'

In the morning, Elise got up as usual and started to get breakfast ready. Cheerios, orange juice, toast for Danny. Coffee and toast for her and Bill. Then she stopped. She didn't want breakfast. She just wanted to go. She went into the bedroom where Bill was dressing. 'That's it.'

'What?'

'Enough. I've had enough. I want a divorce.'

He stopped tying his tie and looked at her in the mirror. Then smiled slightly. 'Don't be silly.'

'Silly? Last night . . .'

'Yes, I'm sorry we rowed.' He put his jacket on and brushed off the shoulders.

'Rowed? Bill, arguing about where to spend Christmas is rowing, or something your mother said. You *raped* me. That's not—'

She didn't get a chance to finish her sentence, as Bill had grabbed her and was in her face.

'Don't say that. Don't ever say that.'

He held her face in his hand, hard. It hurt. She didn't move.

'We are not getting a divorce. You understand? I will not allow it. And if you try, I will ruin you. I'll make sure Danny stays with me and you only get to see him when I say so.'

'You wouldn't.'

'Believe me, I would do whatever it took to make sure that you didn't take my son away from me. So think about it, Elise, think very carefully.'

He let go of her face, and walked out of the room. As he went, he said, 'I'll take Danny to school. Why don't you have a lie-down? You're obviously tired. Take a day to relax.'

'I'm going to the committee meeting for the Crown ball later.'

He shrugged. His voice was relaxed again, as if the exchange had never happened.

'Ah, OK. Oh, by the way, make sure the fifteenth of October is clear in your diary. We've been invited to something that you're going to love. I'll tell you all about it later.'

He smiled at her as he went out of the room, and waved goodbye. Just a normal morning. Just another day. Elise waited until she heard the front door click shut, then she lay on the bed and sobbed.

On her way to the house where the committee meeting was to take place, Elise passed the wedding shops where she had held one of her wedding lists. She and Bill had married in New York, but had lists in London and Los Angeles and Paris as well as their main one at Bergdorf Goodman, to make things easier for their guests. Elise hadn't wanted to do them at all, had liked the idea of individual gifts, or nothing at all – it wasn't as if they were short of money with which to outfit their home – but her future mother-in-law had pronounced the idea 'unthinkable', and so Elise had dutifully done the rounds of the catalogues, selecting tasteful china patterns and crystal champagne flutes and marble-topped cheese boards. The one thing she was really pleased with from the list was her espresso machine. Crisp and soft 600-thread-count linen sheets for the emperor-sized bed, full sets of leather luggage that was almost over the baggage limit before you even put anything in it, so heavy was it with hide and buckles and linings, decanters for the whisky Elise hated and Bill had trained himself to like because he believed it was important to do so; thousands and thousands of dollars' worth of gifts that said 'I'm rich' like nothing else. And none of which would be personal. She doubted she'd even be able to remember who had given her what, until she recalled the embossed leather notebook Bill's mother had presented her with for precisely that reason.

'Note down each gift as it arrives, then you have a log for thank-you letters, and a lovely keepsake for the future,' she had said with a thin smile as she gave it to her over a 'girl's lunch' in Le Cirque.

Thinking about it now, her marriage had been characterised by conflict and Bill's attempts to control her from the moment he had proposed. Everything, every decision, every damn table setting at the reception, it seemed, had been something Elise had tried, and ultimately failed, to imprint her personality on. In the end, everything had been proper, correct, and absolutely down to Bill and his family, particularly his mother, Bibi McAllister III. Everything, that was, apart from her wedding dress.

Thirteen years ago, in 1995, Elise had lain on the sofa overlooking the sea and gazed at her left hand, newly adorned with the diamond engagement ring. She had turned it slightly from side to side and watched how the smaller diamonds set off the greater light of the central stone. A family heirloom, passed down from Bill's grandmother, it was a weighty piece of jewellery on her small slim hand. It was beautiful, no doubt about it, impressive, the way it caught the light and flickered reflective icy flames, and its sheer size meant people's eyes were drawn to it, so she wasn't sure why she was developing the habit of folding her hands together, or covering it with her fingers, and not moving her hands as much when she talked.

She turned her attention from the flashes of the ring to those of the spray on the sea, beyond the dunes and private lane that led to the property. It was the McAllister family summer residence, and one of the best addresses in East Hampton. It was also the only one of their homes in which Elise felt relaxed. The Manhattan apartment was Upper East Side formal, and their family seat in Connecticut was run with all the relaxed bonhomie of a state funeral. Etiquette and proper manners were paramount. Fun, it seemed, was not. Elise was used to a comfortable standard of life herself, but not on this level, of course, and she was also used to a lot more spontaneity and far fewer rules and regulations than this family she was to join employed. Oh well, all brides had to make some adjustments when they got married, she thought, as she shrugged on a white voile minidress over her navy and white striped bikini to protect her fair skin from the sun ('We don't want you too tanned in church, or with ugly marks, do we, dear?') and went outside to find Bill.

He was on the tennis court, face red and sweaty from the intensive lesson his coach was giving him, his expression deeply serious and his eyes focused. She watched as he returned the ball, again and again, thwack, thwack, thwack. Always accurate, well-judged, precisely placed, with the skill of a man who'd spent his childhood learning to be good at a sport, and a socially useful one at that, with the best teachers, the best equipment, and the required streak of determination. Little flair, maybe, but what did that matter when you had the drive and the resources at your disposal that Bill did? As he finished the lesson he walked over to Elise standing watching him at the side of the court, wiping his face with a towel and grinning.

'Did you see? Ace, ace, ace.' He punctuated each word with a swipe of his racket before packing it away.

'I saw, baby. Well done.'

'Hungry? I thought we'd go to the club.'

Elise groaned inwardly. 'Really? I thought we could stay here.' And she stepped forward so the outline of her body was gently brushing against his, and kissed Bill lightly on the mouth. She felt his body react immediately.

'Mmm. You've convinced me.'

And he picked her up and carried her inside, leaving his tennis gear strewn around the court. Someone else would take care of it.

Later, as she lay in the bath watching Bill shave, she caught his eye in the mirror. He winked at her.

'I love it here, Bill.'

'I'm glad. It's where we spent every summer when I was a kid. Happy days.' And he smiled. 'One day I hope our kids will have the same memories. Lazy summer lunches, playing on the beach. Tennis. Fresh air.'

'Know what I'd really like?'

'What's that?' He raised his chin and stuck out his bottom lip as he negotiated the contours of his Adam's apple with the bone-handled razor. Like many of Bill's most prized possessions, it was an heirloom.

'To get married here, on the beach. Have a party in the garden, by the pool. Keep it small.' The words all came out in a flurry, and then she held her breath. She hadn't been sure that she was going to say it until she did, but as soon as she had done, she was sure that she meant it, that that was what she really wanted, a small wedding for family (even though Bill's contingent of that was considerable) and close friends, a barbecue maybe, or a buffet laid out in the beautiful rose garden of the house.

Bill laughed, and rubbed some more shaving cream into his face with the salt and pepper badger hairs of the shaving brush. There was a pause.

'I'm serious.'

'Don't be absurd, darling.'

Elise bristled. 'Why is it absurd? The whole thing's got out of control. It's not about us, it's about your family and their social and business obligations. I don't know three-quarters of the people coming. I've never met most of the people coming to my bridal shower, and I don't even like one of my maids!'

Elise's throat was hot as again she realised the truth of what she was saying, even as she realised how spoiled and petulant she must sound.

'Who? Whom don't you like?'

She closed her eyes. 'Oh, it's silly. Your cousin.'

'Marla? Why don't you like Marla, for crying out loud? She's been nothing but kind to you from the day you first met her.'

It wasn't true, but Elise decided now wasn't the moment to go into it. She had already said too much.

'I'm sorry. Forget it – forget I said anything.'

'How can I forget it? My family and I have spent months planning the perfect wedding. Not to mention the thousands – no, tens of thousands – of dollars that the whole event is going to cost. We're getting married in St Patrick's Cathedral, one of the most beautiful and important churches in the city, if not the

189

country. The Plaza is the top reception venue in New York.'

'I know, I know.' Elise climbed out of the bath and wrapped a thick robe around herself. 'It's going to be fantastic, I know it is. And I know how much work has gone into it all.' She touched his shoulder, but he shrugged her away.

'People are coming to your shower to give you gifts, Elise, to welcome you to the family. My mother's spent hours of her own time arranging it for you. And, I'm afraid, like it or not, a wedding of this scale isn't all about the bride and groom. There are social obligations to be fulfilled.'

His jaw was jutting out as he splashed his face with aftershave and went to the bedroom to select a shirt. 'That's something you're going to have to learn.'

Elise followed him. She'd made a mistake bringing it up. She felt ungrateful and chastened. Her wedding was going to be one of the events of the year.

'I will. And . . . and I'm very grateful for everything your mother's doing for me.'

Bill's face softened slightly and he said, 'I know you're not from the same background, so all this must seem overwhelming sometimes. That's OK. I'll always help you if you're not sure of things.'

He finished fastening the cuffs on his shirt and checked his watch.

'Come on. We don't want to be late for dinner. The Van Hassetts want to introduce us to the Spielbergs.'

That night, they'd had their first major row. Already stirred up by the disagreement about their wedding plans, Bill had started the night defensive. They'd arrived at the Van Hassetts' mansion for dinner on time, although Bill insisted they were late. They'd circulated, Elise on her best behaviour, chatting to the host and hostess charmingly, admiring the newly redesigned pool house and commenting on the exquisite canapés. Bill was approving, proud even, and it was all fine. It was when they had, as promised, been introduced to Steven Spielberg and his actress wife that things had taken a turn for the worse.

Bill had been expounding his theories on baseball formations to the couple when the famous director had looked at Elise.

'Sylvester. You're not related to Pete Sylvester, are you?'

'Yes. He's my father.' Elise smiled proudly while Bill stopped a frown before it fully appeared on his forehead. Elise's stuntman father was not someone he wanted to discuss. He thought he was irresponsible, reckless. A bit of an embarrassment, the way he still didn't even own his own home but just lurched around the world from film set to film set, jumping out of cars and into fake fires like a teenager when in reality he was a sixty-year-old man.

'You look like him. Prettier. Same hair.'

Elise laughed. 'I hated it when I was a child. Too thick, too wild, not blond. The usual. I used to drive us both mad trying to show him how to do a French plait in it.'

While they discussed the films that her father had worked on, industry gossip, friends they had in common, Bill had glowered. And later, in the car on the way home, he had made it clear how he felt.

'I don't think it's appropriate to mention your father at events like that. I know you love him, and that's as it should be, but he's hardly someone that I should be associated with at this stage of my career, is he? He always lets you down. Scandal seems to follow him around like a bad smell, and he's – well, I think it's better if he's not part of our social circle as a married couple.'

Dumbfounded, Elise had exploded. '*He* brought him up! *He* asked me! And what, you want me to lie? Understand this, Bill, I will never deny being my father's daughter, ever. He brought me up, alone. He gave me everything. He's a good man, I love him, and if you ever talk about him like that again, I will walk out of the door and I will never come back.'

Bill was silent.

'And more than that, he's giving me away at our wedding . . .'

Bill's mouth opened . . .

'Or there isn't going to be a wedding.'

And shut again.

There had been a wedding, six months later. A few compromises had been reached between bride and groom and Elise walked down the aisle of St Patrick's Cathedral on the arm of her proud father, who was grinning from ear to ear, as handsome as James Bond in his tuxedo.

Elise had relished the look on Bill's mother's face when she saw her dress. Instead of the simple Vera Wang or Oscar de la Renta gown that Bibi had been hinting about, Elise had kept her choice of dress secret from everyone, and gone to a new designer that hardly anyone had heard of, and who certainly wasn't part of the Manhattan establishment. The dress was constructed from tightly corseted thick silk, pulling her waist in so it was tiny, covered in a layer of fine lace, ivory with just a hint of pale pink. The front of the skirt fell in soft folds down to the ground, where it swished gently against her feet as she walked. The back was a long train, long enough for the grandeur of the cathedral, and the silk at the back was a flash of bright, hot pink. Silk flowers nestled in the folds of fabric, peeping through from under the lace at the back. Layers of tulle made the skirt a gentle A-line that was still slim enough to highlight her narrow hips and long legs. And the cathedral-length veil that she wore was pinned to her hair not with the pearl tiara Bibi had wanted her to wear, but with diamond and feather clips woven into her hair, which tumbled down her back over the fine pink straps of the dress. The effect was elegant and eccentric.

She reached the end where Bill stood waiting for her and let go of her father's arm. He kissed her cheek before taking a step back.

The cathedral was full of people. Many of them were Bill's family and associates, but she'd made sure that enough of her own and her father's friends were represented as well. His fellow stuntmen friends looked amusingly broad-shouldered and swarthy next to the refined examples of American high society, her colleagues from the accountancy firm where she worked, and her friends from her yoga class.

Bill couldn't take his eyes off her during the ceremony. He was calm and determined as he said his vows, his voice ringing out clearly and his hand firm as he pushed the diamond band on to her finger.

'To Elise and Bill!'

The chorus rang out through the ballroom, which was filled with people and flowers and laughter. Fifteen thousand roses gave out their scent from the centre of tables, from their positions twined around columns, from petals strewn over crisp tablecloths. The groom's family crest adorned the front of the stiff white menus, which opened to reveal a six-course menu that read like a grand procession through the highlights of haute cuisine. Scallops, lobster, beef fillet, all served with champagne and fine wines. A dessert station served a variety of exquisite creations crafted by the pastry chef.

When Elise and Bill took to the polished dance floor for their first dance as a married couple, she felt that once this was over, she would finally be able to relax and enjoy the party. She looked into his eyes as the band started to play 'It Had To Be You', and they began to move around the dance floor.

'Hey,' he whispered, 'Mrs McAllister. Lovely Elise. Thank you.'

'What for?'

'For marrying me.'

She shut her eyes and leaned against his shoulder, whispering back, 'Oh, it was my pleasure, Mr McAllister.'

And at that moment, held in his embrace, in her beautiful dress and surrounded by people clapping and wishing them well, it really was.

Pete Sylvester lay on his back looking up at the ceiling of the ballroom. It was pretty impressive, as ceilings went, he found himself thinking, and he'd seen a few in his time. He didn't have long to consider this before the face of his new son-in-law came into view, and behind, his daughter. Man, she was beautiful. He couldn't understand how that stuck-up suck-up McAllister had won her heart and inveigled her into his clan. Load of stuffed shirts they were. But now her beauty was marred by a look of terrible hurt and disappointment. Disappointment in *him*, he realised.

'How could you? Oh, Dad.'

Bill leaned down and pulled Pete up. The room swam, and then came into focus – and almost immediately he wished it hadn't, as it meant that now he could see the disapproving faces staring at him in horrified silence.

The music soon started playing again and the party continued, chatter and laughter quickly smoothing over the crack in the evening where the bride's father had launched drunkenly into a table and fallen flat on his face. But Pete knew smoothing over his daughter's feelings would take much longer, and he also knew he wouldn't have any help from Bill. His new son-in-law, when he pulled him to his feet, had whispered in his ear, 'Fucking loser! You're just a drunken Irish thug, Sylvester. I knew it – and now everyone else knows it too.'

Then, Elise would have been shocked to hear her husband talk like that. Not any more. She sat in the formal drawing room of a tall, narrow townhouse just off Park Lane, and accepted a glass of mint tea from the uniformed butler. The room was fussy, all striped and patterned wallpaper and ugly, chocolate-boxy paintings that were no doubt worth millions of pounds, and swagged and heavy curtains. Two Oriental vases stood proudly on either end of the carved marble fireplace, a gold clock swinging its pendulum smartly in the centre, the rubies inlaid into its face glinting in the sunlight. The mirror above the fireplace reflected the room back on itself. Elise found it depressing and claustrophobic – surely one version of this room was plenty? Apparently not. She reached forward, took a pink Ladurée macaroon from the plate on the polished wood occasional table in front of her, and nibbled on it. Around the room were lots of tiny, uncomfortable chairs, upon which were perched the top ten Crown wives – the women married to the highest-earning and most successful hedge-fund analysts and account executives.

Elise reminded herself that she should be trying to look pleasant and approachable, and smiled around the circle in what she hoped was a friendly but non-committal way. God, she hated these things.

The other women in the room were all professional wives with a capital W, glossed and buffed, tanned and toned. They had set out to marry a rich man, had trained hard to achieve their end goal of merging their joint assets. His money; her looks. Once the deal had been done and celebrated with a lavish wedding reception, they would honeymoon, usually on a private island, with romantic dinners carefully scheduled to fit in with the markets. They spent hours at the gym perfecting their already perfect bodies, they studied the *Financial Times* and the *Economist* so as to be able to hold their own over the canapés at City drinks parties, they networked and manoeuvred and negotiated everywhere they went, all with steely efficiency and the sole aim of securing and furthering their social and financial positions. Power couples. She didn't fit in here.

But who was she to judge them? thought Elise. She was no better. At least they knew what they wanted and went after it; she seemed to have fallen into the job and now she didn't want it any more. Many of them would have killed to be married to Bill. They wouldn't have cared about any of his less pleasant personality traits; they would have seen his status and success as ample compensation for that. She had stumbled blindly into a marriage of the sort that most of them had struggled for years to achieve. They were all very, very nice to her. They asked her to attend Pilates classes with them, and to join them for 'girls' afternoons' at beauty spas, where they lay around getting pedicures and discussing the state of their pelvic floors. It was Elise's worst nightmare, and she knew that they were asking her because it was on their list of good trophy wife's duties. Join the fundraising committee, check; monthly facials, check; daily Powerplate class, check; fortnightly sex, check; befriend the boss's wife – *check*. Elise tried to get out of as many of the invitations as possible, but it wasn't easy. The wives were very determined.

The hostess and the oldest woman in the room at a Botoxed and face-lifted fifty, Toody Wills, tapped a silver pen against her glass, making a ringing sound, and smiled with pearly pink lips, her hair tied back in a girlish ponytail fixed with a bow.

'Ahem! Good afternoon, ladies. Before we start, some administrative business.'

Toody enunciated every syllable of every word she spoke. It took her a very long time to say anything. The circle of perfectly white and straight teeth bared at her made Elise think of a shiver of sharks. She gritted her own teeth, and turned her attention to the agenda that was being handed round.

The meeting droned on, with the biggest excitement coming when two of the women got into something of a stand-off concerning how many celebrities each knew and could expect to attend. Elise let the voices wash over her, mentally running through what she had to do later. Pick up some more coffee beans, answer the batch of dinner and party invitations on her desk, phone the florist . . .

'Thank God that's over. Have you got a cigarette?'

Leaning nonchalantly against the railings outside the house in the September sunshine, one leg crossed behind her, was a striking brunette in a light-fitting tailored suit, with a cropped jacket and wide trousers. Her hair was swept up into a chignon, held in place by a diamond-encrusted spider. Elise recognised her as a new face from the committee meeting. The woman stuck out her hand. 'Cordelia Templeton, darling. You're Elise. My husband's just joined Crown, so I suppose I'm the new girl.'

'That's right. Welcome, Cordelia.'

'Call me Delly. Wasn't that beyond tedious? Hate those things. Come with the territory though.' She spoke with a cut-glass accent covered in smoke.

'Yes, I'm afraid it does.'

'I know a kindred spirit when I see one.' Delly waved her cigarette at Elise. 'We should make a battle plan. Fancy a drink? I'm gasping.'

And without bothering to wait for Elise's answer, she hooked her arm through Elise's and started off down the street, talking quickly all the way to the nearest wine bar with a speed and sharp wit that amused and entertained Elise, making her feel happier than she had felt in ages.

By the time Elise arrived at the restaurant where she was meeting Bill for dinner with two of his clients and their wives, after whizzing home to change out of her jeans and T-shirt into a flippy black dress with lace panels and a softly ruffled jacket teamed with suede Louboutin peep-toes, she felt as if not just a breath but a gale of fresh air had blown through her. Elise had just had time to touch up her make-up, adding smokier eyes, and to put her hair up slightly haphazardly (the three glasses of champagne she'd been persuaded to drink with Delly had left her coordination more than a little skewed) before kissing Danny goodnight and hugging Ines then flying out of the door so as not to be late for dinner. As she was leaving, the phone rang. She paused. Should she answer it? Damnit, she'd better.

'Hello?'

'Is Mr McAllister available, please?'

'No, I'm afraid he's not. This is his wife – can I help?'

'Ah, good afternoon, Mrs McAllister. This is Seth Wharton, calling from the Lenegan and Pearson Bank,' the young-sounding male voice announced in her ear.

Elise prepared to launch into her 'No, we don't need a loan, we've got all the credit cards we need, our house, car and lives are all insured and we don't want to remortgage' speech, but first she tried to deflect him.

'You can reach Mr McAllister on his mobile – do you have the number?'

'Um, I do, but it doesn't appear to be working. I've tried his office already, and they told me he had gone home for the day. I'm sorry to have bothered you.'

'Can I leave him a message?'

'Yes, if you could inform him that we're holding some proceeds from the recent sale of shares, and await his instructions as to how he'd like us to handle it, that would be helpful. Unless you'd like to instruct us yourself?'

Elise hung up the phone. Strange. Bill didn't really deal with banks at work. And they wouldn't usually call him at home. Even if they couldn't get hold of him at the office, they'd leave a message with Crown, or send an email. And why would *she* want to instruct them? Oh, well, she had no time to think about it now, she would mention it to Bill later. She wrote down the message, but instead of putting it by the phone, in her rush to get out of the door, she absent-mindedly put it in her handbag.

As the six of them were being seated around the famous chef's table overlooking the kitchens of the Chesham Hotel, Elise thought back over her afternoon. Delly had regaled her with gossip about the company and its employees, starting with the tale of the PA who'd been fired three months previously after she'd mistakenly sent an email bitching about her boss to 'the man himself, darling, but the worst bit was that they'd been having an affair and it included various, shall we say, *personal details*, that he didn't want known. Of course he couldn't say this was why he fired her, so he made up some excuse, which made *her* so cross she sent the email round to everyone in the company!' She moved on to the rumours about the trader who had died last year, 'Suicide, sweetie, all hushed up by the family because he slit his own throat after his wife found him in bed with the nanny,' and the lowdown on the less salubrious backgrounds of some of the other wives. 'Our Lady Lytham looks down her nose at anyone who's not titled because she snagged old Lord Timmy, but before she got the ring on her finger she was plain old Amy Brown – changed it to Amelia by deed poll at the same time as she left her job as a barmaid in the pub on his estate.' All of her stories were told in a dramatically hushed whisper and with a heavy scattering of winks and gossipy asides. Elise had loved her at once.

As glasses of Dom Pérignon Œnothèque were served with canapés – spoons of steak tartare topped with a single quail's egg, Bill squeezed Elise's thigh under the table and smiled at her.

'You seem happy. Nice day?' He frowned at a tendril of her hair that was tumbling out of its pins, and smoothed a section of it back over her head. She reached back to resecure it.

'Yes, thanks. The committee meeting was – fine. It was fun, actually.' She smiled at him and took another swig of champagne. Bill looked surprised. 'Well, excellent, excellent.' He patted the back of her hand.

And as if by mutual but silent agreement, she turned to her left, and he to his right, to make polite small talk with their dining partners about, respectively, the interior options for a new Aston Martin and the difficulty of finding good help in London, while drinking their *amuse-bouches* of tiny shot glasses of red mullet bouillabaisse topped with caviar foam.

Chapter Fourteen

One month later

Logan stood in the rooftop garden that he had created at Luxury. It was one of his favourite places on L'île des Violettes – a secluded hide-away full of tumbling roses and fragrant honeysuckle and jasmine, tendrils entwined and trained up pillars, espaliered fruit trees lining the white walls. A fountain pattered water into a stone bowl lined with turquoise; he could almost feel its cool water on his tanned skin as he breathed in the densely hot air of the island, and birdsong chirruped gently, piped through small speakers concealed in the walls.

In the distance he could see one of the hotel's light aircraft as it neared the smaller island that was also owned by him, where it would land. The guests would then make the last part of their journey by boat, so that they arrived calmly, slowly, easing their way into the island, and so the blue skies above Luxury's beach and gardens were not constantly dotted with helicopters and planes. It also meant the no-fly zone he had managed to obtain over the hotel could be enforced, and no paparazzi lenses could poke their way into guests' rooms and villas.

He savoured the last few moments of privacy and solitude. They were coming from all over the world, his guests, the favoured few who were attending the party at Luxury. For a moment his confidence wavered. He wondered if he had done the right thing, opening up this place to other people. In his attempts to enhance it, had he destroyed its unique beauty? But it would have been greedy to keep it to himself, and he wouldn't have been able to justify buying the island just to let it sit there. He was a developer. That was what he did and who he was.

Logan remembered that he had been in the middle of a long and very dull meeting when he discovered that L'île des Violettes was his. The negotiations had been dragging on for weeks, and he had half-given up on the idea of ever owning the place; the paradise he had dreamed about for so long. Had tried to accept that maybe it just wasn't meant to be, or not now, at least. Maryanne had started to get sick of him talking about it, never being quite present, gazing into the distance as he mentally drew up plans and imagined what he would build where. So he had tried to forget about it and concentrate on everything that needed to be done at LBI already – and there was plenty of that. Logan Barnes International had risen from the ashes of First, and was thriving. There were always hundreds of decisions to be made, books to be balanced. So far that day he had approved the plans for a new car park that was being built for one of the hotels in Singapore; discussed the cost-efficiency of upgrading the plumbing system of a French chateau; met with three advertising agencies who were pitching for a campaign to promote his hotels with golf courses in an attempt to reach a new, younger market; agreed to upgrade his employee insurance program in the UK to cover dental care; and reassigned the contract to supply his traditionally styled Italian hotels with bathroom toiletries.

At 11 a.m. precisely his phone had buzzed in his pocket; he had smiled an apology to the lawyers, and clicked 'reject'. It was just Johnny, he saw, he'd ring back if it was something urgent. The phone rang again – Johnny. This time Logan made his excuses and went out into the corridor to take the call.

'We got it. No, actually, since it is all yours – *you* got it.'

For a second Logan didn't know what he was talking about. 'Got what?' he said.

'The island, buddy. Your mysterious lady – your other woman. She's all yours.'

Logan held his breath. 'Really? You're not fucking with me? Johnny, I swear—'

'Hey – I wouldn't. Really. Deal's just gone through. I've dotted all the i's and crossed every last t.'

'But I didn't realise . . .'

'What, that we were so close? I know. I decided to keep it quiet until it was for sure.'

From inside the meeting room, the four lawyers looked at each other in surprise as they heard Logan whoop with joy, and then shout at the top of his voice, 'Johnny Stokes, you legend, I fucking love you!'

One of the female lawyers cleared her throat and looked around the room. 'Ahem. I think we can assume this meeting is over.'

Logan chuckled at the memory of their faces as they had filed out of the room. One of them had stopped and ever-so politely offered him his 'Congratulations, Mr Barnes, as you've clearly had some positive news.' To his obvious horror, Logan had hugged him.

Now he looked down over the white buildings that sparkled in the sun, and the lush, tropical gardens that combined a sense of wild paradise with contained beauty, and further, to the beach and the sea. He raised a small pair of binoculars to his eyes, so he could see the first party of guests stepping off the boat, gazing around wonder.

No, Logan was confident that he had destroyed nothing. On the contrary, he had set out to create heaven on earth. And as he watched the reactions of the guests as they disembarked and stood on the polished wood jetty, he knew that he had succeeded.

Nicolo was one of the guests. Logan observed him coolly as he struggled to contain his emotions, as he stepped on to the island. Johnny had asked Logan why he had sent Nicolo an invitation.

'So he can see what he missed out on,' Logan had replied steadily. Johnny had raised his eyebrows.

'Bit risky?'

'Why – what can he do? Keep your enemies close, remember.'

It would be fine. He had assigned Steve Bigby the specific task of watching Nicolo. The man could bring nothing on to the island. Nothing would happen here, not during the launch party. And then Nicolo would be whisked away, to savour the glimpse of Luxury that he had been allowed to see . . .

Elise hated flying, even in a plane as new looking and comfortable as this one. Two other couples were already seated in the spacious cabin, which was outfitted in LBI's signature black and cream Art Deco-influenced style. As she settled into her seat, a man whom she vaguely recognised but couldn't place and who was travelling with a woman with white-blond hair who was so thin her thighs looked the same size as Elise's arms, entered the cabin and sat at the back of the jet. She heard one of the hostesses offering him a drink as she put her bag away and got out the novel she was reading.

'Champagne, Mr Flores?'

The woman made her way round to Elise, who accepted. Maybe it would calm her nerves. It wasn't just the flying she was worried about, she was anxious about spending the holiday with Bill. They hadn't been away together for months. Oh well, they were here together and she might as well try to make the best of it. She rubbed the back of her neck.

'You can't possibly be uncomfortable in these seats,' he snapped from beside her.

She turned to look at him in surprise. 'I'm not, I'm just trying to relax,' she said. 'You know I find flying difficult.'

'You have mentioned it before, yes,' he said. And went back to his newspaper.

The flight had passed in a haze. Once she'd had a facial massage from the therapist on board, Elise had settled down in a cashmere robe to sleep. The interior of the plane had been designed so that each couple had their own area, partitioned off from the rest. Two large and padded armchairs folded out into a double bed, with soft pillows and duvets. There was a fully stocked kitchen in the galley, plus individual fridges in each area, which held a selection of the guests' favourite treats. Elise had poured herself a single glass of pink champagne, and had ordered a lobster roll from the solicitous attendant. It had arrived almost immediately. Even Bill, who could ordinarily be relied on to select the one dish on a menu that was not quite up to par, or to find fault with the running of almost any enterprise, seemed to be impressed. After she had eaten, Elise had drifted into a blissful sleep, eased into it with the rose and violet scented face cream that had been massaged into her temples, so her dreams were as sweetly fragrant as the island she was travelling towards.

L'île des Violettes rose up in front of them now. Beyond the landing stage was a wide white sand beach. A cliffside soared up towards the sky and a cream and black cable car was visible rising through the boughs of the trees.

Jacinta Tramontello's voice shattered the peaceful scene as they reached the pier.

'I'm not getting in *that* thing,' she squawked. 'I suffer terribly with vertigo. It's simply crippling.' Her companion patted her shoulder distantly as one might comfort a yapping dog, but the boatman just smiled.

Bill turned to Elise, saying mockingly, 'Oh dear, sweetpea, I'm not sure you're going to like that very much either, are you?'

She bit her tongue. 'I'm sure I'll be fine.' She was damned if she was going to give him the satisfaction of being right.

'It's no problem, ma'am. There are many routes to Luxury,' the boatman said kindly, and pointed to a small fleet of buggies, in the same black and cream livery, that were waiting nearby.

Nicolo sat on the cream cotton cushions that lined the bow of the boat and drank in the sight of the island coming into view, deaf to the chattering of the other guests. He was strangely nervous. The swift motion through the water created a breeze that whipped his hair back, and made him gulp. The island was close now, and he could see a white-clad figure waiting to greet them at the end of the wooden jetty that was jutting out into the sea towards them.

It was perfect. This wasn't the island of his memories, this was like some super-charged, turbo-boosted version of it. The colours were brighter than he remembered, the sea clearer and a more exquisite turquoise, the air smelled sweeter. As the boat slowed to a stop and he was gently led on to the jetty, he noticed that it was trimmed with silver, and that in the water below it, bright pink and coral and silver tropical fish flickered in the shallows.

He let himself and Vienna be guided to one of a handful of small beach buggies, which chugged the little group through the lush undergrowth, up meandering pathways towards what he knew must be the main buildings that made up the hotel. Even this tropical woodland was beautiful, scented with pine and frangipani and jasmine, tamed and somehow untamed simultaneously. Leaves on sand crunched gently beneath the buggies' wheels, and he could hear distant music, lilting and seductive.

Suddenly the buggy stopped, and Nicolo gazed at the scene before him. He felt dazed, as if he were in a dream. In front of them was a pair of polished silver gates, all curlicues and sinuous curves and flowers opening their petals towards you. The driver of his buggy turned to him.

'You got the key, sir?'

'Mm. The key?'

'The one that came with the invitation. Mr Barnes was very clear that no one can come in without opening the gates.'

Nicolo reached into his pocket, and pulled out the small silver key with the diamond in its end. In the centre of the gates was a small silver keyhole, surrounded by an ornate keyplate, engraved with the words, *Through me you pass into the city of delight.* Dante. They had read Dante at Harvard, had quoted it at each other as undergraduates, captivated by the visceral power of the words. Nicolo shook his head. Why had he come? To be taunted, reminded of everything he had lost? He hesitated for a moment, the key hovering next to the lock.

There was still time to leave, to turn back. He didn't have to do this. And then he looked up, sensing someone watching him. Standing behind an ornate railing on the roof of the main building in front of him, looking down at him, was the unmistakable figure of Logan. *Looking down at him.* 'It was ever thus,' Nicolo thought savagely. Logan raised the glass that he held in one hand, and tilted it at Nicolo, in a mock toast.

Bill and Elise's villa was on the east of the island. After they'd disembarked from the boat and been greeted with refreshing spritzes of lime and violet cologne and cool linen towels, they'd been whisked off in silent electric buggies, past the three main buildings and down a cool, shady avenue of rustling palm trees, to find their villa at the end of the track. There was no check-in, since all of the formalities had been taken care of already, and by the time they reached their rooms their baggage had somehow already arrived.

As Elise walked in the front door, she gasped. A circular room faced her, with a black stone floor that shone like caviar. Around the edge, white suede sofas were covered in silk and velvet and ostrich-feather cushions – hundreds of them. A large crystal chandelier hung suspended from almost invisible fixings so that it appeared to be floating in the middle of the room. A circular skylight let in the rays of fading sunlight, which shone down and caught the droplets of crystal in the chandelier, and made little rainbows on the surfaces everywhere.

The bedroom was more extraordinary still. An eight-foot-wide bed covered in sheets of muslin so fine that they looked like layers of tissue paper was positioned on a slightly raised platform. Posts at its four corners were slim columns of silver, and tiny blue lights seemed to glow from them. Elise stretched an arm out to touch them, and saw that they were tiny, multi-faceted aquamarines. Draped between the posts were yards and yards of pale blue lace, falling in soft puddles on to the dark polished wood floor, like a bride's veil. The wall that the bed faced consisted of soft grey wooden panels embellished with silvery filigree decorations translucent and delicate as spiders' webs. As Bill and Elise gazed around the room, drinking in the beautiful mouldings around the tops of the walls, the immense French-style wardrobe, carved and whitewashed, the oversized indigo chaise longue that stretched languidly out at the foot of the bed inviting feet to rest upon it, the panels began to slowly and silently fold back.

Asha, the butler who had driven them to their room, indicated that he had pressed a button in the wall, and they watched with astonishment as the panels revealed first a plasma screen the full height of the wall, which Asha demonstrated as being of top quality and clarity. Then, with a grin and a flourish, he proudly pressed the button again, and the screen slid to one side. And the vision that was in front of them made them gasp again, as the room opened up to reveal a private infinity pool that they could step into almost straight from their bedside, and which seemed to tip straight into the sea beyond. By now it was almost dark, and the ocean was the colour of Elise's dark blue sapphire earrings. Surrounding the pool were loungers the size of double beds, and cabanas with heavy curtains to shield delicate skin from the heat of the sun. A feeling of coolness rose up from the pool and it was so inviting that Elise could not resist slipping off her shoe and dipping her toes into the water. It was as soft as cotton wool against her skin and she sighed with pleasure.

She took her time exploring the delights of the rooms, moving between them silently. She didn't want to break the spell. In the walk-in wardrobe she discovered a perfectly folded pile of sorbet-coloured cashmere wraps, a wide-brimmed white straw hat and a classic Panama, white and cream silk sarongs, navy Havaianas flip-flops. In the bedroom, a humidor made of inlaid wood, lined with clean-smelling cedar, was filled with some of Bill's favourite cigars – 'A tobacconist's hall of fame,' he had marvelled when he opened it, greedily inhaling their murky scent.

A tall chiller cabinet was hidden in one wall, containing wine, champagne, beer, pitchers of fresh lemonade and tropical fruit juice, chocolates, caviar – tempting titbits in case of sudden hunger during a hot afternoon or a balmy night. The space was set into the structure of the building so it could be accessed from either the inside or out, and Asha could replenish the stocks or deliver new orders without Bill and Elise even having to open the door. A thick book contained ideas and inspirations for dishes that the resident private chef could create. The kitchen never shut. You could order a full English breakfast at 4 a.m., a sushi banquet, a ten-course *dégustation* menu, or a chocolate cake for breakfast and it would be served either in the cabinet, or outside, or anywhere in the villa – in the small private dining room off the main living space, as you swam in the pool, or directly to you in bed.

So many delights awaited them that Elise felt like Danny did when she took him to an ice-cream parlour and let him choose. His eyes flicked from flavour to flavour, desperate not to make the wrong choice, part of him wanting everything at once . . . Her heart tugged as she thought of his dark eyes and what he would think if he saw this place, and for a moment, she wished she was back at home with him. Then she heard the sound of the sea lapping against the shore just a few feet away, and checked herself. No, there was plenty of time to spend with her beloved boy when she got home – she was going to enjoy the break. She mentally raised a glass to Johnny Stokes, Bill's client and the partner of the man whose island this was, for inviting them. She had four days to enjoy being one of the first people to come to the place that she was sure everyone was going to be talking about when she returned to London.

But first, they had a party to get ready for . . .

* * *

Elise stood in front of the full-length mirror, turning from side to side, assessing herself with a critical eye. She was wearing a strapless, full-length dress of shimmering bronze, cut low at the back. The shade flattered her copper-coloured hair and her golden, freckled skin. She turned to the left. The small curve of her belly that remained from carrying Danny was just visible under the fine fabric. She turned to the other side, smoothing the fabric over her stomach, trying to decide whether it was noticeable or not.

'Admiring yourself, are you?'

Bill was leaning against the doorframe, smoking a cigarette. She looked at him in the mirror. He smelled of lime cologne and silk. He was wearing a brand-new and very expensive white tuxedo, and his hair was swept back. He was very handsome. But he was wearing that half-smile that made him ugly, at least to Elise, because she knew what usually came after it.

'No,' she replied, keeping her voice light and calm. 'Just checking.'

'Checking what? Whether everyone's going to be able to get enough of an eyeful?'

He ran his hand over himself in mock imitation of Elise, pursing his lips. 'Ooh, look at me, aren't I sexy? Let's see if I can make Hubby *reaaaally* jealous tonight.'

Elise's cheeks flushed. 'Leave me alone.' She turned away from the mirror and made for the door. She had another dress in the cupboard, something more demure that she had brought with her in case of this very scene. She would put that on instead.

'Leave you alone? That's not very nice, Lisey.'

Bill grabbed her wrist as she moved to pass him, hard, and she cried out in pain. He twisted it behind her, and then tugged her towards him. She didn't cry out again. He was blocking the doorframe with his body. His voice was his own again now. Dark, though. Dangerous. She stood, his strong arm pinning her weak one behind her back. She could feel her flesh bruising, her hand starting to throb as he cut the circulation off.

'Let me go, please, Bill. I'll change,' she whispered.

'You can't change, Lisey. It's in your nature to tease, isn't it? You can't help it. My Scarlet Lady.'

He put his free hand on her behind and pulled her closer towards him, and smiled when she flinched. 'You're teasing me now, aren't you? Teasey Lisey.'

She could feel his erection pressing into her groin. She wouldn't fight him, not tonight. Whatever else happened, she was stuck with him on this island for the next few days, and she knew how unpleasant he could make it for her if she battled him. He kissed her roughly then let her go.

'Not now,' he said. 'Later. We'll play later.'

She forced herself to smile at him. 'I'll just get changed, then we can go and enjoy the party.'

'Don't be silly.' He looked at her as if she was joking. The cloud had lifted, for now. 'Why would I want you to change? You look ravishing.'

He leaned in close and whispered in her ear, 'Ravishing, and oh so very ravishable. Don't change – but take off your panties. I want everyone to see how beautiful you are, and I want to know you're completely naked underneath your dress. OK?'

She nodded. 'OK.'

'Good girl.'

He patted her bottom as she went to get some concealer for her arm, and to do as he had told her. Like a good girl.

Two hundred of the most famous people in the world were standing on the lawn, waiting patiently for the doors of the main house to open and for the party to begin. There was the occasional shuffle and murmur as someone wondered aloud what was going to happen now, but mostly, they were quiet.

Then suddenly, someone at the back of the group cried out 'Oh!' and pointed, and everyone looked up at the sky, which was suddenly lit up with the blazing trail of a light aircraft, apparently writing in pure fire. The word *Luxury* appeared as if it was being written by an invisible hand with an immense sparkler – and then faded.

Two hundred people held their breaths. Silence. And then a cacophony of noise, music, laughter, calls of the fiesta erupted as the guests were surrounded by performers who seemed to appear from nowhere. It was a spectacle unlike anything Nicolo had ever seen before; some kind of otherworldly carnival, or a version of what one might imagine to be a Dante-esque vision of heaven.

A dancer in a Burlesque costume, all corseted and uplifted breasts and sequins and feather headdress, was riding a gilt carousel horse towards him, stockinged thighs gripping the animal, which moved as if by magic. He turned. A tumble of acrobats had lifted the woman who had been standing behind him (and who was Rose Ross, the Supermodel) high up into the air, and were parading her towards the doors. A team of Pierrots carried her companion after them, in a fuschia leather sedan. A tubby statesman, all belly and comb-over, was giggling as a Geisha gently took his hand and drew him along with her.

As everyone was gathered up and the group moved slowly and magnificently inside, the music became louder. The undercurrent of drums drove it, and over the top strings and vocals were layered into a melody that kept gathering pace until people were clapping along with it, faster and faster, their excitement growing with the music. Nicolo's skin tingled. He couldn't help but be as excited as everyone else. The circus of Logan Barnes was on display in all its glorious, Technicolor finery. He relished the drama, the peacock-like splendour of it. It would be all the more satisfying when it was gone.

The singing faded away, and then the strings, until all that remained was the pulsating drums. The performers drew back into the shadows, and a shiver ran through the crowd. They were in a large space, presumably a restaurant or ballroom, but it was unrecognisable as such tonight. The ceiling was swathed in a rainbow of billowing fabric, sparkling with tiny lights, which dimmed even as Nicolo was watching, and a white spotlight focused on a circular hole in the ceiling. Beyond it the sky was black, apart from a single star that burned brightly. Slowly, slowly, the star grew brighter, seeming to get closer and closer. People held up their hands to shield their eyes. And then, from the very centre of it, came an explosion of colour. Flowers rained down on the heads of the waiting guests, and streamers, and tiny sparks, which burned themselves out before they reached the floor. As the room was lit up with lights of every colour, a silver trapeze, with a pair of small feet standing on it, came into view, clad in a pair of jewelled shoes. Then legs, then the rest of the body, and as the crowd realised it belonged to

Antoinette, the superstar singer who had retired from show business five years ago amid a storm of controversy, and who was still the biggest-selling artist in the world, they went mad. The first chords of her most famous hit started up, and when she had performed her opening number and disappeared, two hundred calls for *encore! encore!* following her, a man stepped silently on to the darkened stage at the far end of the room. He stood for a moment, watching the scene below him. And then the spotlight swung over to him, and a great cheer went up. He raised both arms in welcome.

'Ladies and gentlemen, good evening. My name is Logan Barnes, and I'm delighted to welcome you to Luxury.'

Elise and Bill were at the back of the room. Logan had left the stage and was making his way through the party, greeting people, smiling and hugging and shaking hands. The music had started up again, and with it, a swell of chatter as guests turned to their neighbours to share their reactions.

For herself, Elise felt punch drunk. It was almost too much – so much colour, so much beauty. Acrobats tumbled over each other in pyramids and circles and scrambled up columns like multi-coloured insects. In the centre of the room was a huge pool, its water the sort of clear turquoise that you dream of, and inside, floating towards the Perspex sides and waving at the transfixed viewers, were mermaids naked and beautiful. They flicked expertly through the water. Bill had got into conversation with some man, and they were guessing how much the party was costing, and so Elise wandered away towards the pool. As she did so, a mermaid swam up to the glass and waved at her, her hair curling out behind her in tendrils. And then she flicked her tail and was gone. Like the Sirens, Elise thought; beautiful and deadly.

She turned back to Bill, but he was still deep in conversation, so she carried on exploring alone. She came to a pagoda, covered with twisted roses in swathes of palest white moving through sugar pink to deep fuchsia. Sitting on a pink velvet-covered throne in the centre was a film actress, now well into her sixties, but still a famous beauty. She was having her feet, hands and shoulders massaged gently by a trio of dwarves. Elise blinked and moved on, past immense platters of food, piles of tropical fruit on great gilded stands; a pyramid of chocolates and *petits fours* and squares of

210

Turkish Delight. Across the hall were cake stands, on which were spread raspberry tarts that gleamed with luscious fruit, and exquisite little chocolate boxes, piped and decorated with more chocolate. Elise reached out and took one of these; she bit into it, and it had the same ethereal flavour as the chocolate that had arrived with the invitation.

There was a fountain by her side, made of black marble, flecked with silver. It was fizzing – surely, thought Elise, it couldn't be . . .

An attendant appeared at her elbow. 'May I pour you a glass, madam?' she asked, holding out a champagne flute on a small tray.

Elise nodded. 'Please do.'

The woman held the flute under one of the small jets of liquid, filling it expertly with pale gold, and handed it to Elise. 'Krug 1988, madam.'

Elise laughed. Of course. The finest champagne, in a fountain. What else?

'Elise.'

She turned towards the voice.

'Johnny! Thanks so much – what an invitation! I'm overwhelmed.'

'It's my pleasure. Glad to be able to repay your husband for all he's done for me.'

Elise nodded. Johnny was being generous – it was hardly as if managing a big chunk of his investments was doing him a favour since he was one of Crown's most valued clients – but then that was Johnny. A big-hearted, open kind of a guy.

'Where is Bill, anyway?'

'Oh, he's over there somewhere – talking about work again by now, I guess. It doesn't take long.' Oh God, she shouldn't have said that, it sounded bitter, shrewish. She tried to cover it up. 'He's so dedicated, enjoys it so much, he can never wait to—'

Johnny grinned and rescued her. 'I'll catch up with him in a bit. I wanted to introduce him to someone, but you'll be much more popular anyway, I'm sure.'

'Popular with whom?'

'The man of the moment.' Johnny nodded to the man who was standing next to them, his back to them, and touched him on the shoulder.

'Logan, meet Elise McAllister, Bill's wife.'

Logan turned, a polite, practised smile on his face, his hand ready to shake hers. The smile faded.

'Hello. I'm so pleased to meet you,' she said shyly. 'I can't believe we're here.'

She faltered a little. He was staring at her intensely. She would usually feel uncomfortable under such scrutiny, but somehow this time she didn't. If it had made any sense at all she would have thought that it was like looking at herself.

'Logan Barnes.'

'Yes. Elise.'

She somehow knew what his hand would feel like before she took it. And she was right; it was solid, fleshy, firm. *Familiar. Say something,* she told herself. *You should say something about the party, about the island. Something witty or clever.*

'Darling, everyone's dying to talk to you, you mustn't huddle back here with Johnny and . . . ?'

Maryanne looked at Elise, her smile warm, and Elise felt herself blushing, like a schoolgirl caught trying to pretend she was one of the grown-ups. Maryanne was pure glossy perfection tonight, in a dramatic gown of rainbow-hued silk, and a necklace that had been specially designed and made to pick up the colours again – pale blue sapphires, yellow diamonds, deep violet amethysts and pure scarlet rubies, dotted on gold wire so fine it was hardly visible, so the jewels looked as if they were floating around her neck. Her hair was caught up with more jewels and she smelled expensive.

Elise watched as the trio moved away, getting absorbed into the crowd of admirers, all flocking around Logan. As he went, he turned back to her, just for a second, and their eyes met. She held his gaze. And somehow felt as if she was staring into the eyes of a friend, not a stranger. And then he was gone again.

A hand touched the base of her spine, and she shivered. 'Let's go somewhere a bit more private, hmm?'

Bill's voice was soft in her ear. For a moment, she remembered a time when those words would have excited her rather than filled her with dread. She turned to him and smiled.

'Sure.'

She had to find a way to escape.

* * *

'Keep Nicolo away from me. Logan, Johnny – keep him away.' Maryanne's voice was trembling. 'I don't understand why he's here. Why *is* he here? Why didn't you tell me?'

Johnny's eyebrows went up. 'You didn't know?'

Logan put a hand on Maryanne's shoulder. 'I didn't want you to fret about it,' he said soothingly. 'He needs to be here.'

'Why does he? Why?'

'Calm down.' He took both her shoulders now, firmly, and looked her straight in the eye. 'Calm. Down.'

She breathed; seemed to bring her emotions back under control. Then: 'OK. Tell me why.'

'Come on, darling. You know how it works. Keep your enemies close, remember?'

When Maryanne walked away, Logan said to Johnny, 'Steve's keeping an eye on him, isn't he?'

'Never out of his sight,' he replied. 'We're in the driving seat here. Look, I'll check on Maryanne in a bit, OK? Now go and enjoy your party. You did it, man.'

'No, Johnny. *We* did it.' *Keep your enemies close.* It was a maxim that had served Logan well in the past – and it wasn't going to let him down now.

Maryanne's hand trembled as she took another pill out of the vial and slipped it into her mouth, swallowing it with half a glass of champagne. The ladies' cloakroom she was in was styled like a movie-star's dressing room. The mirror above the dressing table was surrounded with clear light bulbs, and the surface of the table held an array of perfumes and cosmetics. The attendant, who wore a black and white maid's uniform, complete with starched cap and pinafore, hovered in the background as Maryanne selected a bottle of Chanel No 5 and sprayed a little on the inside of her wrists. She turned to look at herself sideways on in the mirror. Pushed her shoulders back and sucked her stomach in. She had to be on form, had to play her part as Mrs Maryanne Barnes perfectly, even better than normal. Since her overdose a month ago, she had tried so hard to be a good wife, just as Logan had tried to support her. She had been dutifully going to her counselling appointments, she had even printed off some information about NA and left it lying around. He seemed to trust her again. And as long as she kept things under control this time, there was no reason for anything to change. She just needed to make sure that she didn't go too far; didn't get drunk and get carried away with the pills. Take just enough to keep her steady.

She went back out to the party.

Lucia and Jonty were standing on the wooden bridge over one of the hotel's many pools. It was covered in fairy lights fashioned to look like garlands of flowers, and their reflections twinkled in the water below. Lucia was wearing her third outfit of the evening, a one-shouldered dress splashed with exotic flowers. She took a cocktail shot from a passing waitress in a silver bikini and knocked it back. On the far side of the pool, a young Formula One driver was flirting with Lucia with his eyes. She turned to Jonty, putting her most appealing pout on.

'No, you can't go over there,' he said immediately.

'What?!'

'That's what you were going to ask, isn't it? Can you go and talk to Racer Boy over there. And the answer, my darling, is no.'

'You can't tell me what I can and can't do.'

'Yes, I can. I'm in charge of managing your public image, that's what you pay me for. So, let me do my job. Let's eat.'

Food stalls had been set up all over the grounds of the hotel, each serving different types of cuisine, so guests could stop for a single snail, still in its shell and served with parsley butter, or for a perfectly constructed sea urchin maki roll, or for a cone of chips served with a creamy dollop of truffled mayonnaise. Jonty was piling his plate high. Lucia didn't really do food. She waved a cigarette at him.

'I'll just call him when we get back, you know. I can get his number.'

'Oh, I know you can, sweetheart.' Jonty laughed. 'You can get anyone's number you like – just don't do it here.'

'Why? It's not like there are any press here.'

Jonty was a patient man, but Lucia really was testing his limits tonight. 'Look, darlin', people talk, all right? This place may not have any journos around, but everyone in this gaff is watching you.'

Lucia shrugged smugly. 'True.'

'And if they see you chatting up old Gearstick over there, they're going to notice. The most beautiful girl in the place, and the racing Boy Wonder copping off? Of course they'll notice. So if we want to keep this story spinning about you and Gerry Davies, you need to keep all eyes on that. It's much better publicity than a fling with a petrolhead.'

Lucia nodded wisely as she exhaled her smoke. 'So there *is* a reason I pay you all that money after all, Jonts.'

'Exaggerly. Now if, when we get home, you want to bugger off to Monaco and spend a weekend *ever-so-discreetly* fucking his brains out, then that, my princess, is another matter entirely.'

Lucia thought of the racing driver's muscular thighs. Mmm. She might just do that.

'Also, I didn't tell you earlier, but I've got some good news for you.'

'Oh my God.' Lucia grabbed his wrist. 'Did I get it? Did I get the part?' she demanded.

'Yeah. Jonty got you the part, babes.' He raised his glass to hers and clinked it. 'So, let's celebrate, eh?'

'Absolutely.' Lucia nodded, and handed him her drink. 'Give me ten minutes – I just have to do something.'

'But Luce . . .'

She held a hand up in the air. 'Honestly – ten minutes. Tops!'

She grinned, and raced off towards the hotel. Jonty sighed, downed both their drinks, then looked around for someone to entertain him. One of the dancers approached him.

'Left all by yourself?' She gyrated in front of him sinuously. 'Wanna dance?'

'Yeah, baby!'

And Jonty started shaking his slightly plump, denim-clad booty, in what he was as sure was a hip and funky manner, as the dancer tried to work out what rhythm he was bumping along to so she could dance alongside him.

Upstairs in her suite, Lucia grabbed her BlackBerry and tapped out a message with her fast little fingers.

To: RW Aziz@Azizlawinternational.com
Subject: Heiress/No. 98
Ranj – I got the contract! So we can def. go ahead with buying No. 98. Please get the ball rolling asap. Will be back in London on Wednesday, and will come by the office then to sign anything and go over stuff. Thanks. Xx Lucia.

Lucia flopped back on her bed. In a minute, she would go back downstairs to the party that she could hear was hotting up, but for now she wanted to savour the moment. It wasn't the fact that she'd won the advertising contract that she was so excited about – though she couldn't deny she was proud to have beaten all the other girls to it, and excited that she would be working with one of the best photographers around at the moment; it was what it meant. Because the Heiress contract, just like all the other modelling jobs and PAs she did, was a means to an end; a way of earning her own money that she had been squirrelling away, spending her allowance on the fripperies that everyone expected her to, and that she, admittedly, enjoyed very much, while she watched the numbers tot up in her savings account week by week.

And now she would have enough for phase one of her plan. Enough to enable her to go back to the private investment bank that she had already had a preliminary meeting with, and negotiate a loan. A big loan, that would allow her to put phase two into action. She wasn't going to be just a pretty little doll any longer; she was going to be a businesswoman. She imagined what everyone would say when they found out that Lucia Barnes was going into the hotel business.

Phase two was to buy number 98 Bilton Square, a hotel near Bond Street that was for sale because its current owner had never quite managed to make it work. Tucked away, in a quiet back street that didn't get much through traffic, it had once been a private members' club, stuffy and wood-panelled, and had never quite managed to shake off that image. Lucia had big plans for it. She knew she could make a success of it, make it the flagship of the chain she planned to build. Phases three, four and five of her plan were all mapped out in a document in her pink laptop. First, she had to get her hands on the Bilton Square property – and she had to make sure she did so without anyone finding out what she was up to – especially the hotel's current owner.

Because she knew there wasn't a chance in hell that her father would agree to sell it to her.

Maryanne held her glass of champagne lightly by the stem. She couldn't see Logan, but knew that he would be somewhere nearby, working his way through the maze of rooms, accepting compliments, making jokes, flirting a little – not too much, just enough to make people feel well attended to. She also knew that she should be doing the same. Playing her role of top wife. But at the moment, that's all it felt like – a role that she had taken on somewhere along the line, and didn't really want to play any more. However, she didn't think her husband, the director – always the director – would ever let her just walk off the set.

Charlie pushed the wedge of lime down the neck of his bottle of Corona and took a swig as he watched performers from the Cirque du Soleil. They had created a special show for the launch of Luxury and it was spectacular. His dad sure could throw a good party. Charlie had always been popular at school, and his popularity had definitely been helped by the invitations to his parents' dos that he extended to his friends. Logan and Maryanne weren't like most parents, he knew that. Never had been, even in the rarefied world of the private schools Charlie and Lucia had attended. There was usually a building named after his father at their schools, which was especially handy for Lucia, who would have been expelled from even more of them if it hadn't been for this.

He walked down the beach, kicking the sand. However great the party was, he wasn't really enjoying himself. He was kind of bummed about Belle still. It wasn't like he'd been in love with her or anything, but she'd been fun and sexy, and he missed it. Charlie was a man who liked women and liked having regular sex. And that wasn't the only thing bugging him. He would finish his album, and try to get it released. But there was always this question of whether he should go and work for LBI. Learn the business, end up running part of it in a few years, gain enough experience so that one day he could take over from his father. Did he want to be a hotelier, a property magnate? He had no idea. It was probably what was expected of him. Logan might be indulging him in his music career now, but how long would that last?

Draining his beer, he headed back to do his duty. Find his sister, avoid his mom, with whom was still not on good terms, put on the united family front. It wasn't always easy being a rich kid, whatever anyone might think.

Logan found Maryanne talking to the Mayor of New York in the cigar lounge, with Charlie at her side charming the man's wife. The Mayor was drunk and red-faced, and clearly delighted to be the recipient of her attentions.

'I'm sorry,' Logan said pleasantly, 'but I'm afraid I'm going to have to steal my wife away from you.'

'Aw, and we were having such a lovely chat, weren't we, Maryanna?'

She smiled thinly. 'We certainly were. Do excuse me.'

As soon as they were out of earshot, she said, 'What an awful man! Why on earth is he here?'

'Repaying a favour. You know how it goes. You were handling him very well, anyhow.'

'What do you mean?'

Logan looked baffled. 'I mean you were being your usual captivating self.'

'There's really no need for that sort of sarcasm.'

'Maryanne, honestly, I don't know what—'

He stopped. Realised. 'Come with me. NOW.'

He took her hand and firmly led her out into the corridor and into a bathroom behind the main foyer of the hotel, shutting the door behind them.

'Right, what is it? What's it been tonight? Are you on the painkillers still, or have you moved on to a bit of coke? A few tranqs, maybe? What's the drug *du jour* in your warped little world?'

Her cheeks flushed, but the rest of her skin was pale. Her eyes weren't quite focusing on him as she opened her jewelled evening bag and reached in for a compact.

'Fuck you, Logan. I haven't taken anything. Don't you accuse me . . . You were talking to me as if I was some kind of whore, telling me how I was "handling" him.'

218

'What? I did nothing of the sort. Jesus, I can't even pay you a compliment any more, is that it? It's all about you, isn't it? You can't let me enjoy this one night. You're a selfish bitch.'

Maryanne gasped, and went to slap Logan's face, but he stopped her wrist in mid-air and she dropped her bag. Her make-up and mobile phone skidded out on to the stone-tiled floor.

'Oh, damn!'

She hurriedly knelt down to scoop everything up.

'What's that, Maryanne?' Logan's polished dress shoe kicked the bag out of the way.

'Don't! That's vintage Chanel, you fucking philistine!' Maryanne went to retrieve it as Logan leaned down to pick something up from the tangle of make-up. She stumbled, the hem of her dress catching on her high heel, and she tripped, sprawling on the floor. 'What's got into you now?' Her voice was shrill and hoarse.

Logan straightened up, the small vial in his hand. 'I don't think the question is what's got into me, as much as what's got into you, is it?'

She knelt on the floor, concentrating on putting her belongings back in her bag.

'I knew it. I knew you'd been taking something. But oh no, "how dare you," you said, "how cruel to accuse poor little me." Mean old Logan, poor little Maryanne.'

She stood, her bag dangling from her wrist, a few tendrils of hair beginning to come undone.

'Well, there you are. Well done. You were right. Clever you, right again.' Her eyes were blazing. 'I hope you're happy.'

'No, Maryanne, I'm not fucking happy.' Logan's laugh was bitter. 'You lie, and lie, and lie again – and you think that makes me *happy*? You think I care so much about being right, that I'd rather that, than know that you're doing as you promised and staying off drugs?' He shook his head. 'This is the most important night of my life. And instead of being out there,' he pointed to the door, 'talking to my guests, enjoying the fact that I have finally achieved something I've been trying to do for half my life, I'm in here, in a fucking bathroom, arguing with you because you seem intent on ruining things.'

He slammed both hands down on the marble surround of the

basin, and stood over it for a moment, trying to rein his anger back in, and then Maryanne started batting at him with her bag, pummelling his broad back with her fists.

'How can you? How can you stand there and say to me, your wife, the mother of your children, that this hotel, this building is the most important thing in your life!'

'That's not what I said.'

'It's what you *meant*. "The most important night of my life," you said.'

He turned and put his hands on her shoulders, trying to hold her at arm's length as she continued to swipe at him, tears running down her face.

'Don't put words in my mouth,' he said quietly.

'I don't have to! You're doing it all yourself.'

'You promised me. You promised me, and Lucia, and Charlie, that you were going to try, that you were going to stop.' Logan shook his head. 'They're going to be so disappointed.'

'Oh, you absolute—'

Maryanne reached for the closest object, which happened to be a glass bottle of hand lotion, and threw it, not at Logan, just wherever. It shattered against the wall, sending shards of glass flying. Logan shielded his face.

' . . . shit, you shit, how dare you use them like that.'

Maryanne was sobbing now, really sobbing. The bathroom door opened and one of the security men put his head round it, his eyes taking in the scene.

'Sorry to disturb, sir, we heard a crash – is everything all right?'

'Yes. Thank you.'

He nodded and tactfully withdrew. Maryanne sat on the padded stool in front of the basin, her shoulders hunched, weeping. When she spoke again, her voice was quieter, calmer.

'Don't you dare tell me how the children are going to feel. As if you *know* them. Do you remember, Logan, when they were small, how you said you would never be like your parents? Never be in a position where you didn't know your own children, know what was important to them, what was happening in their lives.'

Logan's jaw was set hard.

'I may be on drugs, I may be an addict – yes, there you are, I said it. But can you tell me what Charlie's favourite band is? The name of his first girlfriend? What subject Lucia got an A in?'

She raised bloodshot eyes. Logan lowered his head.

'You haven't been there, Logan. You haven't been with us for a long time.'

For a moment they stared at each other. Both regretting things they had said. Both unable to *un*say them.

'The thing is, Logan, this hotel, this island – Luxury – it's more important to you than I am. It has been that way for years. And that's not a very easy thing to live with.'

He took a deep breath.

'Neither are you, Maryanne. Neither are you.'

Chapter Fifteen

Logan Launches Last Word in Luxury.
General Manager's *Star's Latest Creation.*
Luxury: Indian Ocean's Sexiest Secret Hideaway.
Rumoured $5 million cost of launch.

It was the day after the launch, and there was only one story, and one name on everyone's lips in the world's media. Luxury.

Logan sat on his private terrace which looked out over the gardens of Luxury and towards the ocean, having his breakfast of fresh fruit and coffee, with Johnny sitting opposite him. They looked like an old married couple reading the Sunday papers, he thought to himself, and grinned. Kirsten appeared on the terrace holding another folder full of clippings from dozens of newspapers and magazines, in scores of different languages. She'd been up all night collecting from the cuttings agency and compiling them for him to go through, and they were still coming in, as different editions were published in awakening time zones. He passed them to Johnny as he finished going through each piece.

'I'll send more to your laptop as they come in.'

'Thank you, Kirsten.'

It was a huge success – that was obvious from the articles. The launch had gone as he had planned. Now the real work would begin – making sure that Luxury lived up to the expectations of the visitors, that the privacy there remained absolutely secure, and that it was able to cover the repayments to the investors. He wasn't expecting it to turn a large profit, if any, but it had to pay for itself. And there were all his other properties to attend to, and new investments to make, new plans to dream up. He was excited at the thought.

Then there was his family. Thinking about them didn't fill him with the pride and joy that it should. They were all worrying him, in one way or another. Charlie with his lack of direction and interest in anything other than hanging out with his band, Lucia with her increasingly racy modelling jobs. And Maryanne . . . Maryanne. His perfect night had been marred by the tawdry behaviour of a woman whom he had once thought unable to ever make a move that wasn't 100 percent graceful, by whom he had been entranced – partly because of her unerring ability to say and do the exact right thing.

He had tried to give her everything. He really had. Had worked to provide her with beautiful homes, wardrobes full of designer clothes, the ability to do anything she wanted. She could go anywhere, buy anything, and still she wasn't satisfied, it seemed. He was at a loss to know what to do.

'You haven't been there. You haven't been with us for a long time.'

Maryanne's words rang in his ears. Was she right? He had tried, all night, as he lay awake, wired with adrenaline from both the party and their argument, to write her words off as drunken ramblings, wild accusations from a woman who was clearly out of control. But he couldn't. In the end he had given up on sleep and got up, flinging his bedroom doors open to let in the sweet, warm air and listen to the silence of the island – *his* magical island. L'île des Violettes was sleeping. The only sound was the ocean swishing against the sand. Despite his turmoil, Logan felt calmed. He padded outside and walked down to the beach, his way lit by the lanterns that were still burning and the morning sunshine and he strolled along the edge of the ocean, letting the water lap over his bare feet and his toes sink into the soft sand.

Maryanne's words had hit home. It was true – he didn't know his children, not as real people, as adults. And it was also true that he seemed to have done the one thing he had always promised himself he wouldn't do. How – *how* could he have been so blind, not to see that he was retreading the footsteps of his father? Cutting himself off, becoming more and more disconnected over the years. It didn't matter that it was work, not whisky that Logan had been burying himself in; the end result was the same. A fragmented family and a whole heap of regret. Not for the first time in his life he found himself wishing he had been born into a different family, one with a normal set of parents and a brother or sister. Ah, what was the point? That was what Johnny had had, and look what had happened to them.

But he could fix it, couldn't he? There was still time to fix things with Charlie and Lucia, if not with Maryanne. The thought hit him in the chest. He didn't think he could fix things with Maryanne. Not just fix her, but *them*. He had never thought that it would come to this. Other people grew apart, let life get in the way of love, but not them. He had fought so hard to win her. How could he have let her go?

He carried on walking. By now the island had begun to wake up and he could hear the sound of voices, of glasses clinking as waiters carried breakfast trays to weary, party-heavy guests. Logan knew he should go back to his suite, meet with Johnny and Kirsten who would be waiting for him. The clear blue sea sparkled brightly, reflecting white-hot light that pricked his eyes. Eyes that were suddenly pricking with their own saltwater. He wiped the back of his hand over his face. The sun was making his eyes water. That was it. That must be it.

Now, he shook off the sadness of the night. He had to focus on the present, on the future. He turned to Johnny. 'I think we can safely say that went rather well.'

In her suite across the hall from Logan's, Maryanne was sitting at her dressing table, drinking an iced coffee and also looking at the headlines. Instead of taking them in properly, she was going over and over the night before in her mind. She was ashamed of the way she had behaved. Ashamed that she had lied – to Logan, and the children, and most of all to herself. Ashamed that the security guard had seen her in such a state, ashamed that she couldn't really remember getting back to her room, ashamed that she was sitting here, in one of the most beautiful places in the world, with hands trembling from the poison she had put into her body, with her throat raw and her eyes puffy from crying, and still craving drugs. Something to fill that aching void in her – in her heart? Her soul?

But even more than the shame, she felt a terrible, wrenching sadness. She had well and truly lost her way, and seemed to have lost her husband as well. Half a joke floated through her head. What was it? Oh yes, it was when she was at school, and she'd told a group of girls who were teasing her that she'd lost her father, not wanting to say that he'd left. Hoping that by using the word 'lost' they would assume that he'd died, and leave her alone. Instead: 'How careless of you,' they'd said. 'How do you lose a whole person? Did he fall down the back of the wardrobe?' And they had twirled off, giggling and laughing. Ah well, she thought, the joke is on you again now, Maryanne. She'd pushed Logan too far, pushed him away, until he had gone – and she didn't know how to bring him back.

Hating herself, she poured a shot of brandy into her coffee and swallowed a painkiller. Just to get her home. Then she picked up the phone and dialled her butler.

'Please have the jet made ready. I'm going back to London. No, not with Logan. Alone.'

Maryanne wasn't the only one preparing to leave the island. Nicolo had been up since five, as usual, though in fact he hadn't been to bed since the party had continued well into the morning. He had marked the beginning of a new day, however, by returning to his suite, showering, exercising, showering again, before ringing the bell for his butler and informing him that he would breakfast on the beach.

Now, Nicolo folded his napkin, finished his glass of water, and stared along the sand. He had come here to see inside the kingdom, and now he was going to bring Logan down off his gilded perch. From inside the very heart of his empire. It was time.

Elise was sitting by their private pool, drinking from a glass of lychee juice. She could hear Bill on his iPhone inside the room, talking to some broker or dealer or whatever. She closed her eyes and let her head tip back.

'No, it's fine, needs must. Yup, OK, *ciao*.'

Bill's footsteps came up behind her. She waited. Sensed his presence. Remembered the night before. When they had got back to their suite, late at night, he had pulled her to the ground almost as soon as they had walked in the door and fucked her on the cool marble floor of the living room. Her shoulder had been jammed up

225

against a chair leg, and had hurt her as he pushed himself into her over and over, but he hadn't cared. And she had learned a long time ago that to tell him he was hurting her had no effects – if anything, in certain moods, it made things worse. She was so tired of living her life according to Bill's moods, under the shadow of fear. The first time he had hit her she had explained it away. Classic. It was an accident, he was passionate in bed, he had got carried away. The second time, she had told him she would leave if it happened again. By the third time, they both knew she was bluffing. By then she had given birth to Danny, an event which, despite bringing her so much joy, also ensured that Bill held all the cards. 'I won't let you leave with him,' he would whisper. 'If you go, you go alone. I will never let you take my son away from me.'

And she had looked around herself, and realised that she was trapped.

She looked up at him now from behind her sunglasses. 'What is it?' she asked. 'Crisis at the office?'

'I have to go back. It's Johnny's account, some issue with the people I left in charge. Useless twats. But as it's him . . .'

'If you have to, you have to.'

'Indeed. I want you to stay though.'

She nodded, and smiled briefly. *Thank God Thank God Thank God*. 'OK. I'd like that.'

'Need the rest, do you?' he sneered at her. She didn't say anything.

'Make yourself useful for once,' he went on. 'Stay here and be nice to Johnny. Make friends with him – with Logan as well, if you can get anywhere near him. They could be important for me in the future.'

He puffed out his chest. Bill was proud of his status at Crown, enjoyed knowing that he was one of the biggest traders there.

'Just try not to embarrass me,' he snapped.

Elise nodded. 'I'll do my best.'

As Bill was leaving the villa, his bag slung over one shoulder, he paused. 'Oh, Lisey?'

'Yes?'

'Can you give me your swipe card for the apartment? I've lost mine. I'll get them to set another up by the time you get back.'

'What have you done with it?'

'If I knew that . . .'

'All right, hang on.'

She took her bag from the wardrobe where it hung, and rifled through her credit cards, gym card, driving licence . . . until she found the pass that allowed them into the car park and main entrance of their apartment block. 'Here.'

As he reached for it she spotted something else in there, a folded piece of notepaper. The message she had taken for Bill before dinner the other night. She paused, and then clicked the bag shut and handed him the card. 'Bye. See you in a few.'

He nodded and took her face in his hand, holding her chin between his strong fingers. 'And no gambling, remember?'

She shook her head a fraction – she couldn't move it much more than that. 'Of course not,' she murmured. 'We agreed, didn't we?'

He kissed her forehead. 'Yes. We agreed.' And then he left.

Why had she not given him the note? Elise asked herself. Even though she'd forgotten about it, it wasn't the end of the world; she could just tell Bill what had happened, pass him the message. But something held her back. Something that niggled at the back of her mind.

People who worked for banks, especially offshore banks who dealt with important clients every day, didn't leave messages with people's wives. And then she realised. They didn't think they were leaving a message with someone's wife who knew nothing about the account in question. The man had said, 'Unless you would like to instruct us yourself?' He wouldn't say that if it were an account of Bill's, or something to do with Bill's work. He would only say that if the account was a joint one, or one that she had privileges on, for example. But why would Bill set up a joint account, or one in her name, without telling her?

Elise picked up the phone and called the suite's butler. 'Has my husband's plane gone already? I forgot to tell him something.'

'Ah, sorry, Mrs McAllister, they're already in the air. I can pass on a message for you?'

'No, no. It's not urgent. Thank you.'

She put the receiver down in its cradle then ran, racing through the bedroom and through the French doors and leaping fully dressed into the pool, letting out a great whoop of laughter as she did so. She sank into the water, feeling it close over her head and fully submerge her. Her dress floated out around her and she kicked her legs. As she bobbed back up and her head broke the surface of the pool again, she laughed again with joy, running a hand through her wet hair. It was as if the island had been shrouded in clouds and suddenly the sun had come out and she could see how beautiful it really was. Not just as somewhere luxurious, full of indulgence, but as somewhere almost mystical. She swam a length of the pool, savouring the thought of three whole days by herself, and then hauled herself out. She was determined not to waste a single moment of it.

The hotel was wonderful, and she loved it, but it was the island itself that really interested Elise. L'île des Violettes had a wildness to it, somehow, bubbling underneath the luxe surface. Wanting to explore, she set off along the beach, in shorts, bikini and T-shirt, intending to see how far round the island's perimeter she could get.

Leaving the beach cabanas behind her, she headed towards the jetty where they had landed what seemed like weeks ago. Time had slowed. Sitting on the end, she dangled her legs in the water and watched as a school of tiny silver fish flocked around her feet. Danny would have been transfixed by them: he loved fish. Danny. Her heart sank and she had a sudden flash of missing him and worrying about what she was going to do. She stood, started walking again. Don't think about that now, she told herself. There's time enough for that.

Further along the beach, the strip of sand narrowed and the undergrowth next to it began to get thicker. Elise couldn't figure out what type of plant or tree it was made up of; it had twisted roots like gnarled fingers, and smelled faintly musty. It was hotter over this side of the island, hotter underfoot – obviously the temperature-controlled beach only went so far.

Elise put her flip-flops back on. The sand had petered out and there was just a stretch of rocky ground rounding the corner. She should probably turn back now, but something made her want to keep exploring. Her calves ached from walking on the sand, and she could feel a patch of skin on the back of her neck burning, but she was enjoying the sensation of her muscles working. Impulsively, she began to clamber over the rocks.

By the time she had managed to get up the rocks and through the patch of what she had now realised must be mangrove trees, Elise was beginning to realise that she had been rather foolish. She wasn't really dressed for exploring; she was wearing the wrong shoes (as usual) and as well as having applied her suncream rather patchily in her enthusiasm to get going, she had forgotten to bring any water. And now she was very hot, very thirsty, and very tired. More worryingly, the tide seemed to be coming in, and she wasn't sure she had the energy to get back over the rocks if it came up any higher. Oh, damn. Should she try and get back now, or should she push on – see if she could get round another way?

Push on, she decided. There had to be another way through. And if the worst came to the worst, and she did get stuck, at least she'd be in the shade. It wouldn't come to that, though. Would it?

She carried on, getting hotter and thirstier and more panicked with every step. Her flip-flops were rubbing between her toes. And then, as she stumbled over a mangrove root and cried out, she looked ahead of her and saw that she was standing on the edge of a clearing.

'Oh!'

It was a large area, with a sandy floor, and what looked like clusters of violets everywhere, and there was a derelict building at its centre. The air felt cooler here, and she could hear the sound of running water. God, she was thirsty. She walked towards the sound, trying to locate it. Was it a stream? Oh no, she wasn't hallucinating, was she?

When she walked around the crumbling building, she saw that the clearing opened out further, and there in front of her was a waterfall. It splashed down into a pool of clear, fresh water at its base. Running forward, Elise lowered her head and drank, then took off her T-shirt and submerged her body in the pool, closing her eyes underwater for the second time that day, in sheer relief. When she emerged, she opened them wide in surprise. For there, standing in front of her, was Logan Barnes himself. He held a hand out to her and nodded towards a small hut.

'Here. I've got some towels over there. I think I can even rustle you up a clean shirt.'

She took his hand and let him pull her up.

'Thank you,' she said, flustered. 'Um, sorry. I got a bit lost.'

'Didn't you just. This isn't part of the hotel, really, you know. But I'll forgive you this once.'

He winced as he noticed the red skin on her neck and shoulder. 'Ouch. We need to get that covered up. Come on.'

He led her to the hut, which contained a desk, an old armchair and a cupboard full of basic supplies. He pulled out a towel and a long-sleeved man's cotton shirt, and handed them to her.

'That'll have to do until we can get you back to the hotel. How on earth did you get over here, anyhow?'

She blushed. 'I've been exploring. Oh God, I sound about six. Sorry. It's just – there's something about the island that makes me feel . . .' She trailed off under the intensity of his gaze.

'Go on. Makes you feel what?'

She thought for a second. 'Makes me feel as though it's calling me in. As though it's mine, somehow, and I have to go deeper. I couldn't resist. Like the Sirens who lured all those men to their deaths. It's . . . it's magical, isn't it?'

Logan continued to stare at her and she laughed, embarrassed. 'Oh dear. You must think I'm quite mad. Maybe I've got a bit of heatstroke.'

'No. I don't think you're mad at all,' he said. 'I think you're the first person I've met who understands why I had to buy this island.'

She had been thinking about him – hadn't been able to stop since they had met at the waterfall that morning – and now here he was, standing in front of her by the oyster bar.

'Another drink?' He nodded his head at the waiter before she'd had a chance to reply. The waiter brought her a white peach Bellini and Logan's beer.

'*Santé.*' He tilted the bottle towards her in the air and held his face up to the slight breeze that was moving over the terrace. 'Better than a rainy night in London, no?'

'Better than anywhere I can imagine, actually.'

'Thank you for agreeing to join me for dinner,' Logan said. 'You certainly look more relaxed than you did this morning.'

She didn't just look relaxed, she looked exquisitely beautiful, he thought. Her simple silk dress fell in loose folds around her slim body, and even the patches of angry sunburn couldn't detract from her glowing beauty.

'I'm so embarrassed about that,' she told him. 'Crashing into your private area, like some kind of demented Davy Crockett.'

'Not at all. I'm impressed you made it there. It must have taken you a while.'

'It did, yes. Thank you for bringing me back the easy way.'

When she had dried off and drunk some more water, Logan had led her down a hidden pathway through the mangrove trees and over a little wooden bridge to where a small speedboat was moored. He had then delivered her personally back to her private section of beach in front of her suite.

They chatted for a bit about the hotel, and he listened as she described her excitement when she first saw the room, and how she'd felt this morning when she'd woken up to the sight of the sea from her bed. Had laughed as she'd told him about feeling like a child at Christmas as she'd opened the wardrobe to discover all the beautiful things inside. Her smile suddenly died. For a few minutes she had forgotten about Bill, his threats, everything. Suddenly it all came back to her. It was like that – caught her unawares. But what was wrong with her having dinner with Logan? Bill had told her to be nice to him and Johnny.

'Sorry,' she said awkwardly. 'I must be boring you, banging on about how wonderful this place is. You don't need me to tell you. You created it.'

'I promise, you're not boring me. Nothing could be further from the truth.'

There was a pause.

'So, your husband was called away.'

'Unfortunately so.'

There was another pause while they both considered just how fortunate it was. Then Logan took charge.

'You like seafood, yes? Good. Let's go for dinner.'

He led her down the sweeping white steps of the oyster bar terraces, through the lobby of the main building and out of a side door. Elise followed him, not knowing where they were heading, but he had an air of authority that made her feel safe. They'd made their way down a path lined with gardenia, their white flowers glowing in the moonlight and their scent filling the air, and then the path opened out on to a small beach where a speed-boat was bobbing in the shallows. She could see the driver behind the wheel. The boat took them a short way out into the ocean. The sea was dark and Elise revelled in the silence. She watched the hotel's lights become smaller.

'Good view of the place from out here, isn't it?' Logan said.

'Yes, wonderful. Like something from a fairytale. I wish my son could see it. He'd love it here.'

'How old is he?'

'He's six. His name's Danny.'

'Good age. Enjoy it. Won't be long before you're dealing with a stroppy teenager.'

She laughed. 'I know.'

'You'll have to bring him here.'

She didn't reply.

'Here we are.'

They had reached what she could see was a tiny white sandbar rising up out of the sea near a slightly larger island. He took her hand to steady her as she stood and then, just as she was wondering whether he was expecting her to wade through the water to dry land, there was a soft whirring sound and an inflatable walkway unfolded from the back of the boat to the sand.

'Slip off your heels, if you don't mind?' Logan said. And then, as she stepped gingerly on to the structure in bare feet: 'Don't worry, it's quite safe. It's got struts that dig themselves into the seabed and support it, so you won't fall in, I promise.'

Elise grinned to herself. So far, Logan Barnes was living up to his reputation as the man with the golden touch. It seemed he'd even found a way to walk on water.

On the beach a low, round table was laid simply, with cushions to sit on next to it. Champagne flutes caught the light from a hundred tiny candles that flickered in the surrounding sand. A few metres away, a chef worked behind a large barbecue, flames licking up around a wok on one side, his tongs turning something over on another area of the grill, before he moved swiftly to chop something on a preparation surface to one side of his workstation.

'Wow.'

Logan patted a cushion and Elise sat down. Next to the table was a mobile wine bar. Made from polished stainless steel, it had two temperature-controlled wine cellars underneath complete with ice-bucket suspended from one side, glass holders, and a wooden serving board. Logan noticed her looking at it.

'A complete self-indulgence, I'm afraid. I like to have a choice of wine with dinner.'

She gave him a look, and he had the good grace to colour slightly.

'You are so smooooth, Mr Barnes,' she said cheekily.

He chucked a napkin at her. It was a long time since anyone had laughed at him, and he liked it. He poured a glass of Krug and handed it to her, and they sat, sipping their drinks as the sea lapped gently against the shore. They were surrounded by water; it was like sitting in the middle of the ocean, Elise thought happily. A crab scuttled across the sand.

Logan pointed to the dark water. 'Look.'

She peered forwards.

'Hang on, you'll see them better if it's darker,' and he motioned to the chef, who extinguished the flares. Elise gasped as thousands of tiny lights seemed to fill the sea, flickering in the inky water.

'What are they?'

'Flashlight fish. They light up to find food and communicate with each other. Clever little things, aren't they?'

She didn't answer, just watched, transfixed.

Then: 'Why have you brought me here?' she asked suddenly.

'Because you're too beautiful to look so sad. It's peaceful here and I thought you'd like it. Hey, and it's my island. My responsibility to make sure all my guests are properly looked after. That better?'

She raised her eyebrows in silent acknowledgement. The flares were lit again and the fish disappeared once more, and then the chef arrived at the table and placed a platter of seafood on a silver stand in its centre – papillon oysters, razor clams, enormous prawns fresh from the sea, and Elise realised how hungry she was.

For the next hour, they feasted on a procession of exquisite dishes: soft-shell crabs sauteed with chilli; a cup of lobster bisque, scallops griddled with lemon juice squeezed over them and served in their shells; curls of baby squid in a tempura batter; slices of fresh tuna sashimi cut thin as rice paper. All around them, the ocean from which their dinner had been caught murmured, soft and inviting. They drank a crisp Sancerre with their dinner. And they talked and laughed as Elise couldn't remember laughing for years. Laughter that made her cheeks ache. After they finished eating the chef melted away, and they were left alone on the sandbank. The soft chug of the boat receded.

'Don't worry. They'll come back for us whenever we want – I've got a radio.'

'I'm not worried.' And she wasn't. She'd forgotten about Bill, about her worries for the future, and it was just her and Logan in the most beautiful place she had ever been in.

'So, did you always want to be a phenomenally successful hotel tycoon?' she asked.

'No, I wanted to be an astronaut. Spent my time in the classroom dreaming about going to the moon.'

'Oh. Well, it's probably a good thing that you went into hotels instead. Much safer.'

'Safer physically, certainly. It's not without its dangers though. Financially, it's all about risk. Luxury – the island – riskiest thing I've ever done. But worth it. Now, what about you? What did *you* want to be when you grew up?'

'A mother. Which I am.' She hesitated. 'I never had a dream job, a big ambition, you know? I just wanted to be happy. I'm not sure how I ended up . . .'

She broke off, and looked down at her lap. There it was, Logan thought. The sadness in her eyes. He decided to take a risk, and he reached out and touched her hand.

'You haven't ended up anywhere. Everything's negotiable, Elise, don't forget that.'

'I just never imagined myself as this corporate wife,' Elise said quietly. 'I'm on the committee for the Crown charity ball – and I have no idea how that happened. How I turned into the sort of woman that actually *did* that. I loathe every second of it, but it's part of my job – if you can call it that. When I get back home I have to find a venue for the ball. Somewhere for hundreds of fat bankers and their thin wives to sit and eat foie gras and pretend they care about the charity that it's all in aid of, when they've probably never even heard of it. And I just can't think of anything more depressing.'

She stopped. 'Sorry. Bit of a rant.'

'Well, I can help you there. Not with the fat bankers and their thin wives, sadly. But with a venue, at least. Bill's been pretty helpful to Johnny, I know. I'm sure LBI can do something to help the cause.'

'I wasn't hinting . . .'

'I know you weren't. It's fine. I'll arrange it. Should win you some brownie points with the rest of the committee at least. In my experience they tend to be a pretty terrifying lot . . .'

Logan took a bottle of cognac from the wine station and poured some into two full-bottomed glasses, allowing Elise a moment to compose herself.

'Don't feel trapped, Elise. It's never too late to make changes.'

'I *am* trapped. It's – it's complicated, my situation.'

Logan took another risk. Turned her wrist over. The bruise on it was darker blue now, and it almost glowed in the moonlight. 'Complicated because of things like this?'

She pulled her hand back and shivered. 'Bill isn't a happy man,' she said. 'Successful, yes. Happy? No. And it doesn't always get expressed in the most . . . healthy way.' Elise swallowed the lump in her throat. She had never admitted it before.

Logan tried to contain the anger that he felt rising up inside him, anger that this lovely woman was treated like this. 'Have you thought of leaving?'

'All the time. But I can't.'

'Danny?'

'Yes.'

He understood, she could tell. She was grateful that he simply nodded, didn't ask her to explain why, or fire questions at her. Just understood. He sipped his drink. 'Well, he's not the only successful but unhappy man. We don't all go around beating our wives, however.'

'I thought you were . . .'

'Happily married? The golden Barnes family, like you see on *General Manager*, right?'

She shrugged. 'I guess.'

'I was, once. Very happy.'

'What happened?'

'Honestly, Elise? The truth is, I still really don't know.'

She had spent seven hours with Logan, and the only time he had touched her was to help her in and out of the boat, and when he had gently patted her hand and examined her wrist. Her skin remembered that touch later, as she tossed in the cool sheets of her bed, sleepless at dawn. Despite herself, she imagined his hand moving up her arm, tracing his fingers along her shoulder, down over her breasts . . . and drawing her lips close to his . . .

Chapter Sixteen

Mark and Logan walked past the front of the hotel, towards Luxury's gates. Mark was as perfectly groomed as always, even in the midday heat. Logan was ready to leave, to fly back to London. He would far rather stay here, on his island. The fact that Elise would be here for another day was an additional draw. But he had obligations, he reminded himself. Luxury wasn't his only property, and he needed to talk to Maryanne face to face as well. As for Mark, he was glad to be staying here. His wife was on the campaign trail, which meant the house was full of flyers and worthy women waiting to hand them out.

'Don't worry, I'll hold the fort here,' he told Logan. 'Everything seems to be running smoothly, on the whole. A few teething problems, but nothing we hadn't anticipated.'

Logan loved the way Mark spoke. So proper. So very English.

'Good man. Everything needs to be running perfectly for the paying guests.'

'Exactly. It will be. Look, I'd better get on. I'll see you, Logan.'

Logan knew he would be as good as his word – Mark was a stickler for detail. But he seemed uncomfortable around him recently. Logan hoped he wasn't going to resign or anything. He had come to rely on Mark to pick up on the sort of fine detail he himself sometimes missed in his quest to see the big picture. Logan made a mental note to have a chat with him when they were next both in the same country at the same time to make sure there was no problem. He couldn't afford to lose him.

All the way back to London in his jet, Logan's mind was full of *her*. Every few minutes he would have to drag his attention back to what he was meant to be doing, but before long she would come into his head again, and his heart would leap and his veins would contract with excitement. She was extraordinary. Intelligent, vital, captivating. He could see the future in her eyes, and he sensed that he was part of it.

The phone rang. It was Rachel. 'I have Fergus Chilman on the line for your interview, Logan.'

'Thank you, Rachel, put him through.'

Fergus was an old friend, and the ghostwriter who was helping Logan write his autobiography. Though he had fallen on boozily hard times recently, Fergus was still a seasoned journalist and interviewer. He'd already prised more details out of Logan about some areas of his life than he was entirely happy with. He was going to have to try and concentrate, stop mooning like a teenager over Elise McAllister, otherwise before he knew it he'd be telling Fergus all about that as well.

'Fergus!' he said heartily. 'All ready for the next instalment?'

'At your service. We were up to your college years. Here, bloody good party that was, mate.'

'So you enjoyed yourself?'

'Bash of the century. Everyone's still talking about it.'

'So they bloody well should be. Cost me enough.'

'I bet. OK, we were up to your time at Harvard. Single guy, Ivy League college . . . there must be some good stories there.'

'I worked hard and was in bed every night by ten.'

'Weren't we all, chum weren't we all. Come on, dish the dirt. Your publishers haven't paid you that stonking great advance so we can all read about how many fucking hotels you've opened, have they?'

Logan roared with laughter. 'OK, OK. But I'm not putting too much sex in. I'm a married man, you know.' Ah yes, a married man . . . Was he behaving like one, though? No time for that now.

'Weren't always, though, were you? Anyhow, you can make it up if you like. Doesn't matter – important thing is, people feel that they're getting a glimpse behind the scenes.'

'All right, I give in. There was this one time . . .'

As Logan was flying back from Luxury, on top of the world, revelling in the stories that had been written about him, someone else was also thinking about those stories. Colette Hardy had read them

238

all, on the screen on her small laptop, sitting in a chair next to her mother's bed. Logan Barnes got to carry on as if she and her mom didn't count, as if what had happened to them – what he had done to them – didn't count.

Flaunting his success, his smug face, his spoiled children. Not for long though. Not for long.

All the way back from the island, Nicolo stewed and fumed and plotted as Vienna slept next to him. For years now, he had more or less managed to keep the rivalry between himself and Logan under control – the usual tussling of two successful entrepreneurs with a history. It was hardly anything out of the ordinary, after all. But somewhere deep inside his heart, the flame had been kept alive. He had stoked it occasionally, if he was honest. Every so often he would get up in the night and spend hours on the internet, charting Logan's upward progress. Thinking of new ways to yap at his heels. Allowing himself sporadic, blissful binges where he tried to chip away at the facade of Logan's brilliance.

Once he had managed to bribe one of the secretaries working in LBI's head office to steal the plans for a new casino in Michigan, pipping Logan to the post by submitting them to the planning department before he had a chance to do so. Logan had sued him and they had ended up in court for almost a year. Nicolo didn't care – he had got in there first, and he was happy to spend time tying Logan up in legal knots.

Logan had retaliated by getting the construction of the place stopped: suddenly none of Nicolo's workers seemed to have the correct visas or paperwork, meaning that he was forced to spend millions of dollars sorting the mess out.

Then there had been the time that Logan had reignited the flame himself by giving an interview to *Forbes* in which he strongly hinted that Nicolo came from a family with links to the Maltese mafia. Nicolo may not have had mafia links but he had as keen a sense of family honour as any Don – and he had lashed out by giving a similar interview, hinting even more strongly that Logan's own business was founded on dirty money. 'Look at the paper trail,' he had been quoted as saying, 'and the truth will out. It's all very well smearing my name, but maybe Barnes should tread more carefully, if he doesn't want people to start digging and joining the dots. It's not hard to see how hotels and casinos can be used to move money around. I should know – I've been accused of the same thing myself in the past.'

Each time, after Nicolo had given in to the impulse for revenge – revenge that he had already taken but was unable to stop taking – he felt disgusted with himself. Like an addict, he would swear off his drug of choice, telling himself that he must have got it out of his system by now, that it was time to move on, leave the past in the past. He wanted to be able to let it go, to pour all of his energies into his own business, his own personal life, instead of being compulsively drawn to Logan's. His business was hugely successful – Nicolo's early flair for marketing and salesmanship had grown stronger as he grew older. He dominated the Californian hotel industry; his properties were hi-tech and appealed to young, flashy travellers looking for a good time. He had every material thing that he could want, an art collection that was the envy of many a gallery, invitations to every premiere and dinner he could fit into his schedule. But he didn't have anything, or anyone, to occupy his heart. He'd never married. Never, since Maryanne, had a relationship with a woman who meant anything to him, whom he could allow himself to trust or rely on. That day, when he had sat on the scratchy carpet of his apartment, the engagement ring he had been about to present her with in his hand, had changed him for ever. He had kept his heart closed, barricaded shut against anyone who tried to make their way in. He could not take that kind of risk again.

So instead of love and companionship he had filled his life with work, with possessions and with a full schedule that should have absorbed all of his attention. And it did, most of the time. He didn't have any real friends, but he had plenty of people who were interested enough in his money and power to pretend they were, and no shortage of women willing to share his bed. Los Angeles was convenient like that. But then every so often, just when he had put it all to the back of his mind, something would spark it off and the cycle that Nicolo had been subject to for over twenty years would start up all over again.

No one had taken it all that seriously. Just two more tycoons, full of testosterone and ambition, playing out their feud in magazines and courtrooms and boardrooms. No one who read the stories and speculated as to which man was on top this time knew what lay behind it; the history that bound them together and which had driven them apart. No one knew the damage that their duelling had already done – no one could have envisaged the damage it would still do.

The worst time yet had been the screening of *General Manager*. Nicolo had been driving on Sunset, talking to his accountant on the hands-free, when he first saw their faces on the billboard poster. Logan Barnes, Johnny Stokes and Mark Mallory. Thirty feet high, they loomed over the highway, arms crossed in front of them, their expressions severe. *General Manager*, the lettering at the bottom proclaimed, *coming soon. Who will be the first to Check Out?*

'I'll call you back,' he had told his accountant, and had pulled into a side road where he could park his car.

He walked round to the front of the billboard. The three faces stared down at him. He stood tall, but was dwarfed in comparison. The irony of this was not lost on him. Logan, the man who had ruined his life. Johnny, the man who had watched while he did so. Mark, the man who had apparently taken his place in the trio. So, Logan was throwing his hat well and truly into the media arena, was he? Jumping on the celebrity gravy train. Nicolo supposed he fancied himself as the Gordon Ramsay of hotels, or somesuch. It made sense. Business life was all about the brand, these days, and TV and the media was the quickest way of developing that brand. Nicolo lit a cigarette, and continued to gaze at the poster. They were going to be everywhere. The show would screen in a few months and their faces would be splashed over the TV, in magazine profiles, on the internet. There would be books, merchandise, promotions. How would he bear it? How could he sit and watch as they raced into the limelight, Logan with his perfect family, Johnny with his perfect bachelor life, Mark with his perfect English Gentleman act? It was so unfair. He should have been there. It should have been him, him married to Maryanne, him as the third member of the group, him with friends and a wife and a real life, not just a pretence of one.

He ground his cigarette into the sidewalk. His lungs felt like they were burning, his skin was crawling. He walked quickly to his car, and sat behind the wheel before starting the engine again, allowing himself five minutes of pure, intense rage; letting it flow through his veins like white-hot lava.

Then he went home, and began to make plans.

The talk of an island, recently purchased by LBI and in the process of being turned into the most exclusive and private hotel in the world, started as a whisper. A whisper that made Nicolo's ears prick up when he first heard it. An island? Secluded, cut off . . . could it be the same island? Industry chatter, in boardrooms and hotel lobbies and in the trade press grew louder. Vienna had mentioned it that time as well. A magical place, that Logan had been lusting after for years . . .

It had to be L'île des Violettes. The place where they had gone together, the three of them, and where they had vowed they would return – but as owners, not trespassers. Two of them had returned, as they had said they would. One had been left behind.

'One man with a dream, at pleasure, shall go forth and conquer a crown . . . and three with a new song's measure . . . can trample an empire down.'

This time, he was determined to prove that one man could also trample an empire down.

Colette would have got the latest batch of articles he had sent her by now, and the money. He had been sending her money for years, but never that much. Enough to pay the bills, just. Not enough to make things comfortable, especially not with a woman who needed as much care as her mother did. It was a glorious entertainment of his own making. The girl nursed a hatred for Logan that ran almost as deep as his own, and Nicolo had taken care to feed it. He had come across her almost by accident. One of the private detectives that he had hired to dig up dirt on Logan had found a reference to her and her mother in some court papers, from the aftermath of the accident, and had tracked them down, seeing if there was anything there that Nicolo might be able to use. She had been just eighteen then. Apparently she blamed Logan for everything that had gone wrong in her life – her mother's accident, of course, and all the repercussions: the grinding tedium of poverty, the opportunities the girl had missed because of having to care for her mother, the jobs she could not do and the childhood that had been snatched away from her. She laid it all at Logan Barnes's door.

It hadn't been difficult for Nicolo to exploit that. He wanted to make sure she retained a keen sense of how unfair life was, of the gulf between her life and the Barnes family's life. As Logan's profile grew, so did Colette's fury and desire for revenge. And now, he had offered her the ideal opportunity to get her revenge, and the money to do it with – as well as the promise of more to come further down the line.

She had jumped at it, as he had known she would. He'd been waiting for years for the right time to use her, and now that time had come.

It was a week since Elise had left L'île des Violettes, and the whole experience felt a bit like a dream. It had been wonderful to see Danny again, less wonderful to see Bill. She sat at her desk now, drinking her morning coffee, holding her cup carefully. Her finger was swollen, but she didn't think it was broken. She could move it at least, that was something. He had bent it back as far as he could, until she had screamed with pain. This time it was because she had gone out for dinner with Delly leaving Danny with Ines but without telling him where she was going. The argument when she got back had been terrible. He'd accused her of going to a casino, and she'd been forced, in the end, to phone up the restaurant and make up some excuse so that they would confirm she had been there, while he listened on the extension. She didn't go to the casino any more, it was too risky. She gambled online, wiping her history every time she shut the computer down, transferring her winnings to the secret savings account she had set up specifically for that purpose. Her nest egg. Her running-away money. It was growing.

She was sure the arguments were getting worse. Or was it her? Was she reaching the end of what she could put up with, what she was prepared to suffer? Could she be getting ready to take the biggest risk of her life? She didn't know. But she did know that something was going to give before too long.

Now, though, she had things to do. Phone calls to make. Danny was safely at school. The house was quiet. Taking the piece of notepaper from her hand bag, she dialled the number on it. As she waited for it to connect she ran through what she would say. *Good morning, this is Elise McAllister, I'm returning your call from* – no, she couldn't say that. *Hello, I'm calling about . . . it's Elise McAllister.* Gah. She was just going to have to do it and hope for the best. *Do it now, before you bottle it,* she told herself. *Deep breath . . .*

'Good morning, Lenegan and Pearson.'

Oh, shit. No going back.

'Oh, good morning, can I speak with Seth Wharton, please?'

'Who can I say is calling?'

'Mrs . . .' Her voice faltered, and she almost hung up the phone. *Oh, for goodness' sake, woman, stop being such a pussy.* 'Elise McAllister.'

'Hold the line, please.'

She let her breath out slowly through pursed lips.

'Mrs McAllister, a very good morning to you. How can I help?'

'Mr Wharton, I'm just calling to check whether my husband got back to you. There's been some confusion.'

'No, he didn't, and I didn't want to harass him. I assumed one of you would let me know when you were ready. After all, the money's not going anywhere.'

'Indeed.' She stopped, suddenly unsure. 'So . . .'

'Shall I recap briefly? I just need to know whether you'd like the proceeds of the sale of the shares, which amounts to three million pounds sterling, to remain with us, or to be transferred to your joint account, as we have done previously a few times, of course, or whether you have some other instruction.'

Christ. What was going on?

She cleared her throat. 'Hmm. Yes. Please do send it to the joint account.'

'Certainly. If you can just confirm the password. Sorry, but I have to ask . . .'

'I quite understand.' She thought furiously. What would he use? None of his usual ones that she knew, presumably. Not her name, not Danny's, not his mother's . . .

'Sorry to keep you, it's just we have a few, I'm just checking.'

'Take your time.'

Then she realised. The password would be something he thought she would have chosen.

'Elise loves Bill,' she said, and held her breath. Did she know her husband well enough?

Seth chuckled. It appeared she did.

'Very touching, if you don't mind me saying so, Mrs McAllister.'

She'd had Seth forward copies of the recent transfers to her phone to the secret email address that she used to play the occasional game of online poker and had stared at the amounts of money that had come into this account set up in their name, and gone out again, into an account in his.

And then she had made another phone call, to her new friend Delly who, as she had suspected, had all sorts of ideas about exactly why someone might set up a secret bank account, and how they would be able to do so.

Finally, she dialled the number of LBI Hotels, and asked to be put through to Logan. She was going to take him up on his offer of a venue for the Crown charity ball. Bill had told her to get more involved in Crown affairs, hadn't he? And he'd instructed her to be nice to Johnny and Logan when they were at Luxury. She was just going along with his wishes. Without realising it, Bill, who expended so much energy trying to shut his wife in, had opened a door for her, through which she could see a sliver of light.

Delly and Elise walked around the hotel ballroom, their heels clicking on the polished floor, listening to the events manager describing the features and benefits. The room was perfect – large, with a soaring ceiling and balcony running round the room, with smaller bars and lounges situated off the main ballroom. The event would have the run of the hotel for the night, according to Logan's instructions, the manager explained. She was a very short woman who nodded briskly as she spoke, as though she was ticking off everything she said on a mental checklist.

'Can we organise priority booking for bedrooms, as well?' Delly asked.

'If guests could please confirm whether they require a room or not a month prior to the event. If there are more guests than rooms, we will organise alternative accommodation and transport them to another of the hotels under Mr Barnes's ownership.'

'Oh, so we ...'

'Mr Barnes has informed me that the entire hotel is to be at the disposal of Crown for this event, including bedrooms, yes. Excuse me.'

The woman's phone gave a beep that was as short and efficient as its owner, and she walked to the far side of the ballroom. Delly clutched Elise's hand and Elise yelped as her fingers were spiked by the corners of Delly's diamond rings.

'You know we are going to be the talk of the town with this – the stars of the Crown committee. Nigel's going to come in his pants when I tell him I've managed to swing this one. Well, that *we've* managed to. OK – it was you, but hey. I can't believe we've got the whole hotel for the night. How long have you been screwing him, anyway?'

'Delly! I'm not screwing anyone. I only just met him. I mean, not that I'd be screwing him even if . . .' She stopped, tongue-tied.

'Don't be embarrassed, darling, everyone does it.'

'No, really. I met him at Luxury. At the launch. He took me to the beach for dinner. It was – it was amazing, actually.'

Delly looked at her sideways. 'I bet it was. The launch of Luxury, eh? Well, if you're really not fucking him, it won't be long before you are. He's obviously got it bad, and men like Logan Barnes usually get what they want. Lie back and enjoy, I say.'

Elise blushed as the manager came back to them.

'Ms McAllister, Mr Barnes requests that you call him as soon as possible. He'd like to discuss the arrangements for the event with you personally. He's sorry he couldn't be here, but you can reach him at any time on this number.' And she handed Elise an engraved business card.

Delly elbowed her in the ribs. 'Told you, darling,' she stage-whispered, before bursting into peals of dirty laughter.

Elise shot her a look that was intended to be the equivalent of a sharp kick in the shins, but which had absolutely no effect on the Sid James-esque cackle Delly was emitting.

'Thank you,' she said politely to the woman. 'I'll be sure to be in touch.'

After they'd finished looking around they had a quick drink and then Delly dashed off in a taxi to another appointment. Elise had a few hours to kill before Danny would get back from school so she walked through Covent Garden, watching the entertainers in the piazza and browsing through the stalls in the market. A string quartet was playing on the lower level, and she stood by the balustrades for a while and looked down on them, their bows making a ballet in the air as they swept over the strings. And as she watched and listened, she fingered Logan's business card in her pocket. Thinking about Logan, but also about what Delly had explained to her with reference to forward-trading.

'Forward-trading, front-running – whatever you call it, it's illegal.'

'Not just frowned on, then?' Elise had been hopeful, to start with. Maybe Bill was just pushing the boundaries? But no.

'Not just frowned on, no. Look, Elise, if you suspect someone you know of doing this, I'd be very careful that you're not involved with them in any business. You don't want to be implicated.' She'd given her friend a piercing look. 'Are you in trouble, Elise?'

'Oh no! You're sweet, Delly, and thanks for explaining – but it's not about anyone I know, God forbid!' Did she sound convincing?

Delly sipped her drink and shrugged a shoulder. 'So you phoned me from the Indian Ocean to ask – but you're not in any trouble. OK.'

Elise blushed. 'It's nothing, Delly. Honestly.'

'Well, just remember what I said. Be careful. And not just with this – with Logan as well.'

Elise had blushed even more deeply, but she didn't bother to deny anything this time.

'I'll try.'

I'll try. She realised now that she had come to a halt in the street, and was standing, gazing into space. She was jerked back to reality by a man in a bright yellow jacket trying to shove a free paper into her hands. She waved it away, and then saw that she was standing by a payphone. She hadn't used one for years, but there was something strangely comforting about picking up the heavy handset and slotting coins into the machine. She did it quickly, without thinking about it too much, because she knew that if she did, she would lose her nerve.

The call made her feel like she was taking all her exams again, waiting for the results of a pregnancy test and late for a job interview, all churned up together. Her hands shook, and she swallowed and tried to steady her breath as the phone rang twice next to her ear.

'Logan Barnes International, good afternoon.'

They met in a small Italian café in Soho, full of flirty waiters and chutes of steam from the espresso machine and little sweet pastries. She was there first, and when he walked in he noticed her straight away, her stillness and poise making her stand out amongst the frenetic hubbub of the place. She glanced up and saw him standing at the doorway, and she smiled as he went to her table.

'Hello.'

'Hi.'

She suddenly felt shy. His gaze was direct. He was probably impatient, waiting for her to get on with discussing the event. He had been brisk on the phone; he just gave her the name of a meeting place and said he would be there. She was embarrassed now, feeling that she had misread him. He was a busy man, he didn't have time to waste sitting around drinking coffee with bored housewives.

'The hotel's perfect – your events manager was so helpful.' She reached into her bag. 'If we could arrange a time to confirm the details I'll organise everything and won't bother you any more.'

'Bother me?'

She looked up. There was that piercing gaze again.

'How could you bother me? Elise, you didn't think I really wanted to talk about your husband's company bash, did you?'

'Um . . .' She didn't know where to put her eyes, so she took a large gulp of her coffee and then tried not to splutter it out again as she winced at its heat. He stood by the table for a moment, and then held his hand out to her.

'Let's go.'

She stood, and took it. He paused and looked around. They were tucked away in a corner, concealed from view. He leaned down to her, and kissed her very lightly on the lips. She didn't move a muscle. Was afraid that if she did, she would fall to pieces, or say something irredeemably stupid. The noise and movements of everyone in the café continued to swirl around them.

'Where?'

He thought for a moment. 'A better Italian place than this.'

She nodded. 'OK.'

And he led her out into the street where he hailed a black cab, telling the cabbie, 'London City Airport.'

She turned to him. 'What? No, I can't.'

'Don't worry. I'll have you home by midnight.' His smile was warm and he took her hand. 'Come on. Rome – it's no distance. It'll be an adventure.'

Elise felt nervous suddenly. However tempted she might be, she couldn't just dash off to Rome for dinner with a man she'd only met once. It was ridiculous. And, if she was really honest, faintly irritating. She took her hand back.

'No. Look, I think you've got the wrong idea about me. Maybe this was a mistake.'

'You getting in, mate, or what?' The driver gestured to the back of the cab, impatient.

Logan waved him away. 'No, sorry.'

He stared at Elise. Damn. He had ruined it, had pushed her too far.

'It's OK, we don't have to go,' he told her.

'I'm not looking for some flash, rich man to come and impress me with his money, sweep me off my feet and take me to Rome for dinner,' Elise said quietly. 'I'm a mother, I'm – I thought you knew me . . .' Then she laughed softly. 'I was about to say that I thought you knew me better than that, but why on earth would you? We don't know each other at all. Look, like I said, this was a mistake.'

She turned back to the road, her arm raising to hail a taxi.

'Please don't go.' Logan took her elbow and pulled her towards him slightly. 'Please. I'm really sorry. I . . . I haven't done this for a long time.'

She lowered her arm again and looked back at him, sighing. 'Well, I'm glad to hear that.'

'I wasn't trying to impress you,' Logan began, then corrected himself. 'Well, I was, but not because I thought you were impressed by money. I just . . . I suppose I just thought it would be fun.'

He faltered.

'Look, the truth is, I haven't got a fucking clue what I'm doing. I've been married for a hell of a long time, and now I think – no, now I'm *sure* – that my marriage is over. My wife is ill. My family is falling apart, basically. And I don't know what's happening between us, between you and me. But I think something is.'

There was a long pause, and then Elise reached up and touched the side of his face.

'Me too.' Then she grinned. 'You said you wanted to have fun, right?'

He raised an eyebrow. 'Yes.'

'Come on then. I've got an idea.'

'Five, four, three, two, one.'

The flag went down and the dogs flew out of their traps, passing by Logan and Elise in a flash of black and grey. A huge cheer went up from the crowd and everyone was leaning forward, tickets waving, the air filled with cries, urging the dogs on. Logan was almost anonymous among the crowd – everyone's attention was on the track.

'Clearwater, get in, my son – go on, Clearwater, show them how it's done!'

Logan threw his head back and laughed as Elise, next to him, let rip.

'Clearwater, you can do it! Come on, Clearwater! Go on, baby, shake that ass! Yes!'

Her arms shot in the air and she let out a huge whoop, then put her finger and thumb in her mouth and whistled. Logan was still laughing as she turned to him, her face joyous.

'What?!'

She hit him gently on the arm, mock angry.

'Why are you laughing at me?'

'I did not have you pegged for a fan of this stuff.'

'I told you I liked to gamble, didn't I?'

'Sure. But I figured, a bit of roulette, a bit of blackjack, not ...'
He gestured to the stadium. ' ... This.'

She winked at him. 'Well, there's a lot you don't know about me.'

'I bet there is.'

She smiled, and looked away. 'Come on, the next race is going to start,' she said excitedly. 'Which dog did you pick for this one?'

There was a lot he didn't know about her, but there was also a lot that Logan *did* know about Elise McAllister. On the flight back to London from the island, he had opened his computer, pulled up Bill and Elise's file, and read about her, his mind full of images of her, sweaty and dirty from her hike, and later, groomed and glossy at dinner. Her skin, that glowed so enticingly, begging to be touched; her eyes that sparkled and crinkled at the corners when she laughed; the way she walked. She had captivated him in a way he'd never thought he would feel again. He had read about her avidly. By the time he landed in London he knew where she had been to college (Brown), where she had got married (Manhattan), whether she had siblings (like him, she was an only child). He knew that she enjoyed the song 'Diamonds on the Soles of her Shoes', but that her husband preferred Beethoven (he had had his secretary fill out the forms, so their in-room CDs had been mostly to his taste, but she had downloaded the Simon and Garfunkel single from the hotel iTunes library. He knew that she read voraciously, loved sushi and champagne and white roses. Most of all, he knew she was beautiful and clever, and utterly wasted on her brute of a husband.

Now, as looked into her eyes, he was desperate to know more. He wanted to know what the skin on the nape of her neck smelled like, and whether she stuck her tongue out when she was concentrating. He wanted to know what she looked like when she woke up, and as she was going to sleep. He wanted to know what her touch would feel like, whether she was quiet and soft in bed or whether she would grip his waist with her thighs and cry out for more . . .

Later, when they had collected their winnings ('Twenty-three pounds! I'll treat you to a bag of fries,' she had said excitedly. 'Don't we have to call them chips here?' he replied), Logan had called for his car to pick them up, and almost immediately regretted it. They had driven back into Central London in near silence, the atmosphere between them suddenly changed with the presence of his driver. Both of them aware that they were being observed, however discreetly, both of them reminded that the hours they had just spent together had been stolen, time out of their real lives, which were elsewhere.

Logan had dropped her off at her riverside apartment and then been driven home to South Kensington. When the car pulled up outside his house in the quiet street, he had hesitated for a moment, not wanting to go in. He looked up at his wife's window; Maryanne's

251

light was on. She would be inside, lying in bed or on her chaise longue – hungover, drunk, high? All three, maybe. Charlie would be in the studio, working musician's hours, sleeping in till late tomorrow. Lucia would be out, no doubt, at one of the many pre-birthday celebrations she deemed necessary as her birthday approached. A wave of tiredness overcame him. His baby daughter would be twenty-one in a week's time. All grown up. Where had the years gone?

'Sir?' Henry's voice was as smooth and calm as ever. 'Do you wish to go somewhere else, Mr Barnes?'

Logan shook his head. He would go inside, go to sleep, and in the morning he would go to work. As usual. Except something had changed, and eventually, something would have to be done about it. He and Maryanne couldn't carry on as they were. They were doing each other no good. He would have to talk to her. But not tonight.

'No, thank you, Henry. Goodnight.'

He got out of the car and went inside.

The next day, Logan called Elise as soon as he got to the office and asked her if she was free for an hour that afternoon.

'I had a lot of fun at the races last night,' he said, 'and I'd like to give you something to say thank you. Don't worry, I'm not going to try to take you to Italy again.'

'Yes,' she had said straight away. She had been awake since dawn, her heart leaping into her throat every time she thought of him. Bill had been pleased when she told him about the hotel, and that Logan had taken her out for dinner after she had been to see the venue.

'You didn't bore him with a lot of chit-chat, did you?' he had asked her. 'Men like Barnes aren't interested in where you had lunch or what your kid did today.'

'I don't think so,' she'd replied. 'He didn't seem to find me too tedious, at least.'

When Elise arrived at the address that Logan had given her, it turned out to be a back street near Shoreditch. Why had he sent her here? Shrugging, she pressed the buzzer by the door and it opened. Logan's voice came out of the speaker next to it.

'Elise? Come up, it's on the third floor.'

There was no elevator. By the time she had climbed the six narrow flights of stairs, she was breathless. Logan was waiting for her at the top. He looked excited to see her, and her heart jumped again. He stood back and waved her through a door.

'Come in, come in.'

She found herself inside a small workshop, crammed with hundreds of wooden shoe lasts, stacked in perfect rows on shelves that reached up to the ceiling. Sample shoes in every style imaginable were displayed on racks, next to cases that contained heels, just hundreds of heels: low kitten heels, teetering stilettos, elegant, slim wedges. She saw huge books full of fabric and materials of every colour. And then there were the glass drawers full of decorations: sequins, feathers, little birds and butterflies, large coloured rhinestones and samples of intricate embroidery. Elise gazed around the room, trying to take it all in at once. Logan watched her with pleasure.

'Amazing huh? This is Mr Warwas.' Logan gestured to a small, moustached man standing nearby. 'It's his workshop.'

Elise smiled, and shook the man's hand.

'I'd like to buy you a pair of shoes. You do like shoes?'

'Oh yes, but—'

'Please? I'd like to treat you.'

Elise nodded. 'Thank you.'

'Good.'

Mr Warwas smiled at Logan, and disappeared into a back room of the workshop.

'Now – what do you think? Something like this?' Logan waved a black patent boot at her, its silver buckles rattling as he did so.

She laughed. 'Hmm. I'm not planning on becoming a dominatrix any time soon, so maybe not?'

'Shame,' he said lightly.

'Really? Is that your thing then?' She bit her lip. 'Dungeons and whips?'

He laughed. 'No, not really. Very pedestrian, me, I'm afraid.'

'Oh, well. I never was much good at walking in terribly high heels.'

There it was again, the unspoken sexual tension. They acknowledged it silently.

'Then I think you should have some practice.'

* * *

253

Elise teetered down the middle of the workshop in vertiginous five-inch platforms. 'Waaah!' She wobbled, and grabbed on to Logan's shoulder. In these shoes she was taller than him, and he put an arm round her waist to steady her.

'Hmm, maybe not those ones,' she said, sitting down and taking them off. 'How did you find this place?'

'People point me towards these things. And I brought my daughter here when she turned eighteen. Lucia loves coming here.'

A reminder of their other lives floated between them. He pointed at a pair of pale blue shoes with kitten heels on a shelf. 'How about those?'

'That's more like it. Bring you back down to my level,' Logan said as she posed in them.

'Oh, I'm not sure about that,' she said, deadpan.

In the end she chose a pistachio-green silk that would be embroidered with lilies in a pale gold thread. The shoes were to be a mule shape, open at the back and with a toe the shape of a dolphin's nose – long and gently squared off at the end – with a medium heel, slim and curved. The heel would be covered in Swarovski crystals in the same light gold colour as the embroidery. And, although she didn't know it, Logan had asked for a single diamond to be set into the leather that sat under the arch of her foot, so that she really would have diamonds on the soles of her shoes.

Afterwards, they walked through the back streets, letting themselves get lost in an area where they were unlikely to see anyone they knew, enjoying the freedom to talk in a relaxed way. Passers-by occasionally glanced at Logan, clearly recognising him, but no one bothered them.

Elise told him about her life, how in her childhood, her father had taught her to play cards at the small folding-table in his trailer on set. How Pete had always told her that she should have running-away money of her own so that she wasn't beholden to anyone. To her surprise she found herself telling him about her secret bank account, and the fact that Bill banned her from playing poker but she did it anyway, online now, building up her nest egg.

'Good,' Logan said. 'No one should tell you what to do, push you around, even if he is your husband.'

She had winced slightly, when he said that. Logan paused.

'It's not my business – although I feel like it is. But if he hits you – you don't have to put up with it.'

She carried on walking, a bit shakily, unsure how to respond.

'I like that you feel that it's your business,' she said eventually. 'But it's my responsibility, my marriage. For better, or for worse.' Elise's smile was wry, and she had a lump in her throat.

Logan nodded. 'Yes.'

They fell silent.

'I don't intend to put up with it for ever though.'

'I'm very glad to hear it.'

She took a deep breath. What did he mean? That he was simply glad she wasn't planning on staying in an unhappy and violent marriage – or something more? She changed the subject. She talked about how she had also inherited her father's love of racing and riding in fast cars. Understanding exactly what she meant, Logan described the trips he and Johnny took, the ski lodge they had bought because they loved the peaceful mountains and their vertiginous slopes. He then told her about Johnny, how they had become friends, and about the day of the awful accident that had wiped out his family.

'How terrible.' Elise's eyes filled with tears.

'I know, it was. But he didn't let it make him bitter. It changed him – of course. But he's never used it as an excuse.'

'Admirable.'

'He's an incredible guy. He's – well, we became each other's family that day, I guess. You'll meet him properly, soon.'

Her heart fluttered at this promise of a future meeting, with its hint of what might be in store for them. What *was* in store for them? For this thing which was not yet an affair, but which was more than the business relationship she had led her husband to believe. Bill. She shivered at the thought of what he would do to her if he found out ... But there was nothing for him to find out. Not yet, not really.

And then, suddenly, there was.

Logan stopped, and reached for her hand. 'Elise?'

She didn't reply. Just waited. He came closer and she let herself be pulled into his arms as he kissed her, long and hard, wrapping her in an embrace that felt like the safest, warmest place she had ever been.

When they broke away, she looked up at him.

'Oh,' she said.

'What is it?'

'It just felt like . . .'

She didn't know how to describe what she had just felt, the strange sensation that this was not the first kiss they had shared, the odd combination of familiarity and overwhelming, thrilling newness that she had experienced when he kissed her.

'Like coming home?'

Tears came to her eyes again, but ones of happiness and relief and excitement this time.

'Yes. Like coming home.'

Chapter Seventeen

It was a month since the opening of Luxury, and the hotel was full of stars.

On the west beach of the island, known as the pink beach because of the flecks of coloured sand that were raked into it every morning before dawn, and the pink candy-striped cabanas and loungers that lined it, Lola and Colm Farlon lay side by side sipping their drinks. Lola was a designer and owner of luxury goods house Farlon, and her husband, Colm, was a notorious hellraiser. Hers, a wheatgrass, pomegranate and acai juice smoothie, his, a 'crack daddy' – a cocktail of champagne and passion fruit juice and Polish vodka. Lola adjusted the shade that was shielding the screen of her iMac from the sun, and frowned slightly. She was checking the progress of the new Farlon website, but something was not to her satisfaction. Colm watched her pretty nose wrinkle as she read the copy.

'Lola . . . Lolita . . . what's wrong?' His voice was sing-song and throaty.

'How many cigarettes did you smoke last night? You sound like a tramp.'

He sighed. 'Beautiful, but cold, my Lola. Not a kind word for a poor Irish boy.' He flopped on to his back and pouted. 'What's wrong with the Farlon empire? Not raking in enough millions today?'

'Don't be flip, Colm. It's the new website.' His hand was stroking her thigh, and she batted it away absently. 'It's our public face: if it doesn't look right, we look shoddy.'

'Can't have that. Not the great Farlon.'

She looked sharply at him. 'Are you drunk already? For crying out loud, it's not even eleven.'

He continued to stroke her, his hand moving to her stomach.

'Stop working, Lola, lovely Lola.' He thickened his accent, mugging an almost incomprehensible Irish brogue. 'To be sure, to be sure, I'll go stark raving mad if you don't throw a boy a little crumb of affection over here.'

Lola looked at him sharply. 'Colm, this is our business. Our name – *your* name. Our future. Don't you want—'

'I do want, yes, I do. I do.' And he pulled the ties on the side of her bikini bottoms suddenly so they unravelled in his hand, and she yelped, and then broke into helpless giggles and allowed him to draw her close to him.

Jacinta Tramontello heard the laughter of the young couple further down the beach and sulked. Oh, for a charming companion like the lovely Colm Farlon with his indecently long eyelashes and his curls of dark hair that she had wanted to pull her hands through since she first saw him on the plane, and his thick eyebrows that he had waggled at her cheekily. He'd recognised her, of course he had, she was still a seriously famous actress, even if she was the wrong side of forty-five, and she rather fancied she'd seen a flash of attraction in those dark eyes as she moved deliberately slowly past him on the Gulfstream. The laughter had stopped now and the voices turned to low murmurs. She tightened her stomach muscles slightly (still tender from their surgical tautening a month ago, but satisfyingly trim) to pull herself up and peer round the corner of her cabana to the Farlons'. As she did so she caught a glimpse of Colm, reaching up with a long, muscled arm to close the side drapes, and his young wife stretched out on the day bed, slim and half-naked and unbearably lovely. He saw Jacinta looking, and held her gaze. His face was knowing and smug as he stared at her, and reached back to touch his wife's breast, gently, softly. Then he let go of the pink striped drape so it fell and concealed them – but not before she had seen him wink at her.

She sat back, cheeks flushed with a mixture of arousal and embarrassment. He knew she'd been watching, and was probably enjoying the thought of the older woman lusting after him, even now as he made love to his gorgeous young wife. Feeling humiliated and in need of reassurance, she turned to the man next to her, who, it had to be said, was proving to be something of a disappointment. He'd made love to her on demand, sure, energetically and for as long as she required, but that was it. There was no flirting to speak of, no excitement, no *fun*. He was sleeping now, full of the laziness of the young and indolent. She touched his shoulder. 'Marco . . . Marco, wake up.'

She tickled him. His eyes opened and she saw them tighten slightly with irritation before he wiped the expression from his face and smiled charmingly at her. She leaned down and kissed him, and he responded. She ignored the slightly mechanical feel of his routine – kissing her lips, then her neck, then her shoulder, before pushing her bikini top aside and moving down to circle her nipple with his tongue – and focused instead on the glorious sight of his perfect body and particularly, his perfect mouth with its full lips and firm tongue, working its way down her torso, his only aim that of her pleasure.

Ten minutes later her pleasure had dissipated entirely and turned back into frustration, and she stared down angrily at Marco's apologetic face.

'This has never happened to me before, I promise,' he told her.

'Shut up! How do you think that makes me feel – to be the only woman you've ever been with who can't excite you? Now get on with it. It's not as if the paps can get at us here, is it? So don't give me any of that tosh about getting caught.'

'You do, you do excite me, you have excited me every night since we got here . . .' A very slight tone of weariness had crept into his voice. That was a big mistake.

'Oh, I'm sorry, Marco, are you feeling a little tired? Have I been placing unreasonable demands on you? Bringing you to the single most exclusive hotel in the entire world, lavishing every luxury upon your handsome head, and only asking for one thing in return?'

'No, not unreasonable. I am having an amazing week.'

But her anger was in full flow. 'And let's not forget the money, Marco. You're not doing me a favour, you're here because I'm paying you – and your "broker". A great deal of money, as I'm sure you're aware. Or maybe you're not? Maybe he doesn't tell you how much you're worth?'

One look at his face told her he knew exactly how much.

'So don't make excuses, don't tell me how much you desire me. Show me, and show me *now*, or I'm sending you home and I won't pay a single penny. And I'll bill you for your share of the holiday.'

He looked at her and forced himself to swallow his loathing of her and of himself, and think of the one person who never, ever failed to excite him. His broker, as she put it, his best friend, his lover, and the one person in the world that he loved.

In the cabana just down the beach, Colm and Lola stuffed their hands over their mouths to stifle their laughter at the exchange they had just overheard.

'Come on, darlin', let's go back to the room. I feel like a line. I want to inhale it off that beautiful body of yours – this bit, just here.'

'Why go back to the room? I want you to do it now. Here.' She was breathing hard, her lips slightly parted.

'Lola, Lola. Naughty girl.'

'Come on. I thought the whole point was that we can do anything here. No risk. No limits. Go on.'

She reached into her canvas bag for the small silver credit-card holder that held a white wrap of cocaine and a twenty-pound note. Then she lay back on the lounger, her breasts small and her nipples hard, flicked the wrap open with one hand and, without taking her eyes off Colm, she poured a line of the white powder on to the skin between her breasts. Then stopped, and, still holding his gaze, she undid the other tie on her bikini bottoms and let them fall open before pouring a second line on to the perfectly waxed skin there.

'I dare you,' she whispered. And with a smile, he reached for the twenty-pound note, rolled it up and lowered his head.

Back in London, Lucia Barnes stood in her mother's dressing room in their large South Kensington house, combing through her wardrobe. It was her twenty-first birthday and she needed something fabulous to wear for the dinner that her parents were hosting for her and just over a hundred close friends, before she changed into the showstopper of an outfit that she already had planned for the party afterwards, to which five hundred guests were coming.

It wasn't just her twenty-first birthday, it was the beginning of a new phase in her life, she felt. She had had her meeting with Ranj as soon as she'd got back to London after the launch of Luxury, had raced round to his impressive offices near Mount Street and signed the papers that officially engaged him as her lawyer, and the ones that created an offshore company called Light.

Then she had put on her brand-new pinstriped suit, and had taken herself off to the investment banker who, to her slight surprise, had looked over her business plan and the plans she had had drawn up for the renovation of 98 Bilton Square, and agreed to lend her the money. All of it. She had walked straight out into the sunny street, gone round the corner to Gucci and bought herself a new handbag to celebrate. Well, she needed to look the part, now that she was almost a hotelier, didn't she? She hugged the thought to herself now as she flipped through a selection of possible outfits. A classic Yves Saint Laurent tux, worn with nothing underneath? A scarlet sheath minidress, to highlight her long slim legs? A gold and cream Grecian-style draped dress, elegant and glamorous? None of them were quite right, none of them felt special enough.

Then she saw it. A fluttery chiffon babydoll dress, dip-dyed so it went from deepest indigo at the hem, which was flecked with tiny star-shaped sequins, through navy, mid-blue, to palest baby-blue over the bust, finally turning cool bright white at the strapless neck-line. The white would highlight her bronzed shoulders and the delicate line of her collarbone, and it was revealing enough to satisfy her desire to show what wonderful shape she was in, while being demure enough to ensure that her father wouldn't start bitching and moaning in front of everyone. Then later, after the meal, she would slip off and change.

She pulled the dress out of the wardrobe and stalked into Maryanne's shoe room to find some suitable heels. She had in mind a particular pair of silver strappy sandals with a little platform that she'd seen recently.

Lucia couldn't wait until it had all gone through and she could see the looks on her family's faces when she told them that she, Lucia Barnes, their daughter, was the new owner of 98 Bilton Square. They weren't going to believe it. But it would be true. She just had to wait a little while longer.

* * *

It was one of her favourite things in the world, standing in front of a room full of people, all of whom were there for the sole purpose of adoring her, looking out at 120 pairs of eyes and basking in their gaze. She couldn't understand how people could be afraid of public speaking. It was as natural to Lucia as being naked. Which was something else she was extremely good at.

'We're all going on to Neon, which is open to our party only – thanks, Daddy – so please make sure you have your tickets with you.'

She waved a set of silver dog-tags in the air, each one of which had been engraved with *Lucia – 21* and which were to act as the tickets necessary for entry to the exclusive Mayfair nightclub, and the guests laughed as the tags tinkled together in the air, sounding like a set of keys – the keys that would gain them entry to the only party to be at in London that night.

'So thanks for coming and thank you all for your generous gifts.' Lucia gestured at a table in one corner of the room at the Ivy Club, loaded with a pile of expensively wrapped presents and stiff bags – Jo Malone, Gucci, Tiffany. Beams of red and green and cobalt-blue light shone through the diamonds of stained glass on to them.

'And thanks to my parents for hosting this fabulous little do.' She looked to one side where Logan stood, handsome in a white suit and shirt. He smiled proudly at his daughter and raised his glass, and saw her noting the empty space beside him. He gave a small shrug in answer to her unspoken question, and saw the flash of disappointment in her eyes before she covered it, and for a second he hated Maryanne for causing it. How could she fail to show up to her only daughter's twenty-first birthday party?

He moved to Lucia's side, put an arm round her, and began the toast to his daughter.

The guests trickled out of the club in a stream of laughter and chatter. Lucia's gifts were being loaded into the back of a black 4x4 by two of Logan's employees, to be delivered to their house where she would spend the next day opening them. Logan kissed his daughter goodbye as she and her friends moved on to the next venue of her celebrations, excited and high and ready for a night of partying. He didn't begrudge her it. You were only young once.

Jonty ushered her into the car. As he did so, Logan noticed that

Lucia was holding her arm slightly protectively around her lower abdomen. The group of photographers had noticed it as well, he was sure, and they were focusing their attention on it, jostling and zooming in to get the best shot. Oh God, she wasn't . . . was she? She'd bloody well better not be pregnant.

He grabbed her arm. 'Hang on a minute.'

'What is it, Daddy?'

'Do you have something to tell me, Lucia?'

Lucia swallowed. He couldn't know, could he? If Ranj had dropped her in it, she'd fucking sue the little . . .

'You know you can tell me anything, sweetie – right? If you're in some kind of trouble . . .'

His eyes went to her belly. Oh, God. Thank fuck for that.

'Daddy! Don't be ridiculous. Of course not. Honestly, I'm . . .' She was going to say she was a good girl, but she stopped herself. That *would* be silly.

'I'm always very careful,' she replied instead, her face a perfect picture of innocence.

He sighed with relief. 'Jesus. Don't do that to me.'

She stood on tiptoe to kiss his cheek. 'Daddy. Just a silly PR stunt of Jonty's. You worry too much.'

'All right. Have fun. Don't let Jonty talk you into anything I wouldn't approve of. Hmm?'

He did his best to look stern. They both knew it was an act. Lucia could wrap him round her little finger.

'I won't. Don't wait up.'

Her fingers waved and she was gone, into the night. Logan watched the car go. His little princess, all grown up. And, though he didn't like to admit it, maybe not such a princess either, if one was going to be realistic. Ah, but she would always be one to him.

In the car, Jonty looked excited.

'Perfect, just perfect,' he gushed.

Lucia was reapplying her lip gloss. 'They totally bought it, didn't they?' she said.

'Hook, line and sinker. Now in a few days I'll get them to snap you in that tunic, nice and loose and ambiguous . . .'

* * *

Logan got his phone out and called Elise. Since their afternoon in Shoreditch the week before, they had spoken on the phone whenever they could, and seen each other twice. Both times had been far, far too brief – a snatched half-hour one lunchtime, a quick drink one evening. They had to be careful. Though nothing more than a few kisses had happened between them, the sexual tension was clear for all to see. The second time they'd met, Elise had gone to the LBI offices and Logan had introduced her to Johnny.

'You remember Elise McAllister, your client Bill's wife.'

'We had such a wonderful time at the Luxury launch, and he was so sorry to leave early but had to get back – well, of course, you know that, it was a – anyhow, Logan's been so helpful and generous about the ball.' She was babbling like an idiot. *Shut up*, she told herself frantically. Johnny had nodded and his eyes had moved between her and Logan.

'I bet. He's a very generous man.'

Elise had blushed. He could tell something was going on, she knew, and she had left shortly afterwards, promising to pass on Johnny's regards to Bill.

'I can tell,' Johnny said to Logan, the moment she had gone. 'And all right, I know you better than most, but it won't just be me who notices.'

Logan had opened his mouth to deny it, but closed it again. He couldn't pretend to Johnny. He remained silent, his hands in his pockets.

'Just be careful,' Johnny said quietly. 'You've got a lot to lose.'

Johnny was right about the fact that they would have to be careful, Logan thought, but he was wrong about having a lot to lose. On the contrary – he had everything to gain.

The phone call was a brief one. Elise was waiting for Bill to get home and she was nervous, but it was enough just to hear her voice for a few seconds. When he had hung up, Logan got into the back of his waiting car and signalled to Henry to move off. He was furious with Maryanne. A hen party ran in front of the car as it sat at traffic lights, a gaggle of girls in fluffy pink bunny ears and with fat thighs squeezed into too-short skirts. Logan didn't notice, was paying no attention to the crowds and bustle of the streets. His anger showed in his face, in his forehead, as he stared out of the window as the car moved through the West End, his thoughts fixed on what he was going to say to his wife when he got home.

Maryanne had given up all pretence of being on top of things, normal, together. What was the point? So instead, she lay in the centre of her shoe room, an empty bottle of wine next to her. She didn't know what time it was. She didn't care. She hadn't been to bed, but instead had just wandered around her suite of rooms, drinking. Logan had taken the pills away from her, but not emptied her fridge. She could drink herself to death for all he cared. Maybe she would. That would show him, Mr Big Shot, I'm in charge of everyone, I'm so important and powerful. La-di-da. Pulling herself upright, she went unsteadily back to the fridge in her dressing room. Poo. Boo hoo. No more wine. Where had it all gone? Maybe Carla had been at it. Never mind. Never never mind mind. She would go downstairs and fetch more. That was it. She had a plan. There. An aim in life. A purpose. Ha!

There was a pack of cigarettes that Lucia had left behind, though. Maryanne rarely smoked, but she was bored. Where *was* everyone? She opened the packet idly. Tucked inside among the beige filters was the familiar twisted paper end of a joint. She pulled it out of the packet. It had been a while. What the hell. She lit it, posing in the mirror as she did so, pouting at her reflection and turning from side to side. Not bad, for an old girl. She felt dizzy suddenly, and sat down heavily on the sofa. The room was spinning in front of her and she felt nauseous. Ugh. The joint was a bad idea, it had given her a headrush. She lowered herself backwards to lean against the arm of the sofa, dropping the cigarette as she did so. She felt horrible. As her eyes dropped shut she let tears leak out from them and as she slid down into unconsciousness she felt utterly, wretchedly sorry for herself.

If Maryanne hadn't refused to have smoke alarms in her room because they would spoil the decoration scheme, then the finely tuned sensor would have detected the cigarette smoke almost as soon as Maryanne lit it, and the fire would have been stopped before it had started. The sprinkler systems would have been

265

triggered automatically, and the worst injury Maryanne suffered would have been wet hair and an angry husband.

But it wasn't until the smoke had wound its way under the door to the corridor outside her suite of rooms that it travelled up to the ceiling and found the sensor located there. This triggered the house's fire control system, and by the time this happened, Maryanne had been lying in the room slowly filling with smoke for fifteen minutes as the woven silk rug smouldered and released its tiny particles of cyanide gas.

At the moment that the spark from the cigarette she'd left in her parents' home caught the silk carpet, Lucia Barnes was leaning over a Bugatti Veyron, enjoying the unusual sensation of being fucked from behind over the bonnet of the most powerful and expensive car in the world. It was the car which excited her the most, though the vehicle's owner was labouring under the illusion that he was the primary cause of her ecstatic moans. The heir to a large construction firm, and one of the most eligible men in London, he was attractive in a rough sort of way, and as he flipped her over on to her back and shoved her further up the bonnet of the car so he could thrust even more deeply inside her, she wasn't complaining. Reaching for her calf and manoeuving her leg so it was hooked over his shoulder, he then paused, his hips pressing heavily down against her pelvis. He looked into her eyes and she returned his gaze.

'The heir and the heiress,' he whispered. 'What a good match.'

And he began to move against her again, harder this time, so she was forced to reach for his waist and hold on to him. He groaned as she squirmed underneath him. 'Oh yeah . . . yes baby.'

'Rob, stop. Stop, for fuck's sake!'

'What?'

She had stopped moving and had scrambled into a more upright position away from him. As he pulled out angrily he followed her gaze, turning to the end of the mews street where he had parked, behind the club where Lucia's party was continuing, to see a police car, two uniformed officers, and the bespectacled film director who was meant to be Lucia's date for the night.

'Oh, bollocks.'

* * *

As Lucia was trying and failing to charm the police with her usually reliable little girl lost act – difficult when they'd been getting such an explicit display just moments previously – someone else whom she had recently fucked was plotting how they were going to get back at her for the state she had left them in afterwards. Lucia Barnes was not someone who was used to clearing up after herself, in any sense of the word.

The street around the private gardens of the square where the Barneses' white-fronted home stood was filled with fire engines and ambulances. Staff and visitors to the house stood at the end of the street, waiting anxiously, and neighbours were ushered out and away from their properties in case the fire took hold. It was a credit to the efficiency of the systems, the fire staff said later, that the house remained largely undamaged.

The front door opened and a stretcher was wheeled down the steps by the paramedics, Logan holding his wife's hand. A shocked ripple moved through the crowd waiting outside. With that oxygen mask over her face, it was impossible to tell whether Maryanne was conscious or not.

Logan only let go of Maryanne's hand as she was lifted into the back of the ambulance, and the paramedics climbed in behind her, quickly and efficiently working on her inert body. He stood behind the open doors, paralysed. *Not again*, was the only thing he could think. *Not again, not now.*

When he'd heard the smoke alarms he'd run straight to Maryanne's rooms, had somehow known that would be the source of any problem. Johnny, who was with him, had cut off the call he was on and dialled 999 in case the automatic link to the emergency services didn't work for some reason. There had been a second when he had almost followed his instincts to run after Logan, but instead he had set off around the rest of the house, gathering together the staff and making sure everyone got out of the building.

When Logan had got to his wife's dressing room, the door was locked from the inside. Smoke was just visible from under it, and he could smell it and feel it as he breathed in. He opened the door of the small cloakroom just down the corridor and soaked a towel to put over his face, and then cast around for some way to get the door open. The tiny cloakroom had little in it – certainly nothing strong enough to break the wooden door.

The next room along was a small office-cum-meeting room used by visitors sometimes. The chair was a flimsy antique and would be of no help, the desk likewise – carved wooden legs were all well and good but were no match for a locked door. Quickly, quickly: there must be something in this house full of expensive furniture and art – art! That was it; he ran further down the corridor to the cinema room and dragged the heavy bronze Henry Moore from the corner of the room. Only a small work, but still weighty, it took all Logan's strength to pull and push it down the hallway to Maryanne's door, where he lifted it and hefted it into the wood. It splintered but did not collapse. What had he thought, that he was Bruce Willis in some action film, and could just burst through? He tried again and the smooth curves of the piece bashed a hole in the decorated wood door. As he pulled it back to try again, Logan felt someone move him firmly to one side, and a group of firemen broke the door down and moved through into the room, holding him back from running in there himself.

Now Johnny steered him towards a waiting Range Rover as he watched the men hook Maryanne up to an IV, to some machine, to all sorts of things. Her body was so small and fragile – surely it couldn't take this sort of intervention twice in so short a time?

'We'll follow them there, give them space in the back,' Johnny said gently. 'Come on, my friend.'

In the hospital the doctors treating Maryanne continued to administer oxygen to her, worried by her fast rate of respiration, signs that she could be suffering from cyanide poisoning from the toxins in the smoke, as well as irritation to her lungs from smoke inhalation. She wasn't regaining consciousness.

Outside the room, Logan and Johnny waited.

'God, I can't believe I'm back here again!' Logan said despairingly. 'What the fuck is going on, Johnny?'

Johnny didn't respond. There was nothing to say. The two men sat side by side, waiting for news.

By the time Logan was allowed in to see her, Charlie had come from what was left of Lucia's birthday party, and the three of them stood at the foot of her bed. Logan moved to her side and gently pushed her hair back from her face.

'Where's Lucia?' he asked his son.

'Um. She's . . .' Charlie trailed off. How did he tell his Dad about this one?

Logan looked at him sharply. 'What?'

'No, it's fine, she's fine. Just . . .'

The doctor entered the room and pulled the door shut behind him. He looked at the group, and then at his notes.

'It might be better if your son waited outside, Mr Barnes.'

'No.' Charlie's voice was definite. 'I want to hear.'

'He can stay.'

'Fine.' The doctor was fourteen hours into a double shift, and didn't really care either way.

'The test results indicate that there is a small amount of cyanide present in Mrs Barnes's blood. Because of the actions of the paramedics at the scene of the incident, however, the outlook is optimistic. It appeared initially that her state was more severe than it has turned out because of her lack of consciousness.'

He made a small 'ahem' sound in his throat.

'However, we are now confident that Mrs Barnes was already unconscious when the fire began.'

It was what Logan had feared.

'This made diagnosing the extent of her smoke inhalation more complex. However, your wife is going to be fine. We'd like to monitor her overnight to ensure that her condition does not deteriorate, and then she should be quite all right to be discharged tomorrow. Although she's likely to feel weakened and somewhat unwell for a few days.'

'Thank you, Doctor. I can assure you that my wife will get plenty of rest.'

In the corridor, Logan stood for a moment, trying to gather his thoughts. *Oh, Maryanne, what are you doing to yourself? To your children? Why are you so unhappy that you're torturing yourself like this?*

Johnny put a reassuring hand on his shoulder. 'She'll be all right, buddy. We'll get her straightened out.'

Logan looked at his friend, who was more like a member of his family. 'I hope so. I've let her down, I think.'

Johnny shrugged. 'We do the best we can. Come on. Let's go and survey the damage. I've phoned Dr Slade.'

Logan turned to Charlie, who was standing a few feet away, and held his arm out slightly awkwardly to put it round his son's shoulders.

'Are you coming? She'll be sedated until morning, there's no use in us staying.'

'Yes. Dad, look, there's something I've got to tell you ...'

Just then Logan's phone rang and he flipped it open. 'Logan Barnes.'

'Good evening, Mr Barnes, this is Sergeant Haworth in the custody suite at West End Central police station. We have your daughter here with us.'

Logan leaned back against the wall of the corridor. He looked at Charlie and sighed. This was what his son hadn't had a chance to tell him, obviously.

'Good evening, Sergeant,' he said heavily. 'What are you holding her for?'

Logan felt numb, as he stood in the corridor outside the room where his wife lay unconscious, waiting to return to his house that had almost been burned down, on the phone to a man who had his daughter in a police cell. He could almost have laughed at the absurdity of it all. Apart from the fact that he couldn't, because it was just too fucking tragic. Everything was falling apart. His heart was split. He veered from feeling fury that Maryanne could be so stupid, to sadness for her and for himself, to humiliation that he was married to such a shambolic wreck. *Ah, but it's your fault that she's like that, isn't it, Logan?* a little voice said. *She was happy once. Happy and carefree. Then she married you, and things started to go downhill. You didn't pay her enough attention, you just worked and expected money and nice things to make everything OK. Stupid Logan.* But no. It wasn't all his fault, he wouldn't shoulder all the responsibility. Maryanne was a grown-up.

No, no, no, that wasn't good enough. He might be angry, but she had almost died. He'd almost lost her for ever. Maybe he already had. She was stumbling through her life, lost in a maze of pain and confusion. He *had* to help her out of it, he had to try harder.

Just a few weeks ago he had been on his perfect island, glorying in the successful launch of Luxury, lapping up the praise and accolades. Maybe that was why? Pride comes before a fall. Maybe his pride had tripped him up, once again. Again . . . his pride had done it before, hadn't it? Kicked his legs out from under him, sent him sprawling. Sent that poor woman Georgia Hardy sprawling to the ground. Maybe this was how he was destined to live – building himself up, and then being punished. He was an international success, he was famous – and he was clearly a total fucking failure at the things that mattered most. Love. Family. Life – real life.

Sergeant Haworth was speaking in his ear. 'Outraging public decency, sir. And perverting the course of justice. Otherwise known as getting caught having *sex-u-al* (he drew out the word, emphasising all of its syllables) 'intercourse in the street and then trying to buy her way out of it by bribing police officers . . .'

There was a short silence.

'. . . I'm sorry to say,' the policeman added, though he didn't sound sorry at all. 'And she's insisting on having a Mr Stokes represent her, who, as I understand it, sir, is your personal legal representative?'

'Yes, that's right. We'll be there right away.'

Logan shut his phone. Part of him wanted to leave his daughter to fucking stew in her own juices. What did the little trollop think she was playing at? She didn't deserve his help – she didn't deserve to be bailed out, *again*. But he knew he would. He was her father; it was his job. Christ knows, he was beginning to realise that he had done little enough else of real value as a parent. He stood up, wearily, and looked at Johnny.

'We need to go.'

By the time Johnny had dealt with the fallout from Lucia's eventful night, placated the custody sergeant who had been subjected to her vociferous complaints and threats for the last few hours, sat in on the interview with her and eventually managed to get her to shut up and let him do the talking, it was seven in the morning, and Logan and Charlie had been waiting on an uncomfortable bench for four hours. They'd spoken little, both of them shaken and exhausted.

'I tried to tell you,' Charlie had said nervously, when they'd first sat down to wait.

'I know you did. It's OK, Charlie, it's not your fault. None of this is your fault.'

He looked up. Lucia stood in the doorway, looking dishevelled, tired and very, very young.

'What is this?' Logan said harshly. 'Another of these publicity schemes you and that fucking idiot Jonty have dreamed up? As if you didn't already get enough attention!'

'No.' Quiet, wary of her father.

'I'm firing him,' Logan went on.

'I pay him. You can't do that.' Defiant. Not for long.

'Really? I think you'll find that I can do pretty much anything I want to, Lucia. Now get in the car.'

And she did.

The damage to the house was minimal. The firemen were leaving by the time the car pulled up outside, and the clean-up had begun. They'd been lucky, overall. Maryanne's rooms would all have to be refurbished, not that she would complain about that, and there was some smoke and water damage to that corridor. Everything would be checked and double-checked for any structural damage, but the early indications were that there was none.

Logan told Charlie to pack a bag, and asked Linny to pack two separate bags for him and Maryanne. He and Charlie would move into his boutique hotel in Soho until the checks on the house had been completed. Maryanne wouldn't be going with them. He still didn't speak directly to Lucia, who was standing sulkily just behind her brother.

'Should I pack?' she asked. 'Where are we going?'

He was too tired to deal with her now. 'Charlie and I will stay at Lexington. You . . .' He turned away. 'Just do what you like. You always do.'

He went to his rooms to nap for half an hour, then changed and headed over to the hospital to meet Dr Slade. He planned to move Maryanne to another of his hotels, Sternley House – the country house he had bought from the Mallory family – where the doctor would help her recover. She wasn't going to like it, he was sure. But it was for the best. As they seemed singularly unable to do it for themselves, he was going to take control of his family.

The private ambulance entered the grounds of Sternley via a winding country road that led into a courtyard at the back of the hotel, out of sight of the main entrance. The doors opened and a tail lift lowered a sedated Maryanne to the ground in a wheelchair. Dr Slade, a tall, good-looking man with thick curly hair, oversaw the process. He walked alongside the chair as the driver wheeled Maryanne into the hotel, through the kitchens and to the lift, which carried them up to the top of the building and the floor which would be her home for the next week. All prior bookings for rooms on the top floor had been cancelled and guests with reservations for these rooms had been generously compensated for their inconvenience with free stays in other LBI hotels, or a free stay at Sternley for a different date. They had been told that essential and urgent repairs were being carried out on the rooms. In reality, the six suites would play host to Maryanne, Dr Slade, a team of nurses working round the clock in shifts, and a bodyguard, employed by Logan to ensure that his wife remained where she was to get the most out of the detoxification treatment, as well as to protect her from any prying eyes.

When Maryanne was settled in the large four-poster bed, Dr Slade inserted an intravenous line which would administer fluids, vitamins and minerals, so that she was hydrated and in as good a condition as possible to begin the treatment. Then he opened her mouth and gently placed a small 100 mg tablet of ibogaine on her tongue, and settled back to observe her. As long as she displayed no allergic reaction to the drug, she could be given the full dose in the morning.

When Maryanne woke up she could feel the now familiar symptoms of opiate withdrawal approaching her from the blurred edges of her consciousness. The nausea, the sweating, shivering fever, the aching joints and limbs that felt so heavy it was as if they were magnetically drawn towards the ground. She opened her eyes, wincing at the bright light. Her mouth felt dry and her lips cracked.

Above her, a handsome face appeared. A cool hand felt her pulse, and looked into her pupils.

'Hello, Maryanne. Don't worry, you're perfectly all right, you're quite safe. My name's Dr Slade. You can call me Jeremy. Your husband's asked me to help you stop taking the pills you've been having some difficulties with.'

Maryanne was confused. Where was she? She tried to sit up, but it was too difficult, and then the same cool hand stopped her.

'Lie back, Maryanne. You're in good hands. You're at Sternley House.'

Sternley House. The name sounded familiar from somewhere, but her head was thick and fuzzy, and she couldn't remember where.

'I'm going to give you a pill now. I want you to swallow it. You're going to feel much better soon. You might feel disorientated, have some strong memories, feel a little sick. But I want you to trust me, all right?'

There was something comforting about the man's modulated voice, and she did trust him, despite her sense of uncertainty. She nodded. He was fixing pads to her chest that led to an electrocardiogram.

'Good. I'll be monitoring you all the way. Here we go . . .'

He gave her a capsule and helped her sit up so she could swallow it with some water. It was large, and her dry mouth struggled to swallow it.

'Well done. Now just try and relax, Maryanne. I'm going to be with you the whole time . . .'

She rested her head on the pillow and allowed herself to drift off into sleep.

The images floated out towards her whenever she closed her eyes. She was awake, she thought, but it wasn't like being awake, not properly. She couldn't control her thoughts, her body was too heavy for her to get up, and she felt sick. A strange noise filled her ears, like a heartbeat, thudding, thudding.

The vision in front of her was clear, like watching television on one of the large plasma screens at home. She saw herself a few years previously, at a party. She recognised the dress she had been wearing as by Versace. Her hands were trembling slightly and she remembered a feeling of anxiety; it crept up on her again now, making her feel panicked like she had then. Then the image changed and she was in the bathroom, washing her hands next to her friend Gerthe, and Gerthe was handing her a couple of Valium and telling her they'd make her feel so much better. And they had; she'd taken them and had instantly relaxed, the feelings of being unable to cope slipping away . . .

She forced herself to open her eyes, and the image stopped. She was in a hotel suite at Sternley. She had remembered where it was now; it was one of Logan's hotels, one of their hotels. How silly that she hadn't remembered before. Who forgets they own a hotel? Suddenly she felt sick, and she leaned forward and vomited into a basin hastily held out for her by the pretty young nurse at her bedside. As she threw up, she shut her eyes again and the visions started up once more.

Flying, soaring over the ocean, she could see the sunlight sparkling on the deep blue sea through the layer of fluffy clouds beneath her, out of the window of their jet. An argument with Logan, he was shouting at her. She'd failed to do something she had promised to do. She'd let him down.

An arm was round her shoulders, helping her to stand. She opened her eyes and saw Dr Slade.

'Can you walk with me, Maryanne?' She tried but her muscles were weak and clumsy; she couldn't get her limbs to move in the right order and she slumped back into bed and shut her eyes again. She heard his voice somewhere in the distance reassuring her, but already the film had started again and she was lost in the images.

She was in New York, and she was drinking, heavily, not for pleasure but to block out the pain, and she remembered the painkillers in the medicine cabinet that Logan had been prescribed for a knee injury that he'd got while doing some kind of stupid sport, she couldn't remember which now. She saw herself walk drunkenly into his bathroom (where was he? he must have been out – he was always out) and count out the pills into her hand and stare at them before swallowing them with a glass of wine.

More noises – a gasping, mewling sound – and then she recognised it as sobbing, a woman sobbing, and it was herself and as she wept the sickening film continued behind her eyelids, moving on to a new scene now, one which she could hardly bear to watch, as she drank herself into a stupor of alcohol and pills while her only daughter celebrated her twenty-first birthday without her there, and eventually passed out cold, alone, surrounded by all her pretty things.

Charlie and Logan were sitting in the dining room of the Lexington Hotel where they were staying following the fire, having breakfast.

'The album's going really well, Dad. It's good. TJ says—'

'Who is this TJ?'

Charlie straightened his cutlery, giving himself a moment so he didn't snap back at his father that he'd told him a hundred times already who TJ was. Logan never fucking listened.

'TJ Burke. He's a top producer, one of the best. He's worked with the Stones, with Madonna, everyone.'

When Logan didn't reply, Charlie knew he was going to have to produce something quickly if he wanted his dad to get off his back.

'We'll have something to play you soon.'

Logan looked up. 'Really? So it's nearly finished?'

'No, not finished – but ready to take to the record companies. TJ thinks we'll definitely get a showcase at least.'

'Look, Charlie, that's all very nice. I'm glad you've made something you're proud of, something you can look back on and think, hey, I made that. It's great.'

The 'but' was coming – Charlie could feel it.

'But ...'

And there it was.

'Don't roll your eyes at me. You're twenty-five. You've had a good few years doing this, and I don't begrudge you that. Hey, I gave you and Lucia the trust funds precisely so you could make these kinds of choices for yourself.'

Logan's smile was brief.

'Even if they weren't the choices I would have made for you. But that's all part of being a parent.'

'Watching your kids make mistakes, right?'

'Not mistakes, necessarily. Different choices, let's say. But I think it's time you thought about making the music more of a hobby. About coming to work for me.'

Charlie took a big swallow of coffee that was too hot and winced.

276

He didn't want to work for Logan. Couldn't think of anything he'd rather do less. He loved his dad, but they were so different. And Charlie just wasn't interested in hotels, properties. He knew he wouldn't be that good at it; you needed passion to really get to the top. He had that passion for music, for playing; he didn't have it for hotels. And the thought of going to work for his dad and being mediocre, the boss's burdensome son, filled him with dread.

'OK, listen. Let's make a deal,' he said, deciding to take charge himself for a change.

Logan looked up. That caught his interest.

'What do you propose?'

'I finish this demo. If we get a showcase and a record deal, then that's what I do. Make an album. If not, if it's not good enough, then OK – I come and work for you.'

Logan thought for a few moments, then held his hand out to his son. The two men shook hands; Logan's wrist with its crisp cashmere suit sleeve and gold watch; Charlie's bare, his shirt rolled up, the hairs on his arm golden, his watch a rugged diving one.

Charlie had to get that record deal . . .

Shortly after his son had left, Johnny joined Logan, arriving at the table with a bulging briefcase. He opened it and took out a pile of papers, began flicking through them, handing Logan marked sheets for signature.

'How is Charlie?' he asked.

'Struggling. Frightened that his mother's going to end up killing herself. I told him he needs to decide about coming to work for me.'

'Think it's the right time for that?'

'He needs some structure. The music stuff's all well and good, but he's not a kid now. More responsibility would be good for him. I'm not having Charlie turn into a nightmare like Lucia. Speaking of whom, what's the latest?' Logan handed a sheaf of signed papers back to Johnny, who exchanged them for the next batch.

'She has to appear at Westminster Magistrates Court in a few weeks' time,' Johnny said. 'As long as she doesn't play up too much in court, she should get off with a fine and a warning.'

'She'd better not expect me to pay any fine.'

'She will.'

'Then she can think again.'

'How's everything on the island?' Johnny asked.

'Seems fine. No complaints – actually, that's not quite true.' Logan sighed. 'I spoke to Mark a couple of hours ago, and he said someone had complained that the sea was too warm.'

'Ha! Hard life, huh?'

'Indeed.'

Johnny checked the schedule on his iPhone. 'So, we're shooting for *General Manager* this afternoon at Chesham Place.'

'Yup. Celebrity management task, right?'

'Yes, should be interesting . . . Anyhow, next week, Toronto – yes?'

Logan nodded. 'We'd better. Occupancy's down in both hotels there, and in Vancouver. I want to find out why.'

'I think we should go to Whistler for a few days while we're over there. Hit the slopes. We could both do with the break.'

Logan shook his head. 'There's too much going on here. Speaking of which, what's happening with Bilton Square? Have we found a buyer?'

'Not firm, but there's interest from somewhere. Don't know who. I'm getting more details.'

'What do you mean, you don't know who?' That rang alarm bells.

'It's a new company, no name attached. Not a public one, at least. I've got someone looking into it.'

'What's the company called?'

'Um . . .' Johnny used his index finger to scroll down an email. Light Hotels.'

'All right. Look, I just think we should get straight back – it's too busy to take a holiday.'

'Not a holiday, just a couple of days. And it's always like this. It's not like there's ever a quiet time.'

'But there are less unquiet times.'

'You need to step back from it for a few days. Recharge. Come on, we haven't been to the lodge for ages.'

'Maryanne . . .'

'Is in good hands. You can't do anything to help her until she's detoxed. And when she comes home she's going to need your support.'

'I don't know.'

'I do. Come on, making you take time off is part of my job. If it were left up to you you'd work Christmas Day.'

Logan laughed and took a swig of coffee. 'I *do* work Christmas Day.'

'Exactly. Let's go to Whistler. Get some runs in, some fresh air. Make plans. It's an order.'

Logan thought about it. The prospect of a few days in the mountains was appealing. What was really holding him back? *Elise.*

Johnny read his mind, saying kindly, 'She'll still be here when you get back. A bit of distance might give you some perspective.'

Logan didn't need perspective. But maybe he did need some time to think about everything, about where the relationship with Elise was going and what he was going to do about it. He decided.

'OK, you're right. Let's do it.'

'Great! I'll tell Jim to get the plane ready. We'll go tomorrow.'

Charlie was heading to record some guitars for his album at a small studio in South London. He was looking forward to it. He was fired up, ready to get to work; keen to prove to his dad that he could make it as a musician.

The studio was part of a converted church, with high ceilings and an old Hammond organ in the corner of the room. The walls of the live room were lined with guitars and bass traps. In the control room they were papered with album covers and pinboards covered in photos of bands drinking and messing around next to ones of topless girls, the recording engineer's young children and gig tickets. It wasn't swanky, like the LA studio, but he preferred it here. It felt like somewhere he could kick back and be himself. His guitar parts were spot on, and he came out of the studio late that night feeling on a high from playing all day. It was coming together, the album; he could feel that the painstaking and mostly incredibly tedious process of making a record was drawing to a close. And it was something he felt he was going to be proud of.

Too wired to go home, he'd decided to head up to the West End, get some late dinner. As he opened the door and made to jump into the back of the 4x4 that was waiting for him in the quiet street, he saw a movement in the shadows a couple of feet away, and spun round, fists up.

'Eek – don't shoot!' The figure standing in front of him was not the mugger or attacker that he had feared. The girl standing holding her hands up in mock surrender couldn't have been much more than five foot tall, although her height was increased by a pair of silver wedge platform sandals, which she wore with opaque black tights, and a black tunic-style minidress, showing off her slender legs.

The girl looked warily at the driver who had got out and was standing over her threateningly. She looked up at his burly form, and then over at Charlie, who was also tall and broad-shouldered, and began to giggle.

'Sorry, sorry, I was just going to ask you to help me, but it's cool. I don't want to bother you.'

'Hey, That's OK.' Charlie looked at the driver, who backed off. He grinned at her.

'You're American as well,' she said.

'Yeah. Well, kind of, I live here now.'

'Me too. Anyway, I saw you coming out of that church so I figured you were safe. It's really stupid, I've been out with my boyfriend and we had a fight and I ran off but I left my purse with him, and now he's left the restaurant and I don't know where he's gone. He's got my phone and everything . . .' She trailed off and looked at the ground.

'And you don't have any money to get home.'

She blushed. 'Pretty much. I'm not one of those druggy con-artists, I promise. I don't want you to give me money, I was just wondering if you could maybe give me a lift.'

'What time did you have the fight?'

'An hour ago – why?' She looked at him quizzically.

'I was just thinking that you probably hadn't had a chance to finish your dinner, in that case.'

He took her to the casino and private member's club owned by the family that adjoined the Lexington Hotel. They sat at the back of the club, at a table that was tucked away and cleverly positioned in the room so that you could see the comings and goings without being easily visible to anyone else. They ordered beers and burgers and chips, and talked almost non-stop for an hour.

The girl, who had told Charlie her name was Jamie, was fun; she was into the same bands as he was, they went to some of the same bars in LA. They chatted about travelling and music, and what it was like being an American in London. Jamie told him she'd been here for six months.

'Studying. Seeing the sights. I love it here. How about you, how long have you lived here for?'

'Oh, a few years, on and off. My parents are here most of the year now, and my sister. I spend more time in LA. It's just that recently . . .'

'What?'

'Ah, nothing. Family stuff, it's boring.'

'No, it's not boring. Tell me about them. What does your father do again?'

Charlie didn't want to spend any more time thinking about his family today. Didn't want to get into the whole, 'Oh, that guy from *General Manager*, wow, what's it like being his son?' conversation. Not with this girl. *He* wanted to be the focus of her attention. He changed the subject. 'Oh, he's in property. Nothing interesting. What about your folks?'

Something passed across her face. 'I don't know my dad. He's never been a feature.'

Charlie frowned. He felt bad having denied his own father, in effect. At least he had one. 'Sorry to hear that.'

'Don't be. You don't miss what you've never known, right?'

'I guess. How about your mom?'

There it was again, a flash of pain, or anger on her face, he couldn't work out which.

'She's just a mom. Just a regular mom.' How she wished that were true. She decided to lighten things up. 'OK. Now for the important stuff.'

Charlie looked at her expectantly.

She reached into the middle of the table and picked up the two jars that sat there. 'Ketchup or mayo on your fries?'

Charlie laughed. This girl was fun. 'Ketchup, always,' he told her. 'I find that whole mayo thing really weird.'

She held up her hand for a high five. 'I am totally hearing you, my man,' she said and they giggled. Later, she looked at him and said, 'Let's dance.'

'I can't dance.'

'Don't be silly, you're a musician, how can you not be able to dance?'

'I just can't. My feet are too big, or too small, or something.'

She raised an eyebrow.

'OK – too big.'

She laughed.

'Don't you need to call your boyfriend?' Charlie asked.

'Um. About that ... I just – well, to call him a boyfriend was stretching it a bit maybe. And I don't think I'm going to be seeing him any more.'

She smiled beguilingly, and Charlie bit his lip to stop himself grinning. This stuff never happened to him.

'OK. What about your stuff – your phone and money? Give me his address.'

Suddenly he was taking control. She liked it. So did he.

'Forty-six, Elsen Street.' She spelled it out. 'It's near Gloucester Road tube, apparently, but I've never been there.'

He scribbled the address on a napkin and motioned a waiter over before handing him the napkin and having a word in his ear. 'OK. Done.'

'What do you mean, done?'

'Your stuff'll be here soon.'

She sat back in her chair. 'Very slick.'

He felt embarrassed. She was laughing at him. And then he realised that she was shifting in her chair slightly, before standing up and leaning into him. Her hair fell in front of his face as she kissed his cheek. At the same time, she put something soft in his hand, before slipping behind his chair and walking towards the Ladies.

He looked down to find that he was holding a pair of silk panties, still warm. Then he got up very quickly indeed and followed her.

Charlie didn't fall for girls often, but when he did, he fell hard. And Jamie was entrancing, so full of fun and spontaneity and so utterly, utterly sexy. She was exactly what he needed – a refreshing break from everything that was going on at home.

And he was exactly what *she* needed. Colette, who had introduced herself to Charlie as Jamie on the street had, of course, known exactly where he would be, had made it her business to find out what studio he was recording at and be there, doing her little girl lost act when he came out. Spending a few weeks being screwed senseless by him was no hardship, since he was just her type. Tightly muscled, surfy, she certainly enjoyed the hours she spent in bed with him as much as he did. The difference was that he was busy losing himself in her, while she was just lying back and thinking of one thing – his father.

Colette was finally going to get her chance to hit back at Logan. She had waited for so long. But now, thanks to Nicolo, she had a plan. He had given her enough money to get her mother into a fancy private hospital while she was away, so Georgia would be well looked after. Colette had told her mother that she was going away to England with a boyfriend, just for a break, and that she'd be back soon – within a few weeks at the very most. She didn't like lying to her when she was so vulnerable, but she didn't have a choice. She was doing it for her, anyhow. Georgia would hardly notice Colette was gone, and soon she would be back, with money to look after her properly, and the shadow of Logan for ever banished from their lives.

The fact that her exquisite body was displayed in all its naked glory on most of the billboards in London was going a long way to cheering Lucia up after the humiliating end to her birthday cele-brations. Her father was still only responding to her in clipped tones, and only when he absolutely had to. He was ashamed of her. The thought made her cringe inside for a second, then she stopped herself. Fuck him. He was such a stiff. It was all about him. You're giving *my* family a bad name, you're making *me* look bad. She was an adult, she didn't see why everything had to reflect on him.

Anyhow, soon she would show him that she wasn't just a pretty face and an empty head. Ranj had made an offer on Bilton Square and he seemed confident that it would be accepted. She had already had a meeting with the interior designer who she wanted to take charge of the renovations, and now that the money was in place there was no reason why the purchase shouldn't go ahead. It was going to cause quite a stir when it was announced. She knew there would be people who would say she couldn't do it, that she knew nothing about the industry, that she was too young. That she had only managed to buy the hotel because of who her father was. Lucia knew she was young, but so had her father been when he had started his first hotel company. And she was buying the hotel in secret, precisely to counter any accusations of nepotism before they started.

Maybe she should have targeted a property that wasn't owned by LBI, but this was so perfect; she had such a clear vision for it, she always had done. She was going to turn it into a ladies'-only club with bedrooms, a counterpoint to the stuffy gentlemen's clubs that still littered the city, with their old duffers stuffing their faces with spotted dick in the dining rooms. It was near all the best shops, it would have a fabulous restaurant able to cater for any diet you cared to name, and she was already in talks with hairdresser to the stars, Jeanine Aslett, about including a salon within the building. Lucia knew she had been born to do this. She had spent her whole life observing how the industry worked, it was in her blood. And whereas other hoteliers might have to research their target market by analysing statistics and tables of figures, Lucia knew what those women wanted, because she was one of them. So there was no way she was going to pass up the opportunity she had created for herself by letting 98 Bilton Square go to some other buyer. And anyhow, buying the hotel from under Logan's nose would be the perfect way of making her point.

She shot the Agent Provocateur assistant, who was packing up an array of underwear in crisp paper packages, an impatient glance. She wanted to get back to her room, where the Formula One driver she had met at Luxury was waiting for her. She had called him following what she was now thinking of as 'the incident' and persuaded him to fly over to see her. It hadn't been hard to do that, since phone sex was one of her specialities. The thing was, none of her usual fuck buddies seemed that keen at the moment. It was amazing how a little kerfuffle with the police could scare people off. A real man wouldn't be worried about being caught with his pants down – not if the girl inside those pants was Lucia, anyway. Screw them. (Or not.)

The assistant was tying up the last package. Classic black satin lingerie sets, a taffeta ruffled corset, sheer pink tulle thongs and French knickers, a red set with little bows and tie sides, a pair of closely fitting black leather elbow-length gloves that buttoned at the wrist, all went into the growing stack of pink and black carrier bags. As she watched the till tot up the total, her phone rang.

'It's Tamara. Lucia, have you seen the posters in town?'

Lucia smiled smugly. 'I know, they're everywhere. For once, Jonty's actually done what he said he was going to. Good job it all went through before my fucking father fired him.'

'Oh shit, you *haven't* seen them.' Tamara's words sounded ominous, but her tone was strangely gleeful. 'Just – go and look. The ones in Tottenham Court Road. Well, any of them, really.'

Lucia sat in the back of the car, unable to believe what she was seeing. The expanse of hoarding showed her standing, back to the camera and her head turned towards it slightly, as she trailed a chiffon robe on the floor, next to the large bed. Her bare bottom was round and high, and her eyes inviting, seductive. But scrawled over the image, in huge, red letters were the words:

THIS DIRTY BITCH GAVE ME GONORRHOEA

She made the driver weave through Bloomsbury and round into the Strand, where she saw the next one, red paint obscuring the beautiful photo. And then Trafalgar Square, and then Charing Cross Road . . . Lucia saw what felt like hundreds of the defaced posters as the car sped her home. At one horrible moment the cab stopped at a set of traffic lights next to one of the posters, and at the same time someone looked in the back window and recognised her. The woman pointed her out to her companion, and they laughed. Lucia's cheeks burned.

She dialled Jonty's number. 'What. The. Fuck?'

'Who's been a naughty girl, then?'

'It's not funny. Was this you?'

'Eh? Why would I do that?'

'Um, I don't know, Jonty – some part of your "brilliant" publicity plans?'

His laugh spluttered down the phone line on for a long time. He could be such a prick.

'I want you to get them taken down, now.'

'And how exactly do you expect me to do that?'

'How the fuck do I know? I don't care what you have to do, just get it fucking done!'

'No can do. Remember, I don't work for you any more. But look, it could be a good thing. Any publicity's good publicity, right? Although Gerry Davies called. He says to tell you that if you contact him again, he'll call the police.'

Lucia squealed with rage.

'And, obviously, they'll be using someone else for the rest of the Heiress campaign,' Jonty went on. 'You'll still get the first payment, but that's it.'

She threw her phone on the car floor. All of her plans, all of her dreams, gone. Without the rest of the money from the Heiress campaign there was no way her backers would still support her purchase of Bilton Square. She began to cry.

The driver looked in the rearview mirror.

'What are *you* looking at?'

'Where to, Miss Barnes?'

Her phone rang again. She diverted it to answerphone and sat back. 'Home. I want to go home.'

'But the house is still—'

'Just take me there.'

She knew that celebrities had to deal with malicious gossip, the tabloid rumour mill. But this wasn't something she could shrug off as spiteful, jealous lies. Because as soon as she'd seen the graffiti she had known exactly who had written it, because it was true.

From a small table outside a coffee shop in Covent Garden Tom Cope, a painter and decorator and part-time model from Bromley, was enjoying the fruits of his long night's labour as people kept stopping and doing double takes at the billboards, trying to work out if they were part of some kind of ad campaign or if they really had been defaced. It had taken him and a group of his friends all night and gallons of red paint to work their way round London but God, it had been worth it. Stupid cow. She had picked him up in a club, treated him like a pet for a few weeks, giving him a taste of the high life, and then dumped him, leaving him with a crushed ego and a burning sensation when he peed.

* * *

286

As Johnny and Logan walked towards their waiting Range Rover in Dean Street, the usual buzz that followed Logan as people recognised him was present, but there seemed to be another, less friendly undercurrent to it.

As they got into the back of the car, Henry turned to them, his brow furrowed.

Logan noticed straight away. 'What's wrong, Henry?'

The chauffeur paused. He hated having to be the one to point this out, but it was his duty as a loyal employee.

'You're not going to like this, sir.' He pressed a button and the window of the car slid smoothly down.

In front of them was the billboard with Lucia's naked body on it, covered in the same lurid red lettering.

THIS DIRTY BITCH GAVE ME GONORRHOEA

Logan stared at it for a long time. The other two men were silent. When he finally spoke, it was slowly and with absolute control.

'Get my bank on the phone. I want any of her credit cards that are linked to my accounts cancelled, I want her access to the trust fund frozen, and I don't want her using the plane or the cars, or any of the family rooms at the hotels.'

Johnny hesitated.

'Do it, Johnny. Do it now. Daughter or not, that girl needs to learn that no one fucking humiliates me like that.'

Maryanne sat on the balcony of her suite at Sternley. She was weak and tired, and her face was pale and free from make-up. Her hair was tied back in a loose ponytail, and she wore a cashmere sweater, wide-legged, soft jersey trousers and suede ballet pumps. Though the sun was shining, there was a chill in the air. Ducks waddled and bickered next to the lake like old married couples, and she found herself missing Logan's reassuring presence.

Dr Slade sat down next to her, putting a glass of fresh juice on the table in front of her. It was an unappealing, sludgy brown colour, and he noticed her suspicious look. 'Wheatgrass, carrot and acai berries,' he explained. 'It's delicious.'

She tasted it. It was as disgusting as it looked and she raised an eyebrow at him. He had the good grace to laugh and shrug apologetically.

'All right, maybe not. It is good for you, though.' He paused. 'How are you feeling today?'

'Pretty wiped out.'

'It's normal. How about psychologically, emotionally?'

'Again – pretty wiped out.' She sighed. 'The visions . . . It was like watching a film of all the worst bits of my life from the last few years. All the things I'm most ashamed of.'

'It's a reasonably common ibogaine effect. Patients report visions of the process of addiction, events from key moments of its progression.'

'So you lose the withdrawal and gain a slideshow of your worst bits.'

'Sort of. Maybe. We don't completely know how it works. But it does detox you in the most painless way I've seen. Compare that to the symptoms you were experiencing after you overdosed and when you've tried to stop before.'

He was right. She hadn't felt those wracking pains and cramps, that unbearable urge to use, and to quell the storm of withdrawal.

'And maybe the memory of the visions, seeing your descent into addiction like that is a cleansing thing. A reminder, in case you are tempted in the future?'

She nodded. Her eyes filled with tears as she choked. 'I'm so ashamed. Of what I've become.'

'Don't be. Be thankful that you're free of the drugs now – because you *are* free of them. Build up your strength again here. Your body's been through a lot, and it needs time to recover. And then look to the future. To your future, with your family.'

If there was a family for her to return to. Unbeknownst to Maryanne, Logan was getting ready to go to Canada, his thoughts taken up with another woman. Charlie was in bed with Colette, lost in her, absorbed by her. Lucia was sitting chainsmoking in the fire-damaged house, unaware that her father was in the process of cutting her off. The Barnes family was fragmenting.

288

Chapter Eighteen

In his office on the island, inside Luxury, with the door tightly shut, Mark played back the recording he had made a few days previously.

'So don't make excuses, don't tell me how much you desire me. Show me, and show me now, or I'm sending you home and I won't pay a single penny. And I'll bill you for your share of the holiday.'

'Come on, darlin', let's go back to the room. I feel like a line. I want to inhale it off that beautiful body of yours – this bit, just here.'

'Why go back to the room? I want to do it now. Here.'

Mark breathed a sigh of relief. It was done. He downloaded the data to a memory stick, which he slipped into his pocket, before getting on with his day's work. He might be betraying Logan, but he wasn't going to let standards slip. He was a professional, after all.

As LBI's Director of Hotels of some twelve years, Mark had worked closely with Logan on many of his new projects – from boutique city hotels to golfing resorts and country-house spas. It was one such English property that had brought about their meeting and Mark's career, when Logan had found and made an offer on a rundown, relatively minor but architecturally interesting stately home in Dorset. The offer had come at the right time for the Mallory family, or what remained of it, since they were in a dire financial situation, like so many other families since the days of the English landowner had begun to fade. A once large and prosperous estate owned by the family and supporting a village of farmers and estate workers had been reduced to a house that was far too big for its inhabitants and long overdue for major repairs, a garden that was unmanageable without a team of full-time gardeners, and an overdraft that the bank would no longer support. By the time Logan arrived in the back of a Jaguar one drizzly November morning, fresh from New York, the east wing of Sternley House had been closed for three years because of an unsafe roof, the ceiling in the ballroom had been partially destroyed by bats and was leaking water on to the floor, and the minstrels' gallery was out of bounds because of woodworm. But as Logan's car brought him through the gardens, overrun with swathes of tall grass and brambles, past the walled vegetable garden which had once been full of lines of raspberry canes and lettuces and sweetpeas but was now just a mass of weeds, he had seen the pale stone of the building ahead of him and had determined that he would return it to a glory that it hadn't seen for decades.

He had made a generous offer which Mark and his elderly mother had accepted swiftly, on one condition. Although Logan's reputation was good, and they trusted him with the refurbishment and conversion into a luxury hotel of their family home and seat, he was still an American, still a stranger, and they were wary. So Mark specified that he must be employed to stay on in the house and help run it, thus ensuring that Logan didn't suddenly decide to turn the beautiful old building into a holiday camp full of screaming brats and Karaoke nights. And apart from anything else, Mark had been in need of a job, not being qualified for much in the real world. So he'd worked for Logan and learned the basics of the hotel industry, and found, to his slight surprise, that he not only enjoyed the work but was rather good at it. He had a natural sense of what people needed and wanted from different sorts of hotel, an ability to provide the right sort of hospitality and welcome – never intrusive, always calmly and smoothly efficient. He had been brought up to be a different sort of host, but adapted to this new role well.

And so he had moved on from Sternley House eventually, though his mother still lived in her cottage in the grounds, and had worked his way up through LBI, growing with the company into the job he had today, that of Director of Hotels. He worked closely with Logan, assisting him in all things to do with the operations and development of the LBI hotel brand, had a large salary as well as share options in the company and use of a private jet whenever he needed it, three homes around the world, and a wardrobe full of his favourite Savile Row suits. But somehow, it still wasn't enough;

there remained a gap in Mark's soul somewhere between the success he had achieved and the things that would make him truly satisfied. Logan had saved his family home, but in saving it had transformed it into something else, something different. It wasn't Mark's domain any longer, it was Logan's, part of the ever-growing, ever more powerful Brand Barnes. And though Mark knew he should be grateful for the fact that the hotel was a chic one, not some shoddy holiday camp with organised games and canteen-style dining, he would never quite get over the fact that he had not been the one to save it. Oh, he had played a part, but was under no illusions that anything he had done had really been under his control. Logan orchestrated, and Mark was allowed to continue as long as he toed the line.

And for years Mark had plugged these feelings of inadequacy as he'd plugged the holes in Sternley's roof all those years ago, but this time with roulette and clothes and fine cufflinks.

There was something rotten in his soul. He knew it. It was familiar, the devil sitting on his shoulder, urging him on. He succumbed sometimes, and was always filled with disgust afterwards. And since his secret craving had been uncovered he hadn't even been able to indulge in it, so it was festering inside him, fed only by his memories.

One person knew what he really liked. Who he really was. It wasn't his wife. Nor was it Logan or Johnny, who had become his best friends in the years that he had been working for LBI, and particularly since they had moved into the media arena with the development and production of *General Manager*. Mark had never had friends like them before. A quiet, serious child, unable to relax and join in the banter of his schoolmates in fear of looking silly, he had always hung back, watching. It didn't help that even as a teenager, his weakness was beginning to make itself known. He knew he was different. His friendship with Logan and Johnny, their trust of him, made what he was doing all the harder. But he had no choice. He could not risk everyone finding out about him. The thought made him shudder.

And if he didn't go along with Nicolo's plans, he would be laid bare as a pervert, a fraud, a traitor. He had no intention of allowing that to happen.

As he sat, biting his lip nervously, Mark's phone rang.

'Mr Mallory? It's Marie Vignes at Les Jeux Sont Faits.'

'Marie, what can I do for you?'

'*Il y a une problème avec Lucia.* She is phoning, insisting on taking a villa, but we have none free. Threatening to get everyone sacked, shouting at my staff . . . I can't get hold of Monsieur Barnes. He is not taking any calls.'

That was strange. Logan was always available.

'Let me try him, Marie. I'll call you back.' Mark dialled Logan's mobile number.

'Yes?'

'Oh, you are there!' Mark exclaimed. 'Marie Vignes has been trying to reach you.'

'I've been in a meeting.' Logan's tone was clipped, and invited no further questions.

'Right.' Mark outlined the problem. He was brief and to the point. 'Your daughter says she can't stay in London because the media are harassing her.'

'Well, she can deal with it herself. She's not to take rooms at any of the hotels – not Les Jeux, not Luxury. Let the individual property managers know, please.'

Mark agreed and hung up. So spoiled little Miss Barnes had finally pushed Daddy too far, had she? Logan's life really was getting complicated. And it was about to become even more so.

Lucia listened to the holding music on the other end of the phone line, picking the nail varnish off her fingers impatiently until Marie came back to her.

'I'm sorry, Lucia, we are not able to arrange this.'

'Marie, listen to me.'

'Non! You will listen! I have been told you are not to stay here. You will find that the other general managers of your father's hotels say exactly the same thing. No more free stays, Miss Barnes.'

To Lucia's shame, Marie was right. She only phoned one other hotel, the LBI place in Paris. The manager there didn't know her as well as Marie, so was more diffident, but the answer was the same. She was not welcome.

Hot tears ran down her chin and she gulped them back, lighting a cigarette and inhaling deeply. Her hands shook. Why was he doing this to her? It was so completely unfair; she was being treated like a pariah by her own father. She hadn't even done anything wrong! It wasn't her fault some guy she'd slept with had given her the infection and she had passed it on. She hadn't had any symptoms, so it wasn't like she'd done it deliberately, or anything. She had better make a plan, though, since she had hardly any money and now, nowhere to stay either. God, her father was a bastard. Well, she wasn't his daughter for nothing. Two could play at his game.

The night before Logan and Johnny were due to go to Canada, Elise managed to sneak away for the evening, telling Bill that she was going to the birthday dinner for one of the women from her Pilates class. They had arranged to meet in his London office, which occupied the top floor of the building which also housed the Lexington Hotel, near the City. She was nervous all the way there. A whole evening together. She couldn't wait, but at the same time, she felt anxious. The lies to Bill were getting more and more frequent, and she was sure she was going to be found out soon. She couldn't imagine what might happen if she was – but the thought of not seeing Logan was worse.

When she arrived at the hotel she took the lift straight up to his office, and knocked lightly on the door. He opened it straight away.

'Hi,' he said, between kisses, on her cheek, her forehead, the end of her nose. Her skin was soft and smelled faintly of roses.

'Hello,' she replied. 'I missed you.'

'I missed you as well.' His kisses had moved to her lips now. She responded, pulling him closer, until he stopped, moved back.

'I want to show you something,' he told her. 'If we don't stop now, we'll never make it.'

'Make it where?'

He grinned. 'Come on. I'll show you.'

'It's like being on top of the world up here, don't you think?'

The wind blew Elise's hair and it whipped around her face. She held it back with one hand and laughed.

'It's amazing!'

They were on the roof of the hotel, looking out over London. The Eye, Buckingham Palace, the Houses of Parliament – half the landmarks of the city were visible from where they stood.

'This reminds me why I love it here,' Logan said. 'All the buildings are different heights. In the States it's all skyscrapers. No variety. It's like peering through a forest. Look at that.'

He moved behind her and pointed towards the city over her shoulder. She was acutely aware of his body against hers, of the smell of his cologne. He kissed her neck. She leaned back into him, savouring the sensation.

'Shall we eat?' He led her around to the other side of the roof, to a corner behind some pipework, where Elise could see some white canvas fabric, fluttering in the breeze. A white Moroccan tent had been pitched – she couldn't tell how – on the roof. Its front was open, the drapes pulled back, edged with a decorative border. The grey asphalt of the roof was covered with a Bedouin rug, stretching back into the tent and spread with a carpet of cushions, from large floor cushions to small sausage-shaped bolsters, all patterned in reds and oranges and deep purples.

She peered round into the tent itself. A low table sat in the centre, covered with food; a bottle of champagne sat cooling in an ice-bucket. Dipping her head, she went inside the tent, slipping her shoes off. Logan followed her.

'I thought we'd picnic.'

She didn't say anything. Couldn't. Just sat for a moment, looking at this beautiful place, a haven which Logan had once again created for her.

'You're like a magician,' she whispered. 'How do you do it?'

'Oh, I can't tell you that, I'm afraid. Magic Circle ethics, you know. You might tell everyone how to pull a rabbit out of a hat, or . . .'

Oh, shut up, Logan, for God's sake! she was thinking. *Stop talking and kiss me.* And then he did.

They were tentative at first. Elise was worried, as Logan's hand ran up the side of her body and down over her breast, that she would feel embarrassed about being naked in front of a man other than Bill. But when it came to it, when Logan pulled her top over her head and laid her back on the bed of cushions, all of her nervousness and worries disappeared. She let go of him so that he could undress, which he did quickly, and then positioned himself above her, cradling her head in the crook of his arm. And quickly, the uncertainty dissolved, and there was no doubt in either their minds or bodies.

The carpet was rough against the skin of Elise's back, and a breeze blew in from outside, running down her body and making the hairs on her arm stand up. Wrapping her legs around Logan, she focused on the sensation of the weight of his body pressing down on to hers. He stopped moving and propped his upper body up on his arms so he could look into her eyes.

'I love you.' He surprised himself by saying the words he knew he meant, but hadn't meant to say.

'I'm sorry,' he whispered. 'Is it too soon?'

'Yes, it is. But I don't care. And I love you too.' The relief was immense, for both of them. Lowering his head, he kissed her deeply and began to move inside her again, urgently.

Later, they drank the champagne and ate the dinner that had been left for them. Logan reached into the cushions and pulled out a glossy black box, handing it ceremoniously to Elise.

'I almost forgot,' he said. 'They arrived.'

She took off the lid, moved aside the silk rose buds that lay on top of the tissue paper, and lifted one of the shoes out.

They were even more stunning than she could have imagined. The pale green silk shimmered, and the embroidery was delicate, a work of art. The crystals glittered.

'Oh, Logan. They're princess shoes.'

'Turn them over.'

She flipped the shoe over. The sole was creamy leather. She stared. The brilliant-cut diamond shone back at her.

'Oh my God. That song, it's my favourite – "Diamonds on the Soles of Her Shoes". How did you know?'

'Hmm, confession time. I read your file.'

'My . . . oh, from the hotel?'

'Yes.' He kissed her breast.

'So you've been checking up on me?'

'No. Reading up on you. It's different.'

'I see.'

His tongue flicked at her nipple. He raised his head for a moment, asking, 'Are you mad?'

She laughed. 'No, I'm definitely not mad.'

She couldn't believe he'd done this. And she couldn't believe she was the sort of woman who could inspire such grand gestures. But one look at his face told her that, at least to this man, she really was. Lying back, she watched lazily as his head moved further down her body.

When she woke the next morning, Elise lay in bed for a while before getting up, letting a hundred fragments of the previous night float through her head. It felt as if the evening had happened years ago, or to some other person. In another life. But was it meant to be *her* other life?

After Logan had dropped her off, driving himself so as to avoid using his own driver, she had headed up to the apartment. Nervous, in case Bill was still up, or got back before she'd got into bed. When she had opened the door and seen his jacket slung over the back of one of the dining chairs, her heart had started to thump. *Please no, please not another row, another fight. Not tonight – not after such a perfect evening.* But the flat was quiet, and when she pushed open the door to their bedroom, she could see that he was fast asleep. The room smelled of stale whisky. She undressed quickly and slid under the covers, careful not to wake him.

Now she stretched, got out of bed and went to her en suite bathroom, holding a bottle of Jo Malone bath oil above the running water. It was early, Danny would still be asleep. When the bath was full, she lay in the scented water until it was lukewarm. Dreaming ... daydreaming ...

Slowly, she got out of the bath and pulled on a pair of jeans and a cashmere vest. Coffee. She needed coffee, maybe then she'd be able to wake up.

The bedroom door was stuck. She pulled harder. Damn, it must be jammed. Yet another thing wrong with this place she lived in that was meant to be so perfect and was in fact a complete pain. Picking up the phone, she rang Ines. She'd ask her to come in early and help unstick the door. The woman's phone was turned off. Damn. She tried Bill's mobile, but he didn't reply. It was stupid, she knew it was, but she felt herself starting to panic. Danny would be awake soon. She needed to get out of the room. Elise forced herself to breathe in deeply as she dialled Bill's office number.

'Crown Asset Management.'

'Bill McAllister's office, please.'

'One moment please.'

'Marjorie Vincent.'

'Marjorie, it's Elise McAllister.'

Bill's assistant was never anything but polite to Elise, who nevertheless sensed disapproval in her voice and manner whenever they spoke or met.

'Good morning, Mrs McAllister. What can I do for you?'

'I'd like to speak to Bill, please.'

There was a short pause.

'I'm afraid he's in a meeting with a client.'

'It's quite important.' She made herself sound firm, confident. She was Bill's wife; she had every right to ask to be put through to him if she needed to. She wouldn't let the woman unnerve her.

'I'm sorry, Mrs McAllister, but he specifically asked not to be disturbed. Not even for you. He did say to tell you not to worry about Danny, he's dropped him off at school already.'

After Elise had hung up the phone she thought about what Marjorie had said. *'Not even for you'*. So he'd given her a direct order not to put Elise through to him. Why? She never called him at work. Why had he thought that she would today? And then it came to her. He'd locked her into her bedroom, like you might a badly behaved child, when you wanted to teach them a lesson. And he'd known she'd eventually phone him at work, which was why he'd planned to refuse her call. The realisation that her husband had locked her in her room was so ridiculous that if it hadn't been quite so sinister, she might have laughed.

Later, she heard the door unlock and Bill's footsteps, quiet on the thick carpet. It was funny how someone's tread, their walk, was so distinctive. The unique style in which they made their way through the world. She continued to unravel a long silver chain that had become wound round upon itself and somehow enmeshed with a pair of chandelier earrings, the little aquamarines and diamonds twisted and tied up with the fine metal. Carefully she worked them apart from each other, making sure she didn't force it and bend anything. She didn't turn to look at her husband. She was glad that her hands happened to be busy when he came in; it gave her something to focus on, helped her remember to go slowly.

'Ines has taken Danny out for his tea. I came home early. Thought we should talk, so you can tell me where you were last night – among other things.'

'What if there had been a fire? Did you think of that? Maybe you did. Maybe that would have been preferable, the thought of me trapped.'

Bill shrugged a little, she could see him do it in the dressing-table mirror. 'There's the balcony.'

She was silent. What was there to say to that, after all? She carefully laid the earrings back in their proper place, and turned to look at Bill. He was standing, self-assured, arrogant.

'Whether you want to talk or not, I've got some things to say. Come downstairs and have a drink when you're ready.'

There was no suggestion of a question in his tone or his body language, as he made his way out of the room and downstairs. Confident in his superior status as the man of the house, the decision-maker, the one in control.

But he was about to realise that the tables had turned.

As Bill's hand swiped across her face, she realised that the tables were never going to turn. Not in her favour, anyhow, not within this marriage. She faltered, and held on to the edge of the table for balance. She could hear him breathing hard: it made her want to be sick. She collected herself for a moment.

'I know about the account,' she said.

'Yes, I figured. Seth told me he'd spoken to you. Left a message with you. I never got it.'

'And I know what you've been doing with the money.'

He didn't say anything. Just sipped his whisky and looked at her. She stared back, defiant.

'How could you, Bill? How could you put us at risk like that, put your son's future at risk?'

'You don't know what you're talking about.'

'I know exactly what I'm talking about. You, forward-trading, front-running . . . It's illegal! You could go to *jail*.'

He inclined his head slightly.

'You worked it out. Clever girl. I thought you probably would. That's why I told Seth to play along, if you phoned him. I wanted to see if you trusted me. And you didn't. Do you know how that makes me feel, Elise?'

'How it makes *you* feel?'

He took a step towards her.

'Yes, me. This is about me, Elise, not you. I'm the one who's put all the work in here, I'm the one making the money. What the fuck do you contribute to this family, exactly?'

Don't listen, Elise told herself. *Don't give into that little voice inside your head that says he's right, that you're nothing, you're no one.*

'I've got the account statements,' she said. 'I want you to give me a divorce. I want you to let me go, no arguments. Or I'm going to give them to Crown, and to the DTI, and whoever else, and let them work it out for themselves.'

Bill shook his head. 'Oh dear. Not such a clever girl, after all.' He smiled. 'It's all in your name, Elise. *It's in your name.* You're my wife. Do you really think anyone's going to believe that you didn't have anything to do with it?'

Hold steady, she told herself. *Hold firm.*

'But by that point, it won't matter. Crown will investigate it – they'll have to. The firm will suffer; you'll probably lose your job. And fine, go ahead and blame it on me, take me down with you. But why? Why not just let me go? Because our relationship is so great? Because you love me so much?'

She laughed, but she was crying as well now, she couldn't help it.

'Fuck it, Bill. Just let me go.' She closed her eyes and sobbed.

'My family don't do divorce, you know that. You knew that when you married me. I am not prepared to embarrass my parents, damage my career, so that you can take my money and piss off with my son.'

'I don't need your money, I don't want any money from you.'

'Because you've got your own money, stashed away in your little secret account?' His laugh was cruel. 'Yes, I know about that too.'

She wept. He knew everything. But she could still expose him.

'So you're prepared to lose everything you've worked for, risk it all? Because whether it's in my name or not, you'd be ruined. You know you would.'

'Ah, Lisey. Nice bluff. But you're not at the poker table now, my love. The question isn't what *I'm* prepared to lose. Are *you* prepared to risk losing Danny?'

He cupped her face in his hand. Stroked her cheek with his thumb.

'I didn't think so. Make no mistake, Elise. If you expose me, you will lose him. Are you prepared for that, Lisey? Are you ready to lose your son?'

She shook her head. That was that, then. He had won.

The three-storey lodge nestled within its own private forest, and as the snow-chains of the SUV chuntered their way through the trees, Johnny and Logan relaxed and enjoyed the drive. Before long, the post-and-beam-constructed building came into view and the lodge's electric gates began slowly opening to let the car through. Over the years they'd both spent many happy weeks here, holidaying, brainstorming with other members of the executive board, and heliskiing – which is what they'd come to do now, ski and breathe in the air that felt like pure oxygen. At the top of the stone steps, by the main entrance, the housekeeper, Judith, waited for them.

'Elise McAllister's on the line for you, Mr Barnes. The switchboard said you'd particularly asked that she be put through at any time.'

Ignoring Johnny's quizzical look, Logan got out of the car quickly and followed Judith into the lodge. He picked up one of the handsets in the great room, keen to speak to Elise. The huge, vaulted ceilings let the bright light stream into the room.

'Elise. Hello, darling.'

'Hello.' There was a pause. 'Where are you?'

'I've just arrived in Whistler. Is everything all right?'

He heard her sigh down the phone line. The sound cut into his heart.

'Elise, what's wrong? Talk to me.'

'I'm very sorry, Logan, but I can't see you again.' The words came out in a rush.

'*What?*'

'I made a mistake. I apologise for any confusion and upset I've caused you.'

'Elise, no! Is this about Bill? Because I told you, you don't have to put up with it. I can help you.'

'I don't want you to help me. I don't need any help. Like I said, I made a mistake, and I apologise for – for leading you to believe there could be something between us. There can't. Ever. Please don't contact me again. Please. Promise me.'

Logan was stunned. 'Right. No apologies necessary,' he said hoarsely. 'I quite understand.' He was surprised by the sheer amount of pain that he felt. 'I promise not to contact you again.'

In her room, Elise spoke again. 'I'm sorry,' she said, but he had gone, and the line was dead.

'I love you,' she added. But there was no one there to hear.

That night, Logan and Johnny sat in the hot tubs on the entertainment deck of the lodge, overlooking the mountains. They'd given the chef the night off, lit the barbecue on the terrace and grilled steaks to eat with homemade bread and dollops of thick, strong mustard. Now, with bellies full of meat and beer, they let the jets of hot water swirl round their tired limbs. Whirls of steam rose into the cold night air, and their breath turned into clouds as they talked and drank chilled bottles of lager.

'I can't believe I've practically disowned my daughter.'

'Lucia's not stupid. Soon as she realises you're serious she'll sort her shit out.'

'You think?'

'I know it. What else is she going to do – go and get a job?'

'Ha. Good point.' Logan reached for another beer.

'You're lucky, you know, Johnny. No children to worry about, no wives to pay for. Not yet, anyway. Going to pop the question to the Park Avenue Princess, are you?'

'Fuck, no.'

'Thank God for that. I was worried I was going to have to be your best man and then I'd have had to lose the rings or something.'

'No. I'd better ditch her actually – she keeps on dropping hints. Don't know why, as I know she's still seeing her ex as well. I don't reckon I'll ever get married. No point, unless it's like you and Maryanne.'

Logan didn't reply.

'I know things aren't good at the moment, but you're all right, aren't you?'

'Fine. Things are going to be fine.' He stood and stepped out of the hot tub, grabbing a thick robe. 'Fancy a whisky?'

Water dripped off him and evaporated on the heated tiles as he walked across the deck, to the bar in the corner of the great hall. Johnny followed him.

'Who is she, Logan? I mean, I know it's Elise, but why her? Why now?'

Logan poured a generous measure into two glasses and handed one to Johnny. In the stone fireplace a fire crackled and spat the occasional spark on to the hearth. Logan turned on the surround sound system, and the chords of a blues guitar filled the room, low and rhythmic and raw. His friend waited patiently for him to speak. When he did so, his voice was thick with alcohol and emotion.

'She's . . . Johnny, you know I will always love Maryanne. She's my wife, she's the mother of my children, she's my family. But it's over between us – our marriage is over. It's gone too far – there've been too many things . . .'

He sighed.

'We've both made mistakes. We've both hurt each other in ways you just can't come back from. And this, Elise, is something . . . I don't know. She phoned me earlier, saying she doesn't want to see me again, saying she made a mistake. I know it wasn't a mistake. I love her, Johnny. I can't let her walk away. I just can't.'

They had stayed up late, not talking any more about Elise, but playing pool and listening to music. They set off early the next morning. The view from the helicopter was astonishing. Bright, white, untouched slopes of powder snow swept down below them for what looked like miles. The sky was the clear blue of a child's crayon, unbroken by a single cloud. Perfect. Johnny put on his sunglasses. The light was hurting his eyes, and making the throbbing pain in his head worse. He felt unusually rough for the amount he'd drunk. Normally he never got hangovers – at least, nothing he couldn't shake off after an hour or so of waking. He'd taken some painkillers with his coffee but they weren't touching this.

The chopper dropped them at the top of the mountain. It looked like the crest of a wave. Logan and Johnny stood for a few seconds, then looked at each other, nodded, and set off, sweeping down the slopes, weaving from side to side, leaving softly zig-zagging furrows in their wake. The cold air rushed past Johnny's face, zipping through his brain, working its way into every cell in his body.

It should have been energising him, but today it was leaving him feeling weak and dizzy, battered. When they reached the bottom of the run he felt out of breath. Logan turned to him, exuberant. 'God I've missed this. You forget what a simple rush it is.'

Johnny nodded.

'You OK?' Logan frowned.

'Yeah, yeah. Let's get the chopper to come round and go higher.'

He'd be fine.

Halfway down the next peak, Johnny realised that he was not fine. The headache and nausea had got worse. This wasn't just a hangover. The dizziness was coming back now, his head feeling light and full of air, and his legs starting to weaken. He tried to slow down, but the combination of the speed he had already gathered and the lack of control he could exert over his muscles made it impossible. His legs splayed dangerously and then, in what seemed to be in slow motion, one leg crumpled behind the other, and he lost control, falling forward and tumbling through the drifts of snow.

The first warning Logan got that something was wrong was the sound of a cry, and he swished to a stop, a plume of snow flaring up behind his skis. He turned to where he had last seen Johnny, just above him and to his left. But he wasn't there. Logan skied quickly over to the side of the mountain, where it fell off and down sharply, and to his horror, saw the body of his friend falling forward, rushing down the steep incline.

He leaned over, craning his neck, but couldn't get down the slope behind Johnny; it was far too steep, too dangerous. He took the radio from the pocket of his ski-suit.

'Get back here now,' he told the pilot, 'and call 911. Johnny's fallen. We're on the west slope. Hurry, it's bad.'

And then all he could do was stand and watch as his old friend's body slowly came to a stop far, far below him, and lay there, his limbs at angles that were wrong, all wrong.

The helicopter landed as close to where Johnny had come to a stop as possible, but it was still some distance from where he lay. The pilot signalled to Logan to go back. There was another helicopter flying in and landing near Logan. He couldn't move, just stood and stared as the pilot, who was trained in mountain rescue and emergency first aid, began to make his way to Johnny's body. He was going to need more than he could provide, much more. If he was even alive still. He was alive, of course he would be. He had to be.

'Come to the chopper, Mr Barnes. We can keep in contact from there.' The pilot of the second helicopter ushered him back and towards the aircraft. 'An air-evac team is on its way.'

Logan nodded. The radio crackled.

'What's the situation?' the second pilot asked.

'He's breathing, but it's bad, he's in a bad way. I'll do what I can, but I don't have the equipment to deal with these sorts of injuries. I need the evac team here now.'

'We've got an ETA of ten minutes.'

'I don't know if I can keep him going for that long.'

Logan grabbed the radio. 'Keep him alive, Phil. Do whatever you have to do, but fucking well keep him alive.'

Johnny was strapped to the board, a tube in his mouth, his head held steady as the team attached a harness and prepared to airlift him off the side of the mountain. They were working quickly, against the cold as well as Johnny's multiple injuries.

Logan waited at the hospital while an emergency medical team worked on his friend. As his next-of-kin he signed the consent forms for Johnny to be operated on. He filled out the insurance forms and confirmed that Johnny was able to pay for any costs not covered by his policies. He waited while Johnny was transferred to the OR, and during the eight hours of surgery that followed. Johnny had no immediate family. No wife, children or parents to rush to his bedside, although his girlfriend Melissa was on her way. But Logan was the one listed as next-of-kin on Johnny's medical records, Logan was the one who had always been there for his friend, his brother, and who would be there for him now. Just a few hours ago he had been envying Johnny his freedom, his lack of dependants. Now, as he lay in an operating theatre with only Logan waiting outside for news, it seemed so desperately lonely.

There was a rap on the door and a doctor in surgical scrubs entered to tell him that Johnny was stable at last, though by no means out of danger. His list of injuries was both terrifying and confusing. The terminology washed over Logan as he listened: Johnny had a basilar skull fracture, an intracranial hematoma, and a diffuse axonal injury, caused by the brain being jolted back and forth like a cocktail in a shaker. This usually resulted in a prolonged coma and multiple injuries to the brain. They would monitor him for increased pressure, the doctor said. A decompressive craniectomy might be necessary to relieve it. There was a strong possibility of seizures.

Eventually the doctor was finished. They sat, waiting. He summed up. 'Essentially, Mr Barnes, your friend is lucky to be alive. He'll be even luckier if he stays that way.'

News of Johnny's accident travelled fast. Logan's phone was going mad. He called Rachel and asked her to fly out immediately. Then he turned his phone off and drove back to the lodge, where he slept deeply for four hours.

When he woke, Logan lay in the double-ended freestanding copper bath that sat on a raised platform. He had always loved the view from here, loved lying in the hot water and watching the light change over the mountain peaks. Now they had lost their beauty and majesty, and instead seemed sinister, foreboding. All he could think of when he looked at them was how Johnny had looked, lying broken on the ground; all he could hear was his cry as he fell, hitting rocks and boulders on his journey down. Logan submerged his head in the hot water, rinsed, and then got out of the bath. He turned away from the window as he called Rachel on the intercom and asked her to arrange transport to New York for himself, and then to remain with Johnny and accompany him to New York as soon as he was stable enough to be transferred to NY Presbyterian, where Logan had the best doctors available standing by. The thought of surgeons operating on Johnny's brilliant legal mind was unthinkable, the prospect of severe brain damage a significant one.

Now, all Logan wanted was to get back to the city. The lodge had lost its magic for him, and he longed to get out of there and away from the mountains. Johnny was in the best hands possible and he should be attending to all the other things that awaited him. But now he would have to do so without the support of the man who had been by his side for even longer than his wife. For the first time in many years, Logan felt as if he was walking through life alone.

Elise saw the news of the accident on the internet. To her shame, she had been guiltily Googling Logan's name, when a news site came up. She watched with dismay as the reports showed him leaving the hospital near Whistler, looking drawn and worried. An image of the mountains where the accident had happened followed, along with an exterior shot of the lodge. One news programme featured a doctor commenting on what were reported to be Johnny's injuries. The prognosis looked bleak.

On impulse she bought a postcard and sent it to Logan.

The only sure thing about luck is that it will change, she wrote on it, and then sent it to LBI's head office address in London.

Chapter Nineteen

Maryanne was bored. Logan was running LBI from the New York offices and spending any free time visiting Johnny, sometimes working from the hospital with Rachel. She'd wanted to go over there as well when she had left Sternley, but Logan claimed he was working almost constantly, and at erratic hours, distracted, not sleeping. He said she needed her rest, time to recover from the stressful time she'd had recently, the fire. She believed him. There was something else though. She sensed that he didn't want to be around her. She couldn't really blame him. Time was when he would have turned straight to her in a crisis; now, he had turned to his executives, to his work, and she had turned to – to whom? Not to Charlie. Her son was buried in the studio, deep in his album. And he was wary of her still, despite her recent detox. He had said he needed to see that she was genuine about getting better before he could trust her again.

God, she would kill for a glass of wine. A crisp Sancerre, or a Pouilly Fuissé – now that would be perfect. She could almost taste it. She sighed and shut the interior design magazine that she had been flicking through in an attempt to find inspiration for the redecoration they would have to do following the fire damage. She was staying in the Lexington now, as her house wouldn't be habitable again for a while. Maybe she would rent somewhere in the meantime, rather than staying here. She stood up and looked at herself in the full-length mirror. In the few days since leaving Sternley after her detox she'd put on three kilos. If she carried on at this rate she'd be the size of a whale in a week and Logan would never want to come home.

Logan. Something was wrong. She could feel it. Something more than Johnny. She'd asked him what was really the matter on the phone the other day, and he'd just answered in astonishment: 'Johnny almost *died*, Maryanne! He still might. No one knows if he'll ever walk again, ever talk, ever wake up, even. I'm sorry if, under the circumstances, I'm not paying you quite enough attention.'

Distraction. She needed a distraction. She could go shopping, but she couldn't really be bothered to deal with all the people everywhere. Clicking open her laptop, she typed in the address of an online designer shop with a same-day delivery service. Two hours later, she had three new handbags, seven pairs of shoes, a pair of suede boots, four dresses, two coats, three jackets, eleven casual tops, and five new pairs of designer jeans. Oh, and three necklaces and a ring. And a pair of sunglasses. The smartly striped black and white bags took up much of the floor space in her substantial suite.

But still she wasn't happy. She missed Lucia, who had been completely unavailable since Maryanne had left Sternley, phoning her only once to say that she was staying with friends.

'Who, darling? I want to see your pretty face. Come on, it's not that bad, you don't have to hide away from me. I'm your mama – nothing you've done is going to make me cross with you for long.'

But Lucia had just made an excuse about having a call on the other line and hung up.

Maryanne was bored and, if she was honest, a bit lonely. Friends had been phoning since the fire, sending flowers and gifts, but Logan had told everyone she'd gone away for a few days to recover. All her engagements had been cancelled, all invitations answered on her behalf. Well, it wasn't a lie, she had needed to recover. But now her children were both off doing their own thing, Logan was thousands of miles away, babysitting Johnny – oh, fuck it. She shouldn't think like that. Demons, demons, making her jealous and spiteful. Of course Logan wanted to be with Johnny. But a little, unworthy part of Maryanne wondered why Johnny was more important than she was. Didn't she deserve some help and attention as well?

Oh, stop it, Maryanne, stop feeling sorry for yourself. That's not going to help anyone. Her mind wandered once more to the bottle of wine she wanted to order from room service – although she knew that if she did, the staff would be straight on to Logan. She shouldn't drink. She'd promised everyone. And she wanted to be better, she really did. She *was* better – Dr Slade had seen to that. So, she should celebrate. Yes! She felt like seeing people again, re-entering society. She would hold a party to celebrate the new her. Rejuvenated, renewed; cleansed and fabulous.

She picked up the phone.

The next day, Maryanne paused before she entered the restaurant downstairs in the hotel, where she was holding a lunch for fifty of her closest girlfriends. On her feet were olive-green silk Christian Louboutin court shoes, with bows like camellias bursting out from their four-inch heels. Her natural-looking blond hair, which had taken four and a half hours to achieve, was pinned up into a gentle chignon, with a sweeping fringe and a few strands free around her face. The up-do showed off her only jewellery – a pair of chandelier earrings that were made from a shower of rare green diamonds. They swung as she moved, dozens of little stones catching the sunlight. Her make-up was subtle, complementing the skin that had been injected with Botox and Restylane, peeled and plumped with creams packed with vitamins, enzymes, fermented marine extracts, fruit acids, anti-aging hormones; all of which variously promised to repair frayed chromosomes, plump up tired skin cells, strengthen collagen, mend DN, reverse UV damage ... Maryanne was determined to present a fresh, polished front to her friends, enjoy her lunch, then tomorrow she would find out where Lucia was staying and spend some time with her, like they used to. Drag Charlie out of the studio for a bit, find out what was going on with him. Her beautiful boy. She would be a proper mother again – it wasn't too late for that, was it? No, of course not. She would look good, she would feel good. She would *be* good. She had to be. She had no choice. Because if she wasn't – if she slipped back again, if she allowed the demons to catch her – everyone was going to leave her and she would be all alone. Maryanne didn't want to be left all alone.

Placing a smile on her face that was as sparkling as the gems themselves, she pushed open the doors to the Orangerie. The room fell quiet, and then was filled with a round of applause from the finely manicured hands of fifty of London's socialites. Wives of Russian oligarchs, aristocrats, celebrities. Women whose combined wealth was far greater than that of various countries. These were the people

Maryanne filled her life with, whom she lunched and shopped and drank with – whom she *had* drunk with, she reminded herself. Maryanne suddenly became very aware that she was standing there alone, as if on a pedestal; polished, admired, but by herself. The room was very big all of a sudden, and full of people that she didn't know, didn't care about, not really. This was just another lunch for them, something to fill the gap in the day, to tick off in their diaries. They weren't the people who mattered. The ones who did were her son, her daughter – her husband. Her family, her only family. Her mother had died years ago, when the children were still quite young. They didn't remember her – luckily. Sativa had been vicious by the end of her life, stuck in the council house where her mother, Ada, had died. And grown drunk and bitter and spiteful. Maryanne saw her as little as she could, not wanting to expose Charlie and Lucia to her vodka-fuelled vitriol. It had been the right decision.

After her father-in-law's death – and Maryanne had never even met him – Elizabeth Barnes had sold the house and gone to live in Australia with her new husband. Logan hadn't seen his mother for years.

The kids had asked about their grandparents sometimes, as they grew up and realised that lots of their schoolfriends had grandmothers and grandfathers to take them out for treats and ice creams, and that they didn't – but they weren't that bothered really. You didn't miss what you'd never had, she supposed. And she had worked hard to make up for anything they might miss out on, to spend time with them and treat them – or she had done so once. Not for a while, it was true. But she would do so again. Her children. They were the ones who mattered.

The applause began to die down. She had to move, had to do something. *Pull yourself together, Maryanne.* And she did. She went towards the tables, began to circulate, greeting her guests. Was she a friend or a freak show for them, she wondered wryly. And as she went from table to table, chatty and charming, Maryanne's smile was wide, her laugh was light – but her heart was heavy and sad.

Rachel looked over the bill for Maryanne's lunch which the restaurant manager had sent through to Logan's office to be signed off. Not only had she provided her fifty friends with individual splits of vintage

Krug at a cost of more than a hundred pounds each, she'd also insisted the restaurant serve the complex and multi-course 'menu prestige' with her own selection of wines, which had not only cost ten thousand pounds, but had also sent the temperamental French chef into a frenzy of rage, and he'd stormed out immediately the meal had finished. In addition to the lunch, Maryanne had given each of her guests gift bags containing products from the hotel's spa. She'd chosen the premium products, naturally: a tube of under-eye serum, a moisturiser that contained white gold, and a cellular-reconstruction night cream sold in the spa shop for a total of two hundred and fifty pounds.

All in all, Maryanne's little lunch was going to cost Logan the best part of thirty thousand pounds. And that didn't include her new outfit or jewellery, the cost of which Rachel would bet at least equalled that figure. Taking a deep breath, she knocked on Logan's office door, not looking forward to being the bearer of this news. Few people would ever guess it, but LBI was in a delicate situation financially. Luxury had cost a phenomenal amount of money to build, outfit and launch, and it wouldn't start making any of that sum back for some time. Logan had put a significant amount of his own money into his dream hotel, so it was up to the other properties to perform even better than usual to cover the shortfall, and there were a couple that weren't doing so. There would be a board meeting to discuss this, along with the consequences and strategy to deal with Johnny's absence, but meanwhile Logan had told Rachel to keep a slightly closer eye on the outgoings, and tell him about any unusually large bills rather than just signing them off as she might have been authorised to do before. Thirty thousand pounds wasn't much in the scheme of things, and Logan could still easily afford it, but he was also aware that the spending habits of his family were prodigious, and could get out of control quickly.

Johnny's absence . . . Rachel had been shocked at his condition when she had visited him, and then accompanied him, unconscious and unknowing, back to New York, the city he loved. His face was covered in cuts and was swollen and discoloured, dark bruises marking the skin under his eyes. He was transported to New York Presbyterian in a specially equipped air ambulance, and Rachel had sat on the other side of the plane and watched as the doctors had monitored him throughout the flight, constantly checking his vital signs. At one point, he'd started to convulse. Rachel had looked up in alarm, but the doctor's voice had been calm and his movements careful and deliberate as he inserted a dose of some drug into the IV that was in Johnny's arm.

'It's because of the injuries he sustained falling,' he said, without looking round. 'His brain was shaken. If you imagine putting a lump of clay inside a tennis ball and then playing a game of tennis with it, that's what his brain suffered. Your friend needs further surgery; this wasn't something the hospital in Whistler had the facilities to deal with.'

Rachel assumed this description was intended to illustrate things without using a lot of technical medical language, but all it did was implant the horrific image of Johnny's head being batted around a tennis court into her mind.

She'd stayed with him for a couple of hours when they arrived in New York, after the medical team had transferred him from the plane into an ambulance, and then unloaded him again at the other end. They were careful lifting him, making sure every movement was smooth and gentle, but still she'd felt anguished at the way this strong man who was usually filled with so much energy was being carted around like a parcel, entirely unaware of what was happening to him. At least, she hoped he wasn't aware of it.

'Thirty thousand pounds? On lunch?'

'And take-home gifts.'

Logan laughed grimly. 'Yes, yes, of course, the take-home gifts – mustn't forget those.' He stood up from behind his desk. 'This is fucking ridiculous. I have no desire to be mean, but all that money on a weekday lunch, for no particular reason? What's next, gold-plated knickers?' He sighed.

Rachel wasn't sure what to say. Her relationship with Logan was good and open. But she still didn't think joining him in berating his wife would be a good idea. Then she smiled. 'Diamonds on the soles of her shoes, maybe?'

She laughed. For some reason, Logan didn't. His face clouded over.

'Sign it off, Rachel. But I'll have to talk to Maryanne about her spending.'

'Of course.' She hesitated. 'I'm sorry if what I said was inappropriate.'

He looked at her, confused. 'What?'

'The joke – about diamonds. I apologise.'

Logan was still thinking about Elise. She hadn't called. He missed her badly. She wouldn't return his calls, and his emails went unanswered. He missed her and he was worried about her. Could she really have meant what she said – that the whole thing had been a mistake?

He dragged himself back to New York and his office, where Rachel was waiting, her expression nervous. 'Sorry, I've got a lot on my mind. Please don't worry – it's fine.'

She nodded, relieved.

'How is Johnny?' Logan continued.

'Stable, they say. Going into surgery. I'll let you know as soon as they get in touch.'

'I'll go over there later.' Logan sighed. 'Is the agenda for the meeting ready?'

'In your inbox. There's also a report from Mark regarding Luxury – he's arriving back here tomorrow – and some updates from Paris and Berlin that you need to look at.'

'Will do.'

'Also, regarding the awards ceremony, the show's film crew will be there, of course, and they want an interview with you and Maryanne after you've collected the award. I'll call Maryanne about that, if you like. Larry Morton want to lend her jewellery for it as well.'

'Good. Yes, if you can let her know about that – when is she arriving?'

He needed to talk to Maryanne before the awards ceremony that she was coming over from London for. The first series of *General Manager* had been nominated for Best Reality Show in the annual TV awards, and he would be going to the ceremony, hoping to collect the prestigious glass trophy. Maryanne would be on his arm, and Mark would be there. Johnny should have been there as well; it should have been the three of them. Logan was reminded again of how much he missed Johnny being by his side, giving him advice, teasing him. He wanted to know what Johnny thought he should do about Elise, about his marriage, about so many things. About Lucia too.

'Oh, and Rachel – where's Lucia?'

Ah. 'We're not sure.'

He looked up sharply. 'She hasn't phoned?'

'Not since Marie told her she wouldn't be able to stay at Les Jeux. Then she called Paris, and they also informed her she couldn't have a room there, according to your instructions.'

'And she's not at the house? Surely she's phoned Maryanne?'

Rachel shook her head. 'No. And Charlie hasn't heard from her either. I called him this morning. He's working in the studio.'

'I see.'

Not knowing what to say was an unusual feeling for Logan. He picked up a pen from his desk, then put it back down again. He wasn't worried about Lucia. Despite having had the access to her trust fund and the credit cards that were linked to his accounts cut off, she still had her own bank account, and he knew there was plenty of money in there, easily enough so that she would be fine for a few months at her normal rate of spending – a good few years at most people's.

But where was she?

Maryanne perched on an upholstered stool in front of a full-length cheval mirror as the woman draped a selection of fine jewels round her neck and wrists; a security guard looked on impassively. She had flown to New York that morning, to join Logan for the TV awards ceremony. She was nervous. She hadn't seen her husband since she had left for Sternley, since the fire at their London house. She knew he was angry with her, about that and about the lunch. He had phoned her, raging, 'You can't just throw my money around like this, Maryanne, it's not fucking on!'

'*Your* money? However big and important you think you are, now you're on TV, getting awards, flying around opening hotels, you're still my husband as well, so it's *our* money. I get a say, Logan, I get to have a say as well.'

'So say something – anything – that explains to me why you needed to drop thirty grand on entertaining a load of women who wouldn't even know your name if you weren't married to me. I'm the only reason you have that money and you know it.'

She had slammed the phone down on him then. He was so arrogant. But he was also right.

The woman placed a pearl and diamond pendant round her neck, fastening it expertly at the back. Maryanne wrinkled her nose. Not that one. But she would buy something. So it was his fucking money, was it? She would show him! The woman removed it and placed it carefully in its velvet-lined case. She selected another, and held it up for Maryanne to see. Ah, now this was more like it. A large, cushion-cut diamond sparkled in the centre of the piece, surrounded by a row of black diamonds, and was suspended from a string of the same darkly gleaming stones.

'I like it,' said Maryanne, and the woman nodded, and put it on her. The necklace lay flat on her skin, and the centre stone was huge and hypnotic. Its stark whiteness contrasted with the darkness surrounding it, and picked up the creaminess of her skin and red-blond hair.

'Get the gown from my wardrobe, will you?' she said, and her maid Carla nodded and disappeared into Maryanne's bedroom, returning with the dress in its plastic protective sheath. She slipped the cover off and held it against up Maryanne so she could view the ensemble together. It was ideal. The stiff black taffeta was dotted with little crystal studs and seed pearls, and was strapless, so her décolletage provided the ideal setting for the necklace. Maryanne reached a hand behind her neck to sweep her hair up loosely with one hand. Yes, up, she thought; it would give a marvellous line to her bare shoulders. The woman from Larry Morton held a simple diamond stud up to her ear, a single five-carat stone cut in the same cushion shape as the central stone of the necklace.

'Yes, those set it off rather nicely, don't they?' Maryanne said. Then she had a thought, and caught the woman's eye in the mirror. 'How much are the earrings?'

'Nine hundred and fifty thousand dollars, madam.'

Maryanne thought for a moment. She wanted to show Logan that he couldn't walk all over her, tell her that people wouldn't know who she was without him. That had hurt her, really hurt her, because it hit right to the heart of what Maryanne thought when she lay sleepless in the night. That she was worthless. Heard the little voice in her head that said, Who are you? Maryanne Barnes, you've wasted your life. You've turned into someone you said you would never be – your mother, someone who turns and runs when things get hard. Who hides in drink and drugs, so she doesn't have to feel. And so his words on the phone had aroused that darkness within her. She was a bad wife, a bad mother; she'd lied, betrayed people who loved her. Proved, once and for all, that she was utterly undeserving of that love.

She looked at the woman. She would buy the earrings. He would see, then; maybe he would finally open his eyes and see her. She needed him to see her again.

'I think I'll keep them. A memento of the evening.'

'Very good, Mrs Barnes. We'll just collect the necklace tomorrow, then. Now. Can I pour you a glass of champagne?'

The woman's hand was poised, the bottle was in her hand. Maryanne could see the droplets of condensation on its side. Just one. Just the one glass wouldn't do any harm, she was sure. It would just make it easier, let her play her part without feeling so empty inside. Yes. It would all be fine.

'Why not?'

The woman nodded, slid the cork out of the bottle with a soft pop, and poured.

The street outside the Royal Hotel was bustling with paparazzi and a queue of limousines waiting to let their passengers out as close to the red carpet as possible, kept in line by a formidable clipboard girl with headset and pointer. Celebrities, directors, actors, even the most famous had to wait their turn. And they were all there tonight – stars of the small screen whose impact was anything but small, ready to collect awards for best newcomer, best comedy, best drama, ready with their speeches tucked inside their tuxedo pockets, ready to plaster on gracious smiles to hide their rage and jealousy if they were to lose, ready to thank their agents and producers and husbands and lovers if they were to win.

In the car, Maryanne and Logan got ready to exit and take their place. They hadn't had any time alone together yet. Logan had been at the hospital, visiting Johnny, and had picked his wife up from her suite with just enough time to get to the ceremony. She knew he was avoiding her. She turned to him now.

'Have you spoken to Lucia? I'm worried about her.'

He didn't look at her. 'No. I'm sure she's fine, just embarrassed. As she should be. Probably lying low, waiting for the whole thing to blow over, hoping we'll forget about it.'

'Maybe.'

There was a pause.

'Is there any news on Johnny?'

'No. No change.' Logan looked out of the window at the line of celebrities moving slowly towards the hotel entrance. 'Come on,' he said. 'We'd better go in.'

'Logan, wait.'

She had to say something. They were like two strangers sitting next to each other, and they were about to go out into the crowd and be filmed and photographed and pretend that everything was normal. It wasn't normal, nothing was normal, it hadn't been for a very long time. Oh, God. Panic began to rise in her chest. She couldn't do it, she couldn't cope. He turned to her, impatient.

'What do you want?'

'I . . .' She swallowed. 'I don't think I can . . .'

He looked at her, hard. 'Maryanne, listen to me. You cannot flake out tonight. I need you to pull yourself together. All right?'

She let out a shaky breath. God, what had happened to her? Once upon a time she had taken all of these events in her stride, but somewhere along the line it had become different. People seemed threatening, worrying, difficult to talk to. She faltered, lost her confidence. Bolstered it with a drink here, a pill there. Just for tonight. She would wait until they were inside then she would take one of the pills that she had hidden in her bag. Just one. Get her through the night. The champagne had helped, just not enough. 'All right. Yes, I'm fine. Let's go.'

Elise watched as Logan stared at the camera. She shivered as she looked into his brown eyes and remembered their evening on the roof of his hotel, how he had touched her, how he had desired her. She looked briefly at Maryanne next to him, dripping in diamonds and perfectly well-preserved in a way that takes not just money, but dedication. Forced herself not to feel jealous, not to imagine herself in Maryanne's place, Logan's arm round her shoulders, guiding her along next to him, whispering in her ear as they took their seats, slipping her hand into his . . . She missed him, missed the future that she had briefly allowed herself to imagine they might be able to share, one where she was with a man who loved her, valued her, thought she was special and worth protecting. Bill, who was out at yet another client dinner, hadn't laid a finger on her since their row, either in desire or in anger, which she was grateful for, at least. He knew he had won the battle, that she wouldn't leave if it meant losing her son.

Her thoughts were interrupted by a small voice from the doorway. 'Mummy, I had a bad dream.'

She flicked the TV off and turned to Danny. 'Oh baby, come here, it's OK.'

He crawled into her lap and she stroked his hair, rocking him until he fell back to sleep and she carried him back upstairs to bed, warm and floppy and heavy in her arms. Her Danny. Her beloved boy. He was worth the sacrifice.

Inside the foyer of the hotel, some of the biggest names in the entertainment industry chitter-chattered over champagne as they waited to be summoned into the ballroom for the ceremony. The red carpet was visible from the foyer, and guests who were already inside tried not to look as if they were peeking over people's shoulders to see who was entering next. Even so, a buzz went around the room when Logan and Maryanne finally arrived in the doorway, *General Manager*'s film crew in their wake, recording everything that was happening.

Logan made a slow circuit of the room, delivering carefully measured doses of his famous charm, complimenting the ladies, shaking hands with the men. They owned the room, he and Maryanne.

And then, just as they were nearing the ballroom doors, there was another flurry of interest in the three people who were entering the foyer.

He had timed it perfectly. Everyone was there, the presentation was about to begin – and then he made his entrance. He stood for a second enjoying the look on all their faces. Him, Nicolo Flores, flanked by two women. One was his girlfriend, Vienna. It was the second woman who attracted all the attention. Lucia Barnes.

Logan turned. The two men stared at each other as Logan took in the scene. Nicolo's face was a picture of smug pride. He had the upper hand. Lucia looked nervous. Maryanne just looked appalled. Then she and Logan turned slowly away from their daughter, and entered the ballroom.

As Logan and Maryanne were talking to Asim Ferat, Melissa's father and the owner of *General Manager*'s production company, a waiter appeared with a tray of glasses of champagne. Logan raised an eyebrow almost imperceptibly at Maryanne as she accepted one. She ignored him. He chose to let it go.

He was aware of Nicolo and Lucia on the other side of the room. Nicolo was glancing over at him occasionally, his body language flamboyant and brash. Logan was studiously ignoring him. Lucia shot her parents defiant looks every so often, which Logan also ignored. He would not allow her and her attention-seeking behaviour to swallow up this night for him. But Jesus, he hadn't dreamed that his daughter would have ever betrayed him like this. Well. There was nothing to be done about it now. He couldn't let people see he was upset – that was what they wanted. He smiled politely as yet another woman who was apparently making it her life's mission to prove that you *could* be too rich and too thin came over to greet them and, no doubt, try and get the inside gossip.

'Helena!' She and Maryanne air-kissed. 'I'm so thrilled you're here, it's been an absolute age.'

She'd noticed the look on his face when she'd taken the drink, of course she had, but she'd pretended not to. She had taken the pill, slipped it under her tongue and let it dissolve, sweetly, in her mouth. Felt the numbing relief begin to spread through her limbs. She sipped her drink now, the two drugs combining in her bloodstream, making everything recede a little into the background. She could move smoothly again; she felt confident, amusing, interesting. She ignored the little voice at the back of her head that said she was walking down a dangerous path, yet again; that she was doing the wrong thing. She was Logan's wife. If Logan wanted her to pull herself together, then she would. She was doing what he wanted: being who he wanted her to be. It was just that these days she needed help to do that. She needed it.

*　*　*

Logan watched as the waiters cleared the plates and refilled glasses, and Maryanne entertained the table, her conversation animated and her hands fluttering around as she talked, her head thrown back, laughing. She was describing trying on the different necklaces earlier.

'And then she put this one on and I knew straight away.'

She sipped her wine, and turned towards a woman to her right as she spoke.

'The earrings are stunning as well,' the woman responded.

'Aren't they?' she simpered. 'Logan bought them for me as a little memento of his special evening.'

A murmur of appreciation passed around the table as the women covered their jealousy with smiles of admiration, and Maryanne lapped it up. The woman's husband leaned across to Logan, and said in a stage whisper, 'You've ruined it for the rest of us – now they'll all want some,' and laughed loudly at his own joke.

While joining in the laughter, Logan flashed a dark look at his wife. First thing in the morning, he'd make her return the fucking things.

In the cloakroom, Maryanne was reapplying her scent, feeling thrilled with herself. She'd got the earrings, and there was nothing at all Logan could do about it. She was on top of the world. Married to the man of the moment. Recovered and renewed.

Kathy Stovell, TV fashion presenter and girlfriend of celebrity chef Henri, the first of the TV chefs to drop his surname in true superstar style, entered the cloakroom and began touching up her eye make-up.

'Hi, Maryanne. Nearly time for the big awards announcements,' she said, applying more lip gloss. 'Is Logan excited?'

'Oh, you know my husband. Takes it all in his stride. Anyhow, I'd better get out there. See you later.'

As Maryanne leaned to kiss her friend goodbye, Kathy touched her on the arm. 'You want a bump?'

She was holding out a little silver vial with a sapphire in its top. 'You know how those speeches can drag on.'

Maryanne hesitated. She shouldn't. If Logan knew ... but why would he? Everything was going well so far, but she was feeling a bit tired – the effects of champagne and wine on an empty stomach that hadn't had any alcohol for a while. This would just pep her up again.

'Can't they just. Thanks.' And she took the vial and used the little silver spoon that was set into the lid to scoop a pile of cocaine out, and then she tipped it on to the side of her hand and raised it to her nose, before pressing a finger to her other nostril and inhaling deeply.

When she returned to the table, Logan leaned in to talk to her, making sure that his voice was low and no one would be able to hear.

'I told you in the car, and I'm warning you for the last time, Maryanne, don't screw tonight up for me as well.'

'What do you mean, "as well"?'

'As well as everything else you've managed to destroy recently.'

She swallowed. 'I think that's very unfair, Logan. You know I haven't been well.'

'And now?'

'And now, I'm very well. You made sure of that.'

He pulled back slightly, looked into her face, and said, 'You're not keeping those earrings.'

She didn't answer straight away. Then: 'Don't try and bully me, Logan. You're not the only one who can throw their weight around, you know.'

'I swear to you, Maryanne, you do not want to push me right now. I'm this close to . . .'

She looked at him. 'To what?'

He forced himself to breathe out slowly.

'Nothing. Just don't spoil this for me, OK?'

Maryanne got up from the table again and excused herself to the other guests, trying to conceal her anger and hurt. Back in the Ladies, she paced up and down the marble floor, busying her hands by washing them, twice, letting cold water run over her wrists, trying to cool her blood, as if it would cool the rage inside her. Why should he get away with talking to her like that? Then she realised she was drunk. Not very drunk, but drunk enough. She had better spend a minute or two in here. Sober up. Pull herself together. Wheee . . . She inhaled deeply, still buzzing from the coke. The tears began to spill from her eyes. He didn't love her any more. It was obvious. No one loved her. Not her husband, not her children, no one. She was all by herself. They had all turned away from her. *Oh help me, help me,* she wailed silently inside her head – but who was she asking for help?

She locked herself in one of the cubicles. *Oh Maryanne. What are you doing? Think calming thoughts, calming thoughts. Don't think about Lucia turning up with Nicolo, don't think about what Logan just said, don't think about what will happen next – breathe, breathe. Ha, ha, ha, exhale.* The panic came again, the edges began to darken and blur, and her heart was thudding; it felt like her chest was being wrenched open by the force of it beating. She forced herself to wait. She had to try and get calm.

When Maryanne left the Ladies, she started off down the corridor, back to the ballroom, where dinner was continuing. Soon they would start to announce the awards. She'd better go back in – she'd be expected to play her part, sit next to Logan, smiling and looking proud of him. Then one of the doors to the ballroom opened, and from it, Nicolo emerged, with another man Maryanne didn't recognise, laughing and clapping each other on the shoulder. Nicolo noticed her, and their eyes locked. She stopped. Oh, God. She began to feel panicky again.

Taking leave of his companion, Nicolo walked towards Maryanne. They faced each other, standing there in the corridor, in their finery – he in a designer tux and polished shoes, she in her ballgown and diamonds. The years flashed between them, and for a moment, they both were remembering a time when they had looked at each other very differently. With love, desire, friendship. Before that look had turned to hate. Hate that she had created, hate that she had caused.

'What are you doing with her?' she whispered.

'With her?'

'You know who I'm talking about. With Lucia. What are you doing with my daughter?'

Nicolo put his hands in his pockets, relaxed. 'I'm simply providing a talented girl with an opportunity. Now what's wrong with that? You should be applauding her, both of you. I thought you were all in favour of the entrepreneurial spirit?'

His meaning was clear. She smarted.

'Anyhow, Maryanne, you don't look like you're in a position to do much to help your daughter, do you? The one whom you claim you care about so much?' He took a step forward, a step closer to her. 'Maybe having a mother who wasn't a junkie would make things a little easier for her.'

Maryanne's hands shook. 'I'm not . . .' She tried to keep in control. 'I do care for my daughter. Very much.'

She wouldn't let him do this – she couldn't let him intimidate her like this. She had to get away. 'Leave my family alone, Nicolo. Do you hear me? You've caused enough damage.'

'*I've* caused damage?' Nicolo shook his head and laughed bitterly. *He* had caused damage? He was the one who had been wronged. All right, he had given in to his impulse to hurt Logan, but he hadn't done anything Logan himself wouldn't have done, anything anyone wouldn't have done. Apart from . . . No. No one knew about that. No one was going to know about that.

'It's a point of view, I suppose. Still, let's not fight about the rights and wrongs, hmm?'

Maryanne's heart was thudding again now; she was desperately trying to keep herself together. *Don't fall to pieces in front of him, you can't, you mustn't.*

'I have no desire whatsoever to fight with you, Nicolo.'

She pulled herself upright, dignified. He had loved her once, then when she had needed him, he had rejected her. Well, she didn't blame him – she didn't want him anyway, she had the better man. Let him remember that. She had made her choice.

'Why would I want to fight with you?' she went on. 'You're nothing to me. I must get back to my husband.'

Calculated, obvious, unsubtle – but still it didn't fail to pierce him. On the surface he remained cool, but underneath his blood boiled.

Maryanne lifted up the skirt of her gown, and stalked past Nicolo. When she was just a few inches away, he turned suddenly towards her, his eyes wide. She felt his eyes on her, and paused.

'What? What is it?'

He stared. Half-reached a hand out towards her. When he spoke, his voice was a whisper.

'You still smell the same.'

She looked back at him in shock. The intimacy of the statement, with all of the weight of memory, hung between them, as did his hand in the air. Her shoulders softened.

'Oh, Nico . . .'

The sound of her voice broke the spell; he swiftly withdrew his hand and marched quickly back into the ballroom.

Maryanne fled back to the Ladies, completely unnerved by what had just happened. There it was again, the panic, the shaking hands. She opened her handbag and took out her pills, clicked out one, two – two? Three.

You still smell the same. He had loved her so. Had been the first to really love her, ever, and she had thrown that away and trampled on it. What would her life be like now if she had stayed with him? she wondered briefly. *No, no, that way madness lies.* She had her husband, sitting out there, waiting for her. *Come on. Time to go.* She stood. Oops – a bit unsteady on her feet. It was probably the shock. She sat down again. Better have another pill, just to make sure. She tipped her head back and swallowed. Sat on the toilet seat and let them take effect, waited for the panic to melt away into the background. There, that was better. That was all she had needed. Why had she ever thought she could do without them? Silly Maryanne. She wouldn't be making that mistake again. They were her friends, her supporters, her companions. Her lovely little pills.

'And now we come to the award for Best Reality TV show, always a hotly contested category.'

The screen above the stage showed a wide shot of the room, the audience seated at their tables, smiling for the cameras, waiting.

'In no particular order, the nominations are *Top Chef* . . .'

A round of applause, and the faces of the show's hosts were flashed up on the screen in close-up.

'*American Idol* . . .'

White teeth sparkled on the screen.

'*Hell's Kitchen* . . .'

More applause.

'And . . .'

Somewhere at the back of the room, there was a loud thud.

'*General Manager!*'

Logan's face was projected on to the screen, his smile wide, the seat next to him empty. From the back of the room, the thud came again. A few people turned towards it; suddenly, the doors open and Maryanne stumbled through them. She giggled, saying, 'Sorreee. Bit of a sticky door. Whoopsee!' She faux-tiptoed through the room to her seat.

The host, Gerald Geras, continued, 'And the winner is . . .'

The light dipped and there was a hush. Maryanne took her seat. Patted Logan's hand. He took it without looking at her and held it down on the table. He could smell the alcohol on her breath. Feel her hot, trembling skin.

'Oopsy, I forgot. Logan's tewwibly, tewwibly cwoss.' She pouted, baby-talking. People were beginning to notice now. The guests at their table looked uncomfortable. The drum roll built up as the audience waited for the announcement of the winner. Logan tried to keep smiling, to look as if everything was normal.

'Darling. Shh. They're announcing the winner now,' he whispered.

'The winner is . . . *General Manager*!'

Cue applause. The lights went up, and orchestral strings swooped, as the cameras panned round to focus in on Logan and to follow his journey from the table to the podium. But as he made his way towards the stage, a ripple of shock spread out from his table.

'What's she doing?'

'Oh my God, she's not . . .'

Maryanne had stood as Logan did, like any wife would. Kissed him, maybe somewhat too passionately, especially as everyone could see his lack of enthusiasm. But when he broke away, she had followed him, holding on to the edge of his jacket as he wove his way through the tables.

'I'm coming with you.' She stumbled on the hem of her dress, almost fell, grabbed him to right herself.

Logan stopped. And with every fibre of his being, forced himself to remember that she was his wife and that, as such, he had a responsibility to her. He took her arm, firmly. Steadied her. She leaned her head against his shoulder, smiling in what she thought was a sweetly girlish way.

He led her up the steps, his grip making sure she couldn't fall again. Reached the lectern, and adjusted the microphone.

'As you can see, my wife and I don't like to be separated even for a moment. Like two teenagers in love, aren't we, sweetie?'

Relieved laughter flooded the room. It looked like Logan, the consummate professional, was going to rescue the situation. But then Maryanne grabbed the microphone.

'So in love that you bought me these lovely earrings.'

Logan smiled, and looked to one side, hoping that he might be able to get Gerald Geras to steer her away. But she was like a rookie stand-up comedian, warming to the mic and the spotlight.

'Aren't they pretty? My husband, Logan Barnes, the winner, bought them for me. *Whooo!* Go, Logan! Mr VIP hotel star numero uno!'

And she waved her arms in the air in a movement akin to a bizarre sort of Mexican wave, which threw her off-balance, and she fell backwards, clutching at Logan again, but missing this time, and just grabbing handfuls of air.

In no time, she was on the floor. The room was agog now, everyone straining for a better view of the spectacle. Lucia had buried her face in her hands. Nicolo was smirking. Logan leaned down to try and help her up, but she batted him away.

'Get off, get off! I know you hate me, I know you do! You just want to get rid of me – you pushed me, you bastard . . .'

She was hysterical now, sobbing. Logan let go of her, and stood back.

The cameras were whirring away. There was nothing he could do to save the scene now. The night was over, ruined. He looked round the ballroom briefly, and the first pair of eyes that found his were Nicolo's. His enemy nodded a mock greeting, then threw his head back and laughed.

Logan felt complete despair. He looked at Maryanne one last time as she sobbed on the floor, then raised his hands in a brief motion of apology to everyone and walked off the stage. Maryanne just lay, writhing and wailing as he left, and attendants and assistants rushed on to try and calm her.

And the cameras recorded it all.

* * *

A few hours later, Logan sat in the chair next to Johnny's bedside, drinking a cup of coffee while the machines beeped and watching TV – the events at the awards ceremony dominating the news channels, recounted by reporters with the enthusiasm of the vulture for a newly discovered rotting carcass. He hadn't slept. Had just sat here, drinking coffee and sitting with his friend. It was the only place he wanted to be right now.

Finally, as morning came, he turned the TV off. It was time to confront Maryanne. He couldn't put it off for ever.

Suddenly, as Logan got up and prepared to leave, Johnny's eyes flickered – a series of tiny muscles moving very slightly. Something was happening, something was stirring within his friend's body. Logan immediately pressed the call button on the wall.

'Johnny? Johnny, can you hear me? It's OK, the doctor's coming. Hang on in there.'

Please let him be waking up, not just twitching in his coma. Please don't let the movement have been that, or worse, the precursor to him dying. Logan couldn't bear for him to die, he needed him. More than ever now, he needed him.

'Please, Johnny. Please stay.'

When Maryanne woke up, for a few blissful seconds she remembered nothing at all of the night before. She drifted pleasantly in a half-sleep, but then a thumping headache and growing sense of nausea impelled her to open her eyes.

Rachel was next to her bed, holding a glass of juice and a couple of Tylenol. She reached out and took them, swallowing them gratefully with a gulp of the sweetly acidic juice. Then she ran to the bathroom and vomited them up again. Rachel waited.

Maryanne emerged slowly, wrapped in a white kimono-style dressing gown. Her face was puffy and pale, with the remnants of her make-up smeared around her eyes, in stark contrast to the glowing, perfectly made-up woman who had started the evening at the awards ceremony last night. She looked old, Rachel realised, old and ravaged.

Maryanne spoke quietly. 'Could you possibly order me some tea, Rachel?'

'Of course.'

327

Maryanne slowly went to the armchair by the fireplace. 'Have you been here all night?' she asked.

'Logan asked me to make sure you were all right.'

'Thank you. It's not your job. I appreciate it.'

'Everything's my job.' She smiled slightly.

The doorbell rang, and they waited while the waiter laid out the tea tray.

'How . . . how bad was it, Rachel?'

Oh, God. Rachel had been dreading this. What should she tell her? Did she really want to know? Then Maryanne solved the dilemma for her.

'I have to know. Please. Tell me.'

Rachel took a breath. Maryanne had closed her eyes, as if she was steeling herself. And then she told her.

She didn't cry, to the surprise of them both. She just sat quietly, her eyes remaining closed, and listened as Rachel outlined the events of the evening as sensitively as she could but without missing anything out, save the gaps that she could not fill. Maryanne could fill in most of those for herself: the panic that she had tried to quell with pills, the line of cocaine in the cloakroom, the urgent gulping of wine and painkillers.

When Rachel reached the end, they sat in silence for a moment. Then Rachel told her, 'One good thing – Johnny's come round now. Well, he's conscious at least; I don't think he's able to speak yet. Logan phoned in the night. We're waiting for more news.'

In fact, Rachel was hardly able to think of anything else, having to force herself to remain with Maryanne, rather than rushing down to the hospital to find out more about Johnny's condition. It was stupid. They wouldn't want her there anyway, wouldn't tell her anything. She wasn't family, or even a friend, really. Just an employee.

'And Lucia?' Maryanne asked. 'Why was she with Nicolo?'

'It would appear she's got a job, working for him.'

Maryanne rested her head back against the chair. 'Oh, God.'

'Yes. Steve was finding out the details. Rebellion, I suppose.'

Maryanne sipped her tea. She couldn't do anything about that now.

'Rachel, could you do one last thing for me? Could you please

328

find me a place in the best rehab centre that has space, and organise my travel there? I think it's time I faced up to this once and for all.'

Maryanne was packing when Logan came into the room. He stood in the doorway for a moment, watching her. She was pale, and her face was drawn and puffy. This wasn't the girl he had married, the girl he'd fallen so in love with that he was prepared to betray one of his best friends in order to have her. She had changed, and he was part of the reason.

She sensed him standing there and looked up. 'Hello,' she said, her voice quiet. He gave her a small smile and walked over to sit on the edge of the bed. It was covered with her clothes, piled up neatly.

'Johnny's come round. I've just been at the hospital. He's awake. Can't talk yet, but he's opened his eyes. It's a start.'

'Yes, Rachel told me. Thank God, Logan, I'm so pleased.'

'So am I. I thought he was going to die, I really did.'

'Yes.'

Logan gestured at the suitcase. 'Going home?'

She took a deep breath. 'No. I'm going to rehab. Proper rehab.'

Logan nodded. 'Where?'

'Rachel found me a place. It's called the Savannah Centre. In the mountains. Fresh air, long hikes, lots of therapy. No bars for hundreds of miles.'

She stopped. 'Logan, I'm so sorry, I . . .'

She put her hands over her eyes. She couldn't face looking at him, and seeing him so disappointed, so betrayed by her. But she had to. She took her hands away, and they were wet with her tears.

'I know I've said it before, but I mean it this time. I'm getting help – proper help, not a quick fix. I don't expect you to forgive last night, but I want you to know – I *need* you to know – that I am truly sorry.'

'I know you are. I know.' He reached out his hand to her. 'But Maryanne . . .'

He couldn't quite say it. A small sob escaped her chest.

'But it's too late. That's what you're going to say, isn't it? It's too late. It's over, and you don't love me any more. Oh no, oh no . . .' Her heart was going to break. She had finally done it. Driven him away.

329

'I still love you. I will always, always love you. You're my wife, you're the mother of my children. But we're not doing each other any good any more, are we? It's not just your fault, it's mine as well. I failed you. I let you down – I let the kids down.'

Maryanne let go of his hand as anger flared up through her grief.

'The only way you let us down was by turning away from us. You turned your back on us, and left me to do everything by myself!'

Logan's face was uncomprehending. How could she say that? 'I didn't! I was working. I was working FOR YOU.'

'You buried yourself in work, you were totally unavailable to me, to Charlie, Lucia. Remember that day Charlie came home and tried to get you to listen to him play, when he was learning the guitar? And you were too busy, always too busy, so you went out the next day instead and bought up the music store for him?'

Logan did remember. 'I didn't know anything about music,' he said, but the excuse sounded lame, even to him.

'You didn't *need* to know anything about music. And Charlie didn't need a load of expensive studio kit that he couldn't even work. He just needed his dad.'

Maryanne carried on putting clothes into the suitcase, her movements jerky.

'Do you remember what you always said, Logan? You told me that you had no relationship with your father, that he was distant, had no idea what was going on in your life. And your mother was the same – worse, even. And we used to talk about how it would be different with us. What happened?'

He was angry now, as well.

'What happened? You tell me. I'm not the only one who changed, Maryanne, you can't lay it all at my door. Come on then, if we're getting it all out in the open. What about you?'

'What about me? I've always been there for the children, I've always known what's going on in their lives. Recently I admit I've – had some difficulties.'

'You could say that.'

'I know, Logan, OK?' She turned on him. 'I know I've fucked up – but it's not just me. And I was a good mother when they were growing up, I know I was. Don't take that away from me. Please.'

330

She sobbed openly. Her face was twisted and ugly in distress. Logan took a deep breath. She was right.

'Yes. You were a good mother.'

'But a bad wife?'

'I didn't say that.'

'You didn't have to.'

'Oh, is that what you want? Me to say "Yes, you were a bad wife, it's all your fault," so you can feel sorry for yourself? Go and drown your sorrows again?'

He was lashing out now, hurt, angry. She shut her eyes. 'I know I deserved that.'

'This is what I'm talking about, Maryanne. This.' He gestured at the space between them. 'This isn't how it should be. This isn't how it used to be. We used to work, and it was right. *We* were right. But not any more.'

She bit her lip. She knew that what he said was true. But to hear the words coming out of his mouth was so, so hard. She closed her suitcase. 'I should go.'

Logan rubbed his head. It had been a very long twenty-four hours. 'I don't want to fight, Maryanne.'

'Neither do I. Not any more. I guess – I guess there isn't much more to be said. I just don't understand how it all went so wrong.'

'No.'

They stood and stared at each other.

'Is this how it ends? It feels like there should be some big scene. Not just two people standing in a hotel room. Over twenty years, and that's it?' She started to cry again. He went to her, and took her in his arms, hugging her to his chest tenderly.

'Oh, Annie. I'm sorry. I'm so very sorry.'

He was telling the truth. He was sorry for so many things – for letting her down, for failing to rescue his wife, for cheating on her, for burying himself in work when she and his children needed him; he was sorry for all the arguments and the anger and, most of all, he was sorry because he was standing here holding her and wishing it was a different woman in his arms.

Chapter Twenty

When Maryanne had left for the rehab centre, Logan had slept for a couple of hours, and then gone into the office, calling the hospital on the way.

'Mr Stokes's condition is stable. His girlfriend is with him at the moment.'

'Has he said anything?'

The nurse's voice was faintly scornful.

'Don't expect miracles, Mr Barnes. He can't talk yet. We don't know how much brain damage he may have sustained. Your friend is still a very seriously unwell man. Opening his eyes doesn't mean everything's all going to be fine, you know.'

'I do know, thank you, Nurse.'

Bloody woman. Now, he was in the the boardroom of his Manhattan office. Around the table, the faces of his board members were solemn. Apart from Johnny, all of them were there.

'Our major problem right now is with the media. I apologise to you all now, because this is my personal life intruding on the business, and it's going to affect all of your working lives as well. I'm sorry for that. But, it is what it is, and we must deal with it as best we can. They're not going to let this one go. Kirsten, this is your area. What's the best way to handle things?'

She thought.

'United front – for now, at least. Maryanne's getting help, we make a statement saying the whole family is behind her, supporting her. We emphasise that your priority is her health, that she needs to be left alone by the press to get well, and hope that they respect that.'

Logan nodded. 'Have the *General Manager* team agreed to destroy that footage? They'll be in breach of contract if they don't, won't they?'

'Grey area. Technically, it seems they own all recorded footage, not you.'

'Make it less grey. I don't want them thinking they can mess me about with this.'

His lawyer, Johnny's second-in-command who had taken his place in the meeting, nodded. 'Although it was on the news channels anyway. They were recording the ceremony . . .' He trailed off under Logan's glare.

'I'm quite aware that the footage is already out there, thank you. I just don't want the show's producers thinking they can use it. Can you imagine how that would look?'

'Sorry, but there's one more thing,' Kirsten interjected. 'We need to make a decision regarding Lucia as a matter of priority.'

Logan's face was stony. 'Steve?'

'She's staying at Nicolo's hotel in West Hollywood. Other than that . . .' Steve shrugged. 'She could be working for him in some way. There's no evidence that there's anything untoward going on. I'm trying to find out more – I've got someone keeping an eye on her.'

Logan nodded.

'I think you should try to make contact with her,' Kirsten said rashly. 'I feel—'

'I appreciate your input, Kirsten, but I'll decide what to do about Lucia myself. Thank you.'

Kirsten pursed her lips slightly, but nodded.

'I'm not going to lie to any of you,' he continued. 'LBI is facing a big challenge. As you know, much of our recent property developments have contained a significant amount of debt financing, which has allowed us to grow quickly, dominate the market share in certain areas, and consolidate our position as the leading luxury hotel group, while allowing control to remain with us. With the construction of Luxury, because of the unusual nature of the project, and because it's by far the biggest project since the company became solvent again, the risk is particularly large. Luxury as a property is not expected to turn large profits. The staff-to-guest ratio, the design-led nature of the property, the high level of service we're providing

. . . all of these things mean that Luxury will be in the red for a significant amount of time.

'However, the balance is viable. Tight, but viable. And I believe Luxury *will* prove to be the comeback for LBI that we have all been hoping for. Now, I'm returning to London. I'll be on all my usual numbers.'

In the street outside the hotel, Logan was surrounded.

'Is there any truth in the rumour that—'

'How's your wife, Mr Barnes?'

'Can you confirm that she overdosed recently?'

'Mr Barnes, can you confirm that Lucia is to receive treatment for sex addiction?'

'Mr Barnes . . .'

'Mr Barnes . . .'

'Mr Barnes . . .'

The questions continued as he got into the car, shielded by one of the security team. He didn't have a personal bodyguard, didn't see the need for it, hated feeling like he had to have someone shadowing his every move. But at times like this, when the press were like a chattering pack of hyenas, there was a distinct advantage in having a team of ex-SAS operatives at your disposal to keep them at bay.

Logan was back in London by the evening, and he went straight to meet Charlie for dinner. It was better for him to be away from New York, away from the scene of the debacle at the awards ceremony. And he wanted to reconnect with Charlie, whom he hadn't seen for a while. The conversation with Maryanne before she left for the Savannah Centre had really brought it home to him just how many mistakes he had made with his family. It didn't matter that he had been trying to do the right thing, most of the time; the fact was that he had got it wrong. But, he could still make amends, with Charlie at least.

He waited in the trendy Japanese restaurant for his son, sipping a glass of rose Sancerre and looking out of the window. The place was buzzing quietly, and outside, London was gearing up for another night. Commuters were making their way home after long days in fluorescent-lit offices, their fingers grimy with the ink from free newspapers.

Motorcycle couriers wove in and out of traffic and drivers honked at their backs, pointlessly. He loved the city.

He was thinking about Lucia. It was his fault, the way she had turned out. He'd spoiled her since she was a small child, she'd had nothing but the best and everything she'd asked for, so he could hardly blame her now for expecting that to continue. When all her classmates went through a Hello Kitty phase, Lucia had insisted that the only possible birthday gift was a $6,000 robot in the shape of the pink-ribboned kitten. When she'd hit her teens and iPods had become the must-have thing, she'd had the headphones customised with diamonds. And that was just the gifts. She was a daddy's girl, and Logan had indulged her, let her get away with murder because she was, at her best, funny and affectionate and loving. She was his little girl. His little girl who appeared to have infected some poor sod with gonorrhoea, and whose bottom was gracing all the bill-boards in London and who was staying in the hotel owned by Nicolo Flores, but still . . . She would always be his beloved daughter.

Charlie flopped down next to him, and motioned to the waiter to bring him a beer. 'Hey. How's Mom? When can we speak to her?'

'Not for a couple of days. They like you to have a few days to settle in. She arrived OK though. She'll call when she's ready, I'm sure. I know she'll want to talk to you both, but I think it's best left up to her to contact us.'

The waiter arrived at the table, and Logan ordered a selection of sushi, and then waited till the man had left the table before continuing. 'It's a difficult thing that she's doing, and we can be really proud of her for doing it. But we should be prepared for her to need some space from everything to get things straight in her head, and that includes us.'

'Yeah, all right.'

'How are you both coping with the press stuff? Kirsten and Steve looking after you OK?'

Charlie shrugged, then grinned. 'Doesn't really bother me. I've been working a lot, and I met a girl.'

'Oh right – who is she?' This was great. Maybe Charlie would open up to him, give him an opportunity to provide some fatherly advice.

'She's called Jamie. She's awesome.'

Charlie carried on eating. Apparently 'awesome' was all Logan was going to get on the subject of the new girl on the scene.

'Have you spoken to your sister?' he asked his son.

'Nope. Won't take my calls. Doubt she'll take yours, either.'

'We'll see about that.'

'She was pretty upset. I wouldn't expect her to just come running.' He picked up a piece of sushi and dipped it in a little bowl of soy sauce.

'What are you saying, Charlie?'

Charlie looked at his chopsticks. 'Well, you like things to happen to your schedule. And sometimes, that's not what other people want. Or need. I mean, I know you're kind of the boss, of the family as well as the business, but sometimes it's like none of us get a say in anything because you pay for it all.'

The last sentence came out in a rush, and Charlie looked shocked at what he had said.

'Right. What about you, then? I take it this means you're saying you've got no intention of working for the company at any point in the future?'

Charlie sighed. 'I didn't say that. I don't know. I just want to do my music.'

'Good. Your music. Well, it's good to know you've put so much thought into things. For fuck's sake.'

Logan removed his napkin from his lap and got up.

'You'll forgive me if I leave you to sort out the bill. I'd hate you to feel I was trying to control you by buying you dinner.'

When he had left Charlie, Logan got in his car and drove, out of London and along the M40 towards Oxford, not knowing where he was heading, not caring where he ended up. He was angry, upset. He had always thought that Charlie would one day follow him into the hotel industry. He'd had images of himself teaching the boy what he knew, grooming him. The two of them working alongside each other, father and son. But Charlie showed no signs of interest, never had done. Logan couldn't force him to join LBI, he just wished he wanted to do so. But then, no one said your children would go down the paths you hoped they would, did they? You could do only so much for them, pay for their schooling, try and teach them right from wrong, give them the confidence to make their own decisions, their own mistakes – and then you had to watch them make them, and stand back, powerless to interfere. For someone who liked – needed, even – to be in control as much as Logan did, it was a very big lesson indeed, and one that he was still learning.

Resting his head back, he watched the motorway unfold in front of him. England. She was just a few miles away. He hadn't stopped thinking about Elise, but he had stopped calling her. She knew where he was. Logan had accepted that he couldn't keep calling her, that he might be making things worse for her if Bill found out, even if she wasn't answering. And, just as he couldn't force his children to do what he wanted, he couldn't make Elise love him.

It wasn't very easy to accept, though.

Elise went through her usual routine of checking that everything she needed was in her handbag: the crucial modern trilogy of phone, wallet, keys? Then chequebook, although hardly anyone seemed to write cheques any more; PDA, so she knew where she was meant to be and what she was meant to be doing; iPod, which she hardly ever used; Oliver Peoples sunglasses in their case; make-up bag containing her capsule selection of products to make any necessary repairs or glam up in case of a sudden change of plan; perfume. Everything was there, in its place inside the deliciously soft white leather of her Bamford holdall. The sun was shining outside. She tried to let it cheer her. It didn't work. God, she missed him! She missed him every hour of every day, and didn't know how this was possible. She'd managed to get through the first thirty odd years of her life without him in it, so why did she feel the loss of him so keenly now?

Since the day that she had told him she couldn't see him again she had focused on Danny, the reason why she had made that decision. As soon as she'd seen her son's cheeky grin and listened to him babbling about a trip to the zoo and how he was going to be an octopus when he grew up, she remembered how in love she was with this boy, and how all the other men in her life faded into monochrome when compared to his bright colour.

The other men in her life. She thought now of the one she was

337

on her way to visit for the first time since they had moved back to London. It was years since she'd seen her father. Relations had been strained since the scene at their wedding. Bill had discouraged her from seeing him, and she'd been angry and hurt that Pete had let his old hellraising behaviour rear its head on such an important day for her. The relationship had drifted, been allowed to falter. Pete had been too ashamed to push things, hadn't wanted to interfere with his daughter's new life and marriage, however much he might wish that she had chosen someone other than Bill.

When Danny was born, they'd attempted a reconciliation. Elise had wanted her newborn son to grow up knowing his grandfather, hearing the stories of riding on the backs of elephants and travelling the world that had so entranced her as a child. Bill hadn't been keen but hadn't tried to stand in her way.

And then, when Danny was a toddler there'd been the two accidents. The first was Danny's. Pete had been looking after his grandson, and drinking and playing cards by the pool instead of watching him carefully. The little boy had nearly drowned – was blue by the time Pete had noticed that the child was being too quiet for a two year old, and was no longer paddling in the shallows but had slipped and was floating under water.

As Elise had stood and watched the small body of her son lying on a hospital table, full of tubes and wires, the pain and guilt were almost too great for her to bear. The only thing that had surpassed it was her anger, which burned hot and dark in her heart. She had been unable to even look at her father afterwards, and he had gone off to film an action movie in Belize.

Two weeks to the day after Danny's accident she had received the phone call telling her that her father had fallen from a boat. The irony that he too, had almost drowned was not lost on her, and she had wondered whether it had really been an accident. But then she'd pushed it out of her head: her father was a stuntman, there was hardly any more dangerous job he could do. He hadn't drowned, but he had broken almost every bone down one side of his body when he had hit the water, hard and from a height. He had also injured his neck, and while broken bones usually mend, spinal cords don't, and Pete Sylvester, who had always been running,

338

jumping, somersaulting, was now a quadriplegic confined to a nursing home.

Which was where she was heading. She wasn't sure exactly what had made her feel she must visit her father, must bury the rage that she still felt and go to him. It had something to do with the dinner on the beach with Logan, when he'd asked about her father; something had tugged in her chest and she'd realised she couldn't ignore the situation any longer.

She didn't even know the place where he was. Bill had organised it all – she had let him take over. She shouldn't have done that, she knew. Her father was her responsibility, not Bill's. But her husband had reassured her; they were married, a team, a partnership. Her responsibilities were his own, he had said gently, and had lifted the burden from her shoulders leaving her free to care for Danny as he recovered – which he had, fully and quickly.

Inside her Audi SUV, she turned on the car's Sat-Nav system and entered the address that she had found in Bill's PDA. She hadn't told him she was going to see Pete. Just another secret. She had quite a list of them now.

Even from the outside, the nursing home looked grim. The net curtains at the windows were grubby, and the gardens in front of the redbrick building were unkempt and uncared for. Much as the patients seemed to be, Elise realised with horror as she walked through the corridors towards the room where she had been told she would find her father. The floors were mucky, and the whole place dark and dingy. She took a deep breath before entering her father's room, and wished she hadn't; the air smelled of urine and bleach and overcooked vegetables.

When she opened the door tears came to her eyes immediately. All the anger she had felt for the last four years – had fostered and nursed even, she realised now – dissolved into the ether with the sight of her beloved dad, lying under a sheet in this horrible place, the only movement in the room that of the ventilator that breathed for him.

'Oh, Dad. Where has he put you?' Her voice was a strangled whisper.

There was a flicker in his face as he recognised his daughter's voice, and he raised his right arm, the only one of his limbs that retained any movement. She went to his side and stood over him so he could see her face.

'Li ...' He could only make a tiny sound, using one side of his mouth.

'I'm sorry, Dad. I didn't know. I should have come. I'm so sorry.'

And she sat in the chair next to him and held his hand as she wept, and the only way he could try and comfort his distraught daughter was with a tiny squeeze of his hand.

She was in shock. Despite everything she knew about Bill, everything he had done, she would never have imagined that he would have left her father to fester in a place such as that. She was beginning to realise that she didn't know her husband at all. The thought of the years her father had spent there, without anyone to talk to, or talk to him, anyone to tell him they loved him, came rushing at her in a terrible wave, and she leaned out of the car and vomited. And although she would dearly have loved to believe that Bill didn't realise the sort of place he had sentenced Pete to, she couldn't. Everything fell into place with a sickening sense of finality: how keen Bill had been to organise everything; the financial aspect he had kept hidden – because, she could see now, the sums involved were so paltry; the address that she had had to hunt out secretly; the very faint hint of a smug expression that had appeared on Bill's face on the few occasions that she had mentioned her father in the past, and the way he had dissuaded her from visiting him, citing her well-being as the reason.

This was her fault.

She didn't go home. Instead, she drove down to Brighton. She parked near the Marina and walked along the seafront, watching as the day turned to evening, and the sun sank down into the silvery sea. Day-trippers were packing up their cool boxes and rugs and returning to their cars with sleepy, pink-cheeked children. Students working the bungee trampolines were clearing up; a few barbecues were being lit on the pebble beach. She walked past a stall selling seafood and bought a white plastic cup of prawns which she ate as she moved on, past fish and chip vans and clairvoyants and souvenir shops set into the arches, and bars starting to fill up, advertising nineties music nights. Nostalgia for party-seekers hardly old enough to have anything to be nostalgic for.

She watched until the sun set completely in the sky. And then she picked up her phone, and did what she should have done a long time ago.

Logan turned the car around and headed straight to Brighton when Elise called. She had been crying.

'I'm sorry, I'm sorry, I didn't mean it.'

He wanted to be there with her, to hold her, comfort her.

'Oh Elise, it doesn't matter, none of it matters any more. Look, I'm coming back, so stay where you are. I'm coming to get you, just stay there.'

He'd never driven so fast in his life, had been convinced he was going to get pulled over, but just pushed on, not caring about anything other than getting to her. He found her still sitting on the seafront, cold now the sun had gone in, her face red from crying. She got up and crumpled into him, her body shaking with sobs, and he stood and stroked her hair and waited for it to subside. Then he had kissed her, and her tears had made his face damp and she'd wiped them away.

'I love you. I love you, I love you, I love you,' he had said, holding on to her tightly and leading her to his car.

'I love you. I couldn't bear it any longer. Seeing my dad lying there, I—'

'You can't stay with Bill any longer.'

She shook her head. 'No, I can't. But I'm so afraid. I'm so scared I'll lose Danny.'

Elise told Logan everything, as he drove her back to London, curled up in the passenger seat of his big car, looking tiny and fragile. He arranged for a member of her staff to collect her car and return it to London. She told him all about Bill's violence, his rages, the dealings she had uncovered, and his threats when he realised she had done so, how he had told her she would lose Danny if she tried to leave or to expose him.

'So that's why you said you couldn't see me,' Logan said.

'Yes. It was the hardest thing I've ever had to do.'

'I won't let you lose your son. I promise you.' Logan touched her thigh with his left hand, steering with his right. 'Trust me, Elise. I

341

will not let him do that. There is no way Bill McAllister will take away your son.'

'OK.'

'Do you trust me?'

'Of course.'

'Good. Remember that.' He stared ahead at the road.

Chapter Twenty-One

Maryanne shook as she followed the nurse through the corridors to the room to which she had been assigned. The woman was dressed not in any traditional nurse's uniform but in casual khaki combat pants and T-shirt. The lodge was full of light and wood, with tall ceilings. The atmosphere was designed to be one of comfort, of natural materials. There were no sharp lines or angles; instead the feeling was of solidity, calm. But Maryanne hardly noticed any of this, and none of it helped quell the feeling of panic that was rising up inside her. Suddenly she stopped in her tracks. She couldn't. She couldn't do this.

The nurse turned to her. 'What's the matter?' Her voice was gentle.

'I'm sorry. I've made a mistake. I can't – I just can't.'

The nurse walked towards her, her body language relaxed. 'OK. I know this is frightening. It's all new, and you don't know what to expect. Maybe we can just go to the room. Then we can sit for a while, and see how you feel then.'

'No. You don't understand, I'm not frightened, of course not. I just can't. I shouldn't have come.'

Maryanne backed away from the woman. She was too hot, and couldn't breathe. Her chest was tightening and constricting, she could feel an itching sensation, as if every pocket of air in her lungs was heating up. She took a deep breath, gasping.

The nurse took her hand. 'Maryanne. Maryanne, try and keep calm.'

'I ...' Her voice came out in a high-pitched wheeze and she stopped trying to talk. Her heart was pounding in her chest, hard, fast. Beating three times as fast as it should be. She must be having a heart-attack. She began to tremble uncontrollably, tears pouring down her face as she gasped for breath. The edges of her vision were growing dark, and there was a rushing sound in her ears.

'Slow and even. Breathe slowly and evenly.'

I can't! she wanted to cry. *I can't breathe at all, I'm dying, I'm going to die here in this corridor, with you staring at me, and it's all wrong.* But the darkness around the edges crept further into the centre, until everything went black, and she passed out. She came round with the nurse sitting beside her on the floor, holding a paper bag over her mouth. The woman smiled as Maryanne opened her eyes.

'It's all right, you're fine. You had a panic attack. How do you feel now?'

Maryanne mentally checked herself. She felt OK. A bit wobbly, like you felt after an adrenaline rush. She sat up.

'I need to see a doctor.'

'You can see someone later. But trust me, you're just fine.'

'I just passed out, and you don't even get me a doctor? I should be in the emergency room.'

'Do you feel as though going to the emergency room might fix you? Fix your problems with drugs and alcohol?'

'What? No, I feel as though going to the emergency room might fix the fact that I've clearly got a heart condition.'

'Your heart is in a bad way, yes. But it's a spiritual problem you need to address, Maryanne, not a physical one.'

Oh, for fuck's sake.

Maryanne picked her way down the large stone steps, over the gravel path and across the lawn away from the lodge. Her fawn suede ankle boots were already muddy. She remembered now how much she hated the wilderness. It was full of mud, and hills, and there was a distinct lack of shops or restaurants. Why anyone would actually choose to live out here was beyond her. Well, she wasn't staying to listen to all of that hot air about spiritual problems and broken hearts. She would just get someone to come and pick her up, and take her back to the city.

She continued storming over the grass, ignoring the fact that her stiletto heels were sinking in the grass with each step she took, and reached into her pocket for her mobile phone. Oh shit, she'd forgotten. They'd taken it away from her, along with her credit cards and keys and jewellery other than her wedding ring, and well, everything. Put it in a safe. Who was she, without all of her things?

Suddenly it was all too much. The exhaustion of the last few days, the shock of what had happened at the awards ceremony, the realisation of the extent of her problems, all rolled into one. She was stuck here. And she sat down on the grass, not caring that it was wet and muddy, and wailed. The thought that she seemed to have done little else but cry recently just made her sob even harder. She was a complete failure – as a wife, a mother, at everything. She couldn't stick a day of rehab, and then she couldn't even manage to leave.

She stayed, eventually. Not for any particularly noble reason, no sudden epiphany, or anything like that. It was more that the thought of going back out into the world, a failure at getting help, to be publicly mocked, to have to face Logan and her children and tell them she couldn't do it, was worse than staying. So she figured she could just stick it out for a few weeks. Get some rest, some fresh air, some exercise. And see what happened.

What happened was that, after a few days of sulking and sleeping, and sitting through the mandatory counselling sessions doing every-thing she could to make sure no one managed to get through to her, she arrived downstairs one morning to be told that she would be taking part in a different kind of therapy session that day. Kurt, the psychologist whose job it was to manage the addicts and make sure they got to sessions, as well as giving them individual coun-selling, greeted her in the hall with a smile that he intended to be energising and encouraging.

'Good morning, Maryanne.'

'Hello, Kurt.'

'With every day comes a new challenge, is that not true?'

Maryanne eyed him suspiciously. What was this leading to? 'I guess so,' she said.

'Don't guess, Maryanne – know. Know and feel in your heart.'

He beamed at her. Christ, there was a load of crap floating around in this place, she thought. People came here to stop taking drugs but sometimes she wondered if they were pumping the happy pills out into the air. The outdoor school was situated some way away from the main building where all of the counselling and group therapy sessions took place. It was behind some outbuildings, and Maryanne had just assumed that it was where laundry and other things she didn't have to bother about went on. Kurt strode ahead, raising a hand in greeting to a man standing next to a large black horse inside a fenced-off square of dusty ground.

As they neared the square, the man walked over to them and then stood and watched them come towards him. He was very tall and he wore a soft-looking pale blue shirt and jeans, his feet in tan leather boots that had clearly been polished and worn many times. All of his movements were considered. When he stood, he was totally still; when he walked, it was with purpose but no extraneous expenditure of energy. There was something immediately reassuring about his silent confidence.

'Sam, this is Maryanne. Maryanne, this is Sam. He's an equine therapist. Well, I'll leave you to it.'

Maryanne and Sam stared at each other as Kurt left. Sam's gaze was steady, unconfrontational. He didn't say anything, or open the gate for her. He just – stood.

'Well?' Maryanne asked eventually.

He smiled slightly. 'Would you like to come in?'

'Not especially. But I suppose that's why I'm here, isn't it?'

He shrugged. She looked over at the horse, which was standing as still as Sam was.

'Don't worry, he won't trample you or anything.'

When it became clear that no one was going to open the gate for her, she sighed exaggeratedly and entered the school.

'So, what are you, some kind of horse whisperer?'

'No. Horse whisperers train horses.'

'And you train people?'

'You can't train people.'

She looked over at him, but there was no indication that he was joking.

346

Humourless asshole, Maryanne thought. This was going to be hard work.

It *was* hard work, but not in the way she was expecting. Sam had handed her a dark brown leather harness and asked her to go to the horse, put it on him and lead him over. Maryanne had bitten her tongue and refrained from ranting about being given pointless and simple tasks in the name of therapy. She could see through their absurd methods, which might work on some of the dim-witted men and women who came here, but they certainly weren't going to work on her. However, she sensed such a complaint would simply be met with a silent shrug.

She stomped over to the horse, bridle in hand, and the animal had immediately shot over to the opposite corner of the school. She'd tried again, and the same thing had happened. When she looked over at Sam in frustration, he'd turned away, and looked out towards the mountains, enjoying the view. Fine. This time she'd snuck up on the horse, coming at it from the side and then suddenly lunging at it. Once again it had eluded her, smartly trotting over to Sam and nuzzling at his neck. He had laughed, and reached into his pocket for a treat. Maryanne had lost her temper then. He'd trained the fucking thing to do that, she'd been wasting her energy trying to catch it; it was some kind of stupid trick to make her feel humble and inadequate.

'I won't be mocked by you or your bloody pet,' she shouted as she threw the harness across the dirt floor in a rage, 'and I won't be manipulated by you people any more, do you hear me?'

'Just about the whole state can most probably hear you.'

'Good. Then the whole state can know that you're all a stupid, manipulative, pretending-you-care-but-just-out-to-make-money bunch of cunts.'

She was shaking with anger. Sam looked up at her, and nodded in acknowledgement that she had spoken, but nothing more. Then he went back to talking to the horse.

She felt like hitting him. Instead she marched out of the school and back to the main house, walked into Kurt's office and announced that she was leaving. 'And as soon as I'm home, I'm going to sue you smug bastards from here to Christmas.'

When he'd calmed her down, which was one of the things he was able to do quite effectively, despite her scathing attitude towards him, he had told her that she would be participating in a daily session with Sam and his horse from now on. They'd spent the next two hours in his office negotiating her continuing treatment programme. Kurt knew that Maryanne was stubborn and needed to feel as if she was in control; he also knew that *he* needed to remain in control of the situation if she was to get well. And he also knew that she wanted to get well, that she was crying out for help and for someone to lead her towards recovery, despite her protestations to the contrary and her posturings about suing the facility. Kurt had been at the centre for ten years and had seen it all before. Everyone came in insistent that they didn't need help, that they knew it all. He just kept doing what he did, and they usually came round in the end.

When they'd reached an agreement, Maryanne went off to take part in a yoga session overlooking the gardens.

The next day, after breakfast and the morning group meeting, she'd returned to the outdoor school. Even though she'd complained about having to do the sessions, and was still smarting from her failure to carry out the task the previous day, there was something magnetic about the man and his horse. Maybe it was just his obvious lack of concern for her – she wanted to push him into showing some kind of reaction. She determined that during the session today, she would catch that bloody horse. For four days she went to the school in the morning, picked up the harness and approached the horse. It wasn't until she stopped trying that she managed it. Or rather, he did. Because it was when she gave up and put the harness down and sat on the dusty ground saying, 'Fine, have it your way. I'll just wait here till you're ready' under her breath, that, to her amazement, the horse came trotting slowly over to her.

'Hello there, boy. Hello, Raff.'

He lowered his head, and she picked up the harness from the ground. He didn't move as she slipped it on over his head, and then slowly stood up. She took hold of the bridle and walked him over to where Sam stood waiting.

'He could tell, then?' She said.

'Tell what? That you'd stopped trying to boss him around?' Sam raised an eyebrow. 'Yes, I think he might have been able to.'

His tone was gently mocking, but this time Maryanne didn't shout and storm off; instead she laughed at herself.

'Oh dear. OK, you win. I get it.'

'It's not about winning. It's just about standing back sometimes, not pushing to make everything happen so quickly. People come to you in their own time if you let them.'

'Yes. So, what next? What's the next lesson according to Sam and Raff?'

Now it was her voice that was lightly poking fun at the man who spoke few words but who, she was beginning to suspect, might have more that was truly worth saying than anyone else she knew.

'No more lessons. Well, not that kind. Now we teach you to ride him.'

From his hospital bed, Johnny lay and watched through tired eyes that were only just getting used to the light again, as Rachel sat quietly by his bed. He reached out a hand and touched her arm gently. She turned to him, joy spreading over her face.

'Johnny? Oh, God! Are you – how do you feel? Hang on, I'll call a nurse.'

She leaned over and pressed the call button. He didn't try and speak – his throat was too dry. But even if he could have done so, he wouldn't have been able to tell the beautiful girl sitting next to him that he had been awake and watching her for the last half an hour, wondering who she was and why she was sitting next to him in this strange room. Johnny watched as a doctor came in, walking briskly but calmly, and came and stood next to his bed.

'Good evening, Mr Stokes. Good to see you. I'm just going to do some tests to see how you're getting on.'

Johnny stared. He had no idea who Mr Stokes was, but he wasn't sure he liked the sound of that at all.

Chapter Twenty-Two

Colette and Charlie did everything together now. His band mates teased him that he was under the thumb – 'pussy whipped' – when the couple turned up at the studio together, thumbs hooked into the loops of each other's jeans. Charlie didn't care. He was in love for the first time in his life, and he didn't care what anyone thought about anything, apart from her.

Her. Jamie was his other half, his soulmate, he just knew it. Ketchup not mayo; vodka not gin; vintage not Abercrombie T-shirts; rock music not R'n'B; sex over most things. They just fitted.

She didn't complain about the time he spent on his music, like other girlfriends had done; instead, she came into the studio with him and she didn't just sit around reading magazines – she had ideas, she liked his music. Most importantly to Charlie, she listened to his music, really listened, in a way that no one else had ever done.

'That section there – have you thought about moving the vocal into the centre?' she would query, in a way that Charlie knew pissed TJ off. But he didn't care.

Or she'd be listening to Charlie's vocal and say 'Loneliness – that's what you're singing about there, isn't it? I can hear it in your voice. Poor baby.' And she would come over to him and straddle him and kiss him deeply, whispering in his ear, 'I'll make it better.'

She did make it better, she made everything better. And she didn't care what anyone thought of her. 'Screw them!' she said. 'We're the only ones who matter now. Not those people walking to work, in their suits, with their briefcases, all stiff and sad,' and she had imitated the formal walks of the businessmen. 'They're just doing what they think they should do, conforming to expectations. Can you think of anything worse?'

Charlie couldn't. She inspired him to push on with his album, 'to prove to your dad that you can do this. That you don't need him or his money – because, Charlie baby, you're gonna make plenty of that yourself.'

She understood him as no one ever had before, saw depths in him that he hadn't even known were there. 'You're a thinker, Charlie, that's what I like about you. You're a deep thinker. Well, it's one of the things I like about you.' Her hand snaked down the front of his trousers, her intentions obvious.

Sex and understanding were a potent combination, and one that Colette had learned how to exploit early in life. She had needed to exploit what she could, after all, because she didn't have much at her disposal. But she did have good looks and a sharp brain, and an innate understanding of men. They wanted to feel special, important – unique. They rarely looked beyond the surface to what lay beneath – the reason for the clever compliment that was just what they had been waiting to hear, the thing their wives never told them, the things their boss didn't see. It was usually pretty obvious what they wanted. What they were lacking, in most cases. The thing they didn't have. You always want what you have not got. The guys who were straight and humourless wanted to feel like they were the fun guy, with all the jokes and the lines. The geeky ones who had always been left out and ignored wanted to feel like, for once, *they* were the interesting ones, not their better-looking friend. She saw what they wanted, and gave it to them on a plate. She became tough, and she did what she had to do.

When she met Nicolo, however, she met her match. He wanted something from her, but he didn't know what yet. They recognised in each other the fire of someone who has been betrayed – by a friend, by a lover, or just by life – and they fed it in each other. Not as lovers, never that. But Nicolo sent her money, keeping her dangling on a string for it because she never knew how much or when it would come, and information about what Logan was doing, in public, sometimes in private, when he had dug up some titbit he knew she would enjoy. She didn't do anything for him in return – not yet. 'There'll be an opportunity, don't worry, Colette,' he'd told her. 'Something will turn up, something you'll be able to do, and we'll both be there. We'll know it when we see it.'

351

And then, when Luxury had been launched, with all the talk of how private and exclusive it was, how no one could get on to the island without a screening process more rigorous than the one for the SAS, it seemed, and the family had been photographed getting on a plane to travel to the island, they *had* both seen the opportunity, and known just how they could exploit it: Charlie.

With Charlie it wasn't a matter of telling him lies, so much – he was talented, she thought, and she'd spent enough time in music bars and gigs to recognise good music. And he was definitely good looking – she had no need to embellish the truth there. He just wanted someone to believe in him, that was the thing he needed, the thing she was able to winkle out almost immediately and provide him with. Someone who told him he could do it, that he was good, that what he was doing was worthwhile. Not to write it off as a hobby, a waste of time, less important than what anyone else was doing. He was gorgeous, and sexy, and funny. She liked him, genuinely liked him, or would have done if she had allowed herself to. If she let herself stop to think about things, she would have felt guilty that she was using him to get at Logan, to find out whatever she could about the family and the company and feed it back to Nicolo.

But she couldn't let herself think like that – she had to remain focused. Logan hadn't given Charlie what he needed. Now she was doing so. If she found herself getting a little soft, enjoying Charlie and his company and his stupid jokes a bit too much, all she had to do was look at the photographs of her mother that she carried in her wallet, one from before the accident, one from afterwards, and everything came sharply back into focus again.

She was staring at a photograph of her mother now. One from before, when she was still able to dance and run and lift her daughter and throw her up in the air, both of them happy and laughing. Now all she could do was speak, her voice always strained with pain. Her dancer's body that had always been so lithe, so supple, was now stiff and paralysed, reliant on machines and other people for any movement.

Colette was in Logan's study, in the Barneses' house in London. It had been redecorated following the fire, and she and Charlie were staying here. Lucia was in the States, with Nicolo, Maryanne had just gone to rehab, Logan was over in New York. The family was all over the fucking place, physically as well as metaphorically. And it meant the house was quiet. Charlie was still sleeping; she had woken up early and slid silently out of his bed, pulled on a pair of jeans and a T-shirt and sneaked downstairs.

The room was formal, businesslike for a home office, with three computer screens and an enormous desk, but then she guessed this just wasn't any home office, one used for domestic filing and paying gas bills. This was one of the places Logan ran his empire from, so he could work wherever he was, even at home. The guy never stopped. She had run a finger along the edge of the desk. Where to start?

Eventually, after poking around for a bit, pulling out files that were full of meaningless spreadsheets, she found something interesting. She couldn't get into any of the computers, they were all password protected, and though she tried a couple of obvious ones, she was forced to admit defeat quite quickly. She was no hacker, and she didn't know what sort of alarm or whatever Logan might have installed in his system. She flicked idly through some receipts, marvelling at how much money Maryanne and her staff spent. Thousands of pounds on a guy to come and replenish the fucking tulips; five hundred pounds a month on designer toiletries for the guest bathrooms; dog food that cost more than her and her mother's weekly food bill. Jesus. She was in a different world. Charlie's world.

The photos were tucked into a small envelope, which was inside an unmarked folder. She almost hadn't bothered opening it. That was probably the point.

Inside were two newspaper articles from after the accident. Neither had photographs of her mother, just named her as *Georgia Hardy, one of the dance troupe who was injured in the accident*. No mention of the extent of her horrific injuries, of what her prognosis was, of the fact that she had a daughter. Just 'one of the dance troupe'.

But as Colette looked at the other things in the envelope, she realised that her mother had been more than one of the dance troupe to Logan. Briefly, at least. In some way. The photo was signed on the back, in her mom's looping, open hand, that Colette remembered from when she was young.

Can't wait to see you on the big night, sexy. Promise I'll make it even more special for you if you come and find me before the show!! Kisses, G.

Colette sat down in the chair behind Logan's desk and drew her knees up to her chest, still staring at the writing on the photograph, flipping it over and looking into her mom's happy, beautiful smiling face.

Then she wiped her eyes, picked up her phone, and dialled Nicolo's number.

The warehouse was cold and the photographer's voice echoed around it as he barked instructions at Lucia. This was nothing like the shoot she had done for Heiress, where she had been made to feel special, like the star of the show. Today she felt more like a piece of furniture, she thought, as the photographer's assistant plonked a large fur Cossack-style hat on top of her head, and yanked it round.

'Ow! You're pulling my hair.'

'So sorry.' The girl rolled her eyes.

'Come on, Lucia, pose, pose, pose.'

She rearranged the scratchy greatcoat so it was falling from her shoulders, and crossed her legs. The Cold War-themed shoot was taking place in a set that had been dressed to look like an old-fashioned wood-panelled office, and she was perched on the edge of the desk, long bare legs stretching out from beneath the coat.

The assistant handed her a buff folder with a red *Top Secret* label emblazoned across the cover.

'Right, peek inside the folder.'

'I'm not comfortable with this.'

'Just get on with it, Lucia.'

She threw the folder to the ground. 'Don't talk to me like that. This isn't what I agreed with Nicolo.'

As she and the photographer stared angrily at each other, Nicolo himself entered the warehouse.

'What isn't?'

She turned to him as he stepped on to the set.

354

'Thank goodness. Nicolo, I don't like this, I feel that they're making me look like a—'

'Defector. Yes, well, that is the theme of the shoot, honey, ain't it?' interrupted the photographer. 'You, changing sides, like a sexy little spy. Phwoar, that's lovely, come on – give it to me, baby . . .'

The camera kept clicking.

Nicolo put a hand on her shoulder. 'Lucia, I know this is hard for you.'

The photographer coughed, and Nicolo twisted his torso a little so he wasn't obscuring Lucia. The man gave him a thumbs-up and carried on.

'But we agreed that this was the best way to send a clear message to your father. He won't listen to reason, he cut you off, and so you need to hit him where it hurts.'

Lucia looked unsure. 'I just think it's too much. He *is* my father.'

'Not really behaving like much of one just now, is he? I know Logan. He'll respond to this. It'll give him a wake-up call, and everything will be fine again. And, you said you wanted the money – needed it for a project?'

She hesitated. The money Nicolo was paying her would make up for the amount she had lost when she was sacked from the Heiress job. That was part of the reason why she was doing this: Nicolo had offered her a large paycheque. And she really, really wanted that hotel.

'Look, I'm trying to help. Despite what your father has probably told you, I'm not the big bad wolf.' He smiled kindly, then shrugged. 'But if you've changed your mind, that's fine. We can call the whole thing off.'

'No, let's do it. I trust you.' Of course she didn't trust him. But for now, at least, she didn't have a lot of choice but to go along with him.

Of course she trusted him, the stupid little tart. One of Nicolo's most useful talents was getting people to trust him, in the face of all logic. It had worked with her mother, and it had worked with her. How could she think Logan was going to see the images of his daughter dressed as a spy, defecting to the other side of the feud that the media had likened to the Cold War, and welcome her back

355

with open arms? Absurd. It was interesting that Logan, who for all his many faults was certainly not a stupid man, had spawned such idiotic children. Interesting, and really rather satisfying.

He checked his email. There was one from Colette, telling him that she was still going out with Charlie, that things were going well, and asking him to send more money. She had discovered something in Logan's office, something that proved Logan had been sleeping with her mother before the accident. Nicolo was pleased. This was all coming together very nicely indeed. Keep her keen to help him, keener still to get revenge on Logan and it might be something he could use – muckspreading about Logan. The perfect husband, as he liked to portray to the outside world. Or not. Especially now that Maryanne was in rehab, facing her demons. A revelation that Logan had cheated on her years before was very good timing – for Nicolo. Logging on to his online banking account, he immediately transferred three hundred thousand pounds into Colette's account.

Back in his office after the meeting, Mark Mallory logged on to his anonymous webmail account and picked up a message from Nicolo Flores: Repercussions from awards ceremony?

Mark clicked REPLY.

Media all over LBI. Maryanne in rehab, etc. Logan still unsure of what Lucia's doing with you and it's clearly rattling him. Long-term prognosis? Not sure, but definitely shaken up by it all. First time I've ever seen him like this, actually. Claims all will come out good but suspect more precarious than he likes to admit.
SEND

The reply pinged back quickly: Security?

Mark typed out a quick reply: Not an issue. I have more authority.

Nicolo responded: Good. Will be in touch shortly.

Mark stared at the screen. He was stuck. Waiting for instructions from the man whose main aim was to bring down Logan and the company for which Mark had worked for years. Mark was in two minds about what he was doing. He knew it was wrong. Betraying his boss, biting the hand that feeds. Deception didn't come naturally to him and he was finding his involvement in Nicolo's plans increasingly stressful. He was sure that the size of his bald patch had increased significantly in the last few months. On the other hand, there was a lump of hatred in his heart for Logan, the man who had swept into Mark's family home and taken it over, done what he, the heir, had been unable to do. Been the saviour, the knight on a white horse, saving the day. No, Mark could never quite forgive him for that. And Nicolo had taken advantage of that resentment, bubbling under the smooth, loyal surface. He'd seen it, and he'd sensed a weakness.

So he'd dug, dug, dug, until he'd found something else that he could use to persuade Mark to be his eyes and ears within the company, a compulsion that Mark managed to keep under control most of the time, but which, occasionally, he couldn't help but feed.

Nicolo seemed to have a network of spies. Mark supposed one of the advantages of owning a string of casinos and bars was that he became privy to all sorts of bits and pieces of information. He knew which celebrities were having affairs, which influential figures in the film industry were fonder of young flesh than they should be, who bought their drugs from whom, and which big-name film star went to great pains to conceal her past as a call girl. He had been keeping close tabs on the people he knew to be in Logan's inner circle for some months when the opportunity he had been waiting for finally arose. He was good at waiting.

When the call had come in he hadn't been surprised, not really. Nothing much surprised Nicolo any more, but this was going to give him a particularly neat way to get what he wanted. He had allowed himself a moment of quiet satisfaction, and of anticipation of the games that were to come. Savouring the knowledge that he would be able to use this to edge his way into the heart of Logan's operations, like an oyster knife sliding in between the crinkled edges of the sealed mollusc to wrench it apart and expose its pale, soft centre.

Mark shut down his email, remembering the occasion that had led to his current relationship with Nicolo Flores.

He'd met the girl in a bar, as was his habit. A particular bar, out of the way, far from the main thrum of Hollywood. She'd been waiting for him at a table in the corner, as had been arranged by phone previously. Dressed simply in a black chiffon top and a black skirt made from some flowing jersey fabric that fell in waves around her slim hips, hair tied back in a low, loose ponytail, her large sunglasses shading most of her face. Glossy pink lips smiled at him as he approached the table and sat down opposite her. His shoulders tingled with anticipation of what was to come. But he liked to draw the process out, make himself wait.

He savoured this as they sat at the table drinking crisp white wine, feeling the tension mount inside him. Knowing she was waiting for him to take the lead, and would then do what he wanted – anything. Anything he could dream up, she would submit to. The question was in her eyes as she returned his gaze. *What do you want today? When are we going to leave this bar and begin the dance properly?* She had met Mark before, knew what he liked and what pattern he liked the evening to follow. The two of them were ensconced in their own world almost in the way that two lovers are – locked into their own private vortex of desire and fulfilment. But this was a business transaction too and Mark always wanted to make sure he got value for the considerable amount of money he was paying.

When he was ready, when he had teased all possible pleasure out of making himself linger, he stood, and motioned with his head for the woman to do the same. As she slipped her soft suede bag over her shoulder her sleeve fell back and he noted with pleasure the gently curving line of her wrist and the delicate skin of her inner arm.

The hotel room was like all the others that he used: anonymous, bland, clean. He checked into a different property under a different name each time and always paid in cash – all the trademark habits of the adulterer or the patron of prostitutes. His girls came from a couple of discreet, specialist agencies, and were selected for their fine features – he tended to choose the ones with an almost aristocratic look, an arrogance or haughtiness. Many men who paid for sex went for the opposite of what they could get in a partner – and so did he, in a way. But Mark, with the stereotypical need of an English public schoolboy for security and comfort was attracted to facial features that reminded him of the girls he was used to at home.

As usual, he pulled the blinds shut and turned on a single lamp, so the room was in shadow, then sat in the armchair in the corner of the room. His legs were crossed at the ankle exposing his scarlet fine knit socks, and his chin rested lightly in his hand. He nodded to her.

She stood in front of him, a few feet away. Just out of his reach. Her eyes met his as she began to undress. Slowly, she undid the shiny little buttons that held the light fabric of her top together, one by one, working from the bottom up, so that the tanned skin of her flat stomach was exposed first, then the curve of her cleavage. When she reached the top, her hand rested on her collar-bone for a moment, holding the two sides of the garment together, and then she lowered her head so her hair fell over her face as she let the fabric fall apart, revealing her bra, which was another layer of black chiffon, trimmed with a line of black satin. Mark bit his lip.

She reached one hand round behind her head and used it to gather up her dark hair, twisting it on top of her head so her neck was exposed. Then let it go again. Mark watched it swish over her shoulders, silky and shimmering. She looked up at him. Held his gaze as she unbuttoned her skirt with one hand at the back, and let it fall to the ground. Stepped out of it, still in her heels. Her French knickers were black like her bra, but the fabric of them was pure satin, with a chiffon ruffle at the hem.

Still watching Mark's face, she touched her nipples through the almost transparent fabric of her bra. They were small and hard, and they pushed the light material out. She rubbed them gently, and now, Mark couldn't help but echo the rubbing movement a little against his suited crotch. He didn't let himself undress, not yet. He would wait again.

He held his breath as she hooked her thumb under the waist-band of her knickers, and ran it along the edge, pulling it away from her skin. She lowered her eyes, at once looking demure and affording herself a glimpse of what was underneath the satin. She smiled slightly, then looked back at him. He leaned forward. She edged the knickers down, just a fraction, then took a step towards him. Stopped. Pushed her shoulders back before undoing her bra with a practised flick of her hand at her back, and removing it.

Covered her breasts with her forearm, holding them up lightly, then splayed the fingers of one hand so one of her nipples emerged from between them.

Now she was topless, standing before him in just her knickers and stilettos. She took another step towards him. He was still fully dressed, down to his polished shoes and perfectly knotted Jermyn Street tie. His eyes were eager, as she put one hand on either side of her slim hips, and began to push the knickers down over them. Very slowly, she edged them down, one side first, then the other. Mark's mouth had gone dry, and he moistened his lips. He could feel his heart in his chest.

She stepped forward again, and now she was right in front of him. He sat upright. There was a palpable tension between their bodies. She paused, and then with one smooth movement stepped out of the pants. Her penis was small, and curved round slightly into her inner thigh, still soft. The skin surrounding it was waxed smooth, and as Mark leaned forward and took it in his mouth very gently, he inhaled the slightly musky scent of her skin.

The video that Nicolo showed Mark the next day, in the cinema room of his 1930s mansion, showed this moment clearly. Mark watched, horrified, at the image of himself on the large screen, sucking greedily on the prostitute's penis, her hand resting behind his head, stroking his hair gently, her bare breasts and curved bottom a surprising contrast to the organ rising up from between her legs. There was more – the camera had captured the whole encounter – but this single image was enough for Mark, as Nicolo paused the video and the picture was suspended, Mark's face contorted grotesquely in a frozen moment in time.

He couldn't take his eyes off his own face; there was something bizarrely, horribly hypnotic about staring at it.

'What's this meant to do – frighten me?' he blustered. 'Come off it. Sex scandals are ten a penny these days. It'll blow over in five minutes. You don't seriously think this is going to get me to do – well, whatever it is you want.'

Nicolo's face showed his amusement as he clicked on the controller, and the screen showed a press image of Mark shaking the hand of a grey-haired woman on a podium, an oversized cheque displayed next to them. The banner above the stage they were standing on read *Action Against Abuse*. The cheque was one Mark had presented to the charity on behalf of LBI some time last year. It was one of Logan's favourites, and it worked to raise awareness of child abuse in various forms.

Mark looked at the screen. It was all right. All was not lost. He was sure he could front this out.

'I don't see the relevance. I act as LBI's ambassador when necessary. Most members of the board do so.'

'The relevance? The relevance, Mr Mallory, is that the "girl" you were with is sixteen – well under California's age of consent, as you know. She had the breast operation last year. Some surgeons are so unscrupulous. Sad, isn't it? Now I'm sure that's something all sorts of people would be interested in. Don't you agree?'

Mark went hot all over, and his guts shivered. He was fucked. He would definitely lose his job if that became public. A transsexual prostitute was one thing. An underage one? Quite another. And it wouldn't just be his job. The shame would taint every area of his life. He knew how these things spread, and how quickly. He had spent a long time getting his life just the way he wanted it. He couldn't lose all of that now.

'What is it you want, Mr Flores?'

Nicolo walked down from the small control booth at the back of the cinema, and sat in one of the chairs on the row in front of Mark. The seating was arranged in four rows, like a public cinema, but the chairs were not the usual cramped burgundy velour but large armchairs covered in ponyskin, with reclining backs and polished metal stands to hold drinks and snacks. As he sat, Mark thought how much he'd like to watch a film here, in different circumstances. One of the classics, *Casablanca*, or a Marilyn Monroe movie.

'Not money, don't worry.'

'No, it doesn't look like you're in need of cash.'

Nicolo smiled. 'Fortunately not. Business is good. But it could be better.'

'Better how?'

And that was how it all started.

* * *

361

Now, on the phone to Nicolo, Mark could hear himself betraying the man whom he had worked for – and with – for almost his whole adult life, and was surprised at the calm, businesslike tone in which he was able to do it. He might have been delivering a presentation full of numbers and sales projections to a room of financiers for all the emotion in his voice.

'Jacinta Tramontello, actress, with her paid companion on the beach, having an altercation regarding the, ahem, nature of his companionship, shall we say. Lola and Colm Farlon, also on the beach, providing some interesting insights into their marital and business relations. Johnson Jones talking to his lady friend about how his record company bought up thousands of copies of his latest single to get it into the charts.'

Nicolo smiled. Finally he had the upper hand. For so many years he had waited, watched while Logan built up his empire, accepted accolades and awards, amassed a fortune on a scale that Nicolo, although very wealthy, could only dream of. No more. Now Nicolo would strike back: he would be the one with the power, in control, and Logan would beg him not to ruin him.

'Well done, Mark. I'm transferring payment to your account as we speak.'

Mark cleared his throat. That was that, then.

'Many thanks. The original recording's in a safe. I'm sending you the details now, with the copy.'

There was a pause while both men keyed in the necessary instructions on their computers. So formal. So quick. Mark looked up into the Webcam. Nicolo was watching him.

'So,' Nicolo said.

'So.' Mark bit his lip. 'There is a final stage to our transaction still remaining.'

'There is?' The screen in front of him showed Nicolo's face still smiling slightly, eyebrows raised in question.

'The video recording.'

Nicolo looked down as he reached into his pocket for a silver cigar-cutter and lopped the end off a Montecristo. Put it in his mouth and sucked slowly and rhythmically as he lit it with a Davidoff lighter.

'The video recording. Aha. No, I don't think so.'

362

'That was what we agreed.'

'I don't think it was, Mark. I don't remember agreeing to that at all.'

'Now you look here. I'm a married man, I have a public image.'

Mark stood in anger, shaking his fist at the screen before realising how absurd he must look. The man was thousands of miles away, for God's sake. He sat again, and avoided looking directly at the screen so he didn't have to see Nicolo's smug, supercilious smile.

'Yes, I know all that. Don't panic, Mark. I've got no plans to out you and your 'lady' friend. Your petite peccadillo will stay our secret. I just like to keep a little insurance, that's all.'

Mark felt sick. How could he have been so stupid as to imagine Nicolo was just going to give him the recording back and that it would all be over?

'Now off you go. You don't have to dirty your hands with this business any more. Enjoy the money. Forget about all of this. May be you should take a holiday? Although I'd suggest you choose somewhere other than Logan's special island – that is, if privacy is important to you.'

Mark reached forward and put his hand over the Webcam, and the last thing he heard before he ripped it from its socket was the sound of Nicolo laughing at his own joke.

Nicolo flicked off the Webcam, still chuckling to himself. Give the video back? *I don't think so.* He'd paid enough to set the whole thing up; he had no intention of just handing the evidence back to Mark like that. No way.

The door to Nicolo's office was shut, he double-checked, before playing the recording. His shoulders tensed with excitement as he listened to it.

' . . . *I feel like a line. I want to inhale it off that beautiful body of yours. This bit, just here.*'

The quality was clear and crisp, the voices familiar and easily audible. Nicolo smiled, and pressed the intercom button on his phone to speak to Vienna.

'Vienna, call Max and tell him to get over here.' He didn't look at her when he spoke. 'And book a suite at the Marmont for tonight. I'm going to want to celebrate.'

In just a few hours the recordings would have been verified by Max, an audio expert, so that when they were made public, there would be no question mark over their authenticity. A handful of influential and famous people, revealing some of their best-kept secrets to the world. But even more damaging was what was unspoken – the implication that this was only the beginning was the really powerful part.

His plan for the recordings was simple yet brilliant. He intended to reach the very people whom Luxury was targeting, so they could see – or rather hear – for themselves how flimsy the claim of total privacy really was. It was typical of Logan's arrogance to believe that he could create something so dependent on the trust of others, typical of his belief that his employees were all loyal to him and would keep their mouths shut. Nicolo knew all too well about loyalty. It didn't exist. Everyone could be bought – all you needed to do was find out the value they put on their conscience. And now Logan would be ruined, shamed and exposed as a fool. Nicolo could hardly wait.

A less imaginative man would simply have sent the recordings to the media, to a news network, or put them on YouTube maybe. Not Nicolo. That was for kids and geeks, and by the time it had filtered through to the people who really mattered, it would have lost its impact. The way he was doing things had an element of the Trojan horse about it, which would only serve to give the whole thing more punch and wit.

Just as the invitations had been hand-delivered to the VIPs on the guest list for the launch party of Luxury by uniformed couriers, the recording would be copied and delivered to a hundred of the most influential individuals on the list (including the ones who 'starred' in the recording), by the very same couriers. He had no need to send it to every single person; this top one hundred would do the job nicely. Especially as he had photographers ready to snap some of the key ones being delivered, images that would come in handy as the story broke. Hopefully he'd get something akin to the photos taken of Cherie Blair on the doorstep of Number 10; that would give the world's media a nice little tie-in to use in their stories about the scandal. For extra panache he was loading the recordings on to slick black iPods, and presenting them in boxes just like the ones Logan had sent his invitations out in. He looked at his watch: 7 a.m. He clicked on the email that he had written to the employee whom he had put in charge of organising the delivery of the iPods, and confirmed that it was time. Nicolo was ready. He hoped Logan was too.

He'd been in touch with Colette again as well. She was making nice progress with her relationship with Charlie, spending lots of time with him, around the family. 'See if you can find out what's happening with the money,' he had said to her. 'I want to know how Luxury's doing financially. It's been open, what, six months now? Do a bit of digging around next time you're at the house – sneak into his office. Get me the numbers.'

Nicolo knew Luxury must have huge running costs. It had had plenty of press since it had opened, and the French President had been the most recent rumoured guest – but no one from the hotel would confirm it, and no one had been able to get a picture. No one, apart from Nicolo. He opened another file on his computer now. Flicked through photographs of the island that he had had Mark take for him. They were dynamite. There were images of things no one had ever seen before, or imagined. Luxury really had become a playground for the world's rich and famous, hadn't it? he thought as he looked through the photos. There was one of a member of the British Royal Family clearly almost paralytically drunk; one of a straight-laced American senator dancing around completely naked by his private pool; one of a famous actress, prostrate and being made love to on the beach. If they got out – well, no, *when* they got out – Luxury would be over for Logan.

Mark pushed his foot down on the pedal of his vintage Porsche, urging it down the long straight road that led to Sternley. It was the only place he wanted to be now; he longed to see the uncompromising lines of its grey walls, and to walk through the avenue of apple trees that led to the lake. Nicolo Flores was never going to give the video back. Mark marvelled at how stupid he had been to believe that he ever would. Some kind of desperation had made him believe it, he supposed; his mind had shut out everything he knew about Nicolo and the way he operated, and bought into the fantasy he had presented Mark with – that he just needed to do this one thing and then he would give him back the video, and no one would ever find out.

He pushed down even harder as he thought about it now. How long had he worked for Logan? Well over a decade, getting on for two. And for all of those years he had known about Nicolo, seen at first-hand some of his attempts to manipulate people and control them. And still, *still* he had let himself believe that it would be that easy. What a fucking fool. His fury and shame threatened to completely overwhelm him, and his hands clenched and slipped on the leather steering wheel of the car because he was gripping it too tightly.

The road narrowed, and the village of Sternley came into view ahead of him. It was a one-track road from here until you arrived at the gates of the house, and then the drive widened out into a broad gravel path. Killer on the suspension of a low sports car though, as every year the stream that ran underneath would rise up and the driveway would become filled with potholes and sharp stones that threatened to rip low-slung undercarriages apart.

Mark would slow then, but for now, he kept up the pace, his mind full of visions of the video recording and the deal he had made in a vain attempt to save his skin. The woman he'd been with – had she been in Nicolo's employ as well? How many times had Nicolo watched him visiting the women whose company he paid for, knowing they were not women, knowing Mark's secret? And who had told him in the first place? Had he set him up, to be filmed with someone underage? Or was it just coincidence? The horrible question of how Nicolo had uncovered his predilection for transsexuals billowed like stormclouds gathering together in his mind.

He couldn't bear it. He had to tell Logan, and warn him about Nicolo. Maybe Logan could find a way to stop him still. He scrabbled in his blazer pocket for his phone but couldn't feel it. Bloody things were too small now, constantly slipping through linings and to the bottom of briefcases. He glanced over at his briefcase on the passenger seat of the small car. Reached with his left hand to click it open. As he did so, the car went over a bump in the road and the briefcase slid forwards.

'Dammit.'

He leaned down for it, his eyes on the road. He managed to open the case, scrabble around then get the phone out from the bottom of the case, and then he glanced down to scroll down to Logan's number. It was at that moment that the Range Rover rounded the corner in front of him. Both drivers were going too fast; neither of them could have put their hands on their hearts and said they were paying full attention to the road. The blame for the accident could feasibly have been split equally between both drivers. But only one of them paid the price for their actions with his instant death.

The slick iPods had gone off to their destinations, the means by which Logan's downfall would be made final carefully loaded on to each one. Nicolo watched with immense satisfaction as they were loaded into the back of a black van on the sidewalk, and driven off. In less than an hour they would all have been delivered. He logged on to the internet from his iPhone and went to HYPERLINK 'http://www.tittle-tattler.com' *www.tittle-tattler.com*. On the left-hand side of the screen was an email address, with an icon inviting you to *Send Tips!*

He clicked on it. He wasn't going to send a tip – but a file containing a selection of photographs, and a video.

From HYPERLINK 'http://www.tittle-tattler.com'
www.tittle-tattler.com 10 a.m.
Some of Hollywood's top stars have been receiving unusual gifts this morning, iPods in shiny black boxes began arriving at mansions and duplexes all over town an hour ago, and my sources tell me they contain some very interesting scenes indeed, taken from the luxury-themed beach resort everyone's gagging to get into, Luxury . . .

From HYPERLINK 'http://www.tittle-tattler.com'
www.tittle-tattler.com 10.30 a.m.
See below for a picture of the new most wanted item in town, the Luxury tapes. Just call you Lumbering Buffoon International from now on, Should we, Logan?

From HYPERLINK 'http://www.tittle-tattler.com'
www.tittle-tattler.com 11.15 a.m.
EXCLUSIVE UPDATE – PHOTOS FROM INSIDE LUXURY
Yes, that's right. I've just been sent images of slebs from inside the so-called 'exclusive' island hotel. The one no one was meant to be able to

get access to? I hear you ask. That very one. And I can tell you, these pictures are hot, hot, hot . . .

Logan was trying to get Lucia to talk to him when his mobile phone began to ring. He ignored it. Then there was a quiet but firm knock on the door and Kirsten entered, her face sombre. He knew as soon as he looked up that something awful had happened, and he stood up straight away.

'Who is it? What's happened?'

His first thought was Maryanne, or one of the children, but Kirsten immediately told him no, 'Your family are fine, don't panic.'

He breathed. 'What, then?'

'It's Luxury.'

And she passed him the computer screen so that he could see for himself.

The photos were bad enough, but with the recordings as well, the impact would be devastating. Already he could hear all the phones ringing around the offices. He gazed at the photos, of naked Senators, of stars behaving badly, listened to the recordings, to the sounds of guests at Luxury well and truly letting their hair down because they were secure in the knowledge that it was private, that there was no way they could be overheard.

'*So don't make excuses, don't tell me how much you desire me. Show me, and show me now, or I'm sending you home and I won't pay a single penny. And I'll bill you for your share of the holiday.*'

'*Come on, darlin', let's go back to the room. I feel like a line. I want to inhale it off that beautiful body of yours – this bit, just here . . .*'

'*Why go back to the room? I want to do it now. Here.*'

He watched, and listened to the recordings, and as he did so he could imagine what everyone would be saying, imagine the internet, that modern-day creation that meant information spread faster than light, filled with chatter about how the hotel had been infiltrated, how the powerful, compelling man who sat in judgement over wannabe hoteliers every week on *General Manager* had allowed himself to be embarrassed like this, about who could have done such a thing . . . and he knew that he was listening to the sound of

Luxury slipping away from him for ever. No one would go there now. It would be – *he* would be – a laughing stock. The whole point of the hotel was its privacy, its secret corners where you could do anything, say anything without fear of being overheard or spied on. That trust was broken now, it had been destroyed and they would never be able to get it back again.

The policeman who had arrived at the scene of the crash half an hour after it had happened, after a dog-walker had seen the wreckage and called the emergency services, had found Mark sitting in the front seat of his car. Staring ahead of him, motionless, still clutching the phone in his hand, Logan's number on the screen. He'd been about to press the dial button when the accident had happened.

He didn't speak when the policeman opened his car door, or when the paramedics gently helped him out of the car. The driver of the Range Rover had been thrown through the windscreen, over the top of Mark's low-slung sports car, and had landed behind him on the road. Mark didn't let go of the phone until he was seated in the back of the ambulance, and the policeman had managed to prise it from his grasp, and call the number that he had been about to ring.

The policeman was nodding, listening as Logan told him that he would send a car to collect Mark once he had been given the all-clear by the paramedics and bring him back to London. He paused and turned as he felt the tap on his shoulder, and saw Mark holding out his hand for the phone.

'I need to speak to him. Is it Logan you're talking to?'

'I have Mr Barnes on the phone, yes. He's confirmed that he's your employer and is going to send a representative to collect you when we've taken your statement and you've been checked over at the hospital.'

'Let me speak to him, please.' Mark's face was pale, almost grey.

The officer passed him the phone, the expression on his face making it clear that he was not happy about something.

'Logan?'

'Mark, thank God you're all right. Look, don't worry about a thing, they aren't going to charge you or anything like that. They just want to—'

'Logan, listen.' Mark spoke quickly. If he didn't get it out he would lose his nerve; follow his instincts that told him to run, hide, anything to avoid telling this man who was being so kind, so considerate, that he had betrayed him in the worst possible way.

'I recorded things at Luxury for Nicolo Flores. He was blackmailing me but that's no excuse. I could have stood firm. I should have . . . Well. It's done now. It was me.'

There was silence on the other end of the line. Mark's eyes were filled with tears. He could imagine how Logan would be feeling; he knew the strength of the blow he had just delivered. He swallowed.

'I'm sorry, Logan. I know how disappointed you must be in me. I am as well, if it's any consolation.'

At the hospital, Mark was checked over. No broken bones, just a few cuts and bruises.

'You were very lucky, Mr Mallory,' the doctor had said. He didn't feel lucky at all.

'We've called your wife,' the doctor continued. 'She's on her way to pick you up.'

'Right.' Mark nodded. His wife was the last person he wanted to see. He felt totally numb. He would have to tell her everything, that he wouldn't have a job any more, try and explain why he would no longer be appearing at Logan's side on *General Manager*, because Logan would surely fire him, have to. Even if he didn't want to, which he would, of course he would. He had trusted Mark and Mark had betrayed him. Logan would need to salvage what he could from the mess, explain to his guests why it had happened. God. What a terrible thing he had done. The full repercussions of his actions were still to come. It would go on and on, interminably. And Nicolo would have the video, always, holding it over him, it would always be there.

Mark's phone rang. He sighed, and answered it.

'Mark Mallory speaking,' he said, as the doctor gestured at him to turn it off.

'You're not allowed to use the phone here,' he said in the background.

Mark waved him away.

'This is Fergus Chilman calling. Look, I'm afraid you're not going to like this, but I wanted to let you know . . .'

The doctor's complaints faded into the background as Mark listened to Fergus, the journalist who was ghost-writing Logan's autobiography, who hadn't yet heard about Mark's betrayal, but who had heard about something else. A video, that another journalist had been sent, from Nicolo Flores, showing Mark with a very young, very pretty transsexual prostitute.

'I just wanted to give you the heads up. What with – well, what with your wife, and the fact that you're all on the TV and everything . . . I'm afraid it looks like turning into quite a big story.'

Sternley was as magnificent as he remembered it. It never disappointed. He'd taken a taxi from the hospital. The officer who had attended the scene had told him they'd rather he didn't travel in the next couple of weeks, just in case they needed to talk to him further about the incident, but that had been it. Astonishing, really, how quickly an accident in which a man had died was written up and filed. The road had been partially cordoned off while they photographed everything and ran through various formalities, but was open again now. Mark didn't know who the man was, he didn't recognise the name. He hadn't asked any details about him, hadn't wanted to know.

He leaned forward as the taxi drove down the long, leafy lane that led to the house, and pulled up at the gates.

'Drop me here, please.'

The thought of returning to Sternley for the first time in so long in the back of a red Vauxhall Astra that smelled of vanilla air freshener and cigarette smoke was more than he could bear.

The air was cold and crisp and he could feel the sharp stones pressing on the leather soles of his shoes as he crunched his way down the drive. The house came into view and his heart lurched slightly as it always did. How could he have signed all this away? Logan had done a wonderful job restoring and renovating the house, keeping it intact, feeling like a private house rather than a hotel, but that had meant that it was *his* now, part of his hotel portfolio, no longer the Mallory family seat. He watched as a gardener on a ride-on lawnmower made his way slowly up and down an area of grass in smooth, sweeping lines.

A couple walked past him, maps provided by the hotel in hand

and matching Hunter wellies on their feet, bundled up for a walk. The woman wore a chocolate-fur hat and was clutching the man's arm. She smiled distantly at Mark as they went past, and then carried on talking. He felt invisible. They didn't know about him. But they would soon. Everyone would. A great wave of shame and regret washed over him. If only he had stayed away from Logan and the deal he offered him, none of this would have happened. Nicolo would not have sunk his claws into him, he wouldn't have been forced to betray anyone, he would have just been able to get on with his life. If he had been a stronger person, if he had kept control, he could have made Sternley into a private hotel himself, even. He could have done that, if he'd just had some fucking balls. Damn his weakness.

He couldn't bear the shame, the humiliation that he knew was coming. Exposed as a traitor, a perve, practically a paedophile, or that's what it would look like, as the boy had been so young. His wife would divorce him and take his children away, he would lose his job, and who would employ him? Someone who betrayed his friends, who hung around in seedy motels picking up boys who looked like girls? No one. The press would hound him, he knew what it would be like. He'd be pictured in the street, looking shifty, every move he made would be scrutinised, he might even be prosecuted. And all because of what? For what? Nicolo Flores, and his insatiable, inexplicable desire for revenge.

Mark carried on walking. His life was over. No one questioned him as he walked through the hall where the reception desk stood – no one ever did as long as you looked as if you knew where you were going, and he certainly did. Down the narrow corridor with the bar to the right, which had once been a rather stuffy dining room, and then left down a corridor which took him past a wooden rack full of pairs of brand-new and clean Hunter boots ready for guests to borrow, and outside again. Across the cobbled stone pathway, through the small gate that was tucked behind a hedge, and he was in the courtyard which held the old barns and storage rooms. He reached into his pocket for the set of keys that he kept with him as a reminder that, whoever's name was on the freehold now, Sternley would always be his in spirit.

To his relief, the locks hadn't been changed and the door opened easily; he breathed in the comforting smell of his childhood – hay combined with saddle soap and old, worn leather and pipe tobacco. He looked around the room. Not much had changed; it was still full of piles of hairy horse blankets and polished saddles, bridles and stirrups hanging from hooks on the stone wall. A cheap kettle and chipped mugs made a makeshift tea station on a small table in the corner, and Mark knew that if he opened the warped pale blue tin with a scratched image of Prince Charles and Princess Diana's wedding on it, he would find a stash of shortbread and bourbon creams. The familiarity of it comforted him. Geoff Harwood, the estate manager whose lair this was, had been with the Mallory family since Mark was a child, and one of the conditions of the sale of the property to LBI was that Geoff would have a job for life. He was still here, Mark could tell by the biscuit tin and the tidiness of the place. Geoff had always been a stickler for order in his workplace. Mark remembered the man's huge hands guiding his own as he taught him how to groom a horse, how to aim for a pheasant or a grouse or even a woodcock, how to whittle a piece of wood into a whistle.

Mark fingered the bunch of keys until he found the second one that he would need. It was small and cold in his hand as he pulled it out of his pocket and moved quickly over to the locked metal cupboard in the corner of the room.

The shot was heard by all of the guests at Sternley, many of whom were in the dining room tucking into a roast rib of beef from the hotel's own cattle. Some of them looked up, and wondered what the noise was. One man, a landowner himself, who was staying in the hotel to celebrate his wedding anniversary, recognised the noise as coming from a shotgun, and cocked his head to listen for further clues as to its source. Then his wife nudged his elbow and told him to stop thinking shop, he wasn't going to bloody well go shooting anything this weekend, so he might as well relax and enjoy his lunch, and he turned to her and smiled. The waiter who was refilling their glasses at the time thought it was strange, because the shot had sounded too close to the main house for any kind of organised shoot, and the estate staff didn't just go around shooting things in the grounds. He looked up and caught the eye of the maître d', who looked as if he was thinking the same thing, and left the room to find out what was going on.

It was Geoff who found Mark's body, slumped over the pile of horse equipment in the storeroom. As soon as he'd heard the shot, he'd known instantly it was one of his own guns; he had cleaned them and shot with them for over forty years, and he knew their particular sounds as well as his own voice. None of the employees would take one of them out without his express permission, and he certainly hadn't given anyone that, nor did they have a key to the gun cupboard. So he had run, his knees aching as they were jarred over the cobbles, until he reached the storeroom with its door wide open, and saw the leather soles of Mark's shoes sticking up from the dusty stone floor. He'd recognised him immediately.

'Aaah, Mark, yeh bleddy young fool, what have you done to y'self now?'

He had gone to him. Ignoring the blood that was everywhere, ignoring the fact that Mark's head was broken, its back a mess of brain and bone and his face battered from the recoil of the gun, Geoff sat down next to him and lifted his shoulders on to his lap. He was already dead, there was no comforting Mark any more, but still the old man rocked slowly backwards and forwards as one might try to calm a small child, or animal, crooning to him under his breath. 'There now, there now lad, that's it, there yeh go, that's it.'

And that was it.

Chapter Twenty-Three

The story of Mark's suicide was everywhere, almost immediately, as Fergus had predicted it would be.

The papers already had photographs of Mark's wife, standing outside their country cottage, looking pale and shocked. 'I had no idea,' she said to the reporters. 'My husband and I had led separate lives for some time. I certainly had no inkling of these allegations.' And she had gone inside and shut the door, firmly. She was telling the truth, Logan knew she was, but there was still something terribly sad about her rush to distance herself from the man who, despite everything, she had at one point shared a life with, had two children by. Still. There was no time to dwell on any of that now. He had to try and limit the damage done, try and somehow contain things at his own press conference, held on the steps of the Chesham.

'Mr Barnes, did you know what Mallory was into?'

'Was the boy underage?'

'Where did the recording come from – was it part of a sex game?'

'Did you know your board member was betraying you? Didn't you have any idea?'

'Logan, we've got a source that says Nicolo Flores is behind this – any comment? Your old sparring partner – has he knocked you out this time?'

Logan had a speech prepared in front of him. He read it out. 'Firstly, and most importantly, I want to pass on my condolences to Mark Mallory's family. He was, whatever anyone is currently alleging, a good man. A good employee, and a good friend.'

He looked straight at the cameras. He would not allow Nicolo, who he knew would be watching, to see the hurt Mark's betrayal had caused him.

'If it is proved that Mark was the one to make the recordings on the island, to take photographs there – and there will be a full and thorough investigation into how this happened – then I know it will also be proved that there was a good reason for that. The recording made of Mark with a companion . . .'

Catcalls and laughter from the press. Logan ignored them and continued.

' . . . seems likely to be the reason why Mark himself told me that he was being blackmailed shortly before his death.'

They had decided not to tell the press that Mark had also confessed to being the mole in Logan's company. Not yet. They needed to investigate, to show potential guests that the place was secure again, if they could.

Logan concluded: 'I have my own suspicions as to who was blackmailing Mark . . .'

Nicolo watched from the comfort of his office in Los Angeles, as Logan gave his statement. Things were getting to him, Nicolo could tell. He looked exhausted, as if he hadn't slept properly in weeks. As he spoke, Nicolo sat up straight in his chair. Was Logan going to come right out and accuse him? He almost hoped that he was . . .

'. . . But I have no intention of giving that individual any ammunition for a libel case.'

He smiled at the cameras. Nicolo fumed.

'Just know this. *You drove a good man to his death.*'

Logan's eyes were hard. Nicolo stared into them. Across thousands of miles, across oceans, their horns were still locked in a seemingly never-ending battle for supremacy.

Nicolo turned the screen off and gazed at the blackness for a moment, then picked up the phone. Logan's words had been a challenge.

The next day was a Sunday, and the *News of the World* ran with the story on the front page. Photographs of Logan, of Maryanne, of Georgia before the accident and afterwards, illustrated the spread, which detailed the affair Logan had been having with the woman who had ended up paralysed when the structure she was performing

376

on had collapsed. Shoddy workmanship had led to her near-death, had taken the use of her legs and arms away from her. The story had everything the tabloids loved – a pretty dancer's life changed for ever, her sweet blonde daughter, a rich man who hadn't cared enough about the woman to do more than pay her off. They hadn't managed to track down the daughter yet – reporters had gone to the last known address for the pair but it was empty. Still, even without that, the story was plenty good enough. Logan's wife was in rehab – that was a bonus, they played that up. *Did Logan's affairs drive wife Maryanne to drink and drugs?* asked the article.

Another woman came out of the woodwork claiming to have slept with him, and by then it stopped mattering to anyone whether it was true or not; the truth didn't matter, it was all about the story.

Kirsten tried to manage the press, but there was little she could do. 'Just keep your head down, and stay quiet,' she advised Logan. 'Go to work, concentrate on the business, on Luxury. This stuff'll blow over soon enough, but until it does, you'll just have to weather the storm, I'm afraid.'

Logan did concentrate on Luxury; he did little else. He spent hours phoning round friends, guests, celebrities who had been due to visit the island and who were now cancelling in their droves. Personally guaranteeing their privacy, promising them that there would be no further problems, that it had been a one-off. Trying to placate the men and women whose secrets had been exposed, and who were now embarrassed and ashamed, their careers damaged. It was no use. Everyone cancelled. No one wanted to visit an island where your most intimate moments could be laid bare before the world.

Still he battled on.

Colette read the story in the *News of the World* alone, in Charlie's bedroom, pleased that she had managed to play a part in what was happening to Logan now, and that she had a front-row seat for the show. She had uncovered the truth. He had fucked her mother, then fucked her over, as if she was nothing. And now he was paying for it. His life was disintegrating. He hardly slept, he was in his office, on the phone to hotel guests, accountants, lawyers, all of the time. He was working every hour God sent to try and save his business, but it didn't look like he was succeeding, not judging by the expression on his face most of the time. He was watching it all fall down. And he was doing it alone. His wife was in rehab and Johnny, who Colette had heard Charlie talk about, was still in hospital. Charlie obviously respected Johnny; he talked about him with real affection.

'Johnny's got out of bed,' he'd said excitedly the other day. 'Rachel just called. He walked three steps!'

Good for Johnny. There had been a time when Colette had hoped to hear someone say those words about her mother, had dreamed that one day she would take those first, tentative steps towards freedom from her paralysis. It had never happened.

Nicolo broke his silence. He knew that his dealings with Mark would come out, so he decided to pull the spotlight back to himself, rather than let Logan announce it and make himself look clever, like some kind of one-man fucking investigative squad. So Nicolo came out and held his hands up, ensuring that he tweaked the truth a little, portrayed himself in a more flattering light. He wasn't going to own up to blackmail. No one could prove that.

'I was approached by a member of Logan Barnes's staff – someone high up in the organisation – who wanted to share some information that he thought was of interest to guests booking into Luxury for what they believed to be a private and exclusive stay. While it is, of course, no secret that Logan and I have had our differences over the years, I felt that as a fellow hotelier, it was my duty to pass this warning on to those people who were most likely to be affected by it, as did my source within the company. Logan Barnes has made overblown claims, that he is unable to back up, about the security of his property – and that information is in the public interest. I admit to delivering the tapes with a certain finesse that was maybe unnecessary, but I'm afraid it's in my nature to be a touch flamboyant. Finally, I'd like to add my condolences to the family of Mark Mallory, the man who originally approached me with this information, and who, I have just been told, tragically passed away this morning. I would like to make it clear that I did *not* leak the video of Mr Mallory with an underage transsexual prostitute, nor did I blackmail Mark, as has been implied. He did not need any coercion from me whatsoever, I'm afraid. Such accusations are unfounded and scurrilous, and my lawyers will respond decisively and with speed, should anyone claim that I did.'

Logan was watching Nicolo's statement on one of the online news channels, just as Nicolo had watched him a few days before. He shook his head. What a fucking mess they had both embroiled themselves in.

Nicolo carried on: 'And I'd also like to extend those condolences to Logan himself. As it seems likely that both Sternley House and Luxury will be out of action in the immediate future, I'd like to take this opportunity to assure guests with bookings at either hotel who are no longer comfortable about visiting the properties, that there'll always be room for you at any of my hotels, Flores Inc.'

Smarmy fucker, trying to sidle in and take his business. Still, it was nothing more than he expected. There was a knock on the door and Kirsten entered.

'Have a seat, Kirsten. Thanks for keeping everyone at bay.' He dropped his fountain pen on the table. 'It's bad, isn't it? It's really bad.'

'It's not good.' Her face was grave. 'We can't control the media – they're a law unto themselves, you know that.'

He nodded.

'And, to an extent . . .' she went on.

'What? Say it. If you think it's all my fault, say so.'

She didn't. But the feud . . . She shook her head.

'No, I didn't mean that. Just that, if you live by the sword . . .'

She was quite right. They'd used the media often enough to their advantage, when it suited them. It cut both ways.

'Did you manage to talk to Lucia?' he asked.

'No. We've been trying, but her mobile's turned off and she's not taking the calls we've been putting through to her at the hotel.'

'Right. Thank you.'

He was silent.

'Anything else I can help you with?'

'No. No, thank you, Kirsten.'

Logan sat in his office after Kirsten had left, thinking. Luxury was sliding through his fingers, he could feel it. More than anything, he wanted to go there now, to go back to the island he loved so much, the clearing that he had kept back for himself, where he had met Elise that day. Elise. The thought of her was the only thing keeping him halfway sane. Everything else was a mess.

Maryanne, Charlie, Lucia ... What had he done to his family? Why, for instance, was he getting his staff to ring his daughter, his little girl? *For fuck's sake, Logan*, he told himself, *be a dad*. He picked up the phone and rang her.

It rang out, and clicked on to her answerphone. Logan took a deep breath, and left her a message.

'I'm sorry, Lucia. I'm sorry that you felt abandoned, let down – that you felt pushed out to the point where you had to go to Nicolo. I ... just want you to know that I don't blame you. For any of it. You're my little girl. My princess. Light of my life ... I will always be here for you.'

Lucia listened to the message from her father. She had seen him at his press conference, looking so tired and stressed. She wanted to go home, but she was desperately ashamed of what she had done. She looked at the photos of herself again, dressed up in the spy costume, the word *Defector* printed across them in red lettering like that which you would get on a folder or dossier. She stared at them and felt sick to her stomach. She couldn't do it to her father. Or her mother, this was the last thing Maryanne needed. No hotel was worth this.

No, she would be brave, she would prove that she was her father's daughter after all. She tore the photos up, and put them back in the envelope with a note to Nicolo.

Sorry. Deal's off. I have to do the right thing. Sincerely, Lucia Barnes.

And as she underlined her surname, she felt proud of herself for the first time in a long while.

Chapter Twenty-Four

Maryanne tried to force herself to listen to the person speaking, but her mind kept on drifting. The room was stuffy and the voice was monotonous. She shifted in her seat in an attempt to wake herself up.

'And then when I finally thought I'd gotten away from him, and had started a new job, I found out I had Hepatitis C. And I took a drink . . .'

Murmurs of recognition spread around the circle of fellow patients and Maryanne groaned inwardly. The whole programme was self-indulgent twaddle as far as she was concerned so far, and the Life Story session was one of the worst. In each session someone would read their potted autobiography that they had spent the last few days writing and then they would read it out to the group, punctuated by sobs and wails and occasionally moments where they announced that they couldn't go on, it was too painful, and would have to be coaxed to the finishing line. Maryanne wanted to hide behind her dark glasses but she had been banned from wearing them by a counsellor who told her they were a barrier to communication and to her recovery. Too fucking right they were a barrier to communication; that was the whole point. There was certainly no one here that she wished to communicate with on anything more than the most basic level.

She gazed around the room as the droning contined. It was comfortably furnished, with photographs of local nature scenes on the walls. Close-ups of autumn leaves, the circles on the inside of a cedar trunk, dew drops on the filaments of a spider's web. Images designed to calm and soothe flustered minds, wired from detoxing. Tedious. She looked out of the window and wished she could just float outside and lie on the soft grass and stare up at the sky. The air was clear up here, and smelled of life and sunlight. That was one Good Thing. She was forcing herself to notice and make a mental note of the Good Things about being here as she did so. She was tugged back into the room by April, the counsellor leading the session, saying her name.

'. . . ask Maryanne to tell her story at the next session.'

Maryanne glanced up sharply. April was looking at her through rimless glasses, her face surrounded by its usual frizz of hennaed hair. Maryannne wished she would get a decent colourist to look at it, and have all the split ends cut off – she could see them from here.

'Oh, I don't think so, April. I'm really not ready.'

'I think you are, Maryanne. You haven't shared much about your life. About your feelings, why you feel you are in this place emotionally. I think you need to start focusing on you.'

Fuck it.

'No really, it's too soon.' She was going to have to bring on the waterworks. It was a good job tears came easily to her. Her eyes welled with them and she raised an index finger to delicately push them back into her eyes.

'I just feel too vulnerable still. It's all too raw.'

April stared at her impassively. Christ, she was a cold bitch. Frigid, Maryanne was certain.

'You're using your tears as a mirror, Maryanne. You're trying to deflect us away from getting closer to you.'

A couple of the smugger members of the group nodded, and Maryanne shot them a hurt look.

'I'm crying because I'm very upset.'

'You're crying because you're trying to get out of writing your life story.'

Now she really was crying, but it was because she was fucking angry. She could tell she wasn't going to get her own way, and she was pissed. She exhaled. Breathe in serenity, breathe out negativity, as they had taught her. Another Good Thing about this place.

'Fine. I'll write my life story.'

She would write the sodding thing then; if a story was what they wanted, then a story was what they would get.

* * *

Sitting at the small desk in her bedroom she took out a pad of paper and a pen. She arranged them at right angles to each other. Took the cap off the pen and held it over the top line of the paper. Put it down again and walked over to open the window. It only opened part-way, like all of the bedroom windows here, but it still let the air in. She went back to the desk and sat down in front of the pad once more.

No, it was no good; the chair was making her back hurt. She picked up the pen and paper and took them over to her single bed, and made herself comfortable on top of the duvet. She started to write.

I was born in Houston . . .

She had intended to invent all but the factual details of her life, using names and dates as a framework and then making up anecdotes about childhood traumas, broken relationships and the roots of her addictions. But it didn't quite work out like that. When she started writing she found that there was something compelling about putting down on paper the blocks of her life, seeing them unfold in front of her. It sparked memories of events she had long forgotten, emotions she had kept buried. It was like revisiting the past, and the people who had populated it. After two hours she had reached the end of her relationship with Nicolo and the beginning of her one with Logan. And her pregnancy with Charlie. The joy that should have characterised those precious months had been tempered by guilt and fear that she would be discovered – and then rejected – by Logan. She thought of Charlie as she wrote, and was reminded of why she was going through this – it was for him and Lucia. Who knew if her relationship with Logan could be salvaged? Or if it had already died. But she would not let her children down any more, by remaining a woman unable to control her drinking and drug-taking, or by staying stuck in such a quagmire of substances that she was unreachable and unavailable to them when they needed her. She would endure the treatment, take her medicine – or stop taking it, rather – and return to them to be a good mother once again.

She went back to her life story.

The day Maryanne went into labour with Charlie, Logan was out of the city. She called him when the contractions became too painful and regular for her to write off as Braxton Hicks, but by that point he was still two hours away and she was alone and afraid. She'd lain in the bath trying to stay calm, and had wept and forgotten how to control her breathing. Then she'd become panicked that she was going to give birth here in her apartment all by herself, and had got out of the bath and phoned him again, half-standing, half-crouching against her bedroom wall as she cried and begged him to hurry up. She needed him and he couldn't be there for her.

And then her fear had turned to rage and she had lashed out at him down the phone line.

'You don't want to be here, do you? You don't want to have a baby. You wish you were free to fuck around and do whatever it is you're doing.'

'Annie, call the midwife. Her number's on the fridge, remember?'

'I can't. I can't do it, I can't . . .' she sobbed.

'Maryanne, listen to me. You have to stay calm. This isn't good for you or the baby.'

She'd let out a wail then; had crouched on all fours on the bedroom floor crying out, listening to the noises that were emerging from her chest; they sounded inhuman, animalistic. She'd dropped the phone and it had clattered to the floor. *The baby is Nicolo's, not yours, but I've chosen you and I'm scared it was the wrong choice, and scared you'll find out and reject me*, was what she wanted to say, but she couldn't. She must bury it, must stand by her decision and make a good home for her child with the man who was now her husband and whom she truly loved.

'Logan! Logan, help me . . .'

She had tried to bury it. She had been so determined to stand by Logan, to be a good wife to him, a good mother to Charlie, and then to Lucia as well when she came along, but the reality of marriage had been harder than she had imagined, right from the start. She felt trapped, hemmed in. She changed her name, but it took her ages to get used to; she felt like a fraud signing it on cheques and till receipts. Maryanne Barnes. Mrs M. Barnes. It felt like she was living someone else's life, playing grown-ups.

She'd managed eventually to get over that, and begin to enjoy being married. As she wrote Maryanne let herself sink back into the memories of those early years, when she and Logan were still

384

lovers in the truest sense of the word. She wrote about the times they hired a babysitter and went out dancing all night, coming home and making love until the sunrise, after which Logan would shower and drink industrial-strength coffee and go into work, and though they would both be exhausted all day, the memories of the night before would carry them through. Times when Logan came home from work early and they would snuggle up on the couch, all four of them. They'd sit there for hours, watching old movies, silly black and white films with men slipping on banana skins and hanging from the Empire State Building, eating buttery popcorn, and Maryanne and Logan would hold hands and marvel at the family they had made.

Time passed, and she wrote on. Wrote on to the place where things began to go bad, very bad. It was after Piccadilly Circus, after all that. After she had tried to leave; in a moment of desperate loneliness and confusion, had thought that going back to Nicolo was the way to solve things, to make things better. She felt so guilty. His reaction had made her realise just how badly she had hurt him. She had never really seen it before. She been too caught up in her new romance, her love for Logan, the first flush of pregnancy to look past that and see the pain she had caused Nicolo.

But then suddenly she did see it, up close, and it was ugly. She felt as if her insides had been scooped out like ice cream. Hollow. The two people Nicolo had trusted, really trusted, had betrayed him. Complicit and together, they had turned against him and left him alone. Maryanne knew what it felt like to be alone. How could she have done that to him?

Her hand ached, but she wrote on. The years passed. Logan and Maryanne's energies were stretched to their limits, in different directions, most of the time. Logan was determined to rebuild his business, to provide the life for Maryanne and the children that they deserved. After all, she had chosen him. He didn't blame her for running to Nicolo when things got so hard; he said it was his own fault. He'd failed her, very badly. No wonder she had tried to get away. Now she was his again, they had a chance to make things right. He promised to make it worth her while, prove to her that he had been the right choice. He poured himself into work.

Maryanne was uneasy at times, during those years; she could see that Logan was not prepared to let anything stand in his way in his ascent back up to where he had been before – and higher, far higher. But she could also see that in doing so, he was moving away from her and the kids, the ones he was doing it all for. She wondered if she should say something, now and then, when she was making French toast for Charlie, Logan having been at the office since half past five in the morning, or when she was going to bed alone for the fifth night in a row, having given up waiting for him to come home. Should she tell him that she'd rather he was here, making waffles and hogging the remote control, getting in her way when she was trying to Hoover the carpet, and if that meant they had no money and had to live in a little apartment in Queen's for ever – well, then, that was OK with her? Should she remind him that the guy she'd fallen for wasn't rich and famous, but someone who was doing what he loved, and that she didn't see much love in what he was doing these days – it was all about the drive, the result, the success? She never did say anything, of course. There was never the right moment, and there just didn't seem much point. So she carried on, believing that it would all turn out fine in the end. Telling herself he was doing what he needed to do, and that her job was to support him.

In 1994 the hotel that Logan's father had entrusted to him reopened, quietly, with no fanfare or red carpet (in contrast to Nicolo's latest casino in Atlantic City which boasted Victoria's Secret models abseiling down its glass sides on opening night). Logan and Johnny were setting their sights on the upper end of the tourist market, and on business travellers who were sick of bland, corporate tower blocks full of beige. They recognised that people longed for something unusual, something they couldn't get at home; and that they wanted top-class restaurants and bars, not just the usual breakfast buffet and whisky and soda set-up. They also felt that the style of a hotel had to reflect its environment, both in terms of the actual building, and its location. The LBI brand would not be one where you walked into a room in Hawaii and it was the same as one in Milan, bar the view outside the window. Their hotels would be as individually tailored as the suits their guests wore.

Number 67, for instance, was a small boutique hotel in Manhattan's Upper East Side, and, in keeping with its location, had the feel of a private house. There was no formal check-in desk, and decanters of wine and and full-sized bottles of spirits replaced the traditional mini-bar. Maryanne had thrown herself into the design of the bedrooms and public rooms, sourcing and refurbishing antiques from flea markets so that every room contained something unique – an old portrait that she'd had reframed, or a polished wood backgammon set on the coffee table. She loved it. She could push her doubts about her marriage to the back of her mind, now that she had something to focus on other than the kids. Charlie and Lucia were happy enough. Charlie was all about music, all the time. As long as he was plugged into his Walkman he was fine. Lucia was seven, and obsessed with ponies and riding in the single-minded way that some little girls are. For her eighth birthday, Logan bought her riding lessons and a complete wardrobe of riding clothes, complete with professional-standard dressage jackets and boots.

The words flowed from her pen filling page after page of her notepad. In 1996 Logan Barnes International opened two more hotels, one in San Francisco and one in Washington. The expansion out of New York meant more time travelling. Maryanne went with him occasionally, but more often he and Johnny travelled together, or he went alone. And with the travelling, inevitably, came temptation. She knew there were other women, had been other lovers for him. She didn't confront him directly. Couldn't really say much, after she had almost gone back to Nicolo.

When he started travelling more by himself, though, she got suspicious. Wanted it to stop. She hadn't actually done anything with Nicolo, after all, and she didn't want a marriage where infidelity was accepted as the norm. She started checking his pockets, under the guise of making sure he didn't put clothes in the wash with tissues inside; asking him dozens of questions about where he was and what he was doing. She was being paranoid, Logan told her she was imagining things. She had to trust him.

So she stopped going through his pockets, checking up on him. He was right, she decided. She had to trust him. It didn't make it hurt less, knowing that she wasn't the only woman he had slept with during their marriage, but she, too, had cheated – first on poor Nicolo with Logan, then on Logan with Nicolo. It didn't matter that she hadn't gone to bed with Nicolo; in her heart she had betrayed Logan, just as she had betrayed Nicolo before him. Logan was right, she was imagining things and if she wasn't careful, she would end up destroying their marriage.

Lucia was ten in 1997, and during the same year LBI expanded into the Caribbean market with the acquisition of a resort in Jamaica and one in Trinidad and Tobago. Charlie had begun to get into trouble at the exclusive Manhattan prep school he attended for not paying attention in class, and for playing hooky to go and hang out in guitar shops and with buskers on the street. Logan stopped his allowance. Charlie didn't seem to care, he just started busking himself. Lucia had tired of ponies and moved on to Girl's World, the disconnected plastic head that she and her friends spent hours playing with styling the hair and putting blue eyeshadow on it and which Logan found so creepy that he bribed her to put it away whenever he was home. Which wasn't often. At the end of the year, while going through her diary to write the annual Christmas letter that she sent out to their friends and acquaintances, Maryanne worked out that she and Logan had spent a total of seventy-two days under the same roof out of the last 365.

The next year, Maryanne wrote, LBI became one of the first hotel companies to introduce online booking for guests. Logan and Johnny built a new library for their old high school, and were invited to rejoin the Russell Club, a private members' establishment that they had been asked to leave following the catastrophe at Piccadilly Circus. They were fast becoming the men of the moment once more. Requests for Logan to speak at business schools and after black-tie dinners came in thick and fast, providing exposure and fat pay-cheques for them both.

Maryanne had stopped working on the furniture and fixings for the hotels by now; Logan had told her they felt it was important to have a 'coherent brand image', the likes of which could only be provided by a swanky design firm, it seemed. So she did the parties instead, which she enjoyed, of course she did. It was great fun – she got to meet all sorts of people, and she was good at it. Dreaming up themes, and creating wonderful entrances, and keeping up with what was happening in the world of fashion and food and all of those glamorous things. And at least she was still involved with LBI, even if she did sometimes look back on the early days and wish that things were more like they used to be then. But people started to talk about her parties and come to her, people outside the company, asking if she could find them a florist for a dinner, or introduce them to that hot new chef that everyone was talking about, for little Simon's Bar Mitzvah.

In 2000 LBI's Millennium Eve Party, conceived and planned by Maryanne, was attended by 2000 guests, and made her one of Manhattan's most in-demand social consultants. Charlie announced that he planned to go to LA the next year to study at the Musicians Institute. Logan, who Maryanne knew had been waiting for Charlie to get bored with music, almost banned him from going, but she had persuaded him to let their son go. 'Let him have his fun while he's still young,' she had said, knowing all the time that Charlie was never going to turn into the sort of businessman his father was hoping for, but telling herself they would cross that bridge when they came to it. Lucia was thirteen and Girl's World, predictably enough, had been discarded in favour of real make-up and boys. She spent every weekend with her gaggle of similarly privileged girl-friends, getting makeovers at Saks Fifth Avenue and debating what shade of Chanel nail varnish to paint their still childlike fingernails. Maryanne wondered now whether she should have sheltered Lucia more, let her childhood last longer. Logan had bought his first property in England by now – a rundown stately home called Sternley House, and his expansion in Europe had begun. He was away for weeks at a time. Maryanne filled her evenings with the parties she planned, and her days with shopping.

When she and Logan took their first holiday together in years – a three-day ski-ing trip at the chalet he had bought near Whistler in British Columbia, it was cut short when Maryanne fell awkwardly and broke her arm and elbow. She was in plaster for six weeks, and three operations followed – the break was a complex one, and didn't heal easily. She was in a lot of pain, a lot of the time. Just sitting around at home, by herself, she got so bored, so she carried on working, taking painkillers to get her through the days, and drinking a little more than she usually did. The painkillers worked during the day, the activity and drinks worked in the evening, but at night she was wakeful and lonely. In the end, she managed to screw up her courage and told Logan she wanted to travel with him more, work on some of the hotels again. The children were older now, they didn't need her there all the time any more. They didn't seem to need her much at all.

To her surprise, Logan agreed. He told her that he had begun to feel as if he wasn't part of his family any more; he never knew what was happening when he was at home, wasn't up to date with any of their jokes and schedules, so it had become easier to stay away, really. So this was an opportunity for him and Maryanne to renew their marriage, and to find their way back to one another. He missed her, he said. Maryanne inhaled sharply as she wrote this. She missed Logan, now, despite everything. Whatever had happened between them, however much they'd hurt one another, they had once been a pair, a partnership. She missed that. They would not have that in the future, she knew. She turned her attention back to the page.

In 2001 then, she and Logan got rid of the design company that had been in charge of LBIs hotels and opened their own, in-house department which she would run, backed up by a team that they had sourced together. She was excited. Their chain of hotels were firmly back on the map as some of the top properties in the world, and she and Logan were going to get back on track as a couple. They had recently signed a deal to take over a small group of boutique hotels in London that had fallen on hard times, and decided to buy a home in London to make travelling between the two countries easier. She had been so happy and optimistic, Maryanne recalled, but getting her marriage back wasn't as easy as she had thought it would be. It was years since she and Logan had spent any real time together, and things had changed. She travelled with him on business trips, but ended up alone in her hotel room while he dined and drank with colleagues in the bar downstairs. 'Bit of a boys' dinner, you understand?' he'd say, and she'd nod and order room service, and a bottle of wine, and look out of the hotel window at whichever city they were in, Prague, or Rome, or Berlin, and realise that she could be anywhere and, in fact, might as well be at home.

She would fall asleep watching TV, and then go shopping the next day, which Logan would always encourage. 'I don't want you to be bored in the meeting – it'll just be dull figures and stuff. Go and buy some shoes, a present for Lucia.' So she did. She became a power shopper, able to empty Gucci of its wares in record time. Lucia loved her for it, as she was always returning from the trips with armfuls of bags and cashmere sweaters and trinkets from duty-free, bought while Logan made one last call before boarding.

By the time of her fortieth birthday, in 2003, Maryanne had realised that the in-house design company ran perfectly well without her, and she suspected that Logan had probably set it up to keep her happy, rather than because he genuinely valued her skills, her opinion. He approved everything anyhow, she didn't have any say, really, and all the designers went to him when they needed a decision on something. She was redundant. Redundant at work, or what had passed for work at one time, redundant at home. Her housekeepers were efficient, the home ran smoothly without her. She became bored. She still took painkillers for her arm, even though the doctor had told her she shouldn't need them any more. What did he know? She was in pain. Her birthday precipitated a bout of age-related angst and insomnia, and she started taking sleeping pills as well. And because she and Logan slept in different rooms by now, there was no one there to monitor the amount she was taking, or to keep an eye on the slowly increasing contents of her medicine cabinet. She threw a Sweet Sixteenth party for Lucia at Boujis in London, and hired the triple Brit Awards winning band Brush to play, at a cost that made even her eyes water. All the girls got Jimmy Choo vouchers in their take-home bags. The next day, Maryanne went back to see her doctor, who told her that she really should try and cut down on the sleeping pills. She promised she would, and he started her on Prozac.

Early the next year, Logan succeeded in buying the island that he had been hankering after for the last two decades, when its current owner died and L'île des Violettes came on the open market. Maryanne had never been there, but Logan had always talked about it as being the place where he had felt happiest, most at peace. 'Why do you want to open a hotel there, then?' she had asked, when he'd told her about his plans. 'Surely it will ruin it?'

He'd looked blankly at her. 'Of course I won't ruin it. What do you take me for? It's going to be beautiful. I want everyone to see how beautiful it is – well, not quite everyone.' Then he'd explained to her what he planned to do, how he would make it available only to the elite of the elite, the hand-picked. 'Do you see? I'm not turning it into some kind of theme park, I'm keeping it exclusive, under control.'

Maryanne had nodded, slightly bitterly. Everything *was* under Logan's control, after all.

When Lucia turned eighteen, Maryanne suffered another bout of depression. She missed Charlie, who was showing no signs of coming back from LA, where he had now formed a band and had bought an apartment. Both of the children had trust funds that enabled them to do pretty much what they liked. Logan believed in teaching them financial responsibility from a young age, and had sent them each to a two-day wealth management seminar when they hit sixteen to help them learn this life skill. With her children grown up, Maryanne felt old. She felt pointless. Logan was impatient. What did she have to be depressed *about*? It was true. She was ungrateful. So she put on a brave face and plastered over the cracks, or tried to, and saved her tears for the night-time, when she was alone. It didn't always work, but the painkillers made it a bit easier to pretend – they made everything a bit easier. The Valium that she had started taking helped a bit, as well, though it did make her feel quite out of it sometimes, so she started perking herself up in the mornings with one of the diet pills her friend Lorna took. Just to get her going first thing. It wasn't like she needed them.

She was reaching the end of her life story now, writing the more recent past. It was painful, but she kept going. She'd gone too far to pull back now. Her life was filling the pages in front of her. She was crying, remembering, writing. In 2006 Logan, Johnny and Mark did the deal to make *General Manager* a reality, and Logan and Maryanne moved their family home to London. Maryanne had had something of a breakdown a few months previously, following a car accident where she had driven into a bollard on the sidewalk. She had spent a week in a private clinic in upstate New York. She was fine, she insisted, just a bit of a blip. She was terribly sorry about the car, it was written off, but the main thing was, no one had been hurt. She'd just been so tired. They both agreed that a fresh start would be good for them all. Charlie was still based in LA, but came home regularly. Lucia complained about leaving her friends but, as she showed no signs of wanting to move into her own place, Logan told her it was tough. The fact that she still lived at home actually suited him just fine, he confided in Maryanne: he could keep more of an eye on her and on her spending if she was at home, so he promised her a new Maserati if she moved without making a fuss. Logan was going to have to be in New York a lot still, as *General Manager* would be filmed partly there, and they still had all the New York hotels of course, but he was ready for a move as well. He'd been in Manhattan a long time. At first, Maryanne liked London. She was invited to all the parties, she made lots of friends, there was plenty to distract her – furniture to buy for the house, dinners to host, new shops to discover.

But before long, the sleepless nights started up again. And the headaches, the awful headaches that seemed to come from nowhere. And then Logan was famous, far more famous than they had anticipated, and everyone was looking at them, all of the time. Everywhere they went she was on show, on display, and then the nerves started, that was new – the paralysing nerves whenever she had to go out or meet people. She felt like an awkward teenager again, all clumsy and dull and gauche, and she suddenly realised why her mother, whom she had so despised for constantly being slightly drunk, had been like that – it just made it so much easier to talk to people without feeling like you were boring them to tears.

That was the final straw really, realising once and for all that she had become more like the woman she had always been so scathing about than she could ever have imagined. So she blotted it out, drowned her feelings and memories with wine and gin, and smothered them under piles of expensive clothes, swallowing endless pills and painkillers.

And still, the pain would not die.

Maryanne was sobbing as she wrote the story. She had never managed to make the pain go away.

She dropped the pen on to the desk. She didn't think she could do this, it was too hard. However difficult it had been to carry this heavy secret with her for so long, she had managed it, hadn't she? All right, she had suffered, but that was no more than she deserved. But this was different: it was coming face to face with herself, and with the mistakes she had made and concealed, and it was just too hard.

393

Putting on a chunky patterned pullover, she went outside.

Raff was grazing in the field next to the outdoor school and he walked over to her for a pat as she neared him.

'I was just going to go for a hack. Want to join me?'

She turned to see Sam behind her on the back of a powerful-looking horse, black and glossy.

'On Raff?'

'He could do with a change of scenery. Looks like you could as well.'

The trail through the forest was shady and smelled of moss and bark. Raff and Maryanne followed Sam and his horse slowly through the dusky woods.

'I don't think I can do this,' Maryanne said softly. Sam didn't say anything, but she could feel him listening. There was something about the gentle rhythm of the horse carrying her, and Sam's quiet strength that made her feel able to talk openly for the first time in years.

'I don't know how to do this.'

'How to do what?'

She paused. 'How to live my life without drugs, without anaesthetic. But more than that – how to tell the truth. My son isn't his father's son. I mean – Logan, my husband, isn't his father.'

She waited for an intake of breath, or other expression of shock or disapproval, but none came. Sam just rode on.

'Neither of them knows the truth. I've kept it secret for well over twenty years. Charlie's grown up seeing Logan as his father, but he's not. His real father is a horrible man, and I don't want him to have anything to do with him.

The ground sloped down, and she leaned back as Sam had taught her as the horses picked their way down the hill, their hooves rustling the leaves on the ground.

'But he's a grown man now, and maybe that decision is his to make. I can't shield him for ever. Control him, I suppose he'd call it. He's very big on not being controlled.'

Sam didn't say anything, but she thought he might have nodded slightly.

'I have to tell them all, don't I?'

'Once you start telling the truth it'll become easier.'

'Maybe. But how do I start?'

They were at the bottom of the slope now, and the trees around them widened into a clearing. Sam pointed to the left.

'Come this way. I want to show you something.'

The forest fell away and they were standing on an area of scrub overlooking an immense plateau. The air was cold and clear as it hit the top of Maryanne's windpipe and made her gasp. They dismounted and gazed out at the mountain range ahead of them.

'Wow.'

'Quite something, isn't it?'

'This is where you bring all the girls, is it?'

Sam smiled. 'Nope. Just the ones who need to remember that it's all pretty simple, really.'

'What's simple – life?' Maryanne laughed. 'Don't joke.'

'It is. We're small. What we do don't matter to anyone in the end, apart from the ones we hurt along the way, or the ones we love. Look at that – it's all been here for thousands of years. It's not going anywhere any time soon. These guys know that.'

He gestured to the horses, who were quietly snuffling around on the ground.

'Just tell the truth, Maryanne. Things'll get a whole lot less complicated once you realise you don't have to answer to no one but yourself and your own conscience.'

'And God?' She covered her emotion with sarcasm. Sam just shrugged.

'If you like. God ain't nothing but our conscience, in my opinion, but call it what you want. Either way, these mountains aren't going to remember what you did or didn't do, the secrets you hid or the ones you told. We'll all be dust soon enough, so you may as well feel good about yourself while you're here.'

He turned to her and his blue eyes were bright and clear.

'Don't you think?'

Later that night, Maryanne sat down and wrote three letters. When she had finished, she went to see Kurt, and told him what was in them. He asked if he could read them. She agreed. If she was going to be open and honest in her life, now was as good a time as any to begin. A fresh start, beginning right now. A new Maryanne.

'I'll send them straight away. Fed Ex?'

She nodded.

'Well done, Maryanne. The truth will set you free.'

She smiled and, to both their surprise, went and hugged the bearded counsellor. For once, she thought, maybe he didn't talk a load of crap after all. Not all of the time.

Chapter Twenty-Five

Bill walked into his apartment after a very long liquid lunch and dumped his briefcase down on the floor. He had a bottle of Krug in one arm and a bouquet of flowers in the other, and he was singing. He was already a couple of bottles of the fizzy stuff down.

'Elise?'

He loosened his tie and took off his jacket.

'Guess who's the new Director of Crown? Who's the Daddy? Oh Danny Boy ...' he sang, and his voice reverberated through the apartment. No reply. No one was home.

He did a little dance in the centre of the living room, wiggling his hips and throwing his arms in the air, then he remembered there was no one else here, and felt foolish. Why was there no one else here? He wanted to celebrate.

'Come out, come out, wherever you are. Come and show Daddy how clever he is, Lisey!'

Yeah. He was going to have a good night tonight. Where was the silly cow? Oh well. If she'd gone out he'd just go back to Blues for the night. The girls there would definitely want to congratulate him in the ways only they knew how.

Then he saw the note propped up against a vase on the glass table, and an envelope behind it.

'*Dear Bill,*' he read out loud, in a high-pitched voice. God, he was drunk. He cleared his throat, and stopped. Carried on reading it to himself.

I've left you. And I've taken Danny. Don't even think about trying to follow us, or taking me to court for custody.

He swayed.

*I know you said you would never let me go, but you don't
have any choice. OK, so you put all of your crap in my
name. It proves nothing. I believed you for too long, I
believed everything you said. I let you beat me down.
My heart, my soul, my spirit, as well as my flesh. Not
any more.*

This couldn't be happening. He was the one who made the decisions, not her, not that bitch – how dare she?

*Speaking of which – I recorded every time. I didn't know
why at first, didn't think I would ever have the strength to
do what I'm doing now. But some small part of me, of who
I really am, not who you tried to make me, stayed alive. And
every time you touched me – no, let's not use euphemisms
any longer, it's too late for that. Every time you hit me,
bruised me, beat me, I took a photograph. They're all here,
in the envelope. That's right, that one.*

He reached for the envelope, tore it open. A sheaf of photographs
fluttered out. Elise's wrist, a vivid purple bruise encircling it,
yellowing at the edges; the remnants of a night where he had held
her down, hard. The side of Elise's face, a thin, inch-long cut on her
cheekbone. She had broken an expensive crystal glass by accident
one evening, and he had scratched it along her skin, in fury. A mark
on the back of her shoulder, from a shove into the doorway. He
looked at the collection and was covered with drunken self-pity.
How could she have done this? Made it look as if he was some
kind of wife-beater, when it wasn't true. It was her fault, she had
driven him to it – pushed his buttons, angered him when she knew
he lost his temper easily. Why hadn't she just done what he wanted?
Then none of it would have happened. White-hot rage overtook
him and he swiped his arm along the table. The vase flew off the
end and shattered on the floor. It wasn't enough. Still the images
taunted him, her eyes taunting him, staring out of the photos at
him, accusing. He started to tear them up, ripping the images of

398

her face, her arms, her legs into pieces, as if by doing so he could obliterate what he had done, pretend it had never happened.

He didn't stop until all of the photos were destroyed and he was surrounded by a pile of pieces of coloured paper. Unrecognisable as images of a woman, of his wife. His wife. Oh, God. What had he done to her? He had broken her. He slumped to his knees among the fragments of Elise.

He reached for the letter again.

You can destroy the photographs but obviously, I have copies. So does my solicitor. And, this might sound paranoid, but he has instructions to give them to the police should anything happen to me. Maybe it is paranoid – but maybe not. I've learned a lot about the depths you are prepared to go to in the last few years, about the strength of your temper.

You have not broken me. I want you to know that. I thought you had, for a long time. Thought you had destroyed everything I knew about myself. But you didn't. I've found a strength that I didn't know I had. And, in a way, it's you I have to thank for it, Bill. Ironic, isn't it, that the man you said I should be nice to if I got the chance, because it might help your career, increase your status, is the one who has made me see that I'm worth more. That I deserve more – and that so does Danny. That's right. Logan Barnes. He has shown me that the old Elise, the one who you tried so hard to wipe out, is still there inside me. I just needed to find her again.

So thank you, Bill. You've set me free. I'm free of you. You will never be able to hurt me again.

Elise

Bill let the letter fall on to the floor, and he sat, leaning against the wall, howling with impotent rage.

Elise arrived at the home just an hour too late. The nurse who gave her the news had been curt, brief. Had just told her that her father had 'passed over', that old-fashioned euphemism, at eleven minutes past five, and Elise's first thought had been to ask what she was talking about. Passed over what? But even as she was opening her mouth she realised what she was being told. He was dead.

'Oh no. Oh no. I was here to . . . But I was going to move him!'

As if that would somehow change things, as if that would mean he wasn't dead, after all.

'I'm very sorry,' the nurse said. 'We have been trying to reach Mr McAllister, but there was no answer.' She didn't sound sorry, she sounded annoyed, and impatient. 'Now, we need to know when the body will be collected.'

'The body.' That wasn't right. Her strong, daring father couldn't have become 'the body'. It wasn't possible. She couldn't bear it. He'd died alone, in this awful place, where she had abandoned him. She had been planning to take him away from here, to move him somewhere decent where he would be looked after properly, and where he could have fresh air and company, but she hadn't done it in time. And now there was no more time.

She had felt so pleased with herself when she had sealed the envelope on the note, and raced out of the house to get Danny and come down here. She was escaping, she was on top, she was going to make everything right. Now she just felt empty and numb. She held her dad's cold hand, stroking the back of it with her thumb. The nurse on duty had grudgingly agreed to let Danny do some drawing in the office with her, while Elise had some time with her father's body. Her father's GP had been, and Elise had phoned the nearest funeral home and arranged for them to come and collect him shortly. Now, all there was left to do was say goodbye.

But how could she say goodbye when she hadn't seen him for so long? She had come here to say, 'Hello, again – here's Danny, your grandson, Dad. Look how he's grown.' Show him photographs, tell him how much she loved him. And that was what she would still do.

'Dad, I know you can't hear me,' she said, tearfully at first but getting stronger, 'but – well, maybe you can. Danny's outside. He's beautiful. So funny. Last week, we were walking . . .'

And she sat with her father, holding his hand, and told him all the things that she had come to tell him.

* * *

By the time the undertaker's van drew up outside the nursing home, Elise was ready. She waited outside her father's room while they covered his body, and wheeled it out to the waiting vehicle. The dour nurse appeared in the doorway.

'Have you taken his personal belongings?' she snapped.

'He didn't have much, did he? Look, if I pay you, can you donate anything worth keeping to charity, and dispose of the rest? I can't face doing it, I'm sorry.'

The woman shrugged. 'Fine. I meant his papers, in the drawer there, though.'

Elise followed her gaze. 'Oh.'

'They were brought in with him. Think it's his will.'

Elise opened the drawer and took out a small packet, and a photo album that was underneath it. Written on the front of the packet were the words *For Elise – my final roll of the dice*, in her father's hand. Seeing his writing brought it home to her. He was really gone. She didn't know what the words meant, but she stuffed the papers into her bag, keen to be gone from this place, and went to collect her son.

Elise and Logan lay in bed, her head resting on his chest, her finger-tips tracing a pattern on his skin. They were in a suite in the Lexington Hotel. Danny was fast asleep in an adjoining room. Confused and exhausted by the day he had had, which had started with his mother gathering him up and not taking him to school as normal, but taking him in the car to do drawings in a smelly place, then bringing him here to this big hotel where he had been allowed to have chocolate ice cream and a lady had given him a teddy bear from the gift shop, he had gone to sleep as soon as his head touched the pillow, his arms wrapped around the bear.

'He'll be all right, won't he?' Elise fretted.

Logan kissed the top of her head. 'He'll be fine. It'll take him some getting used to – it's a big change for him. But kids are tough little things. They adapt.'

She nodded. 'I suppose so.' She lifted her head to look at him. 'And you? Can you adapt? Do the whole thing again, with me and Danny? You've raised one family. Are you sure you want to start over again?'

'Yes. I couldn't be more sure.' He smoothed her hair down.

'Even . . . even though Bill might not make it easy?'

Logan shrugged. 'Ah, I've battled bigger men than Bill, remember?'

'But can you do both?' She pulled herself up on one elbow. 'Your business, the hotels – you've got so much on your plate. I don't want to be a burden to you. I couldn't bear it.'

He turned to her and ran a hand down her side, letting it rest on her hip.

'You could never be a burden to me. I need you, now more than ever. I need you by my side, Elise.' He pulled her closer to him and kissed her gently, with tears in his eyes now. 'A burden. How could you ever think that. Oh Elise . . .'

He kissed her more urgently now, passion rising in him once more. How could her husband have hurt her so badly, this lovely girl, stolen so much of her confidence? He would never let that happen again, Logan vowed, as he moved on top of her. He was going to spend the rest of his life making sure that she felt safe, loved, adored. No matter what.

They didn't sleep that night, the first night they had ever spent together. It felt too momentous somehow to waste on sleeping. Later, they sat up, and talked more.

'I can't divorce Maryanne, you know. Not yet.'

'I know.'

'I'm sorry. I want to be free to be with you completely, but—'

'But she might need you.'

'I'm not the right person to help her, not any more. But it will take time. The kids need her to get well. She needs to get well.'

Elise took his hand. Kissed each finger, one by one.

'It's all right, Logan. I understand. You had a whole life with her. That doesn't disappear overnight just because I came along. It's not like me and Bill.'

'No. So, you'll wait? You don't mind?'

Elise sighed. She didn't think she would mind anything ever again as long as she could stay right here, in Logan's arms. But already the light was starting to creep in around the curtains.

'I don't need you to be divorced to be with me. As long as I have your heart, nothing else matters.'

Chapter Twenty-Six

Nicolo had been at a meeting with one of his hotel managers, looking over the figures that showed the clear growth in his market share from the last few weeks. He was feeling good. His attack on Logan had been a great success. The producers of *General Manager* had announced that it was being taken off air 'indefinitely', and his enemy, Logan, was looking more and more tired and stressed by the day. Life was good.

Nicolo stopped off at the hotel to pick up Lucia, but she had left.

'What do you mean, she's left?' he bellowed at the receptionist.

'Sorry, Mr Flores, she checked out a little while ago, but she asked me to give you this.'

She handed him the envelope. Nicolo looked inside at the pile of torn-up photos, and the childish handwriting on her note, with its little hearts dotting the 'I's. And laughed. So *the deal's off*, is it? That's what *you* think. He shoved the envelope back into the hands of the worried-looking girl behind the desk before striding out of the hotel, calling behind him. 'Shred it. And if she comes back, she's not to be allowed through the doors, understand?'

She nodded.

He arrived at his mansion in under ten minutes. It was at the top of a hill, the road up to it wide and leafy, lined with gated mansions in a variety of architectural styles. His was a white Spanish-style building, behind wrought-iron gates. Security was tight around here. Nicolo parked his Merc in front of the house and ran up the steps and in through the open front door. He strode across the tiled floor of the hallway towards the study at the back of the house where he could hear voices. The hall was a showcase for some serious modern art – one of Warhol's Mao prints was in pride of place facing the front door as you entered, and a multi-coloured Alexander Calder mobile was suspended within the curve of the spiral staircase. Nicolo admired his art collection every time he came through this space; it was a symbol of his success and he liked to look at each picture, almost saying hello to it and letting it remind him of how far he had come.

He paused outside the study door, which was ajar. Vienna was inside, talking. He could see her shadow as she walked around, the phone wedged into the crook of her neck as she lit a cigarette. Her fringe was in her eyes, as usual, and she brushed it away in a movement that always irritated him. A psychoanalyst might have said it was because it reminded him of a similar motion Maryanne used to make that he had found so enchanting, and that the memory hurt him. Nicolo would have said that was bullshit, and it was irritating because it was so graceless and clumsy a movement. He liked things to be elegant, and it jarred. Whatever. He had no interest in navel-gazing. Vienna rested a hand on her hip as she stood next to the French windows which looked out to the landscaped garden and its kidney-shaped pool. Her voice was tense, upset.

'I don't believe you. How do I know you're telling the truth?'

Nicolo listened, breathing quietly, his whole body tense and still.

'He can't have done that. It was Logan – it was *his* fault.'

What was Logan's fault?

'The accident was Logan's fault, Nicolo told me. I asked him about it when we were first together, and he said it was because Logan was sloppy, because he didn't pay attention . . .'

Oh, God. Nicolo moved now, burst through the door.

'Who is that? Who are you talking to?'

Vienna spun around, her face full of fear. She slammed the phone down and flew at him.

'*You* caused the accident at Piccadilly Circus – it was you.'

'Don't be absurd, how could I have done that?'

She ignored his question and said, 'When we were first going out, I Googled you, and we were talking, remember?' She lit another cigarette, her hands moving quickly, pacing.

'I said I'd seen something about the hotel, and wondered how the accident had happened, and you said it was because Logan was

404

sloppy, because he didn't pay attention, you said that – you said it!'

'So what? It's true.'

'No, no, no, it's not, it's not true. That was the woman, that was her.'

'What woman? Vienna, you're hysterical, you're not making any sense.'

She sucked on her cigarette. 'The woman you hurt – the one from the accident. She's in a clinic, in California, she's not far from here. She . . . She . . .'

Vienna sobbed, but carried on.

'She had to have someone hold the fucking phone to her ear, but she told me. That when she was dancing, she noticed that the platform was unsteady, and she looked down.'

'Shut up, Vienna, just shut up. You don't know what you're talking about.'

'I won't shut up!' Her voice was a screech. 'I won't shut up any more! She told me that she looked down, and it was damaged, not because it had been carelessly assembled, but because someone had cut it, someone had deliberately sawn through a strut. She never said anything before, because she cared for Logan. She didn't think it had been his fault – didn't know what had happened. Just put up and shut up. And then she's in this hospital bed, because her daughter's away . . . She has a daughter, Nicolo – did you know that?'

'Yes, I did know that.' He spat the words out, then regretted them.

Vienna waved her arms at him, her cigarette leaving a trail of smoke hanging in the air.

'Of course you know that. You know everything about everything to do with Logan and his family, you fucking freak!'

He slapped her, hard, across the face.

She carried on talking. 'She didn't tell, because she was scared that it would mean she wouldn't get any compensation, and also because she didn't want to make things any worse, but then someone in the hospital showed her the newspaper from England, and she was in it – it was all about her and how she'd been screwing Logan when she was young. And she lay there, in her bed, and thought about it, and realised someone had given her daughter money; over the years, money had appeared from nowhere, and she had thought maybe it was from Logan, but no, because then Colette had called her, and said she was making everything right. And she might be paralysed, but her fucking brain isn't. She's not stupid, and she thought, I wonder who might have done it, who it might have been that likes to hurt Logan, who is always at loggerheads with him? Because over the years Colette's showed her articles, articles *someone* has been making sure she sees . . .'

Vienna paused for breath.

'This lady, Georgia Hardy, has a lot of time to think, lying in that bed with no one to talk to. So, she got one of the attendants to find out how to get hold of you, which wasn't difficult. You're hardly low-profile, are you?'

Vienna laughed; she really was hysterical now, her voice veering between tears and laughter.

'And she left a message for you, at your office, but I recognised her name and called her back. You're a fucking lunatic. You black-mailed Mark, and now he's dead, and you almost killed her. Why are you so obsessed with Logan anyhow? It's weird. *You're* weird.'

He strode over to her and hit her again, her head slamming between his hand and the window. She screamed, and launched herself at him, hitting him, trying to grab at his hair, his flesh, his shirt.

'I'm going to tell,' she panted. 'I'm going to Logan and to the press, and I'm going to tell everyone what you did.'

'No. You're not.' He was holding her against the thick glass of the full-length window, her tiny body pressed up against it.

'Go on then. Hit me again.' She spat in his face. 'Warming your-self up for a fuck, are you? You might as well.'

'I wouldn't be able to get it up. Fucking filthy bitch.'

She laughed. 'Oh, we both know that's not true.'

She raised an eyebrow. Taunting him. Challenging him. Her vacant eyes were surrounded by thick eyeliner and layers and layers of gloopy mascara. It disgusted him, the way she just reapplied her eye make-up on top of the old stuff, never bothering to clean it off and start again.

'Shut up. You will shut up.'

'You can't make me. You can't make everyone do everything, you know? Big man Nicolo – but you're not, are you? You're just a pathetic little boy, running after Logan, trying to get his attention.'

'I said be quiet.'

He closed his eyes. His arm was pressed against her neck. Her breathing was laboured, his weight was constricting her lungs. Her voice was whiny, high.

'Be friends with me, Logan. Look at me, don't leave me behind. Can I be your boyfriend, Maryanne? Oh no, you want Logan instead, boo hoo . . .'

She started to laugh. He kept his eyes closed. His body was hot, the blood pumped through his veins, and all he wanted was for her to shut up, be quiet. Tears fell from his eyes, sweat sprang to his temples, and he just wanted her to please, please be quiet, as he leaned against her, his hands pushing the air out of her; and her laughter stopped and turned into a wheeze, and then she was plucking at his arm, clawing at his skin, a desperate, inhuman noise coming from her, and still he kept his eyes shut, and over and over again he said, 'Be quiet, be quiet, be quiet . . .'

And then, suddenly, she was quiet.

Nicolo went to the dark wood sideboard where his bar set stood. He poured a glass of whisky from the crystal decanter, and then picked up the silver tongs that sat next to the matching ice-bucket. He noted with interest that his hand was quite steady as he dropped two cubes of ice into the glass, and swirled the liquid around in it. No trembles, no judderings. He didn't feel like throwing up. He wondered if this meant he was a psychopath, or a sociopath. Maybe he was in shock. He didn't feel shocked though. He didn't really feel anything.

He pushed Vienna's words to the back of his mind. He had to do two things. He had to get rid of her body, and he had to make sure that what she knew did not damage him. He had already worked out how he was going to do both of these things. He just needed to hold his nerve.

Vienna's body was slumped against the window. He went over to it and moved the upper half of her torso forward so that she was away from the glass, then went to the polished metal panel of switches by the door and pressed the button that controlled the blinds. They slid shut, blocking the view of the room from anyone who might enter the garden, though the house was walled and it wasn't the day for the gardeners. Still, he wasn't going to get caught out. He finished the whisky and went out into the corridor, locking the door behind him. After a quick check of the house to make sure that his housekeeper had left for the day, and that he wasn't going to be overheard, he returned to the study.

'I need some help. Cleaning help, I believe you would call it.'

The voice at the end of the line sounded amused. 'Cleaning help. All right. Where?'

Nicolo gave the man the address. He was someone Nicolo had heard of, a shadowy LA figure who most people heard of eventually, if they hung around the clubs and bars long enough, which Nicolo had certainly done. Everyone knew that he was a man who could clear up other people's messes, as long as the price was right. And Nicolo certainly had a big mess now. So he had taken a deep breath, and called him. He just wanted to get away from the house as quickly as possible. Away from Vienna's body, her eyes, her twisted face ... the memory of her words. *Be friends with me, Logan. Look at me, don't leave me behind. Can I be your boyfriend, Maryanne? Oh no, you want Logan instead, boo hoo ...*

On his way out of the house, he picked up a Fed-Ex envelope that his housekeeper had left for him on the hall table, and then locked the front door behind him.

Half an hour later, D, as he was known, drove the van into the tradesmen's entrance as Nicolo had instructed him over the phone, then shut the gates behind him and locked them. He was careful, he took his job seriously. It was people's lives that he dealt with. Or, more frequently, their deaths. He took his toolbox out of the back of the van. The box was light and plastic, and contained everything he would need to clean the room up. Then he slid back a small metal bolt. The floor of the van that was visible was a false one that D had had fitted by a metalworker friend. It sat above the real floor, creating a shallow area where all sorts of things could be stored and hidden away. He opened the lid in preparation. As he pulled it back, the lid stuck. He tugged harder, but it had jammed. Damn. He would have to mend it now – he didn't want to be trying to get it shut when he had brought the body out of the house. Opening his toolbox, he took out a spanner.

When Lucia was sure that Nicolo had gone, she came out of her hiding place in the cupboard in the large hallway, and padded over to his study door. She hesitated, her hand on the door knob, not wanting to go in. She had to, though. *Come on. Do it.*

She opened the door. The first thing she saw was Vienna's body, obscenely stretched out on the floor. Lucia froze. She couldn't be looking at a dead body, this was ridiculous. People didn't just leave bodies lying around their houses. Not even Nicolo. Fuck. Fuck!

She leaned down, not getting too close, and looked at Vienna's face. Her eyes were closed. Maybe she wasn't dead. Maybe she'd just passed out, hit her head or something. What should she do? Lucia stood up again and gingerly stretched a foot out and nudged Vienna's hip. Nothing. She moved her foot down, and nudged again, her leg this time. Vienna still didn't move.

'Vienna?' she whispered.

Then she looked at her face again, and down to her neck, and saw the purpley-red bruising. There was no way she was still alive.

Shit. What to do. What to do? She looked up as she heard a car door slam. The blinds were shut, but Lucia went to one end of the windows and peered round them carefully. In the back driveway, beyond the garden, she could see the corner of a van, with a man in overalls leaning into the back of it. She was going to have to be quick. She moved away from the window and went to Nicolo's desk, keeping a good distance from Vienna's body. Ugh. The things she did for her family.

D drove carefully; not too fast, not too slowly. He didn't want to get stopped by the police, but if he did, a cursory check of the back of the van would only reveal various bits and pieces of a decorator's equipment. The body lay in the concealed compartment, in the false floor of the vehicle. They would have found it if they'd looked carefully, sure, they'd realise that the van floor was higher than it should be. But no one had picked up on it yet and it had served him well during his career, providing a hiding-place for all sorts of things.

He was a professional. Nicolo had chosen well when he had called on him to do this job. When he got to the turning for the small airfield in the Valley, D drove on past it, before turning off and doubling back on himself, keeping an eye on the cars behind him as he did so. No one was following him. He slowed down as he neared the hangar.

The smoke was thick and acrid, rising up from the canyon and veiling it in a shroud of grey mist flecked with particles of ash. The forest fires had been going for five days now, and thousands of people had been evacuated from the area. Flames continued to lick up the sides of buildings and trees as helicopters and planes were flown in to water bomb the worst-affected areas.

So it wasn't difficult for the pilot D employed occasionally for similar errands to fly his helicopter into a less populated area where there were no news cameras to witness what he was about to do. If anyone on the ground did happen to look up and notice the plane, they would assume it was another craft drafted in to help support the emergency services, or maybe a TV station.

D waited until they were over an area of densely burning fire. There were no houses nearby so the firemen were concentrating their efforts elsewhere, but the flames were strong and showing no signs of abating. Then he signalled to the pilot, who lowered the helicopter until they were as near the ground as they could safely get, and then held position.

And D rolled the body gently out of the chopper, and it fell head-first into the flames.

While D was clearing up Nicolo's mess, Nicolo was on his way to tie up another loose end.

He stood over the hospital bed where Georgia Hardy lay. She stared up at him, fear in her eyes. This was a dangerous man; it was the man who had put her in this position. Who had manipulated her daughter, led Colette to sneak into the Barneses' family, led to the discovery of her affair with Logan. Her eyelids flickered.

'Don't worry,' he said. 'I'm not going to hurt you. I haven't come here to . . .'

He left it unsaid. He had thought about it – thought about killing her. On the way over here, he had thought how much easier it would be if she just died in her sleep. A lack of oxygen to the ventilator that helped her breathe, and it would be over, pretty quickly. But no. Nicolo had killed Vienna, but he was no cold-blooded psychopath. He still couldn't believe he had ended someone's life. It was – it was unreal.

'I came to apologise,' he said.

'Oh.'

'I'm sorry. Hmm. I know that's not really worth anything. Your whole life, your daughter's whole life ... Well. I can't really say anything that will make that go away.'

'No.'

They both looked down at her body.

'I'm hoping you will be able to keep your theory about the accident to yourself, from now on, though.'

He exhaled.

'We both know what I'm talking about. I want to buy your silence. I want you to promise me that you won't make trouble for me, that you'll keep quiet about your suspicions about the accident, and in return I'll do what I should have done a long time ago, and pay for proper care for you.'

She was silent.

'And college for Colette – whatever she needs. Whatever you both need. I know I don't really have any right to ask this, but I'm asking anyway. Because I need this all to be over now. We all need this to be over now.'

Georgia nodded. 'All right,' she said quietly.

There was nothing more to be said. Nicolo could hardly bear to look at her. He left, as soon as he could. He was disgusted with himself. He had fed his addiction to revenge, in the worst possible way. How could he possibly have let it come to this?

Before he left, he had paused by the door.

'I never meant for it to happen like this,' he said. 'I never thought it would ...'

He closed his mouth. What was the point? It didn't matter what he had thought or meant any longer. The only things that counted in the end were the things he had done.

Chapter Twenty-Seven

Maryanne knew in her heart that it was over for her and Logan. For a while now, they had been acting not as a partnership, but as two individuals whose lives were tied together by a complex web of family and work and houses. But still separate, where once they were a single unit. It was sad. So many years together, so much they had built up together. But it was liberating in a way as well. She was going to have to start her life over, learn how she was going to live it, and she would have to do that as an adult, by herself, without the large and imposing figure of Logan Barnes to shelter behind and lean on. Being his wife wasn't just a romantic relationship; it was a job, a public role, a social life.

God, she was sick of talking over her every thought and decision with a team of analysts. She still hankered for her previous method of dealing with things – a bottle of wine, a scattering of little pink pills, and shutting the door on the world. Instead, now, she rode with Sam. She was getting physically stronger; her legs had stopped aching so much after each session and her thighs had become taut and firm. And the physical exertion gave her a focus, some kind of replacement for the oblivion she was drawn to seek. A more pure, meditative quality rather than a dulling one. And it meant she could spend time with Sam, who still didn't say much, but whose presence she found she wanted near her more and more. If she had been allowed to she would have swapped all her counselling sessions for time spent riding Raff, or helping Sam groom and care for the horses in the stables, but she still had to do the rest of the programme.

Now, though, at the end of the long and draining day, she was ready to go down there after an early supper. Reading out her life story had made her relive it all once more, all of the pain and heartache. She had started off falteringly, aware of the group's eyes on her. But then, as she had read, she had forgotten about them and concentrated on the words in front of her, and by the end of the hour she had looked up and felt surprised to see them all in the room with her, so engrossed in the telling of her story had she become. She was sitting in the blandly institutional dining room finishing a cup of peppermint tea, about to leave, when Kurt came in and pulled a chair out opposite her.

'Hi, Maryanne. Are you feeling calmer this evening?'

'Yes, a little, thank you. I'm going to see the horses in a moment as well. They always make me feel better.'

Kurt nodded. 'Mm, yes, they are beautiful animals, aren't they?'

'Indeed. So I'll see you at the meeting tonight.'

'Hold on, please. Maryanne, we – the counselling team and I, that is – don't think you need as many sessions with Raff any more.'

'What do you mean?'

'Well, we've discussed it, and we think you'd be better spending more time in group. Less time out there with the horses. Equine therapy is a wonderful tool, but it's not a substitute for other forms of therapy, and we feel the balance has become a little out of kilter.'

Her face was hot. 'So you're saying I can't go there any more.'

'No, that's not what we're saying. But we don't feel it's appropriate for you to spend as much time there just now.'

'But why? It's the one thing that makes me feel like I might actually be able to survive. And now you say I can't do it any more.'

'Maryanne, you're angry, that's fine. But try and recognise that this anger is part of the reason that we feel you need to take a step back. Your emotions are fragile now, and it's not good for you to be overly emotionally involved with one form of therapy or one counsellor.'

And then she saw it. It was about Sam. They were trying to keep her away from him, when he felt like the one ally she had in the world right now. She stood up and walked out of the dining room, almost running. Despite everything, she still didn't like to make a scene in public. Kurt followed her out of the room.

'Try to remain calm, Maryanne. We can discuss this in more detail at the meeting later this evening.'

413

She ignored him and kept walking. She would not be kept from seeing Sam. Because if nothing else, Kurt's words had made her realise that her feelings for him were far more than those of a pupil for a respected teacher, or a friend. She loved him. That was why he was so comforting to her, why she wanted to spend all her time with him. As she understood this she saw a solution to her problems as clearly as when she had had laser eye surgery. And she wouldn't let anybody stand in her way when it came to love.

Sam was in the stables, combing Raff, when Maryanne came running. She stopped at the door and caught her breath. He looked up and smiled briefly, then carried on grooming the horse with long, sweeping strokes.

'I can't do it without you, Sam.'

'They spoke to you, then?'

She nodded. 'Kurt did. I hate them. I hate it here. You're the only one . . . the only one that isn't a complete shit.'

'Thanks a lot.'

'Sam.'

He stopped and slowly put the currycomb down on a shelf next to him. 'Yes?'

'I love you.'

He walked to the half-door of the stables and faced her. He was so solid, so strong.

'Maryanne . . .'

'Yes?'

He lowered his head. Suddenly his silence wasn't comforting and full of confidence any longer. It felt awkward and difficult.

'Kurt is right. You shouldn't spend as much time here any more. I've got other patients I need to focus on, and you need to get the balance right.'

'No. Didn't you hear me? I love you. It has nothing to do with therapy. I can feel it – we've got a connection between us. You know we do.'

Sam pushed the half-door open gently and she took a step back to let him out of the stable. But then, instead of taking her in his arms and kissing her, telling her that he loved her as well, like she knew he did, he was moving down to the next stable door.

'I have a lot of respect for you, Maryanne. But your feelings for me aren't real ones.'

'Yes, they are, I know they are.'

'You've had a bad time of it. Still are. It's natural that you become attached to people during the process.' He took a carrot from a pail next to the door and went into the next stable along, which held Misty, another of the centre's horses. She followed him inside.

'Attached? I'm not attached, I ... Look at me, will you?' She grabbed his sleeve, and tried to tug his arm round so he was facing her. He gently took his arm away.

'It's for the best, Maryanne, it really is.'

'No, it's not. Not for me, it isn't!' Her voice was high again, and her throat scratchy. She thought she had cried all the tears she would be able to earlier, but it seemed there were more. He finished giving the horse the carrot and tried to guide Maryanne back, towards the door.

'Come on. I shouldn't have let you come in here.'

'I won't come on. Not until you tell me you don't love me as well. That you don't feel anything for me.'

'Maryanne, come on, please, don't do this.'

'Tell me!' She hit his chest in frustration and he let her.

'I don't love you. I'm sorry. Don't be embarassed, Maryanne. This is really common. To transfer emotions to people – to think you feel things you don't really feel.'

'Look at me. Look me in the eye and say it.'

He took a deep breath and raised his eyes slowly. 'I don't love you.'

It took every bit of strength he had to tell her that, because he knew how much it would hurt her. And because, though everything in him knew it was wrong, he felt that there *was* a connection between them. He didn't love her now; she was a patient, a damaged, fragile woman who needed guidance and help, not a love affair. But might he love her in the future? He thought maybe he could.

Maryanne screamed, a wail that came from the bottom of her stomach and she threw herself to the floor of the stable. She couldn't take any more pain, any more rejection, and at that moment she wasn't even really aware of what she was doing, just that she was

415

in agony, writhing agony, and rejected by everyone she had ever felt anything for, and she had to move her body, somehow, to try and make it stop. Hide, curl up, protect herself, anything. Something. Her mind felt like it was shattering, her chest was being torn apart from the inside.

The scream was piercing, and seemed to come out of nowhere and everywhere, and as Sam jumped back in surprise, the horse, too, reared up in shock at the same moment as Maryanne's body dove towards the corner of the stable. She was in desperate search of comfort but what she found instead was his powerful hind legs kicking up behind him as he skittered away from the frightening noise.

'Easy – easy, boy.'

Sam reached up to try and calm Misty while steering clear of his whirling front legs, but it was too late. Maryanne's body was splayed on the ground, and a stream of dark blood was pouring from her mouth. As he looked at her, as he was trying to calm the panicking animal enough to get out of the stable and call for help, Sam knew that the look on Maryanne's face would weigh heavy on his heart for ever.

Rachel entered the room, holding two Fed-Ex envelopes. As she handed them to Logan and Charlie, her mobile phone beeped once and she flicked it open.

'These just arrived for you from Maryanne at Savannah . . . Rachel Mount speaking.'

She turned away to take the call as Logan opened the envelope and began to read.

'Yes, I'm with him now.'

My Darling Logan . . .

Rachel heard the tone in the caller's voice as they announced themselves and asked to speak to Logan, and knew that it could not signal good news. She passed him the phone, and watched as he listened, the letter still in his other hand. He froze and his eyes turned to Charlie, who was reading his letter, the hand that held it trembling.

'Maryanne died two hours ago. There was an accident – Charlie, I'm so sorry. She's gone.'

* * *

Maryanne was gone. Charlie had run out of the room, and Logan had let him go. He would go and find him soon. He had sent everyone else away and shut the door. And then he had put his head in his hands, and cried like he had not done since he was a child. He cried for Maryanne, for the beautiful girl he had met that day on the street, and to whom he had done so much damage. Whom he had loved so much, once, that he was prepared to betray Nicolo – would have betrayed anyone really, if it had meant he could have her. He cried for the fact that once he had got her, he had let her down so badly, had cheated on her, had left her alone, hadn't been there for her. He cried for the girl she had been then, and the woman she had become later – lost, drifting, hurting. He wept for the fact that he hadn't rescued her, hadn't fulfilled the promises he had made to her. Cried for all the times he had shut her out, going to work instead of helping her, cried for their children, whom he had let down as well, cried for everything he had said to her that had hurt her, and everything he hadn't said that she had needed to hear. Sat on the floor of his office, and cried and cried and cried.

My Darling Logan,
I think you know what I am going to tell you already, some-
where in your heart, if not in your conscious mind yet.
We've always known each other so well, you and I, haven't
we? Always been able to talk without talking. So I can't
believe some part of you doesn't know everything that is in
my heart already.
Where to begin? 'At the beginning,' I can hear you saying.
Well, I'm not going to. I'm going to begin at the end –
because we both know that this is the end of our story.
When you proposed to me, you said it was because you felt
that we were already married, in our hearts, and that you
wanted everyone else to know it as well. I'm not going to
talk about divorce, because it doesn't matter. We'll work that
out eventually. But we are no longer married in our hearts,
Logan, are we? We're looking in different directions.
Our children and our past will always bind us together.
Our children. Logan, my Logan. I was going to say that I
have deceived you, but actually, I don't think I have. I think

we have deceived each other. Me, by not saying what I should have said. You, by pretending you didn't know. Because you know, don't you, that Charlie is not your biological son? I am certain you do. Just as I am certain of the fact that you are his father in every way that matters. You have cared for him and loved him from the beginning. And for that, and for everything else, I will always love you and be grateful. It's the ultimate irony, isn't it, that Nicolo should be tied to us all so intimately. The one person you wish you could shake off for ever. But there we have it.

Call me. Come and visit me. I've written to Charlie. I've written to Nicolo as well. You'll be angry about that, but it was the right thing to do. I've spent too long keeping people in the dark, and it has kept me in the shadows as well. There's so much more I want to say, but it can keep until I see you next.

But know always that you made me very happy, for a long time. Anything else is my fault, not yours.

With love, always.
Maryanne

Logan held the letter in between the palms of his hands, as if in prayer. As if by holding on to it he would somehow be able to hold on to her, through these last words that said so much and that still left so much unsaid.

Oh Maryanne, he sobbed. *I failed you. And I'm so very sorry.*

He did know. About Charlie. Had always known. But he had put it aside, put it away. Logan loved him, very much. He had never seen him as anything other than his son, his own son. But he wasn't. And that would have to be faced. Logan picked up the phone.

'Charlie? We need to talk.'

Luxury was also lost. There was nothing more to be done. Everyone who was meant to have been staying there had cancelled, no one was booking. The running costs were huge; Logan couldn't keep it going with no money coming in, it would ruin him completely. He would have to cut his losses, which would be considerable, and close. He had spent hundreds of millions of dollars buying the island and developing it. All for nothing. He sat in his office, looking through the photographs from the presentation he had put together for it. It was still beautiful. But Christ, he had sacrificed so much to do it. He had let the island seduce him, become so important that he had lost sight of everything else.

'*Like the Sirens who lured all those men to their deaths,*' Elise had said. L'île des Violettes had certainly lured Logan to his own downfall.

Logan had set his sights on Luxury, on L'île des Violettes, all those years ago, and he had not stopped until he got what he wanted. And he wasn't the only one who had paid a hefty price.

Dear Nicolo,

I don't know where to begin. So much has happened, hasn't it? There has been so much hate and anger between us all. I wish that hadn't been the case. I fell in love with you, and then I fell in love with Logan. I don't expect you to forgive me for betraying you, but I want you to know that I have always regretted how things happened. I don't blame you for getting back at me in the way you did. You were lashing out. I was looking for comfort in a dark time. We did what we did. Anyhow, blame is a futile emotion, like regret, I have learned in the last few weeks. You can only look forward.

Listen to me. Don't I sound older and wiser than the girl you once knew! Life does that to a person, I suppose.

Still. The point of this letter is not to muse on past actions or what could have been. We've all moved beyond that, I think. The point is that I have something I must tell you. I think I probably should have done so a very long time ago. But I was afraid, and I stuck my head in the sand and hoped the problem would go away. And once you've done that, it just gets harder and harder to speak up, doesn't it? Oh, enough of the excuses, Maryanne.

Charlie is your son. I conceived him the last time that I was with you, I think. Now I'm writing this I find myself wondering if you'll believe me. But it's the truth.

I've written to Logan telling him as well. He didn't know, if that's what you're wondering. Although I think maybe he suspected. Charlie is his son in every way other than genetically. I don't know how this will be resolved. I only know that I have hidden the truth for too long, and if I am ever to get well, I can't hide it any longer.

I haven't told Charlie yet. I suppose the three of us will have to talk about this. Decide what to do next.

I hope that once you have got over the shock of this news, it will make you happy. Charlie is a wonderful boy and I am very proud to call him my son. I hope you will be too. And maybe this will, in time, help to mend some old wounds, even if the initial process is painful.

I don't know how to sign this off appropriately, so I shall simply sign,

Maryanne

The next day Charlie was sitting in the Chesham Hotel cinema when Colette arrived, black and white movies showing silently on the plasma screen in front of him. He stared as Harold Lloyd swung from the minute hand of a large clock suspended in mid-air over busy streets below. Colette watched his face as the flickers from the screen reflected on it. So beautiful, so young looking, and bearing so much grief.

'She loved these films. The really silly ones. Laurel and Hardy falling over, banana skins, all that stuff.'

She walked over to him and put her arms round his neck from behind. 'Hey.'

'Hi.'

'It's weird, because my mom loved them as well.'

'Really?'

'Yes. I told you she was an actress, right? These are the films that she grew up watching, that made her want to act. And I grew up watching them as well.'

'Me too. Whenever I was sick, Mom'd wrap me up in a blanket and put one of these on the TV. She'd sit and watch with me, and man, she had the dirtiest laugh.'

420

There was silence for a moment.

'I'm sorry,' Colette sighed. 'I feel like I shouldn't be here. You should just be with your family.'

'No.' He took both her hands in his and kissed them. 'I need you here. I feel like . . .' He shook his head.

'What?'

How could he say what he really felt, that she was as important as his family, that he wanted her to *be* his family? They hardly knew each other; she'd be gone if he were to say that to her.

'I just need you, OK?'

'Of course. I'm not going anywhere.'

Charlie held tightly on to her hand as they watched the flickering images. He closed his eyes and wept for his mother.

Colette watched the movie. It was true, she had watched them while she was growing up, but not because her mother loved them so much: she was always out at auditions or working. Colette liked the funny walks they did and the way things always turned out OK in the end. They comforted her, somehow.

She shouldn't be here, she knew, whatever Charlie said. He didn't know her. He thought he did, but he didn't; he knew someone else, someone called Jamie, a character she had invented to get into his life, into his father's life. She felt bad. His mother was dead, and she was sitting here, with him asleep on her, deceiving him. Whatever she had set out to do, she had achieved. Charlie did not deserve this. She stroked his hair gently. He just didn't.

There was a knock on the door.

'Come in?' Colette kept her voice soft, trying not to wake Charlie.

The door opened, and Lucia stood there, her weight on one hip. Charlie sat up, his eyes bleary with sleep.

'Luce?'

'Hey,' she replied, and walked over to him. He stood up, and hugged her, and they wept.

Colette left the brother and sister alone for a while, went to sit in the big kitchen downstairs and drink coffee. She had to leave; had to get out of here. Maryanne's death changed everything. Her rage had burned itself out. She had watched Logan suffer, watched everything unfold, and the hotel close, and now she was watching

Charlie and Lucia grieve for their mother. It wasn't right. And she missed her mom.

She went upstairs. She didn't know what she was going to do yet, what she was going to tell him. For the first time in her life, she didn't have any kind of a plan.

Charlie and Lucia were sitting on the sofa. When she entered the room, Charlie held his hand out to her. She walked forward and took it. This was going to be hard. For both of them.

'Charlie, I need to talk to you.'

'OK, babe, but in a sec. Lucia's just telling me something . . .'

'Oh, all right.'

It could wait, after all. She had been deceiving him for months. Another hour or so wouldn't make any difference now.

Lucia had been reading Fergus Chilman's notes for the autobiography one day, and it had been the section about the hotel in Vegas, the first hotel, and everything that had happened afterwards. She had never really known the whole story before, hadn't been that interested, to be honest, but it was fascinating. And as she had read it, something had struck her. She'd gone to Fergus, owned up to reading his papers, and told him of her suspicions. And he had agreed. So, between the two of them, they'd started to investigate further.

'Fergus and I came up with this plan – but everyone had to believe it. Mom, Dad and Nicolo all had to believe it. Daddy had already thrown me out after the party and the posters. I'd lost the contract, so I couldn't buy the hotel any more.'

She had told Charlie about 98 Bilton Square already.

'I just wanted to prove I wasn't stupid. Wasn't some silly little girl who was only interested in shoes and shopping. So I went to Nicolo and told him what had happened, that I was all alone and needed him. And he was only too pleased to take me in, in return for a few things . . .'

Charlie raised an eyebrow, the protective big brother.

'Nothing like that. We agreed on this photoshoot, and that I'd go to the TV awards with him. Prove to everyone that he was the big winner, you see? Well, you know what he's like. Nicolo had given me a key to his house. I went there, when he was giving the press conference after all the Luxury tapes rubbish, and I found the evidence that I was looking for. He definitely blackmailed Mark Mallory. I found the tape. And I also found something else. It was Vienna. He killed her. I heard him kill her. And I saw her body.' She shuddered.

Charlie's face was appalled. 'He killed her? Are you sure?'

Lucia nodded tearfully. 'I promise. He strangled her – well, sort of. I was in the house, looking for stuff, and she came back, and then he came back . . . I hid. They had a big fight. She had phoned up the woman who was hurt in the accident.'

'What?' Colette interrupted her. 'What do you mean?' She had gone pale.

Lucia looked over at her brother's girlfriend. Why was she so interested? Who the fuck was she anyway? 'Yeah – Georgia Hardy. She was the woman hurt in the accident, in Vegas. It was a really long time ago, there's no reason you'd know about it.'

'I know about it.' Colette's voice was harsh. Charlie looked at her in surprise but she ignored him. She had to know, had to find out if what she thought Lucia was saying was true.

'What are you saying? That *Nicolo* caused the accident?'

Lucia nodded. Her eyes were rimmed with red.

'Yes. That's what he and Vienna were arguing about. That's why he killed her. She was teasing him, about Dad, about him loving Mom; he kept telling her to shut up, be quiet, and she wouldn't, and then . . .'

She began to cry. 'She was lying there, she was all . . .'

She shivered. 'Sorry. It was fucking horrible.' Lucia reached in her bag for a pack of cigarettes. With them, she pulled out a DVD and handed it to Charlie.

'That's what he blackmailed Mark with. I don't know if it'll help Dad now. It might do something.'

Colette was staring at Lucia strangely. She stood up slowly. It had all been a lie. All for nothing. She'd done everything for nothing, or to the wrong man – her head was a mess. She had spent her whole life hating someone, and all the time it had been the wrong person. The one who had caused everything, who had set it all in motion, had misled her, fed her anger and hate, given her little crumbs . . . Oh, God. She had to go, get out of here. She turned.

'Jamie – where are you going?'

She couldn't look at Charlie, couldn't bear to.

'I'm sorry. Just – just remember that I'm sorry. Oh, shit.'

Then she had run, out of the house, grabbing her handbag on the way, with her wallet and passport inside, leaving everything else. Charlie had followed her, confused, calling after her.

'Jamie, *wait*, what's wrong? Jamie – please!' He caught up with her, grabbed her arm, stood next to her, pleading. 'I don't understand, babe. What are you sorry *for*? Whatever it is, we can fix it, Jamie, please. Please!'

She was crying.

'I need you, Jamie, I need you so much.'

'No, you don't. You don't need me, Charlie. You don't even know my real name.'

A taxi came and she jumped into it, shoving something into his hand as she did so.

'See? You don't know anything.' She leaned forward to speak to the driver. 'Heathrow, please, as quickly as possible.'

Charlie banged on the window.

'All right, easy, mate! Careful.'

'Jamie, for God's sake. Don't leave me, not now!'

The taxi drove off, the driver shaking his head and tutting.

'Lovers' tiff?' he asked the girl in the back seat, glancing in the rearview mirror. She was curled up like a child, crying her heart out, and didn't answer. Shrugging philosophically, he turned back to the road and drove towards the airport.

What did she mean, he didn't even know her real name? She was Jamie, lovely Jamie, who understood him, who was so much fun, so free and sexy. He walked back to the house slowly. He didn't understand any of it. He sat on the steps of the family home and unfolded the piece of paper she had given him. It was a newspaper article about the Piccadilly Circus accident, and tucked into it was a photograph of a woman. He turned it over. *Can't wait to see you on the big night, sexy. Promise I'll make it even more special for you if you come and find me before the show . . . ! Kisses. G.*

Who was G? He looked through the article, until he came to something he recognised – the photograph of a young girl, named in the piece as Georgia's daughter, Colette Hardy. The thing was, it was the same photograph that Jamie had showed him the other day, when they were laughing at old photos of him in an album, and he insisted she showed him one as well. It was Jamie. It was Colette. They were the same person.

When Colette landed at LAX, she went straight to the hospital to see her mother. Georgia was watching the TV when Colette came in. She flicked her eyes at the set, and Colette stretched over and turned it off. She sat down in the chair next to her mother's bed, laid her head next to hers and cried as she told her everything that she had done.

'Ssh,' Georgia said. 'It doesn't matter now. It's over, darling girl. It's all over.'

Charlie had jumped on a plane to LA and had arrived at Nicolo's mansion, his mother's letter still in his pocket, to find it surrounded by police. Officers on radios were milling around the grounds, and crime scene investigators in their plastic overalls were carrying equipment in and out of the house. Paparazzi were clustered outside, and onlookers, people with nothing better to do, all being kept at a distance. He went up to one of the men who was loitering.

'What's going on?'

'Nicolo Flores – killed his girlfriend, they reckon.'

'Wow.'

'Yeah. Just goes to show, don't it? Rich and famous, or a bum on a street corner. Bitches still drive you crazy.' And he laughed raucously.

'Guess so.'

'One of the press told me they want him for some other shit, too. To do with Logan Barnes? Y'know, the other hotel guy?'

'Yeah, I know who you mean.'

'Apparently some dancer got herself hurt in one of Mr Barnes's hotels, long time ago, and they reckon it's Mr Flores's fault as well.'

'Really?'

'That's what I hear.' The man nodded conspiratorially at Charlie.

'You'd think these rich guys had enough to keep 'em busy, without all this as well, wouldn't ya? Now Nicolo has disappeared. Musta got wind of it somehow.'

Charlie nodded, then walked away. It was over.

Chapter Twenty-Eight

Maryanne had a private funeral, with just Logan, Charlie and Lucia in attendance. It had been a terrible day. The sky had been dark above the mountains that loomed over the small chapel where they buried her. They had decided that she had sounded, in her letters to Logan and Charlie, more at peace here at the Savannah Centre than anywhere else. They didn't want to bury her in Manhattan, or London – the cities were somehow too associated with her addictions, with her pain and turmoil. Here she had finally seemed to be getting well. So here was where they thought she should stay.

The three of them gathered around her grave, watching as the simple coffin was lowered into the ground. They had all been in shock still, the shock of her death and the shock of everything else that had happened – the revelations about Charlie's parentage, Mark's betrayal, the exposure of Luxury, the fights with Nicolo, Lucia's disappearance – it had all hit them when she had died, and they had only now started to realise exactly what they had all lost. Charlie had been hit the hardest; he had gone through the most. Logan had looked at him watching his mother being lowered into the ground, and wondered if he would ever recover. His eyes were haunted, he gazed at Logan unseeing when his father tried to talk to him, and then just went to his room, where he lay for hours on his bed in silence. The family were in London, although Charlie had disappeared for a couple of days after Maryanne's death, refusing to say where he had been when he retuned. Lucia was quiet, grieving, but tougher in a way than Charlie, though Logan worried about what she had seen in Nicolo's house. How it would affect her in the future. She was very young still. But he would be there for her this time, help her through it. He would be a proper father to both his children.

The pastor turned to Logan, and an undertaker stepped forward to hand him a small wooden box full of earth. He reached in, took out a handful, and knelt by the grave.

I'm sorry, Annie. I'm sorry for all the times I let you down. I'm sorry for letting the island, the business, everything else get in the way of what was really important. You, Charlie, Lucia. They're good kids. You did a good job. I didn't tell you often enough, but you were a good mother. And I loved you.

His silent epitaph done, he scattered the earth on top of her coffin, and turned to Charlie, who stepped forward.

Mom. I don't want you to go. I don't want you to be here in the ground. I can't bear it. Why didn't you tell me? Surely you could have told me? I don't know why everyone's been lying to me for so long. I just want you to come back and tell me everything's going to be OK.

Charlie dropped the earth into the hole, and buried his head in his arm. He felt so completely lost and alone.

Finally, Lucia took her turn.

Momma. My lovely Momma. I didn't make things very easy for you, did I? I'm sorry. I should have seen how unhappy you were, but I just selfishly thought you'd be OK. And I didn't know what to say. I never knew what to say. Oh, I'm going to miss you so much. I don't want you to go away and leave me behind.

She dropped the earth, letting it slip through her fingers. Then she turned to Logan and let her father hold her as she wept.

Six months later

The church was filling up, there were at least a couple of hundred people here already for Maryanne's memorial service. Friends, LBI employees, people she had met during the last weeks of her life in the Savannah Centre. A blown-up photograph of her stood at the front of the London church, propped up in a gilt frame. It was of her when the children were young, when she was young. She was sitting on a carousel, astride a painted horse, Charlie and Lucia tucked in front of her, her arms around them, holding them on. Keeping them safe. There was a slight blur in the photo, as the carousel had been going round when Logan had caught it, one spring day in Central Park. They had chosen this photograph because it seemed to sum up everything about Maryanne that they wanted to say. She looked young, and free, and happy, her arms around her two children, her eyes full of love for the man behind the camera.

Logan looked at the photo now, then turned and gazed at the almost-full building and the men and women who were there. Johnny was sitting near the front, on the other side of the church, a bit pale still, with Rachel next to him, holding his hand. The two of them had become close while Johnny was in hospital. He had split up with Melissa and told Logan that he thought he might 'finally have found the one, and she was there, right in front of my eyes, the whole time,' when Logan had last visited him. Johnny was recovering well. He was walking with crutches still, and his leg was kept straight with an external frame with pins that sank into his flesh, but at least he was walking. He would need more surgery, and he wasn't likely to be kite-surfing any time soon – but then, Logan wouldn't put it past him. He wouldn't ever underestimate his friend. He was just pleased that Johnny wouldn't be alone any more, that he would have Rachel by his side from now on. Logan trusted her.

But then, Logan had trusted other people. Mark. His betrayal had wounded Logan deeply. If Nicolo had been trying to make a point, and Logan felt sure that he had, then he had made it well. The poetic justice of Mark's betrayal was not lost on him. He had stolen something from Nicolo that he had loved all those years ago; Nicolo had managed to do something similar to him, many years later. He had taken something from Logan, and that was his confidence that everyone in his life was who they professed to be. Logan had learned a hard lesson. What was it they said, in physics? Every action has an equal and opposite reaction. The reaction didn't have to be immediate to make its mark.

Trust wasn't the only thing he'd lost. He'd lost Maryanne – no, he'd lost her years before, hadn't he? They'd lost each other, in the darkness. Turned away from each other, and then realised, too late, that they didn't know how to find their way back. His relationships with Charlie and Lucia had been damaged, but he thought he would be able to salvage them. Build on them, at least, with work and time.

They had come to him, that day, and told him everything, their faces shocked. They had looked so young, suddenly.

'We must tell the police,' Lucia had said, and Logan had agreed. He had sat with her while she made her statement, painstakingly relating everything she had seen and heard in Nicolo's house, patiently repeating herself while they went over every tiny detail, uncomplaining. He had been proud of her. He had been even more proud of her when she had told him, falteringly, about her plans for 98 Bilton Square. She was nervous of telling him, but he was impressed, as well as surprised.

'Light Hotels . . . Lucia, which means light . . . I should have put two and two together, shouldn't I?' he had said.

'Well, a bit, yes.' She was hesitant when he asked her what she planned to do with it, but her enthusiasm was evident.

'A ladies' club, eh?' Logan had looked over the plans, the designs that she had collated in a leather portfolio.

'Yes, like a gentlemen's club,' she told him. 'I know it sounds strange, but if you think about all the women who come into London to shop, who maybe aren't staying the night but need somewhere to rest and chill out, or who want to stay but they don't fancy being in a big impersonal hotel . . . I really think it could work.'

So did he. He had offered her a deal – he would support her finance application, act as guarantor when she approached the investment banks again.

'You'll be doing it as yourself – no interference from me,' he'd promised. 'No one will be able to accuse you of playing hotels. And it won't be play, it'll be bloody hard work, I hope you realise. You'll have to oversee construction, deal with architects and builders, lawyers, temperamental chefs . . .'

She looked at him and shook her head.

'Um, yes, I do know all that. Honestly, Daddy – where do you think I've been all this time? With my head in the clouds?'

That was exactly what he had thought.

It was obvious that he hadn't really known much about his children at all. Lucia had already made a good start on things, buying the property from him at a fair price, and working hard. She was up every day at six, and out of the door by half-past. She was savvy and determined, and had inherited her mother's design flair. Logan thought she might do rather well. He had underestimated his daughter pretty seriously, it seemed.

She wasn't the only one. Charlie had come to him a couple of months ago with a CD, and Logan had sat and listened to it with him. It was brilliant – even Logan, knowing nothing about music, could hear that. Charlie had poured himself back into his music after Maryanne's death. Logan had been worried that the discovery that Jamie had not been who she said she was would throw him off his game, that the studio would be too full of memories of her to make it easy for Charlie to go back there, but it didn't seem to have had that effect.

'So, what next?' Logan had asked, when they had finished listening and he had congratulated his son. 'A showcase – is that what happens?'

Charlie had shuffled. 'Um, I kind of already did that.'

'Oh. I would have liked to come.'

'Sorry. It's just . . . I needed to do it by myself. Do you understand?'

Logan understood that all too well. Charlie might not be his biological son, but there was something of Logan in him nevertheless. *Not his biological son.* Nicolo hadn't called yet, hadn't been in touch. Logan had asked Charlie if he had contacted him, but he had just shrugged and said no. Logan didn't push it. Charlie would talk when he was ready. He'd taken the news that Nicolo was his father pretty calmly, all things considered.

'Are you surprised?' Logan had asked. 'It must be a pretty big shock.'

Charlie had paused. 'Yeah, kind of. I mean, I wasn't exactly expecting it. But at the same time I always felt different from Lucia. And you and I – like we were different too. So in a way, it makes a weird kind of sense.'

Weird indeed.

'And I got a deal,' he went on shyly. 'Universal are gonna do it, the album. They want to release it next year.'

Logan was proud of them both. Charlie wouldn't be going into

LBI any time soon, and Logan would have to give up his dreams of a father and son business for good. But hey – there was nothing wrong with a father and daughter business one day, was there? Lucia had elbowed him in the ribs when he said that out loud.

'Hey! No planning,' she reproached him. 'You said you weren't going to interfere.'

He'd held his hands up, admitted that she was quite right, so he had. But secretly she was quite pleased.

The island had been sold to a property developer from Dubai who wanted to turn it into a conference centre. The thought was hideous. But he had had to do it. It was time to cut himself free of it: L'île des Violettes had held its power over him for too long. There were things in life that were more important.

And the island had given him something in return. Elise was sitting next to him now, holding his hand. She had been his constant support since Maryanne died, and he hers, as she went through her divorce from Bill. She wasn't asking for any kind of financial settlement, but he wasn't making it easy for her even so. Elise was strong, though, stronger than she herself had ever realised, and she was standing firm. She didn't need Bill's money, didn't need Logan's, either. Her father had left her with a wonderful legacy. The packet of papers that she had taken from the home had contained his will, but it wasn't the worthless document that she had assumed it would be.

Before Pete's accident, it turned out that he had been planning to leave his life as a stuntman, and move on to something just as risky, but in a different way. He and his friend Hans Neuman, a cameraman, had had an idea. And they'd started a company. They'd only just registered the patent for their invention when her dad had had the accident, and shortly afterwards, Hans had died from lung cancer. So Hans's shares had passed to Pete, and the company had just sat there, to all intents and purposes in Pete's nursing-home drawer, until the day that he died and Elise took the papers away with her. She had gone through them and found the company registration. And with nothing much else to do, and intrigued as to what her father had been so keen on that he was going to stop performing the stunts, she had started to investigate it. It had turned out that Pete Sylvester and Hans Neuman had developed iris recognition technology in a pretty revolutionary way that meant cameras could differentiate between live tissue and a high-quality photograph, or a false eye – which they had never been able to do before.

Elise said a silent prayer to thank them both now. She had been playing in a few poker tournaments, and using the money she won to develop the idea. Logan had no problem with her gambling. He encouraged her, was proud when she came home and announced that she had won a place in a satellite tournament, or had had a good night at a private game. He wanted to hear all about it. If she could get the product right, it would revolutionise the security systems that hotels used for ever. She felt as though finally, she was finding out what she wanted to do when she grew up. And she could go to Logan with something to offer. Not from one husband to another, from one man who would keep her to the next. But go as an equal, as his partner.

She wasn't living with him yet. She had rented a small apartment in Brompton Cross, near his house in London, while she got Danny used to the idea of only seeing Bill every other weekend, and gradually introduced him to Logan, and Charlie and Lucia. He had had enough to take in, for a small boy; she didn't want to overwhelm him. And she secretly liked the freedom that came from living by herself, with being able to lie around in her pyjamas eating ice cream for breakfast if she wanted to, being able to paint her bathroom bright pink on a whim, just because she felt like it. She would move in eventually, they would get their own house together and do all the things that people did when they were setting up home and moving in together – argue about wallpaper, and where the TV should go, and leaving the toilet seat up. It would be good. But there was no hurry. They had the rest of their lives together.

Elise turned to him now. He was gazing at the photo of Maryanne. She took his hand and squeezed it. The church was full; the music that had been playing quietened, and the minister stepped forward.

'Ladies and gentlemen. We gather here today to celebrate the life of Maryanne Rose Barnes . . .'

Outside, after the service was over and the guests had filed out, past Logan and Charlie and Lucia who stood at the doorway, thanking them for coming, Logan strolled over to Elise who was standing a short distance away. They walked together towards the gates.

'I let her down badly, you know,' he said.

She didn't deny it.

'I don't want to do the same with you.'

'You won't.'

'Won't I?' His face was worried.

'No.'

'How do you know?'

She shrugged. 'I just know. We won't let you.'

'You won't let me. OK.'

'No. And when I say "we" . . .'

He looked at her, his expression questioning. 'Yes?'

'I mean me, Danny . . .'

She paused. He held his breath.

' . . . And whatever we decide the next one should be called.' She touched her belly.

'Really?'

She nodded. 'Twelve weeks. Here.' She reached into her bag and pulled out a scan picture. Logan gazed at it, transfixed.

'Wow.'

'I'm sorry – I didn't keep it a secret deliberately, I just wanted to be sure.'

He hugged her to him. 'It's fine. Wow.'

'I know.'

Logan gently ran a finger down her belly, then looked into her eyes. 'So, am I finally going to be able to get you to move in with me now?'

'I think I'd better.' She wrapped her arms round his neck. 'Although actually . . .'

'Actually what? Elise, if you're planning on bringing up my baby anyway other than under the same roof as me, you'd better think again. I—' He broke off. 'Why are you laughing?'

She kissed him. 'Don't look so outraged. I was just going to say, before you so rudely interrupted, that actually I was rather wondering if now we might get married.'

'Ah. I see. Yes. Yes, I think that's a very good idea indeed.'

Epilogue

Nicolo Flores sat at the bar of the beachside café, drinking a beer and raising a glass to Maryanne on the day of her memorial service. Raising a silent toast to the only woman he had ever truly loved. It was like the old days in San Diego, almost. Apart from the fact that Panama was hotter, dustier.

He had enough money here to last him for a while. He still didn't know quite how they'd worked out that he had been behind all of LBI's problems, from Georgia Hardy's fall, to the orchestrated lawsuits, to paying money into Colette's bank account every month. His revenge had cost him a pretty penny. Had it been worth it? Logan wasn't the only one who had paid a heavy price.

The evidence was out there, gone from his office and into the hands of the cops. He still didn't know who had taken the photograph of Vienna's body lying on his study floor, that was in all the reports about the incident. D had taken her body from the house and destroyed it, but there was still that photo . . . Someone must have been there before D came over. Ah, he wasn't too worried. With no body they'd have a problem making anything stick. Still, he wasn't planning on going back to the States for a long time. He had got away just in time, had transferred as much money as he could, and had been on a flight out of the country even as the police were battering his front door down. Thanks to a phone call from someone who he certainly hadn't expected to help him.

He paid for a second beer and took it with him as he walked to the newsagent a few yards down the seafront. This one wasn't for Maryanne. This one, he raised to his son. One day, he intended to share a beer with him. Meet him face to face, as father and son, for the first time.

For now, though, he settled for raising a glass to his picture in a silent salute to the young man who was responsible for his freedom.

'Thanks for the tip-off, Charlie.'